100

FRANCIS FORD COPPOLA'S

Zoetrope
ALL STORY

2

steve Almond

Rick Bass

Karen E. Bender

Pinckney Benedict

David Benioff

Jennifer Egan

Alicia Erian

Peter Greenaway

T. E. Holt

Rebecca Lee

Rick Moody

Francine Prose

Margo Rabb

Stacey Richter

Touré

Mary Yukari Waters

FRANCIS FORD COPPOLA'S

Zoetrope

ALL STORY

2

Edited by
Adrienne Brodeur
and Samantha Schnee

Introduction by
Francis Ford Coppola

A Harvest Original • Harcourt, Inc.

ORLANDO   AUSTIN   NEW YORK   SAN DIEGO   TORONTO   LONDON

www.HarcourtBooks.com

Library of Congress Cataloging-in-Publication Data
Francis Ford Coppola's Zoetrope all-story 2 / Francis Ford
Coppola; edited by Adrienne Brodeur and Samantha
Schnee; with an introduction by Francis Ford Coppola.
p.   cm.
Sequel to: Francis Ford Coppola's Zoetrope all-story.
"A Harvest original."
ISBN 0-15-601368-1
1. Short stories, American. 2. Short stories, English.
3. Motion picture authorship.   I. Title: Zoetrope all-story 2.
II. Brodeur, Adrienne.   III. Schnee, Samantha.
IV. Coppola, Francis Ford, 1939–   V. Zoetrope
(New York, N.Y.)
PS648.S5F733 2003
813'.0108—dc21   2003003940

Designed by Lydia D'moch
Text set in New Aster
Printed in the United States of America
First edition
K J I H G F E D C B A

CONTENTS

to particular budgets to certain casting procedures—is there only to ensure maximum control by the financiers. The business end wants as much control for as little investment as possible. So for me, what made the experience with the magazine exceptional was that we—Adrienne Brodeur, the magazine's founding editor, and I—ignored the rules and made things up as we went along. We broke with conventional wisdom as to what a literary magazine had to be. And fortunately we didn't have to conform because we weren't taking anyone's money.

That's the unholy bargain that has existed, I guess, from the beginning, from the days of the Vatican. In 1200, the Vatican was one of any number of Christian churches that were spread all around Italy. What had been the Roman Empire continued to be the Roman Empire. And the difference between the Vatican and the other churches is that it really demanded, in return for its finance, or the equivalent of finance (its sanction, its approval), a whole bunch of things that you had to accept. And that's pretty much the bargain now with business and, particularly, business related to the arts. In order to possess the Holy Grail of creativity, you need financing and distribution. And, in order to get that, you have to give up so much in the way of control, which is to say, be forced to conform to the goals of that entity.

The real purpose of the magazine, as I originally conceived it, was to connect wonderful writing, new writing, into other areas of my company. But now I am finding that I'm less interested in the other areas of the company, so I'm in a real quandary. To use a Middle Eastern metaphor, it's like my companies are the harem, and I want to close it down, except there is one in there I don't want to lose. I do know that I am confirmed in my experience of collaborating with Adrienne Brodeur to make our own rules and bring *Zoetrope: All-Story* to fruition, and I believe that my initial concept was entirely right—that forging a link to new writers, before they've been discovered, before they're already sought out by agents and companies anxious to exploit them, was a good idea.

We did discover many great new writers, Melissa Bank being one. Bank's "The Girls' Guide to Hunting and Fishing" is a good illustration of the problem I'm talking about. That story, which emerged in the first year of the publication and was such a bright light, got bogged down once it was turned over to the film division, with its obligatory procedures and its partnership with a bigger company, which moved like molasses. By the time the big studio actually really looked at and considered the story, it was rejected as being dated, which is the ultimate irony.

After a very successful debut and five-year run of *Zoetrope: All-Story* in New York, I decided to move the magazine, as well as my film division, back to San Francisco. I was forced to reconsider how I was going to organize the interaction of the magazine with the other parts of the company, namely film, internet, and television, to make it achieve the end I had always hoped it could. And it was clear that the solution wasn't going to be speedy, which is to say that it wasn't going to be what I earlier envisioned: *Oh, yeah, you know, we've found a great story, let's get going with a film.* I hadn't counted on the sluggish, three-year development process with the studios, and that all the while the overhead just kind of keeps on rolling along like Old Man River, and that the projects that ultimately hold the hope of recovering the overhead are slow to happen. So, I proposed to my company

that we either abandon this idea or figure out a way to keep
it alive in a more efficient way. We decided that the best solution was to eliminate the New York offices—really, the
magazine being the least of the burden—and bring everything to San Francisco, where we could consolidate things,
sort of like when companies do mergers. We had talented
personnel there in different fields that I thought maybe
could work in new areas, and that by my direct involvement,
we could navigate through the next two or three years, with
a kind of fresh mandate.

In the introduction to *Zoetrope: All-Story*'s first anthology, I
talked about my dream studio in the clouds, and how there
would be all these different sorts of areas within the same
location. Well, I think we had the basis of that in New York.
The only missing element was myself, and when I'm not
present, the different divisions tend to fall into business as
usual, for example, the people in film: although they were
fascinated with the fact that they could be more involved
with the magazine and were always talking about inviting
film directors to meet fiction writers at parties so they could
get to know each other, they didn't actually do it. The different divisions needed to get their projects going and fell into
grooves that had already been worn by the industry, which
is to say, worked through agents and conventional legal
agreements. From afar, it was hard to keep saying, "Let's go
a new way," whereas in this new setup, in San Francisco, it
is more like the dream studio I envisioned.

I recall some comments made by Roman Polanski, when I
was young. The great film school in the clouds then was
at Lodz, in Poland. After the war, that great film school
spawned the most wonderful traditions and, of course, great

artists like Polanski and others were brought to the light in this postwar Polish film group. And I, as a young student, wished I could go there. When I've asked some of the people who went there what it was like, they've told me it wasn't really the professors that made it great, although they had some great teachers who later went on to become heads of many film schools around the world, including the USA. But what I've been told was really great about that school was the front porch where the students would eat and visit with each other, and it was the conversations and the debates and the cross-stimulation that happened on the front porch that really was the film school. And I've always believed in the idea of a studio in which different kinds of artists and associates come to work and rub elbows getting lunch—that the interplay and the ideas that are going to be tossed out is what is stimulating. And I want to provide that, which is why I've always put an emphasis on a great café, or a great place for food, because if you have the wonderful food and the other trappings of the Bohemian setting, then you attract the kinds of people who appreciate and want to be in the vicinity of those things, and vice versa, and this would stimulate creativity.

I'm a big believer that human drive can produce some very positive things or very negative things, and in the arts, they can be very positive in that they cause people to want to be together, to share ideas, and to impress and stimulate one another. And that's what explains the odd phenomenon of schools of art or cinema popping up in different weird places in the world. One turns up in Italy all of a sudden. And then the legacy of Roberto Rossellini spawns fifty wonderful directors. You can't tell me that the extraordinary Italian food and the more extraordinary Italian women didn't have something to do with it. Then, suddenly, another pops up in Japan, and we have another period of great, great fertility. And in France. Or in Germany. Or now in China and Mexico. Iran. What explains how that happens? I think it's the Front Porch Theory. That was what I understood to be the success of the Lodz school.

Zoetrope: All-Story is all about change. I like to think that the magazine is always capable of reinventing itself, which is one of the reasons why we established a guest designer concept. With that concept the designer had total creative control of the look, format, and graphic treatment of the magazine. And my thought was that this would always provide a stimulus for change, which would sometimes uncover some really great innovations, that might be kept for a while. The only sure thing in life is change, and the magazine will keep changing. I hope among other things to totally reinvent the format in the period of the next year or so. And I hope there'll be candidates for other formats that will be more in harmony with the profession of publishing and printing and digital printing and digital on-demand publishing. I mean, I have no idea what this magazine in terms of its format and look will be in a year. But I know that it will be interesting and I look forward to getting to hammer that out.

Best wishes,
Francis Ford Coppola

FRANCIS FORD COPPOLA'S

Zoetrope
ALL STORY

2

stacey **Richter**

THE CAVEMEN IN THE HEDGES

There are cavemen in the hedges again. I take the pellet gun from the rack beside the door and go out back and try to run them off. These cavemen are tough sons of bitches who are impervious to pain, but they love anything shiny, so I load the gun up with golden Mardi Gras beads my girlfriend, Kim, keeps in a bowl on the dresser and aim toward their ankles. There are two of them, hairy and squat, grunting around inside a privet hedge I have harassed with great labor into a series of rectilinear shapes. It takes the cavemen a while to register the beads. It's said that they have poor eyesight, and of all the bullshit printed in the papers about the cavemen in the past few months, this at least seems to be true. They crash through the branches, doing something distasteful. Maybe they're eating garbage. After a while they notice the beads and crawl out, covered in leaves, and start loping after them. They chase them down the alley, occasionally scooping up a few and whining to each other in that high-pitched way they have when they get excited, like little kids complaining.

I take a few steps off the edge of the patio and aim toward the Andersons' lot. The cavemen scramble after the beads, their matted backs receding into the distance.

"What is it?" Kim stands behind me and touches my arm. She's been staying indoors a lot lately, working on the house, keeping to herself. She hasn't said so, but it's pretty obvious the cavemen scare her.

"A couple of furry motherfuckers."

"I think they are," she says.

"What?"

"Motherfuckers. Without taboos. It's disgusting." She shivers and heads back inside.

After scanning the treetops, I follow. There haven't been any climbers reported so far, but they are nothing if not unpredictable. Inside, I find Kim sitting on the kitchen floor, arranging our spices alphabetically. She's transferring them out of their grocery store bottles and into nicer ones, plain glass, neatly labeled. Kim has been tirelessly arranging things for the last four years—first the contents of our apartment on Pine Avenue, then, as her interior decorating business took off, other people's places, and lately our own house, since we took the plunge and bought it together last September. She finishes with fenugreek and picks up the galanga.

I go to the living room and put on some music. It's a nice, warm Saturday and if it weren't for the cavemen, we'd probably be spending it outdoors.

"Did you lock it?"

I tell her yes. I get a beer from the fridge and watch her. She's up to Greek seasonings. Her slim back is tense under her stretchy black top. The music kicks in and we don't say much for a few minutes. The band is D.I., and they're singing: "Johnny's got a problem and it's out of control!" We used to be punk rockers, Kim and I, back in the day. Now we are homeowners. When the kids down the street throw loud parties, we immediately dial 911.

"The thing that gets me," I say, "is how puny they are."

"What do they want?" asks Kim. Her hair is springing out of its plastic clamp, and she looks like she's going to cry. "What the fuck do they want with us?"

When the cavemen first appeared, they were assumed to be homeless examples of modern man. But it soon became obvious that even the most broken-down and mentally ill homeless guy wasn't *this* hairy. Or naked, hammer-browed, and short. And they didn't rummage through garbage cans and trash piles with an insatiable desire for spherical, shiny objects, empty shampoo bottles, and foam packing peanuts.

A reporter from KUTA had a hunch and sent a paleontologist from the university out to do a little fieldwork. For some reason I was watching the local news that night, and I remember this guy—typical academic, bad haircut, bad teeth—holding something in a take-out box. He said it was *scat*. Just when you think the news can't get any more absurd, there's a guy on TV, holding a turd in his hands, telling you the hairy people scurrying around the bike paths and Dumpsters of our fair berg are probably Neanderthal, from the Middle Paleolithic period, and that they have been surviving on a diet of pizza crusts, unchewed insects, and pigeon eggs.

People started calling them cavemen, though they were both male and female and tended to live in culverts, heavy brush, and freeway underpasses, rather than caves. Or they lived wherever—they turned up in weird places. The security guard at the Ice-O-Plex heard an eerie yipping one night. He flipped on the lights and found a half dozen of them sliding around the rink like otters. At least we knew another thing about them. They loved ice.

Facts about the cavemen have been difficult to establish. It is unclear if they're protected by the law. It is unclear if they are responsible for their actions. It *has* been determined that they're a nuisance to property and a threat to themselves. They will break into cars and climb fences to gain access to swimming pools, where they drop to all fours to drink. They will snatch food out of trucks or bins and eat out of trash cans. They avoid modern man as a general rule but are becoming bolder by the hour. The university students attempting to study them have had difficulties, though they've managed to discover that the cavemen cannot be taught or tamed and are extremely difficult to contain. They're strong for their size. It's hard to hurt them but they're simple to distract. They love pink plastic figurines and all things little-girl pretty. They love products perfumed with synthetic woodsy or herbal scents. You can shoot at them with rubber bullets all day and they'll just stand there, scratching their asses, but if you wave a little bottle of Barbie bubble bath in front of them they'll follow you around like a dog. They do not understand deterrence. They understand desire.

Fathers, lock up your daughters.

Kim sits across from me at the table, fingering the stem of her wineglass and giving me The Look. She gets The Look whenever I confess that I'm not ready to get married yet. The Look is a peculiar expression, pained and brave, like Kim has swallowed a bee but she isn't going to let on.

"It's fine," she says. "It's not like I'm all goddamn *ready* either."

I drain my glass and sigh. Tonight she's made a fennel-basil lasagna, lit candles, and scratched the price tag off the wine. Kim and I have been together for ten years, since we were twenty-three, and she's still a real firecracker, brainy, blonde, and bitchy. What I have in Kim is one of those cute little women with a swishy ponytail who cuts people off in traffic while swearing like a Marine. She's a fierce one, grinding her teeth all night long, grimly determined, though the object of her determination is usually vague or unclear. I've never wanted anyone else. And I've followed her instructions. I've nested. I mean, we bought a house together. We're co-borrowers on a thirty-year mortgage. Isn't that commitment enough?

Oh no, I can see it is not. She shoots me The Look a couple more times and begins grabbing dishes off the table and piling them in the sink. Kim wants the whole ordeal: a white dress, bridesmaids stuffed into taffeta, a soft rain of cherry blossoms. I want none of it. The whole idea of marriage makes me want to pull a dry cleaning bag over my head. I miss our punk rock days, Kim and me and our loser friends playing in bands, hawking spit at guys in BMWs, shooting drugs...and living in basements with anarchy tattoos poking through the rips in our clothing. Those times are gone and we've since established real credit ratings, I had the circled-A tattoo lasered off my neck, but...But. I feel like marriage would exterminate the last shred of the rebel in me. For some reason, I think of marriage as a living death.

Or, I don't know, maybe I'm just a typical guy, don't want to pay for the cow if I can get the milk for free.

Kim is leaning in the open doorway, gazing out at the street, sucking on a cigarette. She doesn't smoke much anymore, but every time I tell her I'm not ready she rips through a pack in a day and a half. "They'd probably ruin it anyway," she says, watching a trio of cavemen out on the street, loping along, sniffing the sidewalk. They fan out and then move back together to briefly touch one another's ragged, dirty brown fur with their noses. The one on the end, lighter-boned with small, pale breasts poking out of her chest hair, stops dead in her tracks and begins making a cooing sound at the sky. It must be a full moon. Then she squats and pees a silver puddle onto the road.

Kim stares at her. She forgets to take a drag and ash builds on the end of her cigarette. I know her; I know what she's thinking. She's picturing hordes of cavemen crashing the reception, grabbing canapés with their fists, rubbing their crotches against the floral arrangements. That would never do. She's too much of a perfectionist to ever allow that.

When I first saw the cavemen scurrying around town, I have to admit I was horrified. It was like when kids started to wear those huge pants—I couldn't get used to it, I couldn't get over the shock. But now I have hopes Kim will let the marriage idea slide for a while. For this reason I am somewhat grateful to the cavemen.

It rains for three days and the railroad underpasses flood. The washes are all running and on the news there are shots of SUVs bobbing in the current because some idiot ignored the DO NOT ENTER WHEN FLOODED sign and tried to gun it through four feet of rushing water. A lot of cavemen have been driven out of their nests and the incident level is way up. They roam around the city hungry and disoriented. We keep the doors locked at all times. Kim has a few stashes of sample-sized shampoo bottles around the house. She says she'll toss them out like trick-or-treat candy if any cavemen come around hassling her. So far, we haven't had any trouble.

Our neighbors, the Schaefers, haven't been so lucky. Kim invites them over for dinner one night, even though she knows I can't stand them. The Schaefers are these lonely, New Age hippies who are always staggering toward us with eager, too-friendly looks on their faces, arms outstretched, like they're going to grab our necks and start sucking. I beg Kim not to invite them, but at this stage in the game she seems to relish annoying me. They arrive dressed in gauzy robes. It turns out Winsome has made us a hammock out of hemp in a grasping attempt to secure our friendship. I tell her it's terrific and take it into the spare room where I stuff it in a closet, fully aware that by morning all of our coats are going to smell like bongwater.

When I return, everyone is sipping wine in the living room while the storm wets down the windows. Winsome is describing how she found a dead cavebaby in their backyard.

"It must not have been there for long," she says, her huge, oil-on-velvet eyes welling up with tears, "because it just looked like it was sleeping, and it wasn't very stiff. Its mother had wrapped it in tinsel, like for Christmas."

"Ick," says Kim. "How can you cry for those things?"

"It looked so vulnerable." Winsome leans forward and touches Kim's knee. "I sensed it had a spirit. I mean, they're human or protohuman or whatever."

"I don't care," says Kim, "I think they're disgusting."

"Isn't that kind of judgmental?"

"I think we should try to understand them," chimes in Evan, smoothing down his smock—every inch the soulful, sandal-wearing, sensitive man. "In a sense, they're *us*. If we understood why that female caveman wrapped her baby in tinsel, perhaps we'd know a little more about ourselves."

"I don't see why people can't just say 'cavewoman,'" snaps Kim. "'Female caveman' is weird, like 'male nurse.'

Besides, they are *not* us. We're supposed to have won. You
know, survival of the fittest."

"It might be that it's time we expanded our definition of
'humanity,'" intones Evan. "It might be that it's time we welcome all creatures on planet Earth."

I'm so incredibly annoyed by Evan that I have to go into
the bathroom and splash cold water on my face. When I get
back, Kim has herded the Schaefers into the dining room,
where she proceeds to serve us a deluxe vegetarian feast:
little kabobs of tofu skewered along with baby turnips,
green beans, rice, and steamed leaf of something or other.
Everything is lovely, symmetrical, and delicious, as always.
The house looks great. Kim has cleaned and polished and
organized the contents of each room until it's like living in a
furniture store. The Schaefers praise everything and Kim
grumbles her thanks. The thing about Kim is she's a wonderful cook, a great creator of ambiance, but she has a habit
of getting annoyed with her guests, as if no one could ever
be grateful enough for her efforts. We drain a couple more
bottles of wine and after a while I notice that Kim has become fed up with the Schaefers too. She starts giving them
The Look.

"Seriously," she begins, "do you two even like being
married?"

They exchange a glance.

"No, c'mon, really. It's overrated, right?" Kim pulls the
hair off her face and I can see how flushed she is, how infuriated. "I think all that crap about biological clocks and baby
lust, it's all sexist propaganda meant to keep women in line."

"Well, I haven't noticed any conspiracy," offers Winsome, checking everyone's face to make sure she's not somehow being disagreeable. "I think marriage is just part of the
journey."

"Ha," says Kim. "Ha ha ha." She leans across the table, swaying slightly. "I know," she pronounces, "that you don't believe that hippie shit. I can tell," she whispers, "how fucking lost you really are."

Then she stands, picks up her glass, and weaves toward the back door. "I have to go check the basement."

We stare at the space where Kim was for a while. Winsome is blinking rapidly and Evan keeps clearing his throat. I explain we have an unfinished basement that's been known to fill with water when it rains, and that the only entrance to it is outside in the yard, and that Kim probably wants to make sure that everything's okay down there. They nod vigorously. I can tell they're itching to purify our home with sticks of burning sage.

While Kim is gone I take them into the living room and show them my collection of LPs. I pull out my rare purple vinyl X-Ray Specs record, and after considering this for a while, Winsome informs me that purple is a healing color. We hear a couple of bangs under the house. I toy with the idea of checking on Kim, but then I recall the early days of our courtship, before all this house beautiful crap, when Kim used to hang out the window of my 1956 hearse, which was also purple, and scream "anarchy now!" and "destroy!" while lobbing rocks through smoked glass windows into corporate lobbies. It's difficult to worry about a girl like that.

It doesn't take long for the Schaefers and me to run out of small talk. I have no idea how to get them to go home; social transitions are Kim's jurisdiction. We sit there nodding at each other like idiots until Kim finally straggles back inside. She's muddy, soaked to the bone, and strangely jolly. She says there's about a foot of water in the basement and that she was walking around in there and it's like a big honking wading pool. She giggles. The Schaefers stare with horror at the puddle spreading around her feet onto our nice oak floors. I put my arm around her and kiss her hair. She smells like wet dog.

I come home from work a few days later and find Kim unloading a Toys "R" Us bag. I notice a diamond tiara/necklace set with huge, divorcée-sized fake jewels stuck to a panel of pink cardboard. Again, she seems happy, which is odd for Kim. In fact, she's taken to singing around the house in this new style where she doesn't sing actual words, she goes "nar nar nar" like some demented little kid. It drives me crazy, in particular when the game is on, so I tell her to fucking please cut it out. She glares at me and storms off into the backyard. I let her pout for a while, but I'm in the mood to make an effort, so I eventually go out and find her standing on a chair, hanging over the hedge, gazing at the alley. I lean in beside her and see a caveman shambling off with a red bandana tied around his neck, like a puppy.

"That's weird."

"Look at his butt."

I look. There's a big blob of pink bubble gum stuck in his fur.

"God," says Kim, "isn't that pitiful?"

I ask her what we're having for dinner. She looks at me blankly and says I don't know, what are we having for dinner. I tell her I'll cook, and when I get back from picking up the pizza she's nowhere to be found. I walk from one empty room to another while the hairs on my arms start to tingle. I have to say, there's a peculiar feeling building in the household. Things are in a state of slight disarray. There's a candy bar wrapper on the coffee table, and the bag from the toy store is on the kitchen floor. I yell Kim's name. When she doesn't appear I turn on the TV and eat a few slices straight from the box. For some reason that starts to bother me, so I get up and get a plate, silverware, and a paper napkin. Kim walks in a little while later. She's wet from the waist down and all flushed, as if she's been doing calisthenics.

"I was bailing out the basement!" she says, with great verve, like basement bailing is a terrific new sport. Her hair is tangled around her head and she's sucking on a strand of it. She is smiling away. She says: "I'm worried about letting all that water just stand down there!"

But she doesn't look worried.

On the news one night, a psychic with a flashlight shining up under his chin explains there's a time portal in the condemned Pizza Hut by the freeway. Though the mayor whines he wasn't elected to buckle to the whim of every nutbar with an opinion, there are televised protests featuring people shaking placards proclaiming the Pizza Hut ground zero of unnatural evil, and finally they just bulldoze it to shut everyone up. A while after that, the incident levels start to drop. It seems that the cavemen are thinning out. They are not brainy enough for our world, and they can't stop extinguishing themselves. They tumble into swimming pools and drown. They walk through plate glass windows and sever their arteries. They fall asleep under eighteen-wheelers and wander onto runways and get mauled by pit bulls.

It looks like we're the dominant species after all; rock smashes scissors, *Homo sapiens* kicks *Homo sapiens neanderthalensis*'s ass.

As the caveman population drops, the ominous feeling around town begins to lift. You can feel it in the air: women jog by themselves instead of in pairs. People barbecue large cuts of meat at dusk. The cavemen, it seems, are thinning out everywhere except around our house. I come home from work and walk through the living room and peek out the back window just in time to see a tough, furry leg disappear through a hole in the hedge. The hole is new. When I go outside and kick around in the landscaping, I find neat little stashes of rhinestones and fake pearls, Barbie shoes, and folded squares of foil wrapping paper. They can't see that well but have the ears of a dog and flee as soon as I rustle the window shades. One time, though, I peel back the shade silently and catch a pair skipping in circles around the clothesline. One of them is gripping something purple and hairy, and when I go out there later I find a soiled My Little Pony doll on the ground. They are not living up to their reputation as club-swinging brutes. More than anything, they resemble feral little girls.

Also, our house has become an unbelievable mess. Kim walks through the door and drops the mail on the coffee table, where it remains for days until I remove it. There are panties on the bathroom floor and water glasses on top of the television and scraps of food on the kitchen counter. I ask Kim what's going on and she just says she's sick of that anal constant-housekeeping-bullshit, and if I want it clean, I can clean it myself. She looks straight at me and says this, without flinching, without any signs of deference or anger or subtle backing away that had always let me know, in non-verbal but gratifying ways, that I had the upper hand in the relationship. She tosses an orange peel on the table before marching outside and descending into the basement.

I stand there in the kitchen, which smells like sour milk, shaking my head and trying to face up to the increasingly obvious fact that my girlfriend of ten years is having an affair, and that her lover is a Neanderthal man from the Pleistocene epoch. They rendezvous in our moldy, water-stained basement where he takes her on the cement floor beneath a canopy of spiderwebs, grunting over her with his animal-like body, or perhaps behind her, so that when she comes back inside there are thick, dark hairs stuck all over her shirt and she smells like a cross between some musky, woodland animal gland and Herbal Essences shampoo. Furthermore, she's stopped shaving her legs.

The next day, I duck out of the office claiming I have a doctor's appointment and zip back home around noon. I open the door with my key and creep inside. I don't know what I'm looking for. I think I half expect to find Kim in bed with one of those things, and that he'll pop up and start "trying to reason" with me in a British accent. What I find instead is an empty house. Kim's car is gone. I poke around, stepping over mounds of dirty clothes, then head out back and take the stairs to the basement. When I pull the door open, the first thing to hit me is the smell of mold and earth. I pace from one side to the other and shine my flashlight around, but I don't see anything suspicious, just an old metal weight-lifting bench with a plastic bucket sitting on top. Maybe, I think, I'm making this whole thing up in my head. Maybe Kim just goes down there because she needs some time to herself.

But then on my way out, I spot something. On the concrete wall beside the door, several feet up, my flashlight picks out a pattern of crude lines. They appear to have been made with charcoal or maybe some type of crayon. When I take a few steps back, I can see it's a drawing, a cave painting of some sort. It's red and black with the occasional pom-pom of dripping orange that looks like it was made by someone who doesn't understand spray paint.

I stand there for two or three minutes trying to figure out what the painting is about, then spend another fifteen trying to convince myself my interpretation is wrong. The picture shows half a dozen cars in a *V*-shaped formation bearing down on a group of cavemen. The cavemen's flailing limbs suggest flight or panic; obviously, they're in danger of being flattened by the cars. Above them, sketched in a swift, forceful manner, floats a huge, God-like figure with very long arms. One arm cradles the fleeing cavemen while the other blocks the cars. This figure is flowing and graceful and has a big ponytail sprouting from the top of her head. Of course, it's meant to be Kim. Who else?

I go upstairs and sit at the kitchen table, elbowing away half a moldy cantaloupe, and hold my head in my hands. I was hoping it was nothing—a casual flirtation at most—but a guy who makes a cave painting for a girl is probably in love with the girl. And girls love to be loved, even high-strung ones like Kim. I admit I'm hurt, but my hurt switches to anger and my anger to resolve. I can fight this thing. I can win her back. I know her; I know what to do.

I put on rubber gloves and start cleaning everything, thoroughly and with strong-smelling products, the way Kim likes things cleaned. I do the laundry and iron our shirts and line everything up neatly in the closet. I get down on my knees and wipe the baseboards, then up on a chair to dust the lightbulbs. I pull a long clot of hair out of the drain. There's a picture of us in Mexico in a silver frame on top of the medicine cabinet. I pick it up and think: that is my woman! It's civilization versus base instinct, and I vow to deploy the strongest weapon at my disposal: my evolutionarily superior traits. I will use my patience, my facility with machinery and tools, my complex problem-solving skills. I will bathe often and floss my teeth. I will cook with gas.

A little after five Kim walks in and drops the mail on the coffee table. She looks around the house, at the gleaming neatness, smiling slightly and going "nar nar nar" to the tune of "Nobody Does It Better." I stand there in my cleanest suit with my arms hanging at my sides and gaze at her, in her little professional outfit, pretty and sexy in an I-don't-know-it-but-I-do way, clutching her black purse, her hair pulled back with one of those fabric hair things.

"God, I can't believe you cleaned," she says, and walks through the kitchen and out of the house into the yard and slams the basement door behind her.

Kim is so happy. The worst part is she's so disgustingly happy and I could never make her happy all by myself and I don't particularly like her this way. For a couple of weeks she walks around in a delirious haze. She spins around on the porch with her head thrown back and comments on the shape of the clouds. She asks why haven't I bothered to take in the pretty, pretty sunset, all blue and gold. Like I fucking care, I say, forgetting my pledge to be civil. It's as though someone has dumped a bottle of pancake syrup over her head—she has no nastiness left, no edge, no resentment. Her hair is hanging loose and she has dirty feet and bad breath. She smiles all the time. This is not the girl I originally took up with.

Of course, I'm heartsick; I'm torn up inside. Even so, I do my best to act all patient and evolutionarily superior. I keep the house clean enough to lick. I start to cook elaborate meals the minute I get home from work. I groom myself until I'm sleek as a goddamn seal. I aim for a Fred Astaire/James Bond hybrid: smooth, sophisticated, oozing suaveness around the collar and cuffs—the kind of guy who would never fart in front of a woman, at least not audibly. She has a big, inarticulate lug already. I want to provide her with an option.

Kim takes it all for granted, coming and going as she pleases, wandering away from the house without explanation, hanging out in the basement with the door locked and brushing off my questions about what the hell she's doing down there, and with whom. She doesn't listen when I talk to her and eats standing up in front of the refrigerator with the door open, yelling between bites that it's time for me to go to the store and get more milk. One evening I watch her polish off a plate of appetizers I have made for her, melon balls wrapped in prosciutto, downing them one after another like airline peanuts. When she's finished, she unbuttons the top button of her pants and ambles out the door and lets it slam without so much as a glance back at me. Without so much as a thank you.

I trot out after her, figuring it's about time I give her a suave, patient lecture, but I'm not fast enough and she slams the basement door in my face. I pound and scream for a while before giving up and going up into the yard to wait. The night is very still. There's a full moon and the hedges glow silver on the top and then fade to blue at the bottom. I get a glass of iced tea and pull a chair off the patio, thinking to myself that she can't stay down there forever. I think about how maybe I'll catch the caveguy when he comes out too. Maybe I can tie on an apron and offer them both baby wieners on a toothpick.

After a while I hear a rustling in the hedges. At that moment I'm too miserable to be aware of the specifics of what's going on around me, so I'm startled as hell when a cavegirl pops out of the hedge, backlit in the moonlight, and begins walking toward me with a slow, hesitant gate. I sit there, taking shallow breaths, not sure whether or not I should be afraid. She has a low brow and a tucked, abbreviated chin, like Don Knotts's, but her limbs are long and sinewy. When she gets closer I see that she looks a lot stronger than a human woman does, and of course, she's naked. Her breasts are like perfect human pinup breasts with bunny fur growing all over them. I can't unstick my eyes from them as they bob toward me, moving closer, until they come to a stop less than an arm's length from my chin. They are simultaneously furry and plump and I really want to bite them. But not hard.

She leans in closer. I hold very still as she reaches out with a leathery hand and begins to stroke my lapel. She lowers her head to my neck and sniffs. On the exhale I discover that cavegirl breath smells just like moss. She prods me a few times with her fingertips; after she's had enough of that she just rubs the fabric of my suit and sniffs my neck while sort of kneading me rhythmically, like a purring cat. It's pretty obvious she likes my suit—a shiny sharkskin number I've hauled out of the back of the closet in the interest of wooing Kim—and I guess she likes my cologne too. For a minute I feel special and chosen, but then it occurs to me that there's something sleazy and impersonal about her attention. I'm probably just a giant, shiny, sandalwood-scented object to her. The moon is behind her so I can't see her that clearly, but then she shifts and I get a better view of her face and I realize she's young. Really young. I feel like a creep for wanting to feel her up, more because she's about fourteen than because she's a Neanderthal.

She swings a leg over and settles her rump onto my thigh, lapdance-style.

I say: "Whoa there, Jailbait."

The cavegirl leaps up like she's spring-loaded. She stops a few feet away and stares at me. I stare back. She tilts her head from side to side in puzzlement. The moon shines down. I reach into my glass and draw out a crescent-shaped piece of ice, moving with aching slowness, and offer it to her on a flat palm. She considers this ice cube for a good long time. I hold my arm as still as possible while freezing water trickles off my elbow and my muscles start to seize. Then, after a few false lunges, she snatches it from my hand.

"Nar," she says. Just that. Then she darts back into the hedge with her prize.

I remain in the moonlight for a while, shaking with excitement. I feel almost high. It's like I've touched a wild animal; I've communicated with it—an animal that's somehow human, somehow like me. I'm totally giddy.

This is probably how it was with Kim and her guy when they first met.

I guess I'm a complete failure with every category of female because the cavegirl does not come back. Even worse, Kim continues to treat me like I'm invisible. It's painfully clear that my strategy of suaveness isn't working. So I say screw evolution. What's it ever done for me? I go out drinking with the guys and allow the house to return to a state of nature. The plates in the sink turn brown. I shower every other day, every third. Kim and I go days without speaking to each other. By this time there are hardly any cavemen left around town; the count is running at one or two dozen. I go to the bars and everyone is lounging with their drinks, all relaxed and relieved that the cavemen aren't really an issue anymore, while I continue to stew in my own miserable interspecies soap opera. I don't even want to talk to anyone about it. What could I say? Hey buddy, did I mention my girlfriend has thrown me over for the Missing Link? It's humiliating.

One hungover afternoon I decide to skip the bars and come straight home from the office. Kim, naturally, is not around, though this barely registers. I've lost interest in tracking her whereabouts. But when I go into the kitchen, I catch sight of her through the window, standing outside, leaning against the chinaberry tree. It looks like she's sick or something. She's trying to hold herself up but keeps doubling over anyway. I go outside and find her braced against the tree, sobbing from deep in her belly while a string of snot swings from her nose. She's pale and spongy and smudged with dirt and I get the feeling she's been standing there crying all afternoon. She's clutching something. A red bandana. So it was him. The one with gum on his butt.

"Where is he?"

"He's gone," she whispers, and gives me a sad, dramatic, miniseries smile. "They're all gone."

Her sobs begin anew. I pat her on the back.

So she's curled over crying and I'm patting her thinking well, well; now that the other boyfriend is gone she's all mine again. Immediately I'm looking forward to putting the whole caveman ordeal behind us and having a regular life like we had before. I see all sorts of normal activities looming in the distance like a mirage, including things we always made fun of, like procreating and playing golf. She blows her nose in the bandana. I put my arm around her. She doesn't shake it off.

I should wait I know, I should go slow; but I can see the opening, the niche all vacant and waiting for me. I feel absolutely compelled to exploit it right away, before some other guy does. I turn to Kim and say: "Babe, let's just forget about this whole caveman thing and go back to the way it was before. I'm willing to forgive you. Let's have a normal life without any weird creatures in it, okay?"

She's still hiccuping and wiping her nose but I observe a knot of tension building in her shoulders, the little wrinkles of a glare starting around the edge of her eyes. I realize I'm in grave danger of eliciting The Look. It dawns on me that my strategy is a failure and I'd better think fast. So I bow to the inevitable. I've always known I couldn't put it off forever.

I take a deep breath and drop to one knee and tell her I love her and I can't live without her and beg her to marry me while kissing her hand. She's hiccuping and trying to pull her hand away, but in the back of my mind I'm convinced that this is going to work and of course she'll say yes. I've never made an effort like this before; I've only told her I love her two or three times total, in my life. It's inconceivable that this effort won't be rewarded. Plus, I know her. She lives for this. This is exactly what she wants.

I look up at her from my kneeling position. Her hair is greasy and her face is smeared with dirt and snot, but she's stopped crying. I see that she has created a new Look. It involves a shaking of the head while simultaneously pushing the lips outward, like she's crushed a wasp between her teeth and is about to spit it out. It's a look of pity, pity mixed with superiority; pity mixed with superiority and blended with dislike.

"I don't want a normal life without any creatures in it," Kim says, her voice ragged from crying, but contemptuous nonetheless. "I want an extraordinary life, with everything in it."

The Look fades. She brings her dirty, snotty face to mine and kisses me on the forehead and turns and walks away, leaving me on my knees. I stumble into the house after her. I can smell a trail of scent where she's passed by, cinnamon and sweat and fabric softener, but though I run through the house after her, and out into the street, I don't see her anywhere, not all night. Not the night after that. Never again.

Some psychic with a towel on his head says the cavemen passed through his drive-through palm reading joint on their way back to the Pleistocene epoch, and I finally go over and ask him if he saw Kim with them. He has me write him a check and then says, Oh *yeah*, I did see her! She was at the front of this line of female cavemen and she was all festooned with beads and tinsel, like she was some sort of goddess! He says it in this bullshit way, but after some reflection I decide even charlatans may see strange and wondrous things, as we all had during the time the cavemen were with us, and then report them so that they sound like a totally improbable lie.

It's bizarre, the way time changes things. Now that the cavemen are gone, it seems obvious that their arrival was the kind of astonishing event people measure their entire lives by; and now that Kim is gone it seems clear that she was astonishing too, regal and proud, like she's represented in the cave painting. I once thought of her as sort of a burden, a pain-in-the-ass responsibility, but now I think of her as the one good thing I had in my life, an intense woman with great reserves of strength, forever vanished.

Or, I don't know; maybe I'm just a typical guy, don't know what I have until it walks out on me.

I've been trying to get over her, but I can't stop wallowing in it. One night we hold a drum circle on the site of the old Pizza Hut, and I swear that after this night, I'll force myself to stop thinking about her. This drum circle is the largest yet, maybe a couple of hundred people milling around, having the kind of conversations people have these days—you know, they were annoyed and frightened by the cavemen when they were here, but now that they're gone they just want them back, they want that weird, vivid feeling, the newness of the primitive world, et cetera. My job is to tend the fire. There's a six-foot pyramid of split pine in the middle of the circle, ready to go. At the signal I throw on a match. The wood is soaked in lighter fluid and goes up with a whoosh. Everyone starts to bang on their drums, or garbage can lids, or whatever percussive dingus they've dragged along, while I stand there poking the flames, periodically squirting in plumes of lighter fluid, as the participants wail and drum and cry and dance.

We are supposedly honoring the cavemen with this activity, but in truth no one ever saw the cavemen making fires or dancing or playing any sort of musical instrument. Apparently the original Neanderthal did these things; they also ate one another's brains and worshipped the skulls of bears, though no one seems anxious to resurrect these particular hobbies. Still, I admit I get kind of into it. Standing there in the middle, sweating, with the sound of the drumming surrounding me while the fire crackles and pops, it's easy to zone out. For a moment I imagine what it might be like to live in an uncivilized haze of sweat and hunger and fear and desire, to never plan, to never speak or think in words—but then the smell of lighter fluid snaps me back to how artificial this whole drum circle is, how prearranged and ignited with gas.

Later, when the fire has burned out, some New Age hardcores roll around in the ashes and pray for the cavemen to come back, our savage brothers, our hairy predecessors, et cetera, but of course they don't come back. Those guys look stupid, covered in ash. When the sun comes up, everyone straggles away. I get into my hatchback and listen to bad news on the radio as I drive home.

YOU

There really is no English sound that is equivalent to the French *u* sound. Try the following for best results: Say the sound *oo* as in Sue while trying to say *ee* as in see. As you try to make the sound, concentrate on puckering your lips as if you just ate a very sour pickle. That's about as close as you can get. If you say *oo*, don't worry, you'll be understood. This is a foreign sound that requires concentration and practice.

—THE IDIOT'S GUIDE TO FRENCH

Ellis Hartsall had given you trouble from the start. He was one of those boys who'd signed up for French only to decide that it was a language for girls. There were always one or two of them every year. It didn't matter how many times you explained that 50 percent of the population of France was male, and that none of them felt emasculated by their native tongue. Boxers, racecar drivers, construction workers, rock stars, high school jocks—they all pursed their lips in order to properly pronounce words like *tu*. "Fine," Ellis would say, "*tout.*" You'd tell him that was a completely different word, meaning *all* and not *you*, and he'd shrug, and you'd send him to the office.

"What do you want me to do about it?" Derek Finton, your principal, asked one day in October. You'd been sending Ellis to him since school began in September, and still he returned to class unwilling to participate.

"Tell him he has to say *tu*," you said. "The right way."

"Two?" Derek said. He was tilted back in his swivel chair, hands clasped behind his head. Most of the faculty made fun of the fact that he had a perspiration problem, but for you, the damp circles under his arms seemed honest. Teaching was hard work. You yourself had ruined several blouses over the past seven years.

"No," you said, "*tu*. It's the informal *you* in French. But you have to make your mouth go like this—" You formed your lips into a near-kiss.

"*Tu*," Derek said again, mimicking you.

"That's better," you said.

"Can all the other kids do this?" he asked.

"No," you said. "But they try. Ellis won't even try."

"So grade him down."

"I feel he should try," you said firmly.

"Carrie," Derek said, "Ellis is pretty much a lost cause. Let's not waste too much energy on him, okay?"

You thought about this for a moment. About your hideous salary and all the weekends you spent grading. You thought about how you'd always admired Derek and his occasional indifference toward the children, and finally you said, "All right."

"Good," Derek said.

"What do you do with him when I send him here?" you asked.

"Well," Derek said, "I talk to him for a few minutes. Try to find out what the problem is. Then I send him to a study hall."

"What does he say the problem is?"

"He says he should've taken Spanish."

In class the next day, when it was the same old story with Ellis, you finally gave him detention. *"D'accord,"* he said amiably. This was his trick—a willingness to speak French at the very instant he was reprimanded for not doing so. Whenever you sent him to the principal's office, he said, *"Au revoir, Madame Adlon. À demain."*

That afternoon, you barely noted his arrival in your classroom, his odd habit of ducking through the doorway with his guitar case, even though, tall as he was, he would've cleared it. "Where should I sit?" he asked, and you shrugged and said, "Wherever." You expected him to choose his assigned seat at the back of the room, but instead he plunked down front and center, directly across from you at your gray metal desk.

This unnerved you a little. You'd never really seen him up close before. Even when he stood before you, his face was too high, on another plane. Now, for once, you weren't looking into his nostrils. It was his eyes that fell on your horizon line, and they were green behind a pair of round silver glasses. His untrimmed hair curled softly at the edges, and you had an urge to clip some of it and seal it in a plastic bag.

"Is this really detention?" he asked. "Or can I do my homework?"

"You can work on your pronunciation," you said.

"Oh," he said glumly.

"C'mon," you said, "make your mouth like this and say *tu.*"

He watched you very closely as you pursed your lips. He seemed to be taking the whole thing very seriously. Then he said, "I wish I could, Ms. Adlon. I really do. But I can't. It's too gay."

"Gay," you said. "What does that mean?"

"You know what it means."

"Happy?" you said.

He laughed. "Yeah. Happy. That's what it means."

"You know," you said, "if you took Spanish, you'd have to speak with a lisp. Isn't that gay, too?"

"I thought that was only Castilian Spanish," he said.

You looked at him. He wasn't supposed to have known this.

"Do they teach Castilian Spanish here?" he asked.

"No," you said, "they don't."

He smirked. Like he'd really gotten you. Then he said, "*Barthelona,* right?"

You nodded.

"Yeah," he said, "I guess that's pretty gay."

"Just not as gay as saying *tu,*" you said.

He shrugged. "I don't know. They're about the same."

Asshole, you thought. Derek was right. If he didn't want to say *tu,* he didn't have to say *tu.* Grade him down and forget about it. "Okay," you said, "let's go home."

"Already?" Ellis asked, suddenly sounding deprived.

"Sure," you said. "Why not?" In your irritation, you pushed your chair out too quickly. One of the back legs got caught in the nap of the indoor-outdoor carpet, and you ended up flipping backward. The blackboard covered the wall behind you, and you hit your head on the edge of the chalk tray going down. Somehow, you managed to stay seated while on the ground. It was a strange position to be in, with your legs up in the air like that. Because of your skirt, it seemed pertinent to pull them together.

"Ms. Adlon?" Ellis said. He hovered above you, looking worried.

"Aren't you going to laugh?" you said.

"No," he said, "of course not."

You felt around the back of your head for blood, disappointed when there was none.

"Maybe you shouldn't move," Ellis said, squatting down beside you.

"Of course I should move," you said. "I'm going home."

He smiled. Light spittle connected his upper lip to the bottom one.

"Say *tu*," you said.

He was very close to you now, and you could smell the soap on his neck. You could see the spot on his right shoulder where his guitar strap probably fell. You wanted to ask him to sing you a song—something by Teenage Fanclub or Big Star. You wanted him to say, "Who are they?" then invite him over to your place to see your record collection. You wanted to tell him you'd been a deejay in college, that you'd slept with several of the guys who'd called in to your radio show, that one of them had eventually become your husband. You wanted him to know that you weren't just any old French teacher.

But you didn't say anything. And he didn't say *tu*. He said, "Hold on, Ms. Adlon," and he gripped the back of your chair and within seconds you'd been righted. "Who's the president?" he wanted to know, and when you told him, he said, "You're going to be okay."

He lay a hand on your forearm then, and it was like pumice. Like being touched by your grandfather. You looked

down at the dry skin coating his large knuckles and wondered how a sixteen-year-old had gotten so worn out. In
your dizzy head you heard his calloused fingertips riding the
neck of his guitar.

You found yourself thinking about him on the drive home.
How he hadn't laughed at you when you'd fallen, how he'd
been strong enough to lift your chair with you in it. You
thought about Derek Finton calling him a lost cause, when
maybe this wasn't the case. You began to feel slightly special
that you'd brought out the humanity in such a troubled
young man. Maybe it wasn't so bad, you thought, being a
teacher.

Normally, you hated it. You hated that you'd abandoned
radio. Never in your life would you counsel anyone to have
a fallback career, you'd decided. It was the cruelest of fates.
A job you couldn't help but do well, and would therefore do
forever. That said, there were worse things than having to
speak French for a living. You loved the language, loved that
the students were all so shy that you got to do most of the
talking. And you had a good accent. You'd known this since
your junior year abroad, when you'd perfected the trick of
blending in. There was nothing more pleasing than the look
on a Parisian's face when you revealed your true country of
origin. A near despair over the fact that they weren't so special as they might've thought.

You got off on making the French feel unspecial. On
punishing them for inventing a language that would become
your fallback career. You knew you'd met your husband the
second he called up the radio station at SUNY-Oneonta to
request Charles Aznavour, his accent dripping through the
receiver. You responded to him in French, and he accused
you of being a citizen of the world. You found this charm-

ing, and invited him to pick you up when your shift ended. He arrived with a bicycle, which he clearly intended to ride you home on. Instead, you took it from him and rode yourself home. He tracked you down a few hours later, furious. You apologized for taking off like that, and agreed to have sex with him despite your period. When it was over, you pointed to an oval blood clot you'd deposited on his leg, and he screamed. He was one big ball of reactions, and at the time you couldn't have imagined liking anyone more.

A year or so after you were married, however, he started seeing a therapist. A woman named Kay who advised him that it wasn't in his best interest to let you push him around. You didn't necessarily disagree with this, only you resented the fact that you now seemed to be married to two people. Sometimes, in the middle of an argument, Bruno would call Kay up and ask who she thought was right. She would invariably tell him that he was, at which point he would get off the phone and say, "I sink it would be best if I backed away from zeese conversation." The two of you never spoke English in private. Speaking French was your greatest intimacy—a way for you to escape yourself, and for Bruno to feel more at home. To have this disrupted by Kay's untranslatable psychobabble was too much, and you began to punish Bruno by reverting to English yourself.

You and Ellis had this in common. A refusal to speak French with someone who desperately wanted you to. When you did it with Bruno, he pouted and tattled to Kay. When Ellis did it with you, you pouted and tattled to Derek Finton. And the advice came back basically the same: not much you can do about it, try not to get too worked up. Part of you wished you could brainstorm with Bruno, or even just commiserate. It was hard dealing with unwarranted belligerence. You couldn't imagine how he'd lasted this long.

At home, you flipped through the mail and checked your phone messages. There were three from Bruno, who was in Potsdam for a few days, dealing with a public pool that had been dug and left. This was his job, cleaning up other people's messes. He worked for a surety that sent him all over New York state, estimating what it would take to complete construction jobs in default. There was nothing pre-emptive about it. Work was only work if someone had fucked up, had not done their job properly. It seemed wrong to you somehow, capitalizing on the mistakes and failures of others, but Bruno disagreed. "This isn't *schadenfreude*," he'd say, "it's engineering." Still, you couldn't help but picture him at the edge of that Olympic-sized pit upstate, rubbing his palms together.

Then you felt guilty. Bruno was a good man. His messages said, "Miss you," "Love you," and, "Call me," respectively. Only you didn't feel like calling. You'd already called yesterday and the day before that and the day before that. What more was there to say other than everything was exactly the same? Sure, you'd fallen over in your chair, and sure, a student had helped you up. But so what? Your head was fine. No stitches had been required.

You deleted the messages, happy to see the red zero in the window again. Then you went in the kitchen to make yourself some dinner. This was the best thing about Bruno being gone—not having to eat right. It wasn't as if you subsisted on Ring Dings and Pringles or anything, but you definitely got tired of the salad course. Sometimes you just wanted pasta with butter and garlic, or scrambled eggs, or a lamb chop fried in olive oil. You weren't French. You didn't need every meal to be complete.

After dinner, you washed your dishes, then went to check your e-mail. You'd told your students they could write to you anytime with questions, but so far you hadn't heard a peep. Secretly, you were relieved. You hadn't really meant the offer. It was just something you'd done to try to seem nice. Today, though, you received your first message. It was from a willowy girl named Marie Du Pont who wanted to know if she could start a French Club. *That way,* she wrote, *we could do French-based activities such as traveling to Montreal or food.*

You wrote back saying that a French Club was a very good idea, and that Marie should feel free to raise the issue in class the following day. If enough people were interested, you wrote, you'd be happy to supervise. You didn't mean any of this. In reality, you were furious at the thought of having to do extra work.

Later, as you lay on the couch listening to Dolly Parton sing about a woman who slept with a silver dagger, the phone rang. You weren't going to get it, except that Bruno sounded frantic over the machine. "Hello?" you said, stumbling into the kitchen and grabbing the receiver off the wall.

"Oh," he said, "thank God."

"What do you want?" you said.

"What do I want?" he said. "Didn't you get my messages?"

"No," you lied.

"Of course you got my messages," he insisted.

You didn't say anything.

"I thought something had happened to you," he said.

"What could possibly happen to me? Nothing happens to me."

"I thought you'd hurt yourself."

"I'm not eighty," you said.

He laughed at this.

"What do you want?" you asked again, softening a little.

"Just to hear your voice, to speak a little."

"Is this enough?" you asked him.

He sighed. "Maybe."

"I have to go," you said.

"Why?"

"Because," you said, "my favorite song is coming up."

He paused for a moment, then said fine. After you'd hung up, you turned the stereo off and went to bed. You had no favorite song. How could you possibly, when there were so many of them?

Early the next morning, before your alarm went off, you had an orgasm in your sleep. This had never happened to you before, and you lay in bed for some time, questioning its authenticity. It was just too hard to believe that your body could be so magnanimous.

You ate a bowl of Cheerios for breakfast, then headed off to work. On the way, you tried to remember what you'd been dreaming about at dawn. Or whom. But you couldn't. Your own dreams bored you just as much as anyone else's.

In the teachers lounge before homeroom, Lauren Breslow approached you and said, "Derek says you're having problems with Ellis Hartsall."

You were sitting at a round table, drinking a cup of coffee. "I wouldn't exactly call them problems."

"Don't take any guff," Lauren said. "I mean it. Give him an inch, he'll take a foot."

"Okay," you said.

"I would know," she added.

It was true. Lauren had had a terrible time with Ellis in tenth-grade art. He'd been defiant in the face of her academic demands. He'd used foul language and submitted portraits of her in varying states of undress. The last one had depicted her with thick calves and drooping breasts, glaring out at the classroom. It was deeply unflattering, and you'd had to push her to retrieve it from the trash and show it to Derek Finton. He promptly suspended Ellis and removed him from Lauren's class altogether. Later, as you comforted her in the teachers lounge, you were surprised to hear her say that she would miss him. "I just don't understand," she cried. "All his other drawings made me look like a centerfold."

That afternoon, as your fifth-period Intermediate French class began shuffling in, you busied yourself at your desk. You didn't want Ellis to think you were waiting for him, that you'd finally recalled your dream from that morning. In it, he sat beside you in your fallen chair. With one hand, he kept reaching around to touch the underside of your plastic seat, except there was a hole in it, and in your panty hose, too, so that his fingers passed straight into your vagina. *"Bonjour, Madame Adlon,"* you heard someone say, and you looked up to see Marie Du Pont. She was wearing a scoop-neck T-shirt that hinted at cleavage.

"Oh," you said, "hello."

She smiled at you and took her seat. You were about to return to your busywork when Ellis walked in. You watched him set his guitar case by the classroom door, then lope toward you. "How's your head?" he asked, tapping his own.

"En français, s'il vous plaît," you said, and he shrugged and walked on.

"Vous avez mal à la tête, Madame?" Marie asked.

"No," you said.

She turned to look at Ellis in the back row, but he was fumbling around with a notebook.

After the second bell rang, you asked the students to please take out their *French in Action* textbooks and open to the dialogue at the beginning of chapter three. Marie raised her hand.

"Yes?" you said.

"*Pardonnez, Madame,*" she said, "*mais est-ce que je peux annoncer le Club Français?*"

"Oh," you said, "right. Go ahead." You couldn't bring yourself to speak French with her. Her accent was too perfect. She was a show-off, as you'd once been, and you were interested in cutting her down.

"*Merci, Madame,*" she said, standing. Then, without invitation, she came to the front of the class and positioned herself beside you. "*En Français?*" she asked, and you shrugged and said, "Either way."

She nodded. "Well," she said, turning to her fellow students, "I was just wondering if anyone would want to start a French Club? We could maybe raise money for a field trip to Montreal, or else have a dinner with a whole bunch of courses. Stuff like that."

There was an awkward silence during which no one raised their hand.

"*Personne?*" Marie asked softly.

When there was still no answer, she looked to you for help. As much as you wanted to dislike her, you only felt sorry for her now. It was one thing to make fun of the kids in the teachers lounge, to grade their essays based on the first paragraphs, to make up lectures as you went along. It was quite another, however, to keep them from pursuing their true interests. You couldn't seem to manage it. Finally you sighed and said, "I really think this could be fun, people. We could eat and watch movies and listen to Charles Aznavour and—"

"How do you know about Charles Aznavour?" Ellis interrupted.

"*Pardonnez?*" you said.

"Charles Aznavour," he said, "how do you know his music?"

"En français, s'il vous plaît," you said.

You thought he'd give up then, as he usually did, but after a brief pause, he said, *"Comment vous savez Charles Aznavour?"*

You smiled at him. You couldn't help it. *"Parce que j'étais un disc-jockey à l'université,"* you said.

Some of the kids laughed. Even Marie. But not Ellis. *"Vraiment?"* he said.

You nodded.

"What kind of stuff did you play?"

"En français," you prompted.

He hesitated for a moment, then said, "Never mind."

"Anyone want to start a French Club?" Marie asked.

Ellis raised his hand. "Sure," he said, "I'll be in the French Club."

Again more laughs. But Marie turned to you excitedly. "Is that enough?" she asked. "Is two enough to start the club?"

Of course it wasn't. Five wasn't enough. But you went ahead and said that it was.

At three o'clock, after the elephant train of buses had pulled away from the curb below your third-floor classroom, you, Marie, and Ellis convened the first meeting of the French Club. You asked Marie where she'd gotten her beautiful accent, and she revealed that her father hailed from Lyon. *Ha,* you thought, *cheating.* To her face, though, you said, "Well, you sound like you were born there yourself."

"Merci, Madame Adlon," she said, clearly pleased.

"What kind of music did you play on your radio show?" Ellis asked.

"Ellis," you said, "this is a French Club, not a music club. If you want to have this conversation, you need to do it in French."

"*Merde,*" he said. Then he laughed.

"That's enough," you said.

"*Sacrebleu,*" he said.

"Enough cursing," you told him.

He shrugged.

"Anyway," Marie said, "I was thinking we could either take an overnight trip to Montreal, or else go eat at my dad's restaurant."

"Your dad has a restaurant?" you asked.

Marie nodded. "He said he'd give us free dinner if we promised to speak French all night."

"That's very generous," you said.

"What about Montreal?" Ellis asked.

"Montreal might be a little expensive," you told him.

"But I want to go on a trip."

"Maybe if more people join the club, we can talk to Principal Finton about a fund-raiser."

"That guy hates me. He'll never let me go."

"You don't know that," you said.

"What about dinner?" Marie asked, turning back to him again. "Don't you like *haute cuisine*?"

"I can't talk French all night," Ellis said. "I just can't."

"Sure you can," you said. "I'll help you."

"*Moi aussi,*" Marie said warmly.

That night, you got an e-mail from Ellis. It read: *What kind of music did you play on your radio show? I'm not in French class right now, or French Club, and I really want to know. You said we could write to you about anything. Please answer. EH.*

It seemed very intimate to you, the lack of salutation, the initials, and you toyed with the idea of responding similarly. In the end, though, you wrote: *Ellis, thank you for your interest. On my college radio show, I played American Music Club, My Dad Is Dad, Big Dipper, The Bats, The Go-Betweens, The Stars of Heaven, and Squeeze, to name a few. I also liked Public Enemy quite a bit. What kind of music do you listen to? I notice you have a guitar. Sincerely, Ms. Adlon.* You tried to convince yourself to delete the question—to not make this into a conversation—but it was too late. Some other part of you had already hit SEND.

You ate another pleasantly meager dinner, then listened to Bruno's answering machine message. "I hope you're well," he said. "This pool business is taking a lot longer than anyone expected." To reward him for having called only once, you stretched out on the couch and dialed his hotel. When he picked up, you said, "I'm having a problem with one of my students."

"Oh yeah?" he said. You heard the crackle of a soft pack and the flint of his Zippo. "Which one?"

"Remember the kid who drew naked pictures of Lauren Breslow?"

He laughed. "Of course."

"Him."

"Well," Bruno said, exhaling lightly, "this isn't surprising."

"No," you said. "I suppose not."

"What's the problem?" he asked.

"He won't say *tu*."

"So?"

"He needs to learn the pronunciation."

Bruno laughed again. "This piggy boy? Are you sure?"

"What do you mean by that?"

"It just doesn't sound like French is going to make much of a difference in his life."

"Of course it will," you said. "It's discipline. He needs that."

"Well," Bruno said, "this is a very difficult sound to make. Just because you can do it doesn't mean everyone else can."

"Everyone else should at least try," you argued.

"He won't even try?"

"That's what I'm saying."

"Why won't he try?"

"Because," you said, "he thinks it's gay."

"What?"

"Men who speak French seem gay to him."

"I'm not gay," he said.

"I realize that."

"Neither is half of France."

"That's what I told him."

"*Tu,*" he muttered to himself. "How can this be gay?"

"I think it's the position of the mouth," you said.

"Tell him if he kisses a girl, he has to make this position. Tell him that the men of France are such great lovers because of *tu.* Tell him when I go down between your legs and say *tu,* you come like a fucking animal."

"I'm not going to tell him that," you said.

"Fine," he said, "don't."

"What kind of way is that to talk?" you asked him, though actually, you liked it. You liked anything that didn't sound like a therapy session.

"C'mon," he said, "have sex with me over the phone."

"No," you said.

"Speak French," he said, and you said no again.

———

The next day, when Ellis refused to read a line of dialogue with the word *tu* in it, you gave him another detention. "Can I come, too?" Marie asked. "For French Club?" She was looking particularly pretty in red lipstick and a short black skirt, and you told her no.

He arrived at three o'clock and took his assigned seat at the back of the room. You asked if he was prepared to say *tu* yet, and when he said no, you told him he could just sit quietly until he was. He sat quietly for a while, then said, "Ms. Adlon? I'm ready to say it."

"Go ahead," you said, looking up from your grading.

"You can't look at me," he said. "You have to stand over there." He pointed to the windows.

"Why?"

"Because," he said, "it's embarrassing. You only said I had to say it. You never said you had to watch me say it."

You thought for a moment, then said, "Fine," and carefully pushed your chair out.

When you'd reached the window, he said, "Turn around."

You did as he instructed, looking out onto the bus lane, the faculty parking lot, the well-tended athletic field.

"Ready?" he asked from behind you.

"Yes."

He cleared his throat. "*Tu as des grands mamelles. Tu me donnes une érection.*"

You didn't move, just stayed facing the window, looking down at your red Civic. You were afraid to turn around and find him smirking, when you were taking this pretty seriously. He'd finally said *tu*, after all. He'd used the word correctly in two complete sentences: *You have big breasts. You give me a hard-on.* Just because the content was objectionable, did it mean you hadn't broken him? Lauren Breslow had faced a similar dilemma with his pornographic pictures.

"So what if he draws me naked?" she'd once said. "At least he's doing his assignments."

You hadn't quite understood her at the time, but now you thought you did. It was inappropriate what he'd said to you, yes. And you'd let him know this. But if there was any chance at all that it was true, you weren't sure you were ready to go to Derek about it. To have Ellis removed from your classroom when he might have more to say.

Eventually, you did turn around. And he wasn't smirking, just sitting there looking as unhappy as ever. You snuck a peek at his crotch, but his pants were too loose to verify his previous statement.

"Was that okay?" he asked nervously.

You didn't answer him. You went to your desk and began packing up your things.

"Ms. Adlon?" he said.

"You can go now," you said, though you hoped he'd stay.

"Can you give me a ride home?" he asked. "The late bus doesn't go by my house."

"No," you said.

"But I don't have a ride," he said.

"How'd you get home yesterday?" you asked, zipping up your briefcase.

"Marie."

"Sorry," you said, "no."

"Don't be mad, Ms. Adlon," he pleaded. He got up from his desk and shoved his hands in his pockets. "I really like you. I like the bands you listen to."

"Detention is over," you said, and you walked out.

He followed you at a polite distance through the empty halls of the school, out past the line of late buses, into the faculty parking lot. "Ms. Adlon?" he said as you opened your car door.

You didn't answer, just threw the briefcase in the backseat.

"Can I borrow money for a taxi?"

You got in the car and shut the door behind you. He knocked at your window. "Ms. Adlon?" he mouthed, and you unrolled it.

"Are you going to tell Principal Finton on me?"

"No."

"I learned how to say those things from Marie. From a dictionary she has."

You started rolling the window back up.

"Wait!" he said.

You stopped.

"Could you at least take my guitar home with you? So I don't have to carry it on the walk?"

You thought about this for a second, then popped the trunk.

"Thank you," he said, running around to the back of your car.

You waited until he'd closed the trunk before driving off. In your rearview mirror, he put his hand up in a wave.

You didn't know what to do with the guitar when you got home. Leave it in the car or take it inside. You opened the trunk and looked at the case. You opened the case and looked at the guitar. You'd never seen it before. It was a reddish-brown acoustic with edges that darkened to black. The lining of the case was blue velvet, and when you touched it, the oil from your fingertip left a faint stain. There were a few picks floating around, a steel tuning fork, and a folded piece of notebook paper. You picked this up and unfolded it. Inside were the words to "Up the Junction" by Squeeze. You folded the paper back up and closed the case, then the trunk on top of it.

Inside, there was a message on your answering machine from Bruno, complaining about the incompetency of the general contractor who'd underbid the pool, and an e-mail from Marie. She'd sent it to both you and Ellis, inviting the French Club to her father's restaurant that Saturday. Mr. Adlon was invited, too, she said, but you wrote back telling her that he was unfortunately out of town. After hitting REPLY ALL, you went out to the trunk and got the guitar.

For a while, you sat on the couch with it, the worn leather strap slung over your shoulder. You strummed it a little, only you didn't know how to play. Eventually you put it back in the case. You fondled the picks lightly, then gave in and went for the tuning fork. It was like a long skinny U on a stick. Nowhere near as substantial as your vibrator, yet as you lay back on the couch and put it inside you, there was relief. It was cold like a speculum, but not prying. If you twisted the handle with your fingertips, you felt the thick, rounded tines churning against you like eggbeaters. You came not from this, but from raking yourself lightly on the outside. From closing your eyes and thinking of Ellis doing it for you.

Afterward, you didn't wash it, just let it air dry. You called Bruno and said, "I think I have a crush on one of my students."

He laughed and lit a cigarette. "Really? A teenager?"

"Yup." You were back on the couch again, stretched from end to end.

"Interesting," he said. "Which one?"

"Remember the kid who drew naked pictures of Lauren Breslow?"

"Him again?"

"Uh-huh."

"Wow," Bruno said. "A delinquent."

"He's changed," you said. "He doesn't draw those pictures anymore."

"What does he do?"

"He says *tu*."

"Really?" Bruno said. "You finally got him to do it?"

"Uh-huh."

"And now you're in love," he said.

"A little."

"I guess I can understand that."

"You can?"

"Sure. Kay says we're attracted to people who mimic our experience with parental love. If our parents were stingy, then we'll try to find a stingy mate."

"What an idiot," you said.

"What have you got against Kay?" he demanded.

"Nothing," you said.

"She helps me," he said. "Don't you want me to feel good? To be my own person?"

"Be whoever you want."

"Thank you. I will."

"Good. So will I."

After you'd hung up, you opened the guitar case again. You took out the tuning fork and put it back inside you. You fell asleep like that. All night you dreamed of wood and wire and how they vibrated to make a pretty sound.

In class the next day, when Ellis wouldn't say *tu*, it seemed different. More of a conscious miss. "Detention," you told him, and he nodded.

When he showed up at three, you said, "I'm sorry, I don't have your guitar."

"That's okay," he said. He took the seat in front of your desk, sliding down into a slouch. He stared directly at you, and you stared back.

"I took it out of the trunk last night," you said. "I didn't want anything to happen to it."

"I appreciate that," Ellis said.

"Do you want to try to say *tu* again?" you asked.

"Sure," he said.

You waited.

"*Tu as mon guitar,*" he said.

"Very good," you said.

"*Tu as un mari qui n'est pas chez toi,*" he continued. "*Tu voudrais j'embrasse tes mamelles.*"

He was right: You did have his guitar. You did have a husband who wasn't home. You did want him to kiss your breasts. "Your accent is really improving," you said. "There's no reason you should feel shy about speaking in class."

"Thank you," he said.

"I'll remember your guitar tomorrow," you told him.

"I can't really wait until tomorrow," he said.

"Oh?"

"My mom let me drive her car today, in case I got detention. I could follow you home and pick up the guitar then."

You shook your head. "I don't think so."

"But I have band practice."

"Sorry," you said.

You drove slowly, so as not to lose him. You stopped at all yellow lights, and even some stale green ones. Though you'd told him not to follow you, now that he was, you'd decided there was nothing you could do about it. Anyway, he had a right to his guitar. You should've put it back in the trunk that morning. Only you'd wanted more time with the tuning fork. It was actually in your purse right now.

His mother drove a blue Geo Metro. It was way too small for Ellis, who seemed to be dipping his head forward so as not to hit the roof. You couldn't see his legs through your rearview mirror, but you imagined his knees sandwiching the steering wheel, his feet spring-loaded against the pedals.

At your house, you pulled into the driveway, while he parked at the curb. You got out of your car first, then he got out of his. He started walking toward you, and you waited by the driver's side door. "Ms. Adlon?" he said, stopping a few feet away from you. He was facing the sun, which caused him to squint a little. "I know you said I couldn't come for my guitar, but I really need it."

His jeans were too big. Not the kind that were supposed to be worn that way, but as if he hadn't been eating. He lifted a hand to shield his eyes from the sun, and his T-shirt raised up to reveal a slice of stomach. It was smooth and slightly sunken and cut down the center by a swath of dark hair. You felt vaguely punished by the way it disappeared beneath his waistline.

"Fine," you said. "I'll go get it. Wait here." You headed up the curving walkway Bruno had lined with rhododendron.

"Ms. Adlon?" you heard from behind you.

You stopped and turned around. "Yes?"

"May I use your lavatory?"

"No," you said. There were clean panty hose drying on the shower rod.

"What about a drink of water?"

You thought for a moment, then said, "Okay."

He followed you inside and you told him to wait in the foyer. When you returned from the kitchen with his water, you found him in the living room, flipping through your record collection.

"Thanks," he said, taking the glass from you.

"Your guitar's right there," you said, pointing to the case beside the coffee table.

He didn't seem to hear you. He didn't drink his water. "This is quite a collection," he said.

"Thank you."

"Do you know how many you have?"

You shrugged. "About a thousand." Actually, it was 1,239. Only you thought it might be silly to say.

"Wow," he said. "I only have, like, four hundred CDs."

"That's a lot."

"Not compared to a thousand."

He was going to flip through each and every one, you soon saw, and you went and sat on the couch. "Where are your shoes?" you asked him after a minute.

He looked down at his sock feet. "Oh," he said, "my mom doesn't allow shoes in the house."

"I'm not your mom," you said.

"Wow," he said, pulling one of the records out. "The Violent Femmes."

You got up then and went to pour your own glass of water. As you stood at the sink, you wondered about Ellis's mother. How she'd managed to train him to do anything. "Ms. Adlon?" he said. You turned around to find him standing in the doorway.

"Yes?"

"Could I have some more water?"

"Sure," you said.

He stepped in and handed you his glass. You returned to the sink, and as you stood with your back to him, he said, "You have a message." Suddenly you heard the bleep of the answering machine, followed by Bruno's voice. "Hello, how are you? I should be home by Tuesday. Don't run off with your student before I get there."

You turned around and looked at the answering machine, then Ellis. "What do you think you're doing?"

"Nothing," he said quickly.

"Who said you could listen to my messages?"

"Sorry," he said. "I was just trying to be helpful."

"No, you weren't," you said. "You're never helpful."

"Sorry," he said again.

"Here," you said, handing him the water.

He drank it down in one gulp, then gave the glass back. "Thank you."

"That was a private message from my husband," you reiterated. "You had no right to listen to it."

Ellis nodded. "Is he French?"

You ignored him and returned his glass to the sink.

"Is that why you're always trying to get me to say *tout*? So I'll sound like him?"

"It's *tu*," you said.

"I could never sound like that guy," Ellis said, and suddenly he seemed depressed.

"Why would you want to?" you asked.

He shrugged. "So we could run off together."

"I'm not running off with anyone, okay? It was a joke."

"If you like me, Ms. Adlon, you should know that I like you, too."

"That's enough, Ellis," you said, moving past him into the living room.

"That's why I said all those French things to you," he said.

You went and stood by his guitar. He joined you a moment later, kneeling down beside the case. "Want to hear a song?" he asked.

"No."

"One song before I go."

Again, you didn't answer. Your new way of saying yes.

"Just one," he said, opening the case, lifting the guitar out. Once he'd arranged the strap over his shoulder, he fished around for a pick. He strummed a couple of times, then, dissatisfied, searched the case again. "Ms. Adlon," he said, "have you seen my tuning fork?"

You shook your head.

"My uncle gave me that tuning fork."

"Maybe you left it at home," you said, feeling guilty about upsetting him for no reason.

"I guess," he said, though he didn't sound convinced.

"If you're going to play a song," you said, "do it now. Otherwise I need to get some grading done."

"All right." He unfolded the lyrics to "Up the Junction" and stood up. "I haven't had much time to practice," he warned.

"Don't worry about it," you said. You sat down on the couch then, expecting him to face you. Instead, he set the lyrics on the armchair opposite you and turned his back in order to read them. You'd never heard of such a thing—a rock star who hid his face—and as he began to play, you craned your neck a little, hoping for a glimpse of his profile.

But you couldn't see him. You could only hear him, his voice steady, yet possessed of a lovely strain. You wished you could know if his eyes were closed, or if any of the lyrics made him smile. You wished you could know if you made him smile. In the end, though, you had to settle for watching his back muscles expand and contract as he launched into the final verse with particular fervor. When he was finished, you clapped and said, "Very nice."

At last he turned around, slightly out of breath. There

was moisture on his brow and he raised an arm up to wipe it with his T-shirt sleeve. "Thanks," he said. "I know you like that band."

"Yes," you said, "I do."

He stared at you for a second. "Well, thanks for the water."

You watched as he lifted the guitar over his head, then laid it back in its case. Before he could close the lid, you said, "Hold on a second," and went for your purse. You took out the tuning fork, still sticky and smelling of you, and held it up. "I found it."

"My tuning fork," he said.

"I just need to wash it," you said.

"Why?"

"Because I used it."

"For what?" he said.

"Nothing," you said. "I'll be right back."

He stood up then and said, "Don't wash it."

"It'll just take a second," you said, heading for the kitchen.

"No," he said, and he came over and took it from you.

"Give me that," you said.

"What did you use it for?"

"Nothing."

He brought it to his nose and inhaled. "I know that smell," he said.

"Don't you have band practice?" you asked him.

He shrugged. "Not really."

"Give me that," you said again. He didn't put up much of a fight, and you took the fork in the kitchen. As you stood there at the sink, washing it, you were aware of him behind you. Not in the doorway, but at your back, breathing. You knew that if you were to make any sudden moves, he would run. So you didn't. You pretended not to notice as he slipped his arms around your waist. Brought his head down beside yours. Moved his hands up over your breasts. Only when you felt his erection pressing against your backside did you finally say, "Excuse me."

He released you immediately, as if he'd been reprimanded. You dried the fork on a dishtowel and handed it to him. "Here," you said.

"Show me how you used it," he said.

"No."

"*Tu as un beau vagin,*" he said.

"That's enough," you said, and you took him by the elbow and led him to the front door.

Later, you called Bruno to tell him that Ellis had serenaded you. "At school?" he asked.

"No," you said, "at home."

He was quiet for a moment. You heard the Zippo. "Our home?"

"Yes," you said. "He followed me in his car." You told Bruno about the guitar then, how you'd brought it in the house for safekeeping, then forgotten to put it back in the trunk.

"What song did he sing?"

"You wouldn't know it."

"Was it good?"

You thought for a moment, then said, "His voice is a little flat."

"I hope you didn't tell him that."

"Of course not. I clapped."

"Listen," Bruno said, "I think you should be careful."

"What do you mean?"

"I think you should only see him in school."

"What about the French Club dinner?"

"What French Club dinner?"

"One of the students started a French Club this week. We're going to her father's bistro tomorrow night."

"Well," he said, mulling it over, "just try to keep your distance."

The restaurant was one of those places you'd passed a million times and never really thought much of, due to its location in a strip mall. Inside, however, Monsieur Du Pont had gone to some lengths to create a murky European atmosphere. The place was lit with candles and wall lamps, making the white linens the brightest things in the room.

Marie met you at the front door in one of her short skirts, then took you back to the kitchen to meet her father. He was tall like her, and his hair glittered with gray. *"Bon soir, Madame Adlon,"* he said, shaking your hand, and you complimented him on both his daughter and his restaurant. In return, he complimented your accent. You told him a little about your year in Paris, and he described an excellent cup of hot chocolate he'd once had in your neighborhood. Finally he led you back to the dining room, where Ellis stood waiting by the front door.

You wondered if his mother had told him to wear the suit, or if it was something he'd decided on his own. Whatever the case, the sight of him made you ache. Unlike his regular clothes, these actually fit. For the first time, you had a real sense of his body—where his legs began and ended, how broad his shoulders were. Suddenly, it seemed, he was coming out of hiding.

Introductions were made, after which Monsieur Du Pont led the three of you to a corner booth. You expected Ellis to sit next to Marie, who had left him ample room, but

instead he slid in beside you. *"Mais je suis seule!"* she complained, her mouth collapsing into a pout. Her father spoke
to her gently about being childish, then left you to look over
your menus. A moment later, Ellis closed his and said, "I
know what I want."

"En français," Marie reminded him.

"Tais toi," he said, which meant *shut up.*

"Why are you talking to me like that?" she asked, sounding hurt.

"Like what?" he said. "You just told me to speak French."

She looked to you for support then. "Break it up, you
two," you said.

"What did I do?" Ellis asked.

"You're not going to get a free dinner if you keep speaking English," Marie told him.

"Fine," he said. "I'll pay."

Monsieur Du Pont arrived to take your orders, and both
you and Marie chose the lamb. *"Et pour vous, Monsieur?"* he
said, turning to Ellis.

"I'll have the steak."

"Ah-ah-ah," Monsieur Du Pont said, waving a finger. *"En
français, s'il vous plaît."*

"Right," Ellis said, "le steak."

"Ellis," you said, "that's enough."

He looked at you, then back at Marie's dad. *"Pardon,"* he
said. *"Je voudrais le bifteck."*

"Ah," Monsieur Du Pont said. *"Très bien."*

After he'd gone, Ellis said, "We forgot to order wine."

"We're not ordering wine," Marie said.

"Don't kids in France drink wine with their dinner?"

"You're not having wine," you told him.

"Garçon!" he called, and a waiter in a white shirt approached your table.

"Oui?" he said.

"Yes," Ellis said, "this is a French Club dinner, and for an authentic French experience, we feel we should have some wine."

"My father will say no," Marie said. "He could get in trouble for serving minors."

Still, the waiter said he'd check, and moments later, he returned with a bottle of Merlot and three glasses. Once they were filled, Ellis raised his in a toast, saying, *"Vive la France!"* He followed this with a large sip.

Everyone began to loosen up a little then. Ellis talked about his band's upcoming gigs, Marie revealed that she'd just won the lead in the school's production of *Annie Get Your Gun,* and you admitted that you missed radio. "Why didn't you stick with it?" Ellis asked, and you launched into a discussion of the fallback career. But even as you warned the two of them against it, you couldn't help but feel like a phony. No one had forced you to become a French teacher, after all. They'd only suggested that radio was very competitive, and you'd taken that and run with it.

The food came and you all fell silent for a while, cutting into your meat. You were left-handed, and a couple of times you and Ellis bumped elbows. "Here," you said, scooting over to give him more room, and he chased you with his right thigh until it was nestled against your skirt. You couldn't imagine that Marie had seen this, but still, she chose that moment to ask, *"Où est votre mari, Madame Adlon?"*

"He's in Potsdam," you said. "He's in charge of getting a pool built there."

"En Octobre?"

"It was supposed to have been built this summer," you told her. "But the contractors screwed up. That's his job. Fixing other people's screwups."

Ellis nodded. "He should be home by Tuesday."

"How do you know?" Marie said.

"He doesn't," you said. "He's making it up."

The waiter came then to refill your wineglasses. Marie put a hand over hers and you put a hand over Ellis's, leaving only yours to be topped off. After the waiter left, Ellis reached for the Merlot and refilled his own glass.

"Enough," you said, taking the bottle from him, but it was too late. He'd already drained the last drop.

At the end of the meal, Monsieur Du Pont asked that Ellis ride home with either him and Marie, or you. "It wasn't a lot of wine, I realize," he said, "but I'd rather not take any chances." Ellis said he understood, and Marie looked happier than she had all night. Then he turned to you and asked if you were ready to go. "No!" Marie said. "Ride home with us!" and her father spoke to her gently about letting people do as they pleased.

In the car, you asked Ellis where he lived, and he gave you your own address. You asked him a second time and he said the same thing. "C'mon," you said, "help me out here," but there was no response.

You drove in silence for a while. You were headed toward your house, but taking the long way, hoping something might happen to put a stop to the evening. An accident, maybe.

"Hey," Ellis said, "slow down."

You eased up on the gas pedal.

"Are you drunk?" he asked.

You were a little, but you said, "No."

"You know why I ordered wine?"

You shook your head.

"Because," he said, "I don't want to come too fast."

When you didn't say anything, he said, "Alcohol is good for that, right?"

"I don't know," you lied.

"Well," he said, "it is."

At your place, he went straight for the answering machine and pressed PLAY. "Hello," Bruno said, "it's me. Have you screwed your student yet? Try to wait. I'm almost home."

"What did I tell you about doing that?" you scolded Ellis halfheartedly.

"Sorry," he said.

You went and got the phone book out of the kitchen drawer and looked up Hartsall. Meanwhile, Ellis played Bruno's message again. "It's me, isn't it?" he said. "He's talking about me."

"Your mom's name is Catherine?" you asked.

He nodded.

"Okay," you said, closing the phone book, "let's go."

He sat down at the kitchen table. "May I have a glass of water?"

"No," you said, putting the phone book away.

"I'm hungry," he said. "How about a sandwich?"

"We just ate."

"I always have a snack before bed."

You looked at him. He really was very thin. "What do you want?" you said.

"Peanut butter," he said. "Do you have that?"

You went to the cupboard and got the peanut butter out. You smeared some across a piece of bread, then put it on a plate and brought it over to him. "Thank you," he said. He took a large bite and chewed for a long time. After swallowing, he said, "Could you sit down while I eat? You're making me nervous."

You hesitated for a moment, then pulled out your chair.

"Thank you," he said.

"Just hurry up," you told him.

"That's not very French," he said. "They never hurry a meal."

"I'm not French," you told him.

"Your husband is."

"So?"

"Haven't you adopted his ways?"

"No."

"Why not?"

"I have my own ways."

He smiled. You weren't sure you'd ever seen him do this before, and your ache returned with a vengeance. "Remember that day you fell over in your chair?" he asked.

"No."

"That was a good day," he said. He cleared his throat. "I saw your pussy that day."

"You couldn't have," you said. "I was wearing panty hose."

"I saw it through your panty hose. You weren't wearing any underwear."

"No one wears underwear with panty hose," you said. "That's why they have a cotton panel."

"Did you do that on purpose?" he asked. "Fall over in your chair?"

"What?"

"It was just weird," he said, putting down his sandwich. "It was like—" He got up out of his seat then and stood behind you. Before you knew it, he'd tilted you backward and onto the floor, just as you'd been that day in the classroom. You whooped a little in surprise, then said, "Okay, put me back."

"In a minute," he said, hovering over you.

"No," you said. "Now."

He crouched down beside you on the floor and slipped a

hand between your knees. The blood started rushing to your head, and as it mingled with the wine that was already there, you went dizzy.

"There it is," Ellis said now, pushing your legs apart a little. "I see it again."

"Put me back," you said.

He took a few moments to ease your skirt up around your hips. "Now I can really see it," he said.

Soon you felt his hands beneath the waistband of your panty hose. He rolled them down just far enough to expose you, then used his fingers to pull you apart. You'd been wet since the moment he'd slid in beside you at dinner, and now, as the open air hit you, there was a cooling effect. After a moment, he let go of you and reached inside the pocket of his suit coat. "Look," he said, and he produced the tuning fork.

"Put that away," you said.

"Show me how you used it," he said.

"No."

He was quiet for a moment, then said, "Can I try?"

When you didn't say anything, he returned his hands between your legs. You closed your eyes as he pulled you apart again, then eased in the tuning fork. "Is this it?" he said, moving it in and out of you. "Is this what you were talking about?"

Still you didn't say anything.

"Ms. Adlon?" he said a few moments later.

"Yes?"

"I just came in my pants."

You opened your eyes then. He was still crouched down beside you, holding the fork.

"Sorry about that," he said.

"No," you said, "don't worry about it."

You looked at each other. He smiled at you again, and you put a hand on his knee. "Can I use your bathroom?" he asked, and you nodded.

He tucked the fork back inside his jacket, then stood up. The phone rang and Bruno came over the answering machine. "Where the hell are you?" he snapped. "Is your boyfriend still serenading you with his shitty voice? Call me."

He hung up, and Ellis looked down at you. "What's he talking about?"

"Nothing," you said, pulling your legs together.

"You told your husband I have a shitty voice?"

"No," you said, "of course not."

"Then why would he say that?"

"I don't know."

"You're lying," he said. "You're a fucking liar."

"Don't curse," you said.

"I can't fucking believe this," he said. He sounded a little out of breath.

"Ellis," you said, "could you help me up, please?"

"I mean, you're my favorite teacher."

Finally, you rolled sideways off the chair and onto the linoleum floor.

"I think I'm going to throw up," Ellis said.

"The bathroom's just down the hall," you said, pointing.

While he was gone, you stood, pulled up your panty hose, and brought down your skirt. You righted the chair, then went to the sink and splashed cold water on your face. As you were drying yourself with a paper towel, Ellis came back and said, "I'm leaving."

"I'll drive you home," you said.

"No thanks," he said, heading for the front door. He stopped then and turned around. "I'm sure you did that on purpose. That day you fell in your chair. I'm sure you wanted me to see your pussy."

"That's not true," you said. "That was an accident. No one wears underwear with panty hose."

He shook his head. "I never heard of that. I bet Principal Finton hasn't either." Then he walked out, your DNA tucked safely in his pocket.

Later, when you went to the bathroom yourself, you saw that he had indeed been sick. Not just in the toilet, but outside it, along the rim, and onto the floor. You spent a good while cleaning it up, then went to lie down on the couch. You tried to think of what song would be best at a time like this, but couldn't come up with anything.

It was then that you thought of the pool in Potsdam. Not the abandoned pit left by the general contractor, but the freshly poured concrete Bruno would've arranged for, the pumps and drains, the high and low diving boards jutting out over the deep end. When people arrived in their swimsuits and flip-flops the following summer, they'd have no idea that only a year earlier, the whole thing had almost fallen through. They'd know nothing of the insurance man, whose job it was to run toward a mess, and not away from it.

steve **Almond**

THE EVIL B.B. CHOW

On Friday, a delivery guy comes to my office with roses in a terra-cotta bowl. Everyone is dying of curiosity, which, of course, so am I. It's not that there aren't men who would send me flowers. There just aren't any men right now.

The card says, "Looking forward to meeting you, Maureen—B.B. Chow."

B.B. Chow?

Marco, my Chief Gay Underling, appears on the other side of my desk. He glances questioningly at the flowers.

"A friend," I say.

"Does this friend have a name?"

I hand him the card.

Marco runs his fingernail along the rim of the bowl. "Correct me if I'm wrong, but we don't know any B.B. Chows. Do we?"

"No," I say. "I don't believe we do."

"Sounds like the villain in a Bruce Lee picture," Marco decides. "Like, the Evil B.B. Chow." He does this lame little chop-socky sequence that culminates in him banging his shin against my glass coffee table.

I sit there for a puzzled little moment, listening to Marco yelp and watching the sun bling off this ridiculous desk they gave me when I became creative director of *Woman's Work*. It's covered with transparencies of young mothers paring ink stamps from potatoes and oven-roasting their own pot-pourri. There's always some kid close at hand, gazing at the proceedings in that eerie modulated child-model fashion. The moms exude a *wholesome yet edgy* energy that's almost (but not quite) lascivious.

Then it hits me: B. stands for Brock. Brock Chow. The man my dear aunt Bev has assured me is an *extremely* handsome doctor. Did I make a date with this man? I check my daily calendar. There, in non-photo blue, are the words *Bev date*.

"Wait a sec," Marco says suddenly. "You didn't send yourself these flowers. We're not there yet, are we, boss?"

"Be gone," I tell him. "Go spread malicious gossip."

This is what authority has granted me.

B.B. Chow does not mention the flowers. When I thank him, he blushes, says he hopes they weren't too elaborate. He's about my height, five-seven. A couple of inches shorter, given these absurd mules I tromp around in. A slim guy, narrow through the shoulders and hips. He's got these big, trustworthy features and black hair that falls across his brow like a crow's wing. I can't quite tell if I'm attracted to him or not.

We do one of these new Belgian bistros for dinner and it's clear right away that he's not too familiar with the protocol. When the sommelier comes by, he gets confused and orders an appetizer. The whole dual-fork scenario spooks him. I seem to be a slob magnet. In most cases it's these guys who came from money and can't find a more productive way to express self-loathing. But there's nothing practiced to B.B.'s dishevelment. He looks genuinely befuddled, sitting there with his napkin jammed into his sweater collar like a bib.

B.B. is unlike most of the guys I end up dating in one other way: he's not a loudmouth. He speaks so softly I have to lean forward to catch what he's saying. It turns out he's a resident, training to become a pediatric surgeon.

"That must be pretty intense," I say.

"I guess. You know, most of the cases aren't that serious. It maybe sounds more dramatic than it is."

B.B. is obviously more comfortable asking questions, so I lead him through the little tap dance of my life: the condo I just bought in the South End, my new job, my fierce and inexplicable crush on Pedro Martinez. I also tell him that I'm divorced. I've learned not to hold that in reserve, because it generally freaks the single guys out. They either relegate me to this suspect category of fallen woman (Hester Prynne, Ivana Trump) or they assume I was somehow abused, and it's now upon them to rescue me. I'm not sure which is worse.

"You look pretty young to be divorced," B.B. says.

"I was only married four years," I say.

"What happened?"

I pause for a moment. "It was kind of a complicated situation."

B.B. nods in such a way that he might actually be bowing. "I'm sorry," he says. "That's probably none of my business, huh? I only meant that it must have been a real disappointment."

I'm not sure what to say. We're lodged in one of those moments of intimacy that's come a bit too quick. B.B. peers at
me, in an effort to convey that he *understands* my disappointment. The problem is, I don't feel especially disappointed. I
was married to a man who couldn't operate a washing machine. I got out. The end. "I'll tell you what," I say, "I could go
for some dessert. Something involving chocolate."

I've invited B.B. to a play out in Jamaica Plain, at this
collective art space full of collective art space people. My
date looks like a total square. He seems to be making people
nervous, which I somewhat enjoy. You can see them squirm-
ing in their torn batik. B.B. is oblivious. He thinks the whole
thing is aces. Loves the play, which is a version of "Endgame"
done in the soap-opera medium. Loves the party afterward,
which is in the condemned loft next door. He asks the cast
members all sorts of sweet, dorky questions. (Example: "Did
Beckett have all that nudity in the original version?")

What I like about B.B. is this unchecked enthusiasm. It's
a relief, frankly, to hang out with someone who plunges
through life without the almighty force field of irony. Who
doesn't mind expressing his desires, even if he looks a bit
goofy.

"I mean, he *asked permission* to kiss me on the cheek. I've
been involved with men who don't even ask permission to
come in my mouth."

"Tell me about it," Marco says.

The latest crop of candidates for our Mad About Mom
section lies between us. There's Sharon Stone (and body-
guard) walking little Roan through Piccadilly Circus; Catherine Zeta-Jones looking lumpy and blissed out with her diaper
bag. "Demi Moore is so *over*," Marco says. "Everything she
touches is over."

The truth is she looks radiant. They all look radiant, as if they've drifted into this universe for a single incandescent moment, only long enough to be captured on film. This is what we sell our readers, this illusion of you-*can*-have-it-allness. And we're successful precisely because, beyond all the aspirational blather, back in the drab universe of the day to day, you can't have it all. Not if you want sleep.

The phone rings and Marco snatches it. "Maureen Fleming's office. May I ask who's calling? I'm sorry. She's in a meeting. Yes, I'll let her know. No. No. Goodbye." He shrugs. "Do we know a Mr. Bok Choy?"

As gay underlings go, Marco is unacceptably cheeky. But he's also a decent listener when he wants to be, and he's nursed me through the entire history of my recent romantic pratfalls. *Behind-the-Music* Man (who quoted from the program verbatim). The Incredible Rowing Man (he seemed to confuse my body with an oar). The Sperminator (let's just not discuss this one). Marco coins these sobriquets to keep the lineup straight, and I adopt them to remind myself that these men are only temporary decisions, which can be rescinded.

The phone rings again. "She's busy at the moment, Mr. Choy," Marco says.

"Give me that," I tell him. "Try to remember that I rule you."

B.B. sounds flustered. "I thought you were in a meeting."

"It's over," I say, and motion for Marco to scram.

"I just wanted to say what a nice time I had Friday."

"Yeah. It was nice."

"Can I see you again?"

"Sure."

"When?"

"Well," I say. "I'm kind of booked this weekend."

"Yeah, I am too. This weekend, I mean. I didn't mean this weekend or anything. I meant, like..." I can hear him breathing, this sort of wounded rasp.

"Are you OK?"

"Yeah," he says. "A little nervous, I guess. Not sure, you know, if you like me."

"I'm still getting to know you."

"Yeah," B.B. says. "Yeah. Right. I'm sorry. No big deal. Maybe next week. I'm pretty busy anyway, you know, at the hospital. Maybe next week." He's speaking too quickly, too loud. It's always been a weakness of mine: I can't stand to see others in pain. You want an executive summary of the last two years of my marriage? *Ta-da.*

"Wait a sec," I say. "What about an early dinner on Sunday?"

So there I am, at the Au Bon Pain in Cambridge, on Sunday at five, face to face with a focaccia that looks like a giant, cancerous crouton. B.B. is wearing a Harvard Medical School polo shirt, his skinny arms poking out, the same shirt he wore under his sweater last time. It strikes me as odd that this eager beaver is wearing the same shirt. (I know he went to Harvard.) So I sort of make a joke: "Hey, I've seen that shirt somewhere before."

B.B. looks like I just punched him in the mouth. "Sorry," he says. "These shirts come from the vending machines in the lobby. Sometimes, when you've been on the same rotation for a while, you need a fresh shirt."

And now I see the situation: he's come straight from the hospital, probably left right in the middle of his shift, which would explain why his fingers are stained the color of earwax (betadyne), why he looks frazzled and drawn, why he keeps glancing at his pager.

"You shouldn't be apologizing," I say. "I'm the one who was just an asshole."

"I must look like shit," he says.

"You don't look like shit."

He plucks at his shirt and forces out a laugh. "You should see my closet."

"Look," I say, "you didn't have to cut out on work to see me."

"I wanted to," B.B. says.

There's his face, propped up on his palms like an eager little display.

"I'm flattered," I say. "But there are other times. I mean, I'm not going anywhere."

B.B. takes a deep breath. "I should chill out a little, huh?"

"Maybe a little," I say, and smile. "Hey, I've got a question. What's the second B. stand for?"

"Blaine," he says.

"Brock Blaine Chow?"

"Yeah, you know, that was my parents. They wanted to find these super-American–sounding names. The Brock part comes from Lou Brock. My dad was a baseball fan. That was his big thing, you know, the American pastime."

"What about Blaine?"

"Yeah, I think the idea there was Paine. Like Thomas Paine. Give me liberty and all. That was kind of like a spelling error."

And now for some reason this annoying little Post-It comes tearing out of my wonkbrain and it says: Common Sense. Thomas Paine wrote "Common Sense." Patrick Henry is the guy who said, "Give me liberty or give me death." But I'm not about to correct B.B. because he's already blushing so fiercely his cheeks look maroon.

"Would you like to get an ice cream?" he asks.

I know I should be scooting along. I've got my own rounds to make, the event schedule I keep overbooked to stamp out any late-weekend embers of anguish. And here's this guy who's obviously, at the very least, neurotic. At the same time, I'm touched by his candor, his overwrought confessions.

It's the first day of spring and the streets finally smell again: tar and garbage, sweet sesame oil, old perfume. Everywhere, the righteous folk of Cambridge are strolling the polleny avenues, letting the breeze sift their hair. Not even the punks around the T can muster a decent rage, just bits of loud theater, and Harvard Yard seems almost bearable in this mood, rid of its suicide. Students are draped across one another, unbearably young, auditioning for sex in chunky shoes. "B.B.," I say, taking his arm. "I like you."

B.B. comes over to my place for the next date. I've decided to revive an old recipe (baked salmon drizzled in gorgonzola, on a bed of orzo) and sconced the lights with colored paper and done all the other inane shit my own magazine recommends in its "Kindling the Flame" column. B.B. buzzes and all I can think is: I hope he doesn't wear the same shirt.

He's wearing the same shirt.

He's also wearing surgical pajamas and paper slippers, and carrying a medical bag. In he breezes, calm as you please, kisses me on the cheek, says he's sorry he's late, asks if he can use the bathroom. Sure. No problem. I'm thinking: enough already. What is this guy's *deal*?

B.B. emerges five minutes later in a full tuxedo. With tails. There are some men who can't carry off a tux. My ex, for instance, always looked hopelessly overmatched, tugging at his cummerbund like a spoiled kid. But B.B. looks smashing. His hair is slicked back. His pleats are razors. The black lapels sharpen his features.

We finish off the second bottle of wine and sort of stumble to the couch and now we're really quite close and his skin smells like plums and clay and his eyelashes are so delicate—I've never seen eyelashes so delicate—and I can feel my face get warm and fuzzy as his lips come toward mine.

Sadly, B.B. is not much of a kisser. He presses too hard, and he doesn't know how to modulate the whole mouth-opening-tongue-moving-forward thing. All effort and no technique, which is a marked difference from the guys I usually date, who generally seem to be auditioning for the well-hung/feckless love interest on *Sex and the City.* And yet, I can't help being flattered by his bungling persistence. If push came to shove, I could hog-tie B.B. Chow (I've got at least ten pounds on him). But there he is, groping away at my muslin culottes, smashing his mouth against my bra-cup, whispering *you're so sexy, how can you be so sexy?*

It's gotten late by this time, or early, and I already know I'm going to be a wreck tomorrow, that my gay underlings will watch me in their strange, protective, perversely unjealous manner, and fret amongst themselves.

"We should probably call it a night," I say.

B.B. checks his watch. "I've got to be at the hospital in a couple of hours," he says. "Maybe I could just stay here."

"That's not such a good idea."

B.B. leans forward and looks directly into my eyes. "I want my body next to yours. We can just sleep, but I want to be next to your body. You have such a beautiful body." He's managed to control his voice, but his legs are trembling. It's excruciating. Like watching Oliver Twist ask for more porridge.

"You can stay on the couch," I say. "I'll fix you a place."

"Oh spare me," Marco says. "*Spare* me."

"I don't have time for this." I clap my hands unconvincingly. "Go fetch me Evian."

But Marco just sits there, rolling a gummy bear between his fingers. He's not going anywhere until he's secured a full admission.

Which of course he does, how B.B. managed to prolong negotiations, how I managed to relent, blouse by bra by panties, my outfit wrung into colored bulbs on the floor, knowing I shouldn't, knowing the sort of message it sends, but also somewhat relishing throwing off the shackle, ceding to the reckless volition of my sexual adulthood, the old drama of desire stirred against self-protection.

"What's his dick like?" Marco says.

"Stop it," I say. "Don't ask me that kind of shit."

"It's small, isn't it? How small? Uncooked hot-dog small?"

"What it is, the thing that really freaked me out, he's got no hair on his body. Not even under his arms. Just this smooth little, like, pelt. And he doesn't know how to caress. I thought, you know, he's a surgeon. He'll have these delicate fingers. But he's more of a groper. Like being groped by a twelve-year-old."

Marco makes a despicable yum-yum noise.

There's a note on my desk informing me that Phil, the publisher, wants to meet at four to grill me about the Summer of Fun issue ("Not fun enough!"), our new sex columnist ("She looks like a terrier!"), and *occasions for synergy*, a phrase he acquired recently and now chants through the long cappuccino afternoons. When he's done with me, he'll schtup his personal assistant, Mandy, perhaps in his actual office.

Here's what has me baffled: the sex was good. I can't quite explain this to Marco. But somehow, the fact that B.B. Chow can't really kiss or fuck or even fondle, the fact that he makes me feel like Xena the Warrior Princess, these things *turn me on*. It's like the bar is set so low with this guy, we can't help but get over. Which we do. We get over. Twice. Despite all the flubs, the sighing misfires, what comes through is how enraptured the guy is, enraptured by *me*.

And how, just before he left in the morning, stripped of his tux, back in medical scrubs and swaying in the door frame like a eucalyptus leaf, he says this thing to me: "Will you be my girlfriend?" without a lick of irony—with, instead, a look of utmost and moist vulnerability, as if his life depended on the answer.

I don't know what to say. I mean, we've spent the night together, had sex, orgasmed more or less simultaneously. What does that make us? Steadies? I'm not saying I don't understand what he's asking for. It's just such a weird feeling to be on the receiving end of this kind of need. I feel like I should be able to turn to some impartial referee and say: *flag him, flag him, that's gender preemption!*

We've both got these intense schedules. But somehow, rather than slowing the tempo, everything speeds up, launches us into that delirious, two-gear existence, work to bed, bed to work, the narrowing of the social field, the cultivation of babytalk, the entire goopy works. B.B. calls me from the hospital to tell me how much he misses me. He ends every conversation with the same question: "When can I see you?"

This is not to say that I don't have my moments of doubt. The first time I visit B.B. at his apartment, for instance, I spot a photo on his bookcase. A petite blonde, her hair gathered into a ponytail where the roots turn dark. She's wearing a leotard top and cradling a white puppy in her arms.

"Who's this pretty lady?" I call out.

B.B. comes rushing out of the kitchen with a bottle of wine in one hand and a corkscrew in the other. He sees me examining the photo and looks stricken. "That was a mistake. I apologize." He marches right over and shoves the photo behind his bound copy of *Prenatal Renal Failure.*

"You don't have to do that," I say. "That woman is a part of your life."

"Not anymore. She's my ex."

"OK. She's your ex," I say. "Does that mean you're not allowed to tell me anything about her?"

"She was an awful cook."

"Where does she live?"

"I don't know," he says brusquely. "Prince Street, I think."

"In the North End? That's right near my friend Marco. He's on Salem."

B.B. shakes his head vehemently. "She means nothing to me. Nothing. You're my girlfriend now." He drops the corkscrew and puts this big move on me, backing me against the bookshelf. The whole thing feels so . . . *staged.* As if I'm playing the role of B.B. Chow's New Girlfriend and he needs scenes like this to keep the action rolling.

"It's like a vortex. I've been sucked into the B.B. Chow Vortex."

"How does he make you feel?" Marco says. He's camped on my loveseat, disemboweling a turkey wrap.

"Great," I say. "Horny. Desirous. He notices my shoes. He tells me my feet are beautiful. I mean, you've seen my feet."

"The admission of desire always entails a larger wish," Marco says.

"Who the hell are you, Kung Fu? Quit being so goddamn wise." He's right, of course. My body has started yearning dumbly for permanence. My cheeks are hot all the time and I've stopped obsessing over the skin around my eyes. I feel like the heroine of one of our features: *How I Fell for the Doc Next Door.* But it's not the just the hormones with B.B. There's something else at play, the terrifying possibility— after years of betting on dumb sexy long shots of the heart, half-knowing how the ride will end—that I've finally found the guy who will love me back. It's enough to send shivers down my thighs.

"Don't tell me how I feel, OK? Tell me what to do."

"What do you want to do?"

"I want to be able to trust this guy," I say quietly.

Marco drops his slice of turkey and looks at me for a long moment. "Maybe you can't handle this guy because he's able to take care of you."

We've been together for a month now and for the first time, on a muggy Friday night, something is wrong. B.B. says the right things, but without conviction. He's just present enough to avoid a direct confrontation. But the slow poison of distance hangs around us. When we get back to my place, he climbs onto my bed without undressing.

I lie down next to him. "What's wrong?"

"Nothing."

I place my mouth very close to his ear. "Either you talk about what's going on," I murmur, "or get the hell out of my bed."

B.B. takes a deep breath. "There's this girl," he says.

"What girl?" The back of my neck bristles.

"Last night," he says quickly. "At the hospital." B.B. stares at the ceiling and sighs. "She had what we call cranio-synostosis. The sagittal suture fuses too early and the fetal brain distorts the calvarium into an aberrant shape."

"English," I say. I'm looking at B.B. in profile, the shallow black well of his eyes, the wet budding of his lips.

"There's no room for the brain," he says. "It grows in the wrong direction, you know. But there's this surgery. To correct the situation."

"What happened?"

"The chief of the unit, you know, he performed the operation. Dr. Balk. He let me assist. It was going fine. You know, they have to cut the cranium and fuse the bone. Then all of sudden her vitals started to drop, you know, the vitals..." His voice does a little choked thing. "The respirator, something, there was something wrong. Balk was busy trying to reshape this girl's skull, threading the bone mulch. Her skull, you know, she looked great. But her numbers kept dropping. It wasn't the blood; they gave her another unit of blood. Once the bone is cut, you know, there's no way to control blood loss through the marrow."

The smell of B.B. is suddenly overpowering: a rind of surgical soap soured by sweat. In the park across from my place, the skate rats have gathered under the willows to tell lies. I can hear them spitting at one another and laughing. Further north, on Tremont, jazz is reeling out from the cafés.

"She looked fine, you know, but she wasn't, like, strong enough. It's what we call operative failure. The heart gives up." His chest starts to heave and I wrap myself around him; pull his head to my bosom, run my fingers through his thatched hair, in the half light of my bedroom, this awkward

healer of children with his soft soft lashes, his big broken
cheeks. "I'm sorry," he sobs. "I'm so sorry." And now I can
feel myself throwing the last anchor of discretion overboard,
giving in to the pleasure of giving in, of tending to his tears,
his hurt, his deep want of love.

And it's more than this really. I can see now that B.B. is
as devastated by this loss as by our ardent duet, that what
he's offering me, what his tears offer, is the deepest measure
of love: unfettered access to his emotions.

He moves as if injured the next day, though we manage
to have a good time, puttering around in pajamas, watching
cooking shows, collecting ourselves for some goofy Sadie
Hawkins soiree in Somerville. We take the T over, what the
hell, watch dusk firing up the Charles, unfolding hopeful
pink panels onto the gray rooftops. B.B. is wearing this
suede jacket I bought him, even took the sleeves up an inch
with the sewing machine I thought I'd never use again. He
looks so adorable that I spend most of the night checking
him out from across the room, thinking about his smooth
little butt, only half-tuned to the sad angry buzz of gossip
that rises from the party with the cigarette smoke.

Later, in the quiet of my bedroom, we make love, and
again when the dawn breaks, a languorous morning session.
B.B. runs out to get some fresh juice and comes back with
flamboyans and snapdragons.

Phil the Publisher comes bouncing into my office in his
dreadful linen suit, full of dumb suggestions. He makes au-
thoritative hand gestures while I pretend to jot notes. This is
our Monday morning ritual. He nods at the stack of proofs
on my desk. "Did you come in yesterday?"

"No," I say. "Did you?" What I actually want to say is:
"Uh, Phil, why do you smell like pussy? Have you been pork-

ing your assistant again?" But the whole situation is just too pathetic.

He finally leaves and I start thumbing through the glossies. What I'm actually doing is trying to remember what it meant to give a shit about all this: the grinning semi-famous with their hairdos and rescuing platitudes, the sweet, standing water of self-help. The phone rings and rings. Marco is out sick.

I finally punch up the line.

"Hey," B.B. says.

I can hear all the hospital bustle in the background and I picture him cradling the phone in the crook of his neck—his long, smooth neck—and smile. "Hey loverboy."

Silence.

"Are you OK?" I say.

B.B. says something, but so softly I can't quite hear him.

"What is it, honey?"

"I can't do this," he says.

"Do what?"

"I'm still in love with Dinah," he says quickly. "It's not fair for us to spend any more time. Not fair to you."

"Wait a second," I say. "What are you talking about?"

"I'm still in love with Dinah."

"What?"

B.B. starts crying.

I feel, in my chest, the slapping of wings around a dark emptiness. Then the endorphins come roaring in and my heart does the little two-step into rage. "Why are you telling me this on the phone? Why am I hearing this from a god-damn piece of plastic?"

"I'm sorry," B.B. sobs.

"You've got to be kidding." I slam the phone down.

The lesser gay underlings, sensing a disturbance in the

Boss Force, have clumped outside my office. In Marco's absence, one of them will soon be nominated to check in on
me. I regulate my breathing and call B.B. back. He comes to
the phone in tears.

"Stop crying," I say. "Be a man, for crying out loud. Be a
man and tell me how long you've known this."

"A couple of days," he whispers.

"So you knew on Saturday, when I gave you that jacket?
And you knew at the party. And you knew when you fucked
me Saturday night, and Sunday morning. And last night.
And when you brought me those fucking flowers? You knew.
But you didn't have the guts to tell me, is that your testi-
mony, you little piece of shit?"

B.B. blows his nose. "I was trying to make sure, you
know, I wanted you to have a great weekend. I felt I owed
you that."

And here I find myself, in my ripening thirtyish cyni-
cism, newly confounded by the perversity of male logic. Best
to dump someone on a high note? Is this the way men
think? As if love were a discrete property, something one ac-
crues, like money or promotions? But surely B.B. is em-
pathic enough to recognize I had gone into full meltdown.
And this must have made him panic. He's one of those men
who conducts his love life like a catch-and-release program.
Though it's worse than that actually, because B.B. made me
feel safe by showing me *his* insecurity. While my ex, for instance, played himself in public as a seducer and a tough,
then wound up clinging to me for years. Which just goes to
show how little women can know of their men—because
men know so little of themselves.

Or maybe this is just the line they run. Maybe they know
what they're doing the whole time. They'll give you an office

and a desk and a title. But, in the end men win, always, because they can better withstand their own poor behavior.

B.B. is saying something, sniveling about what a fool he is, as if even at this point we might collaborate in a final scene, commemorating his guilt. I want to shout: *I was going to teach you how to kiss! You can't do this!* But giving him anything else, a single word, seems absurd.

I call Marco at home and the machine picks up. The glossies are staring at me, tireless and beatific in their gospel of self-improvement, urging me and all the other me's in the bleary sorority of millennial womanhood to find our G-spots, to insist on equal pay, to revamp the drapes and consider a diaper service, to do anything but succumb to our own truest feelings of rage and inadequacy.

I tromp across the godforsaken Government Plaza, through the fishy stink of Hay Market and into the North End. I could just barf at the quaintness of it all: the zephyrs of garlic and dusty bricks, the old paisano peddling shaved ice under the weather-stripped cupola. But I need some tea and teary commiseration and I need Marco's bullshit wisdom and I need a hug.

Marco lives on Salem. But the moment I see the sign for Prince Street, I start thinking about Dinah. Dinah who lives on Prince Street. There must be something she possesses that I don't, some emotional or sexual power, some nonthreatening poise. *Something.* Because otherwise he would've chosen me. And now it occurs to me that I have wound up near Prince Street not entirely by chance, that some darker, unraveled part of me is hoping to find and confront Dinah. So that, rather than hurrying on to Salem surely the prudent course—I find myself sort of hov the corner, though what I'm actually doing (it occurs to me unpleasantly) is *skulking,* a verb I had hoped to avoid during my brief tenure on Earth.

The old man selling shaved ice smiles at me.

"You want-a eat a good meal?" he says.

"No."

"Good-a calamari."

"No thank you. Really."

He continues to smile at me, suspiciously now, and I flee onto Prince Street and begin checking the numbers on the apartment houses in a very obvious way, then looking down at an invisible slip of paper in my hand, as if I'm part of the census bureau, a special agent sent out to ask the locals random questions, such as *Is there a skinny little slut living on the premises who might have stolen my Chinese boyfriend?*

I've been at this for anywhere from fifteen minutes to perhaps an hour, when a strange thing happens: a woman strides out of the building across the street with a tiny white dog. She looks just like the photo. Dyed blonde hair, leotard top. Her waist is the circumference of a baguette, and she has that ducky dancer walk, mons pubis thrust forward, like a pregnant woman minus the child.

I cross the street and walk up to her: "Can I say hello to your dog?" I'm wearing a tailored suit and pumps—an outfit that favors the irrational gesture.

Dinah shrugs. "Sure."

I bend down. "Hey there. What's your name?"

"Charmie," Dinah says.

"Hey there, Charmie." Then I look up and say, "Hey there, Dinah."

"*He-ey.*" Dinah cocks her head. I can see her rifling through her little change-purse of a mind, trying to recall how she might know me.

"You don't know me," I say. "I'm a friend of Brock Chow's. He told me you lived around here."

"Oh."

"Actually. I used to go out with Brock. But he just broke up with me. Just a few minutes ago. He told me he's still in love with you."

Dinah takes a half step backward; little tremors of dread vine the skin around her mouth. I keep petting her dog. The fur around its eyes is the color of dried blood. A cumulonimbus has drifted over the spires of downtown, where it hangs like a vast gray anvil. I imagine how this would play in the magazine. *Hex His Ex: How to Confront the Woman Who Stole Your Man!* (Maybe a Photoshop illustration of a voodoo doll in a miniskirt?)

"Do you have a few minutes?" Dinah says. "Like, to talk?"

The moment I step into her apartment, I know I've made a mistake. The decor is what Marco would call Early Porno. Popcorn ceilings. A particle-board entertainment center. There's dust on the sills, crusty dishes in the sink, a *to do* list yellowing on the fridge. The air smells sharp and rotten and a dull wet chopping noise comes from down below, a butchering sound.

"Sorry about the smell," Dinah says. "There's, like, the landlord put out some of those poison traps. My roommate's boyfriend said he'd find . . . whatever it is."

"You have a roommate?"

"She only spends about half the time here."

I'm just about to ask Dinah where, precisely, a roommate would stay, when I notice a door located *behind the stove.*

"Do you want some juice?" Dinah says. "We've got some great juice." She pulls a plastic cup from the cupboard, the kind they give away at baseball games.

"That's OK," I say. "I'm actually supposed to be visiting a friend."

"Yeah," Dinah says. "Anyway, you know, Brock's started calling me again." She gestures, indicating that I should take a seat.

"I sort of figured."

"You have to understand about Brock. He's so, like, insecure. He'll be with one girl, but then he starts thinking about his last girlfriend. It happened to me, too," she says. "He left me for this girl, Tina." She touches the sleeve of my blouse and her hand lingers there for a moment, as if what she really wants is to play the material between her fingers. "It's not even his fault, really. His parents, you know, they put a lot of pressure on him."

Dinah picks up her dog and traverses the room. She wants me to see how graceful she is, I think. She plops Charmie onto her desk. On the wall behind her is a sampler that reads *I'm a dancin fool, what's your excuse?*

"And it's not like I called him back," she says. "He's a great guy and all. I think it's amazing what he does. But I've really been trying to do some work on myself, like, interpersonal stuff. And Brock is someone, you know, he can be a little, like, too much."

The phone rings and we both freeze. "I'm going to let the machine pick that up," Dinah announces. Charmie starts darting around the desk. The machine clicks on and Dinah's desperately cheery outgoing message fills the room. Then there's a long beep and we both stand there not looking at one another.

Whoever it is hangs up.

"How long were you guys involved, anyway?" Dinah says.

"Not long."

She nods and her ponytail bobs. "Were you guys, like, intimate?"

"Listen," I say. "I should really get going."

"Yeah, I just wanted, you know." Dinah makes a little tossing gesture. "Brock is kind of a confused guy. But he's got a good heart. The work he does, you know, it's really the work of saints. I remember one time, right before we broke up, he came back from the hospital and he was just, you know, wiped out. Because he'd seen this little girl die during an operation. There was something wrong with her skull."

The air seems to thicken around me, and I have to lean against the door to support myself. "Do you have a bathroom?" I say.

"That's the one thing that's kind of weird about this place," Dinah says. "The bathroom is actually, like, in the hallway."

I stumble out the door and into the bathroom and drop to my knees over the bowl, which is stained with what I hope is rust, and my body begins to clench.

Dinah's outside asking if everything's OK, do I need anything? "I'm OK. Just girl stuff."

"Maybe I could get your number," Dinah says through the door. "In case you want to talk some more."

"Sure," I say. "Just give me a minute." I sag back from the toilet and glance at the milk crate full of magazines under the sink. Right on top is Cher's face, winched by countless surgeries and beaming from the cover of our Survivor's issue, alongside Tina Turner and Oprah. Dinah has every issue of *Woman's Work* dating back three years. She's folded down the corners of certain pages. I feel ready to weep.

Down below, on the orange sidewalks, with their steadying smell of baked yeast, I want to feel vindicated, to know that

B.B. dumped me for this wreck, that he's simply one of *those* men. And I want to feel relief, that he wasn't in my life long enough to do much damage. I've been in far worse entanglements, where the shared data was extensive and the smells haunted my clothing for weeks. Most of all I want to feel my rage again, at the world of men, who never tire of exploiting our ability to care, our hard-wired weakness for weakness.

I know I should toddle off to Marco's now and have a good cry and listen to his sweet useless pep talk and pretend to make sense of it all. But there's nothing in me but weariness. I'm weary of moving through life in this way, punished for my capabilities, betrayed by the glib promises of love. I'm weary of managing these disappointments. I'm weary of my body's gruesome tick. And I'm weary of telling women it can be different.

In this mood of enervation, I wander the docks, the old schooners burdened under ornate masts, the colonial cemetery dressed in gravestones, names and years in elegant rows, and roasted garlic everywhere, everywhere tourists in their pink summer legs and dusk on the bricks, rain gutters fat with pigeons and rooftops sprigged with antennae, the sediments of beauty, I mean, and the widows on their stoops, done with the suffering of men and silent before the soft click of bocce balls. There is so much time in this life for grief. So many men lying in wait. And here, tonight, there is a harvest moon, which hangs so heavily yellow above the sea it might be God, or my heart.

ZOG-19
A SCIENTIFIC ROMANCE

Zog-19 is learning to drive a stick-shift. He backs up, judders to a stop, and stalls. It's a big Ford F-250 diesel that he is driving, and it's got a hinky clutch. The two shovel-headed dogs in the bed of the truck bark hysterically. On Zog-19's planet, there are no cars and trucks with manual transmissions. There are no motor vehicles at all. Zog-19 shakes his head, flaps his hands, stomps in on the hinky clutch, and twists the ignition key. The Ford rattles back to life. Zog-19 decides that he will sell the Ford at the first opportunity, and replace it with a vehicle that has an automatic transmission. In his short time here on Earth, Zog-19 has had about all he can stand of stick-shifts.

A woman watches Zog-19's struggles with the truck. She squints her eyes worriedly. She thinks she's watching Donny McGinty fighting the hinky clutch. She is Missus McGinty, she is Donny McGinty's wife. Zog-19 is not in fact young McGinty, but he resembles McGinty down to the most minute detail. Even McGinty's dogs believe that Zog-19 is McGinty. The problem is, Zog-19 does not know how to drive a stick-shift, and McGinty does, McGinty *did*. McGinty knew how to do a blue million things that Zog-19 has never even so much as heard of on his own planet.

The Ford leaps forward several feet, stops, lurches forward again, dies. Missus McGinty shakes her head in disbelief. McGinty has never before, to her knowledge, had a bit of trouble with the truck, though that clutch often defies her. She is a small woman, and her legs aren't long enough or strong enough to manipulate the truck's pedals. Around her, around Missus McGinty and Zog-19, McGinty's little dairy operation—a hundred acres of decent land in the river bottom, inherited upon the death of McGinty's old man, and twenty-five complacent cows—is going to wrack and ruin. In the days when McGinty's old man ran the place, it gleamed, it glistened. No more, though. There are so many things that Zog-19 doesn't know how to accomplish.

Zog-19 waves to Missus McGinty from the truck. He wants badly to allay her apprehensions about him. "Toot toot," he says.

On Zog-19's planet, no one communicates by talking. All of Zog-19's people are equipped with powerful steam whistles. Well, not steam whistles exactly, because they sound using sentient gases rather than steam. The Zogs use their whistles to talk back and forth, using a system not unlike Morse code. On Zog-19's planet, "Toot toot" means "Don't worry." It also means "I love you" and "Everything is A-okay, Everything is just peachy-keen."

Zog-19 frets that McGinty's best friend, Angstrom, will notice the substitution. Zog-19 is not so good at imitating McGinty yet, but he is working hard to get better. Zog-19 is a diligent worker, even though he is not entirely sure of what it is that he's supposed to accomplish here on Earth, in the guise of the farmer McGinty. He does know that he's supposed to act just the same as McGinty, and so for the moment he's working like heck at being McGinty.

"Goddam it hurts," Angstrom says. He's got his arms wrapped around his middle, sways back and forth. He looks like a gargoyle, he looks like he should be a down-spout on some French cathedral. Angstrom's belly hurts all the time. Maybe it's cancer, maybe it's an ulcer, maybe it's something else. Whatever it is, Angstrom can feel the blackness growing within him. At night, his hands and feet are cold as blocks of ice. The only thing that scares him more than whatever's going on inside him is how bad the cure for it might be.

Doctors killed Angstrom's old man. Angstrom's old man, strong as a bull, went to the doctors about a painful black dot on the skin of his back. The doctors hollowed him out, and he died. So now Angstrom sits on a hard chair in his kitchen and rocks back and forth, looking like a gargoyle.

"Toot toot," says Zog-19. He likes Angstrom. He's glad McGinty had Angstrom for a friend, that Angstrom is by default Zog-19's friend now, but he wishes that Angstrom felt better. He worries that Angstrom will notice that he isn't McGinty. He wishes that he knew just a bit more clearly what his mission might be. He wishes that, whatever it is, someone else, someone more suitable, had been chosen for it.

Zog-19's planet is made of iron. From space, Zog-19's planet looks just like a giant steelie marble. The planet is called Zog. Zog-19's people are called the Zogs. Donny McGinty had a magnificent steelie marble when he was a little boy. He adored the slick, cool feel of the steelie in his hand, he loved the look of it, he loved the click it made when he flicked it against other marbles. He loved the rich tautness in the pit of his stomach when he sent his beloved steelie into battle, when he played marbles with other kids. When he was using that steelie as his striker, he simply could not be beaten. He was the marbles champion of his grammar school up in the highlands of Seneca County.

Those were good days for McGinty. McGinty's old man was alive, Angstrom's old man was alive, the little dairy farm shone like a jewel at a bend in the Seneca River, and Angstrom's belly didn't hurt all the time. It seemed, when McGinty held that heavy, dully gleaming steelie in his hand, like they might all manage to live forever.

Zog-19's planet is a great hollow iron ball, filled with sentient gas. Zog-19's people are also made of iron, and they are also filled with sentient gas. When they walk, their iron feet strike the iron surface of the planet, and the whole thing rings just like a giant bell. With all the ringing, and all the tooting, Zog-19's planet can get very noisy.

Missus McGinty talks. She talks and talks. She keeps on talking about Angstrom, how she wishes that Angstrom would go to the doctor. He should go to the doctor, she says, or he should quit complaining. One or the other. She talks about Angstrom to avoid talking about McGinty. She has noticed all the changes in him lately—how could she not?— but she doesn't know that he's been replaced by Zog-19. She just thinks he's very, very sad about the death of his old man.

She has a great deal to say on the subject of Angstrom. He should wash more frequently, for one thing. It worries Zog-19 when she talks so much. On his planet, every time you talk through your whistle, you use up a little of your sentient gas. You've got a lot to start off with, so it doesn't seem to be a big deal at first; but little by little, you use it up, sure as shooting. When all the sentient gas is gone, that's it.

Zog-19 watches Missus McGinty's mouth for tell-tale signs of the gas. He watches to see whether it's escaping. He thinks maybe it is. He does not want Missus McGinty to run out of sentient gas.

"You should wash more too," Missus McGinty tells him. "You're getting to be just like old dirty Angstrom." It's true, Zog-19 does not wash himself frequently. He is used to being made of iron. Washing frightens him. He has only recently been made into a creature of flesh, a creature that resembles McGinty down to the last detail, a creature that can pass muster with McGinty's dogs, and he has trouble recalling that he's no longer iron. Do you know what happens when you wash iron? It *corrodes*.

"You smell like a boar hog," says Missus McGinty. "I don't even like to be in the same bed with you anymore." Zog-19 knows that she's only saying these things because she loves him. On his planet, no one talks about anyone they don't love. They can't afford to waste the sentient gas. She loves him, and she loves Angstrom too, she loves him like a brother. She and McGinty have known Angstrom all their lives. Zog-19 imagines that, once he is better able to imitate McGinty, once he forgets that he used to be made out of iron, he'll be able to love her as well.

But here's another thing that scares him: When a person on Earth touches a piece of iron, he has noticed, they leave behind prints, they leave behind fingerprints. No two people on Earth, he has heard it said, have the same fingerprints. All those fingerprints, and every one different! No one on Zog-19's planet has any fingerprints at all. And these human fingerprints are composed of body oils, they are acid in their content. Unless they are swiftly scrubbed away, they oxidize the iron, they eat into it, they etch its surface with little ridges and valleys and hollows, they make smooth pristine iron into a rough red landscape of rust. Almost nothing could be worse for someone from the planet Zog than the touch of a human hand.

In the year 2347, space explorers from Earth will discover Zog-19's planet. The space explorers will leave their rusting fingerprints all over the iron surface of Zog. During their visit, the space explorers will discover that the sentient gas which fills the planet, and which coincidentally fills and animates the Zogs themselves, makes the space explorers' ships go very, very fast. Because they like to go very, very fast, they will ask the Zogs for the gas. They will ask politely at first.

Because the gas makes their planet ring so nicely under their iron feet, the Zogs will refuse it to them. The space explorers will ask again, less politely this time, more pointedly, and the Zogs will explain, with their thundering whistles, their immutable position on the matter.

War. At first, it looks as though the Zogs will easily win. They are numerous and powerful, and the space explorers are few, and a long way from home. The Zogs are made of iron (to the space explorers, they look like great foundry boilers with arms and legs and heads), and the space explorers are made of water and soft meat. Their bones are brittle and break easily. "Toot toot," the Zogs will reassuringly say to one another as they prepare for battle. "Toot toot!"

But one of the space explorers will think of a thing: he will think of a way to magnetize the whole iron planet. He will think of a way to use vast dynamos to turn the entire planet into a gigantic electromagnet. He will get the idea from watching a TV show, one where a big electromagnet-equipped crane picks up a car, a huge old Hudson Terraplane, and drops it into a hydraulic crusher.

McGinty used to see this show in reruns every now and again, before he got replaced by Zog-19, and he was always amazed by what happened to that car. Every time the show played, the crusher mashed the car down into a manageable cube, not much larger than a coffee table. "Look at that," McGinty would say to Angstrom whenever the show was on. "That's my old man's car that's getting crushed."

McGinty's old man used to have a car just like that one when he was young, when he was McGinty's age, and he and McGinty's mother (though McGinty had not been born yet) would run around the county in that big old powerhouse of a car, blowing the horn in a friendly way and waving to everybody they knew, which was pretty much everybody they saw. McGinty does not know it, but he was conceived in the back seat of that Hudson Terraplane.

His old man wanted to sire a child, he wanted a son, and McGinty's mother was only too happy to oblige. While they were making love in the back seat of the Hudson, McGinty's mother's left heel caught the horn-ring on the steering wheel a pretty blow, and the horn sounded, just as McGinty's old man and his mother were making McGinty. And the sound it made? Toot toot.

"We don't make love anymore," says Missus McGinty, "not since your father died." Zog-19 has never made love to anyone.

On his planet, they do not have sex. They do not have babies. When a Zog runs out of sentient gas, it is simply replaced by another full-grown Zog more or less like it. Where do these new Zogs come from? No one knows. Perhaps the planet makes them. Once, the best thinkers on the planet

Zog gathered together for a summit on the matter. They thought that they'd put their heads together and figure the thing out—where do new Zogs come from?—once and for all. But once they were all together, they got worried about losing all their sentient gas in the course of the palaver. They worried that they themselves would have to be replaced by the as-yet-unfathomed process of Zog regeneration. And so they figured, "What the heck?" and they went home again.

Missus McGinty leads Zog-19 into the cool bedroom of their farmhouse. She draws the shades. She does not ask him to speak. She undresses him and sponges him off with cool water. He does not corrode. She undresses herself. She is not built like a foundry boiler. Her pale, naked skin is luminous in the darkened room. She has a slender waist and a darling little dimple above each buttock. When he sees those dimples, Zog-19 says, "Toot toot."

Because she is only made of water and soft meat, Zog-19 is afraid that he will hurt her when he touches her. He is afraid that his dense, tremendous bulk will crush her, like the Hudson Terraplane on the TV show. He is afraid that his iron claws will puncture her skin. When she draws him to her, and when he enters her, he becomes momentarily convinced that he has injured her, and he tries to lift himself away. But she pulls him back again, with surprising strength, and he concedes, for a time, that he too is only made of water and meat.

So the space explorers will magnetize the planet, and the feet of the Zogs will stick to it like glue. Think of it! Poor Zogs. All they will be able to do is look up at the sky as the Earth ships descend. They will look up at the sky, and they will hoot at one another with their whistles. They will not say "Toot toot" because things will not be A-okay, things will not be hunky-dory. Instead, as the space explorers land and rig up a great sharpened molybdenum straw that will penetrate the surface of Zog and siphon off the sentient gas, the Zogs will whistle "Hoot hoot hoot" all over the planet.

To the Earthmen who are setting up the molybdenum straw, it will seem a very sad sound. It will also seem very loud, and every Earth space explorer will be issued a set of sturdy ear-muffs, to prevent damage to sensitive human eardrums. And the sound will mean this: it will mean "I'm sad" and "The end is near" and "We are most definitely screwed."

The loafers that hang out at the Modern Barbershop in Mount Nebo, where McGinty used to get his hair cut, and where Zog-19 goes now in imitation of McGinty, are convinced that the death of McGinty's old man has driven McGinty around the bend. They chuckle when McGinty says to them, "Toot toot." They try to jolly him out of the funk he is in.

They are by and large elderly fellows, the loafers, and they tell McGinty stories about his old man when his old man was young. They tell him stories about his old man roaring around the county in his big old Hudson Terraplane, a car so well-made that, if McGinty's old man hadn't smashed it into a tree one drunken night, that car would still be out on the road today. All the loafers agree that nobody makes cars anymore that are anywhere near as good as that faithful Hudson.

They tell him other stories too. They tell him how, when he was a little boy, he and his old man used to sing a song, to the delight of everybody in the barbershop. McGinty's old man would set young McGinty up in the barber's chair, and the barber would drape a sheet around young McGinty's neck and set to work with his comb and his flashing silver scissors and his long cut-throat razor, and McGinty's old man would stand before the chair, his arms spread like an orchestra conductor's, and he and young McGinty would sing. And the song they sang went like this: it went "Well, McGinty is dead and McCarty don't know it. McCarty is dead and McGinty don't know it, and they're both of them dead, and they're in the same bed, and neither one knows that the other is dead."

There was a fellow named McCarty who always loafed at the Modern Barbershop, a tough old guy who had been a frogman in the Second World War, so it was like the McGintys were singing a song about themselves and about McCarty. The loafers at the barbershop loved the song when McGinty was a little boy, and remembering it now they love it all over again. They love it so much that they laugh, laugh really hard, laugh themselves breathless, and pretty soon it is hard to tell if it's a barbershop full of laughing old men or weeping old men.

Of course, when McGinty's old man sang the song, back in McGinty's childhood, both McGinty and McCarty were alive, even though the song said they were dead, and that made it all the funnier. But now McGinty really *is* dead, and McCarty really is dead too, carried off by a wandering blood-clot a decade before, and they are both buried out in the graveyard of the Evangelical Church of the New Remnant north of town, which is kind of like being in the same bed. None of the song was true before, and now a lot of it is true, and so it isn't all that funny.

"Poor McGinty," says one of the loafers, when they have all thought of how the song is true and not so funny anymore. And nobody knows whether he's talking about McGinty, or McGinty's old man.

———

Before long, the Earth spacemen, with their very, very fast spaceships, will manage to conquer the entire universe. Everywhere they go, the people who live there will ask them, "How in the heck do you make your spaceships go so darned fast?" The space explorers will be tempted to tell them, because they will want to boast about the clever way in which they defeated the Zogs, but they will play it cagey. They will keep their traps closed. They won't want anybody getting any ideas about using the sentient gas themselves.

Before long, also, the sentient gas that fills the planet of the Zogs will begin to run out. There will be that many Earth spaceships! And the space explorers will become very worried, because, even though they will have conquered the entire universe, they will nonetheless continue to think that there might be something beyond that which they might like to conquer as well.

McGinty and Angstrom also used to sing a song. They used to sing it when they got drunk. They used to sing it back in the days when McGinty's old man was alive, when Angstrom's old man was alive, back in the days when even McCarty, the tough old frogman, was alive. They would sing it while they played card games, Deuces and Beggar Your Neighbor.

They used to sing it to girls, too, because it was a slightly naughty song. They used to love singing it to girls. And the song they sang went like this: it went "Roll me over in the clover. Roll me over and do it again."

It was a simple, silly song, but it seemed to be about sex, and that was unusual in a place where almost nothing was about sex. So little was about sex in the Seneca Valley in the days when McGinty's old man and Angstrom's old man were alive that, weirdly, almost *everything* seemed to be about sex.

Anything could make you think about sex in those days, even a silly little song, even a silly little song about clover. Clover is a kind of fodder that cows and sheep especially like. A clover with four leaves is said on Earth to be particularly lucky.

In addition to the hundred acres of decent bottom-land, McGinty's old man also accumulated a little highland pasturage to the north of the valley, where he kept a few fat, lazy sheep. These mountain pastures were almost completely grown over in sweet clover. When McGinty and Angstrom sang the song, when they sang "Roll me over in the clover," McGinty was always thinking about those pastures. He was thinking about rolling over a girl in the mountain pastures. He was thinking about rolling over a girl he knew who had sweet dimples above her buttocks. He was thinking about rolling her over in the cool mountain pastures.

And now Angstrom tries to teach the song to Zog-19. He cannot believe that McGinty has forgotten the song. Zog-19 understands that it's a song that he's supposed to know, supposed to like, and so he makes a diligent effort to learn it, for Angstrom's sake. Angstrom has been drinking, an activity that sometimes eases the pain in his belly and sometimes exacerbates it. For the moment, drinking seems to have eased the pain.

"Roll me over," sings Angstrom in his scratchy baritone voice.

"Over," sings Zog-19, in McGinty's pleasant, clear tenor.

"In the clover," sings Angstrom, waving a bottle.

"Clover," answers Zog-19. He does not know yet what clover is, but he likes the sound of it. He hopes that someone will teach him about clover, clover about which McGinty doubtless knew volumes, about which McGinty doubtless knew every little thing. He hopes that someone will teach him soon.

All this time, while they will have been out conquering the width and breadth of the universe, the space explorers will have kept the planet of Zog magnetized, with the poor old Zogs stuck to its surface like flies stuck to a strip of flypaper.

The Zogs will still manage to talk back and forth between themselves. Mostly, what they will say is "Hoot hoot hoot." Sometimes one among them, a Zog optimist, will venture a "Toot toot," but he will inevitably be shouted down by a chorus of hooting.

Zog-19 wants the spinning radiator fan of the Ford F-250 to stop spinning, and so he simply reaches out a hand to stop it. On Zog, this would not have been a problem. The spinning steel fan blades might have struck a spark or two from his hard iron claws, and then the fan would have been stilled in his mighty grip.

On Earth, though, it is a big problem. On Earth, Zog-19 is only made of water and soft meat. The radiator fan slices easily through the water and meat of his fingers. It sends the tips of two of the fingers cartwheeling off, sailing away to land God-knows-where, slashes tendons in the other fingers, cross-hatches his palms with bleeding gashes. Zog-19 holds his ruined hand up before his face, stares at it in horror. He knows that he has made a terrible mistake, a mistake of ignorance, and one that it won't be possible to remedy. He wants to shout for Missus McGinty, whose name he has only just mastered. He struggles to come up with her name, but the pain and terror of his hand have driven it from his memory. All that he can come up with is this: he calls out, "Hoot hoot hoot" in a pitiful voice, and then he collapses.

Probably by this point you have questions. How is it possible to know what will happen to the Zogs in the year 2347? That might be one of the questions. Easy. The Zogs have seen the future. They have seen the past too. They watch it the way we watch television. Zog science makes it possible. They have seen what happened on the iron planet a million years ago, and what happened five minutes ago, and what will happen in the year 2347. They can watch the present too, but they don't.

They have seen the space explorers from Earth. They have seen the depopulation of their planet, they have seen it emptied of its precious sentient gas. In fact, that episode of their history—a holocaust of such indescribable proportions that most Zogs can be brought to tears merely by the mention of it—is by far the most popular program on Zog. Every Zog watches it again and again, backwards and forwards. Every Zog knows by heart all its images—the Zogs stuck helplessly to the planet's iron surface, the molybdenum straw, the descent of the Earth ships on tongues of fire—and all its dialogue. They are obsessed with their own doom.

Another question: What is Zog-19 doing on Earth, in McGinty's exact form, with McGinty's wife and McGinty's dogs, and with McGinty's best friend, Angstrom? And: How was the switch accomplished? And what the heck happened to the real McGinty?

In a nutshell: Zog-19 was sent to Earth by a Zog scientist who was not enamored of the program, who hated what Fate held in store for Zog. His name was Zog-One-Billion, and he was a very important fellow. He was also brilliant.

Being brilliant, he was able to invent a device that allowed him to send one of his own people to Earth in the guise of a human being. The device allowed him to examine Earth at his leisure, and to pick one of its citizens—the most likely of them, as he saw it, to be able to put a stop to the upcoming extermination of the Zogs—as a target for Zog replacement.

Zog-19 didn't go willingly. He had to do what Zog-One-Billion said, because he had a lower number, a *much* lower number. The higher numbers tell the lower numbers what to do, and the lower numbers do it. It makes sense to the Zogs, and so that's how Zog society is arranged. Zog-19 couldn't even complain. Zog-One-Billion wanted him to be some un-known thing, a farmer named McGinty a galaxy away, and so Zog-19 had to be that thing that Zog-One-Billion wanted.

In all the excitement, the selection of McGinty and the sending of Zog-19 across the galaxy, Zog-One-Billion failed to explain to Zog-19 what precisely he was to undertake in order to avert the Zog apocalypse. It's possible that he didn't really have many firm ideas in that direction himself. There's no way of knowing because, as he sent Zog-19 on his long sojourn, he gave a last great toot of triumph and went still. His sentient gas was depleted.

What is known is this: it's known that, during his sur-veillance of Earth, Zog-One-Billion came particularly to like and admire human farmers. He saw them, for some reason, as the possible salvation of Zog. It is believed that he re-garded farmers thus because many farmers own cows. Cows were particularly impressive to Zog-One-Billion, especially the big black-and-white ones that give milk. These cows are called Holstein-Friesians, for a region in Europe; or just Holsteins for short.

There are no cows on Zog. There are no animals what-soever. Cows burp and fart when they're relaxed. That's why it's a terrific compliment when a cow burps in your face, or if it farts when you're around. It means you don't make the cow nervous. You don't make all its innards tighten up.

McGinty didn't make his cows nervous. McGinty's cows were always terrifically relaxed around McGinty, as they always had been around McGinty's old man, and it's believed that this reaction in some way influenced the brilliant scientist Zog-One-Billion, that this lack of nerves on the part of the cows of McGinty attracted the attention of Zog-One-Billion from across the galaxy.

Perhaps the great Holstein-Friesians fascinated Zog-One-Billion because they reminded him of Zogs, because they reminded him of himself, with their great barrel bodies and their hard, blunt heads. Perhaps the burps and farts of the Holsteins reminded him of the sentient gas within himself, the sentient gas within every Zog, the sentient gas within the planet of Zog, the gas that made the iron planet ring in such an exotic and charming way. And yet— this would have been particularly impressive to Zog-One-Billion—cows never run out of gas, no matter how much of it they release. They manufacture the stuff! They are like gas factories made from water and soft meat.

And what happened to poor McGinty, the good-looking young dairy farmer with the beloved shovel-headed dogs and the beloved dimpled wife? Sad to say. Like the released sentient gas of Zog-One-Billion, McGinty simply...went away, when Zog-19 replaced him. Drifted off. Dispersed. Vanished. Zog-One-Billion believed that McGinty's vanishment was the only way to save his beloved planet. If Zog-One-Billion, a very important Zog, was willing to make the ultimate sacrifice for the salvation of his planet and race, I suppose he reasoned, who was McGinty to object to making the same sacrifice? Of course, it wasn't McGinty's race or

McGinty's planet, but there was no good way, given the enormous distances that separated them, for Zog-One-Billion to ask him.

Oh, McGinty is dead and McCarty don't know it. McCarty is dead and McGinty don't know it. They're both of them dead and they're in the same bed, and neither one knows that the other is dead.

Just when it looks like the ships of the space explorers will run out of sentient gas, the planet of the Zogs having been utterly depleted in this respect; just when it looks like the space explorers will have to stop going very, very fast, one of their number (he was the same one who thought of magnetizing the iron planet of the Zogs) will remember a thing: he will remember that the Zogs themselves are filled with the self-same sentient gas. That gas is what makes the Zogs the Zogs, and each Zog is filled with quite a quantity of the stuff. He will remember it just in time!

Zog-19 cradles his wrecked hand against his chest. The hand is wrapped in a thick webbing of bandages. Zog-19 works hard to forget what the hand looked like after he stuck it into the blades of the radiator fan. He tries to think about what the hand looked like before that, the instant before, when the hand was reaching, and the hand was whole. Angstrom has just been by, and he brought the greetings of all the loafers down at the Modern Barbershop, who shook their heads sagely when they heard the news about the hand. Angstrom tried to interest Zog-19 in a rousing chorus of "Roll Me Over in the Clover," but Zog-19 couldn't forget about the hand long enough to sing. It did not take Angstrom long to leave.

Now Missus McGinty is with Zog-19. She holds his head cradled against her breasts. Zog-19's hand stings and throbs too much for him to take interest in the breasts, either. He does not know about healing. On Zog, no one heals. They are a hardy bunch, the Zogs, and usually last for thousands of years before all their gas is gone and they settle into de-animation. And all that time, all that time, the scars that life inflicts upon them gather on their great iron bodies, until, near the end, most Zogs come to look like rusted, pock-marked, ding-riddled caricatures of themselves. Zog-19 has no idea that his hand will not always hurt.

He is working very hard to listen to what Missus McGinty is telling him. She says it to him over and over, the same five words. And what she says is this: Missus McGinty, lovely dimpled Missus McGinty, says, "Everything will be all right. Everything will be all right." Zog-19 knows what that phrase means. It means "Toot toot." He wants to believe it. He wants very badly to believe that everything will be all right.

Zog-19 is also working very hard to forget that he is Zog-19. He's not worried about the Zog extinction now. Right now he's worried about Zog-19, and about making Zog-19 believe that he is not made of iron, that he is made of water and soft meat. He is concerned with making Zog-19 believe that he is actually McGinty. He understands that, if he cannot forget that he is Zog-19, if he cannot come to believe that he is in fact what he seems to be, which is McGinty, he will— by accident, of course, by doing something that water and meat should never do—kill himself dead.

And so the intrepid space explorers will begin sticking sharpened molybdenum straws straight into the Zogs and drawing out their sentient gas. The Zogs will make a very good source of the gas, and the space explorers will be able to keep on going very, very fast. There is nothing beyond the universe they have conquered, they will discover that disheartening fact after a while, but they sure as heck won't waste any time getting there.

Drawing out the gas will deanimate the Zogs, of course. Magnetized as they are, the emptied iron Zogs won't seem to the space explorers much different from the full Zogs, except that they will be quiet, which won't be a problem. It will be, in fact, a decided benefit. Once they have deanimated many of the Zogs, the space explorers will find that they can take their ear-muffs off. It will be more comfortable to work without the ear-muffs, and so productivity and efficiency will both rise. They will go on sticking molybdenum straws into Zog after Zog and drawing out the sentient gas, until there will be only one un-emptied Zog left.

This depletion will happen quickly, because once a space explorer hears about Zog and what the sentient gas can do, he will go there as quickly as possible (of course, he will leave much, much more quickly, thanks to the properties of the sentient gas when combined with Earth spaceships) in order to get his share. Most of the space explorers who come to Zog will never have seen the Zogs before they were magnetized, and so they won't be able to imagine why it might be a problem to empty a Zog of his gas. Except for the Zog's subsequent silence, it will seem the same afterward as it did before.

Everyone knows that the gas will run out—how could it not? And how could they not know?—but this knowledge will just make them swarm to Zog faster and faster, in ever-increasing numbers, because they won't want the gas to run out before they get there. What a dilemma.

———

Zog-19 rounds up his cows in the early morning for milking.
It's still dark when he does so. Missus McGinty stays in bed
while Zog-19 gathers the cows. Later, she will rise and make
him breakfast, she will make him some pancakes. But now
she is warm in bed, and dawn will brighten the sky soon,
and she can hear Zog-19's voice out in the pasture, calling in
the cows. He whoops and hollers, he sings out, and sometimes his voice sounds to her like a whistle, and sometimes
it sounds like a regular voice.

The cows come trotting eagerly up to Zog-19. They follow him into the milking parlor. They are ready to be milked.

The cows are not nervous around Zog-19. Zog-19 is not nervous around the cows. The cows are large and black-and-
white, they are noble Holstein-Friesians, and some of them
weigh nearly a ton. If they wanted to, they could rampage
and smash up the barn and smash up Zog-19 and smash up
any of the water and meat people who got in their way, even
though they themselves, the cows, are made only of water
and meat, and not iron. Lucky for Zog-19—lucky for all of
us!—that they never care to rampage.

Zog-19's favorite cow burps directly into his face. This
is, as previously mentioned, high praise from a cow. A tag in
the cow's ear reads 127. On Zog's planet, that number would
make the cow the boss of Zog-19, since it is a higher number
than 19. She would be able to tell him what to do, and he
would have to do it, whether he wanted to or not. She would
be able to tell him to go to some other planet for some half-
understood reason, and replace some poor sap who lived
there with his wife and his dogs, and Zog-19 would have to
do just what she said.

Here, though, that number doesn't make the cow the
boss of Zog-19. It doesn't make her the boss of anything, not

even of the other cows with lower numbers. It's just a number. Cows never want to rampage, and they never want to be the boss.

When the cow burps in Zog-19's face, her breath is fragrant with the scent of masticated clover.

The last surviving Zog will be named Zog-1049. That is not a very impressive name for a Zog. Zog-1049 will only be more important than a thousand or so other Zogs, and he will be less important than many other Zogs. He will be much less important, for instance, than Zog-One-Billion, the Zog who sent Zog-19 to Earth to take McGinty's shape. Zog-One-Billion had a very impressive name, even though he didn't really know what he was doing. Zog-1049 will be, as you can see, more important than Zog-19, though not by much.

The space explorer's hand will rest on the big red button that will plunge the molybdenum straw into Zog-1049. He will wonder how much sentient gas the last Zog contains. He will wonder how far his ship will be able to go on that amount of gas, and how fast it will be able to get there.

Zog-1049 will say to the explorer, "Toot toot?" The space explorer will have heard it a million times, from a million Zogs, and still he won't know what it means. He won't know that it means, "Don't you love me? I love you. Everything is hunky-dory."

When Zog-1049 realizes that the space explorer means to empty his sentient gas through the molybdenum straw no matter what he says, he will begin to hoot. "Hoot hoot hoot," he will say. He will hoot so long and so hard that he will expend a lot of his own gas this way. The space explorer will hate to hear Zog-1049 hoot so. He will know that it means the supply of sentient gas inside Zog-1049—and thus the supply of sentient gas in the entire universe—is dwindling ever faster. He will decide to stop contemplating Zog-1049 and go head and empty him.

The space explorer—whose name, by a vast coincidence which you have perhaps already intuited, will be Spaceman McGinty; he will be the great-great-great-however-many-greats-grandson of Missus McGinty and Zog-19—will take a final glance at this last of all the Zogs. He will take in the great iron foundry-boiler body, the sad, wagging head, the iron feet pinioned to the planet's surface by surging electro-magnetic energy. He will take it all in, this pathetic, trapped creature, this iron being completely alien to him, and useful to him only as fuel. And he will think he hears, as though they come to him from some realm far beyond his own, the lyrics of a silly song. They will ring in his head.

Roll me over in the clover.

Clover? Spaceman McGinty will never have seen clover. He will have heard of it, though, a family legend, passed down through the generations. Certainly there is no clover on Zog.

Roll me over and do it again.

The song will be a happy one. Looking at Zog-1049, and hearing the clover song in his head, Spaceman McGinty will feel unaccountably joyful. Looking at Zog-1049, Spaceman McGinty will think of cows, another family legend, great wide-bodied Holstein-Friesians, and he will think of clover, of a single lucky four-leaf clover, and of crickets hidden within the clover, and of sheep trit-trotting across mountain pastures, and of dogs at his heel. He will think of a little farm in a bend of the Seneca River, now lost forever. He will think—unreasonably, he will admit, but still he will think it—of McGinty his distant forebear, who for a time could say nothing but "toot toot" and "hoot hoot hoot," but who fi-nally regained the power of human speech.

He will not know why he thinks of these things, but he will think of them. He will feel the joy of reunion, he will feel his family stretching out for hundreds of years behind him, and before him too, a long line of honorable men and women, almost all farmers but for him, but for Spaceman McGinty. And his family, somehow, impossibly, will encompass poor old Zog-1049. What a peculiar family, these McGintys!

And remembering the cows, and the clover, and the farm, and the family, and the happy song, Spaceman McGinty will stay his hand.

Without the sentient gas that resides within Zog-1049, he will think, he will at last be able to settle down, this formerly peripatetic Spaceman McGinty, he will put down roots, perhaps he will find a planet somewhere that will accommodate him, where he can bust the sod like his ancestors and build a little house and even—dare he think it?—have a few cows, maybe some sheep, maybe some dogs. His blood will call him to it. And on this farm he will have the time he needs to think about the dark ringing hollowness at the core of him, the hollowness that has driven him out into the universe to discover and to conquer. And perhaps by its contemplation, he will be able to understand that hollowness, and even to fill it up, just a bit.

Zog-19 has discovered McGinty's sheep pastures, high up on the ridges at the northern end of the county. He has driven the Ford F-250 up there. He no longer wants to sell the Ford, because he has mastered the stick-shift. He drives the truck as well as McGinty ever did, even though he is missing the tips of a couple of fingers from his right hand, his shifting hand. A lot of other things are coming along as well, but the farm still looks like hell, it still looks like an amateur's running it. McGinty's old man would have a fit if he were to rise up from the grave and have a look at it. Rust everywhere. Busted machinery. Still, progress is progress.

The hand is healing up all right, but at night the thick scar tissue across the palm itches like hell (it's a sign of healing, so Missus McGinty says, and she does not complain about the scar tissue or the missing tips of the fingers when Zog-19 comes to her in their bed), and he can sometimes feel the amputated finger joints tingling and aching. Sometimes, quite unexpectedly, he can feel McGinty in that same way, poor vanished McGinty, he can feel the pull of the man when he is performing some chore, when he's hooking Number 127 up to the milking machine, when McGinty's dogs come dashing up to him, when he runs the wrecked hand over Missus McGinty's dimples.

Sometimes Zog-19 feels as though McGinty is standing just behind him, as though McGinty is looking out through his eyes. Is there any way that McGinty could come back from the void? Zog-19 does not know. Zog-One-Billion didn't mention the possibility, but then of course there are a blue million things that Zog-One-Billion never mentioned, including stick-shift automobiles and spinning radiator fan blades.

McGinty's dogs are with Zog-19 now, scrambling and scrabbling across the metal bed of the truck as it rumbles along the rutted mountain road, their nails scraping and scratching, in a fever of excitement as they recognize the way up to the sheep pastures, as they recognize the pastures themselves. It is lonely up here. It makes Zog-19 feel like he's the last creature on the planet when he comes up here.

He parks the truck, and the dogs are over the side of the truck bed and away, they are across the field before he can climb down from the cab. They swim through the clover like seals. Zog-19 shouts after them, he has learned their names, but they ignore him. Zog-19 doesn't mind. If he was having as much fun as they are, leaping out at each other in mock battle, rolling over and over in the lush, crisp grass, growling playfully, he would ignore him too.

He strolls over to a sagging line of woven-wire fence, leans against it, breathes in, breathes out. He watches the sheep that drift across the field like small clouds heavy with snow. He has learned that he will have to shear them before long, that is part of his job, that is part of McGinty's job. He thinks that probably he can get one of the loafers down at the Modern Barbershop in Mount Nebo to tell him how to do such a thing. They seem to know pretty much everything that a man who wanted to imitate McGinty might care to know, and they're always happy to share. Needless to say, nothing on Zog ever needed shearing. Still, he imagines that he can handle it.

He whistles for the dogs, and they perk up their ears at the summons, then go back to playing. He smiles. He knows. After a while, they will tire. After a while, McGinty's dogs will run out of steam, and they will return to him on their own.

Spaceman McGinty—the only space explorer still on Zog—will shut down the great dynamos. It will be his final act before leaving the planet behind forever.

And the last Zog, unimportant Zog-1049, the final, last, and only Zog, will find himself his own master again. But how Zog has changed during his captivity! He knew something bad was happening, but trapped as he was, he could not imagine the scope of it, the impossible magnitude of the disaster. He will take up wandering the planet, he will pass through the rows upon rows of deanimated Zogs, empty, inert Zogs in their ranked silent billions. He will use his whistle, he will release his sentient gas, the last to be found anywhere, in copious, even reckless, amounts, calling out across the dead echoing iron planet for any compatriot, for any other Zog who is still living. "Toot toot," he will call. He will call, and he will call, and he will call.

Zog-19 enjoys a hearty breakfast. He's eating a tall stack of buckwheat pancakes just dripping with melted creamery butter and warm black-strap molasses. He's never eaten anything that made him happier. He cleans his plate and offers it to Missus McGinty, who refills it with pleasure. McGinty always liked his pancakes and molasses, and to Missus McGinty this healthy appetite, this love for something from his past, a forgotten favorite, is a sure sign of McGinty's return.

He's been gone from her a long time, someplace in his head, gone from her in a way that she can't imagine, and she's awfully happy to have him back. What brought him back? She does not know. She cannot venture a guess, and she does not care. She has wept many bitter tears over his absence, over his apparent madness, the amnesia, the peculiarity (small word for it!), but she thinks that maybe she won't be crying quite so much in the days to come. Watching Zog-19 with his handsome young head low over his plate, tucking into the pancakes with vigor, his injured hand working the fork as of old, working it up and down and up again like the restless bucket of a steam-shovel, she can believe this absolutely.

And what of the planet Zog? Depopulated, hollow Zog? Well, the space explorers, once they have finished with the sentient gas, the space explorers will feel just terrible about what they have done. They will be determined to make amends. And so they will do what Earth people can always be expected to do in a pinch: they will go to work with a great good will.

They will send all kinds of heavy moving equipment, bulldozers and end-loaders and cranes and trucks and fork-lifts, to Zog. They will work, and they will work, and they will work. They will raise up a great monument. They will move the bodies around, they will use the inanimate husks of the Zogs in building their monument (the materials being so close to hand, and free), they will pile them atop one another in great stacks that will stretch up and up into the Zog sky. They will use every deanimated Zog to make the memorial, every single one.

Zog-1049 will almost get swept up and used too, but he will hoot desperately at the last minute, just as the blade of the snorting bulldozer is about to propel him into the mounting pile of the dead. The good-natured fellow who is driving the bulldozer will climb down, laughing with relief at the mistake he's nearly made, almost shoving the last living Zog into the memorial to the Zog dead, and he will brush Zog-1049 off, leaving some acid oil on Zog-1049's sleek iron body, and he will direct Zog-1049 to a safe spot from which to watch the goings-on without getting into any more trouble. The bulldozer operator will shake his head as Zog-1049 totters off across the empty landscape, hooting and tooting. Poor old thing, the bulldozer man will say to himself. He's gone out of his mind. And who can blame him!

Soon enough, the memorial will be finished. And it will be, all will agree, a magnificent testament to the remorse of mankind at their shocking treatment of the Zogs.

The memorial will be this: it will be a single word, a single two-syllable word, written in letters (and one mark of punctuation) tens of miles tall, the word itself hundreds of miles across. It will be a huge sign, the biggest sign ever

made, a record-breaking sign in iron bodies, across the face
of the iron planet, and, when the planet revolves on its axis
so that the sign lies in daylight, so that the fierce sun of that
system strikes lurid fire from the skins of the defunct Zogs,
it will be visible from far out in space. It will be a word written across the sterile face of the steelie, the face occupied
now only by eternally wandering Zog-1049; and the word
will be this: the word will be **SORRY!**

Spaceman McGinty will, in the end, find himself on a sweet
grass planet (plenty of clover there! and the breeze always
blowing out of the east, blowing clover ripples across the
face of the grass) far out at the raggedy edge of the universe.
No one will live on the planet but McGinty and a primitive
race of cricket people who communicate solely by rubbing
their back legs together. The cricket people will live hidden
in the tall grass, and McGinty will never so much as glimpse
one of them, not in his whole life on their world. He will
hear them though. He will hear them always. Their stridula-
tion will make a soft, whispering, breezy music to which, at
night, former Spaceman McGinty will sometimes sing.

And what will he sing?

Sometimes he will sing *McCarty is dead and McGinty
don't know it. McGinty is dead and McCarty don't know it.*

And other times he will sing *Roll me over in the clover.*

And still other times he won't sing at all, but will simply
dance, naked and sweating and all alone, former Spaceman
McGinty will dance along on the balls of his bare feet in the
soft rustling waist-high grass of that lonely place.

All that, of course, is in the very-far-off future.

Zog-19 is back in the sheep pastures. He feels relaxed, and
he burps. A crisp breeze has sprung up, and he watches it

play over the surface of the pastures, he enjoys the waves that the breeze sends shivering across the tops of the sweet clover. So much like water. Water used to frighten him, but he doesn't worry about it now.

McGinty is dead. McCarty is dead. Angstrom is dead.

The dogs are chivvying the sheep over in the far part of the pasture. They are pretending that something, some fox or coyote or wolf or catamount, threatens the sheep, and they must keep the sheep tightly packed together, must keep them moving in a tightly knit body, in order to save their lives. The dogs love this game. The sheep aren't smart enough to know that there's no real danger, and they're bleating with worry.

"Hi," Zog-19 calls out to the dogs. More and more these days, he sounds like McGinty without even thinking about it. "Hi, you dogs! Get away from them woollies!" The dogs ignore him.

Let the dead bury their dead. That is what Missus McGinty tells him. There are so many dead. There is McGinty's old man, there is McCarty, there is Angstrom's old man, there is Angstrom, there is McGinty (though more and more these days, Zog-19 feels McGinty in the room with him, McGinty behind his eyes), there are the Zogs. What could Zog-19 do to prevent the tragedies that have unfolded, to prevent the tragedies that will continue to unfold in the world, across the galaxy? He's only a dairy farmer, he's a man who lives among the grasses. His cows like him. They are relaxed around him. They burp in his face to show their affection. What is there that a man can do?

"Toot toot," says Zog-19, experimentally, but it sounds like an expression from an unknown foreign language to him now.

Let the dead bury their dead.

Missus McGinty has come with him to the sheep pastures. Later in the day, they will shear the sheep together. It turns out that Missus McGinty is a champion sheep-shearer, Seneca County Four-H, Heart Head Hands and Health, three years running. They'll have the sheep done in no time. Right now, though, they're in the act of finishing up a delicious picnic lunch. They're sitting together on a cheery red-and-white checked picnic blanket, sitting in the wealth of the wind-rippled field of clover, Zog-19 and Missus McGinty. Around them are the remains of their meal: a thermos still half-full of good cold raw milk, the gnawed bones of Missus McGinty's wonderful Southern-fried chicken, a couple of crisp Granny Smith apples. Yum.

McGinty would have given the dogs the chicken bones, but Zog-19 will not. He worries that they will crack the bones with their teeth, leaving razor-sharp ends exposed, and that they will then swallow the bones. He is afraid that the bones would lacerate their innards. That's one difference between Zog-19 and McGinty.

"Roll me over in the clover," Missus McGinty sings in her frothy alto voice. She's lying on the checked picnic blanket, and she plucks at Zog-19's sleeve. Her expression is cheerful but serious. She's fiddling with the buttons of her blouse. She takes Zog-19's hand and places it where her hand was, on the buttons. Zog-19 knows that it's now his turn to fiddle with the buttons.

The dogs are barking. The sheep are bleating. The buttons are beneath Zog-19's hand. Missus McGinty is beneath the buttons. The crickets are chirring loudly, hidden deep within the clover. McGinty is standing behind Zog-19 somewhere. The sun is hot on Zog-19's head. There is a four-leaf clover in this pasture, he knows. Somewhere, in amongst all the regular clover, there must be at least one. His head is swimming with the sun. He feels as though, if he does not move, if he does not speak, if he doesn't do something, something, something, and pretty damned quick, he is going to burst into flame.

Zog-19 can't know it, but it is time for him to resume the line that will lead to that far-off Spaceman McGinty, the one who will spare Zog-1049. It is time for him to sire a brand-new McGinty.

"Roll me over and do it again," Missus McGinty sings. The button comes off in Zog-19's hand. It is small in his scarred palm, like a hard, smooth little pill. He tosses it over his shoulder, laughing. He tosses it in McGinty's direction. He tugs at the next button down. He wants that one too. He wants the one after that one. He wants them all. He wants them all.

The wind ripples the clover, the wind ripples Missus McGinty's chestnut hair.

RICK MOODY

THE CREATURE LURCHES FROM THE LAGOON

More Notes on Adaptation

Just got back from another conference where I talked about what it's like to have your book adapted into a film. A weekend in Miami was promised. Sunburn and some pool time sounded pretty good.

I shouldn't be dismissive and ungenerous about questions on the subject of my book, *The Ice Storm,* and its adaptation, because the movie brought me a large audience that had no prior knowledge of my work. It paid for the down payment on my house. I got to meet interesting and gifted people. I got to witness the machinery of cinema up close. Yet I feel ungenerous just the same. When I hear them coming, these questions about adaptation, I feel my heart sink. I start to get bored almost immediately. Why? Why do I feel ungenerous and dismissive about the facts of my adaptation? Well, because I'm a *writer,* first of all, and I therefore make things out of words, and I think the multifary of earthly creation is best refracted in *words*. Sometimes I think words are so beautiful so flexible so strange so lovely that they make me want to weep, for their mystery and imof forage and fifty gallons of water *every day*, but the colossus of culture is far larger than the largest ever herd of these pachyderms. The vanished buffalo of the plains wouldn't get close to its massiveness. Often *we are it*, the repast, we are the thing that culture needs. The people you meet on the street are the thing that the media finds appetizing, because it likes to observe conflicts between these people, between you and me, especially without having to get involved—as in Jerry Springer, *Survivor, et al.* A little conflict can provide a lot of nutrition, it can drive a narrative, and the bigger and more lasting the conflict, the better it works. So there's the presumption of a personal conflict between myself and the makers of the film of my novel, as between all novelists and filmmakers. *There must be some conflict there; there always is.* A political difficulty. Somebody has to get slain in the helter-skelter of this combat. *Which is top?* The movie or the book? Though this is like asking about the translation of a certain poem. Which is the better English version of the *Odyssey* of Homer? Chapman's? Or that one that recently came out of the University of California? Neither of these translations *is* Homer, because there is no exact equivalent. Homer in English is not Homer, since his poem was written in ancient Greece, and Chapman's was written in eighteenth-century England, while that recent translation was written in the United States of America, which didn't exist at the time that the Greek epic poet was composing his lines. *No exact translation.* At the moment of a translation or adaptation is a loss, a falling away from the spirit of the original, a depletion. A photograph is not a thing, even a word is not a thing, but a cinematic adaptation of a word (a sequence of moving pictures) is by its nature farther from the world of the actual and is thus artificial, like the prose paraphrasis of a poem, a falling away, a capitulation to the ingenuine, a capitulation to the culture. Reporters and people who come to readings, they are keen to exploit this difference, this space of discrepancy and depletion, because it hints at a conflict. *So what did you think of the movie?*

Since I'm a failed musician, music is always pretty close to me when I'm working, and each of my books has had certain songs or records that were central to its composition. While I was writing *The Ice Storm,* I listened only to music that was released in 1973. I had piles of cassettes from the period, some progressive rock monstrosities, some stuff from California, and a whole bunch of those Rhino Records samplers that specialize in songs like "Delta Dawn" and "Billy Don't Be a Hero." I've thrown out a lot of these things since 1992, when I finished the book, so I can't tell you exactly what was on them, but I did make a tape of '73 favorites for Tobey Maguire, an actor in the film, which, it's my impression, he didn't like very much. The point here is that music is always implicit in novels, in mine anyhow, is always just outside the margin of the work. I had a friend who included a flexi-disc with his first novel, and there was a point when I thought about having my brother's band record songs mentioned in my own book so that I might shrink-wrap these songs onto the novel when it was published. But this actual music would subvert the immanence of music in novel writing, the incredible power of music described in words, the music suggested by words, the very music of prose. Film, meanwhile, because it's *synergistic,* brings the music out of the wings and into the production. This is an awesome responsibility, and it was one of the areas where I was most worried about Ang Lee's film of *The Ice Storm.* Not because I had any doubts about Ang's ear, but more because what music was occasioned by the composition of my book was so close to my heart. Turned out that the studio financing Ang Lee's film, since it had budgeted *The Ice Storm* modestly, didn't leave much money around for buying well-known songs, and, anyway, Ang and producer James Schamus wanted to have *an actual score*, not one of those film soundtracks that merely traffics in the nostalgic radio music of an earlier time. That's how we ended up with some rather *recherché* song choices as incidental music—"Dirty Love" by Frank Zappa, "The Coconut Song" by Harry Nilsson, etc. What was interesting about the score (by the Canadian composer Mychael Danna) was that it sounded really *eastern* to me. It had a lot of gamelan in it. Mostly, this score was used to accompany montages, landscapes, barren trees of New Canaan, and while it had nothing particularly to do with the era, it was eerily appropriate. Indeed, though the film of *The Ice Storm* now summons in me few feelings at all (I've seen it too many times), the soundtrack to the film, with that mournful score, can bring up in me waves of regret about the past.

I wanted to make movies when I was younger. I was at Brown, and they had a really good film program, and I had made a couple of super-8 films while I was in high school. Around me were Todd Haynes and Christine Vachon and others of their ilk, filmmakers gathering up their filmmaking ambitions. But I arrived at a decision, you know, that I didn't want to *collaborate* with anyone that much, didn't want to try to learn how to construct a story while negotiating with other people. I mean, of course, that the medium of cinema is inherently collaborative, as many have observed. Therefore, when you make the argument that a film reflects *a director's point of view,* are you reflecting the medium as actually practiced? What about the role of the producer? Is Andrew Sarris's *auteur theory* not a particular argument, *voice* of the director, but I think this argument is sophistry. It's an attempt by artists stuck with an inflexible storytelling medium (cinema) to argue for flexibility. I'd suggest that film, almost entirely, is in the third person. In narrative filmmaking, anyway. In films in which the characters do not address the camera. Mostly, therefore, cinema renders depictions of *community*, people in collision, not depictions of individual consciousness, which is the province of language. Music *feels* like consciousness, painting depicts the sensation of observing, but language can describe the actual experience of consciousness, because it can record sensory data and the experience and interpretation of this sensual material. One of the first things you give up when you sign the option agreement in which your book is given over to filmmakers is this consciousness. If your book is in the first person, you may have to content yourself with a *voice-over*, often considered a difficulty by producers of popular entertainment. Or you may simply find that the point of view of your first-person narrator (in my book, he concealed himself as a third-person narrator, only to venture forth with the *truth of his identity* at the end of the story) is stripped away immediately, to be replaced, again, by portraiture of the community. Your first-person narrator may get more *face time*, but that will be the only real vestige of his former role. This arrangement works well when it is drama that is being depicted, conflicts between individuals, but it is an arrangement that doesn't at all favor the mysterious adventure of consciousness, the dreams and volitions and complexities of consciousness, the varieties of consciousness, the way one mood or habit of being merges with and becomes its opposite so fluidly. Consciousness is hard to make palatable in movies and is probably boring when it is attempted at all. There are some trade-offs on which filmmakers have relied in order to delude you into believing that this is human psychology being depicted at the multiplex—a *dream sequence,* a flashback. But these equivalencies almost always feel cumbersome.

Which reminds me, there's a shot in *The Ice Storm* of a hard-boiled egg on a countertop. I could never figure out what that shot was doing in the movie. It's only there for a split-second, just before Joan Allen goes on her shoplifting spree. For a second, on a countertop, an egg, without a character, just an egg. Whose egg? Ang's egg? James Schamus's egg? My egg? Turns out it was meant to be the Ozu shot in *The Ice Storm*: the iteration of domesticity, as this domesticity gets left behind. See how difficult abstraction is to render in the movies?

Centrally, in both book and film of *The Ice Storm,* a boy is accidentally electrocuted. My apologies for giving away part of the story, but I imagine most people who care to have either seen the film or have heard about this electrocution from others. It took me a long time, while writing the novel, to figure out how to execute this poor, unfortunate boy, and it was a turning point in my life as a writer. Before that time, both in my first novel and as I embarked on writing *The Ice Storm,* I had felt confined by the difficulties of getting published. I thought there were certain ways that I was supposed to behave if I were going to get published. Poor Mikey Williams (he had his surname changed to Carver in the movie, *for legal reasons*) was the ritual sacrifice that enabled me to start thinking about what I *liked* to do as an artist, what material called to me, what my own voice sounded like, and so forth. In fact, the opening of the third section of the book, wherein Mikey meets his demise, summoned in me the beginning of the kinds of longer sentences that came to characterize everything I've written in the ten years since

I finished *The Ice Storm*. I know, therefore, that Mikey's sacrifice, as surely as if I were a Mayan priest and poor Mikey were laid out on the stone slab before me and quartered, made the gods smile. Because nature is disjunct, nature is cruel, nature is discontinuous, nature is lumpy not smooth. Children die, and planes go down, safes fall out of the sky. And yet cinema is that popular art in which no child is supposed to be slain. Again, there's this matter of the very large investments. *Are you going to kill the kid?* This was reported to me as an anxious question lodged by the studio financing *The Ice Storm*, which studio was probably even more anxious when word came back that Ang and James, indeed, intended to *kill the kid*. In the seventies, you could still get away with this kind of thing: in *The Conversation*, say, or in *Bonnie and Clyde*, you could get away with a movie photographed in the dark, mortal hues, but not in an era of family entertainment. Adultery, child sexuality, accidental deaths of adolescents? Not demographically sound. And yet *The Ice Storm* got made. The sacrifice worked. Or maybe it was just Ang's good luck ceremony. On the first day of shooting. His ceremony involved a bowl of rice and some bowing. It was dignified and strange. And it worked.

I liked going down to the set when they were making the movie of my book. I also liked leaving the set. Mostly I went while they filmed on location in New Canaan, Connecticut, because it was easy to get there. They filmed, the first day, in the park where I had once played intramural soccer. Soccer was the one sport I was good at back then, and I couldn't help but feel that the triumph of my career as a soccer player would stand the film in good stead. Yet there were all these people around, big union guys driving trucks, trailers everywhere, a guy whose job it was to stand around looking like Kevin Kline until the real Kevin Kline was through with makeup, etc. It took two or three hours, this one setup, and by the end of it I was bored as hell. When I had imagined the story, in 1989 or 1990, somewhere back there, it was about isolation in New Canaan, about the ways that the WASPs of the Northeast could sit surrounded by people, nonetheless besieged by loneliness. Now here was this gigantic production, with Teamsters, trailers, arc lamps, hair and makeup people. Would it be possible for all these people to produce this silence, this conversational fear, this embarrassment and discomfort of northeastern WASPs on a crowded and disordered set; would it be possible for them to create the illusion of things they didn't have around them and perhaps had never experienced? This gets to the *uncanny* feeling of adaptation, and by this I mean the uncanny in the way Sigmund Freud used the word: familiarity and discomfort in equal measure. *Unheimlich.* My experience was made all the more *unheimlich* in that the crews were actually in my hometown, one of my hometowns, anyway, and had requested permission to film at my old junior high school, right across the street from the park. This request was apparently denied when the town of New Canaan got a look at the script and, thereafter, at *the book* (they'd ignored my novel when it was first published). My own town refused to allow filming at my junior high! They said the book didn't reflect New Canaan's spirit! What could be a better example of *das unheimlich*? At least for this sojourner in the unearthly realm of adaptation. Eventually you begin to forget your childhood and remember only the photos yellowing in albums in the closet and you adhere to these photos as though they were themselves the memories. But even if the movie of your novel is not filmed in your hometown, *das unheimlich* still obtains, because of the collision of your imagination (the images that clogged your head when you were getting this stuff down on the page) with the collectivity of the film crew, the director, the producers, the studio suits, the director of photography, the editor, etc. As when I saw the final cut: on a gray day in January of 1997. Ang and James invited me to one of those plush, underpopulated screening rooms in midtown with seats so comfortable that they ruin the local theater by comparison. There were six people in attendance, Ang Lee, James Schamus, myself, my father, my partner Amy, and a foreign distribution person I didn't meet. Ang sat right behind me throughout, so that on top of other ironies, I worried that I might sneeze or shift uncomfortably in a way that would make a mockery of the seriousness of his work. I remember beginning to sob at some point toward the end of Ang Lee's *Ice Storm*, partly out of relief (*because the movie was so good I wouldn't have to simulate pleasantries afterwards*), partly because it was genuinely sad, but also because the story before me was so removed from my own imagining that it was no longer necessary to think of it as my own. I had successfully given away my book, and this was a bittersweet thing. The movie, that is, is the fraternal twin of your novel. Same family, but with only coincidental resemblances. The night they screened *The Ice Storm* at the New Canaan Playhouse *das unheimlich* became actual and environmental: there was a winter storm. The trees and power lines and sidewalks and roads of my hometown were coated in ice.

The film world has too much riding on its investments to be less than beautiful. Not since my adolescence had I felt like the ugliest, most awkward person in a room, but I sure felt that way during the year or so they were making the movie of my book. For example, when I went to rehearsals, and met the principal actors in the film, Kevin Kline, Joan Allen, Tobey Maguire, and Christina Ricci. *I was really scared,* of course. I had never met a movie star before, not even once, hadn't even seen one up close. Nonetheless, James Schamus, producer and screenwriter, asked me to come to a rehearsal and have lunch with the actors who were supposed to play the Hood family in *The Ice Storm*. I think the idea was that Tobey Maguire, who was saddled with the burden of the *Rick Moody part in the film,* should see what an awkward and eccentric guy I was, in preparation for his performance. What I took away from that luncheon (besides the incredible brightness and intensity of the actors, particularly Joan Allen and Kevin Kline), was how *beautiful* everyone in the movie was. Of course, this had nothing to do with the book. The characters in the book looked like real people. They had bad skin, multiple canker sores, glasses. They were puffy, they didn't exercise enough. These actors, on the other hand, were beautiful. They were so beautiful that you couldn't think of anything to say in their company, except *You are incredibly beautiful!* Sometimes I was irritated by all this beauty, since it didn't seem to have anything to do with my vision of how people lived. And at the party after the opening of the film Sigourney Weaver came up to me to thank me for writing the book and held my hand for a moment, and I was completely seduced and charmed and grateful that the actress Sigourney Weaver had read my book and was holding my hand for a moment. Still, at the same time, I couldn't help but feel that the culture of movies (leaving aside Sigourney and the kindness of her gesture) was trying to tell me something: *We make beauty, and we are going to give you access to our beauty, and we hope that you will go back out there and say nice things about us.* I would like to oblige, really. But is this beauty *true*?

If there's a word that best summarizes my feeling about my own adaptation and those of some of my acquaintances, that word is *ambivalence*. Do I think that the film world and everything it touches is venal, cutthroat, cruel, thoughtless, careless, heartless, boorish, dim-witted, and sinister? Pretty much, I do. Do I think that book publishing, and therefore the endeavor of writing, can be just as bad? Yes, I do. Do I regret having signed the option agreement in my own case? No, I do not. Would I advise others to do so? Under the right circumstances, yes. Do I think that most people who sign option agreements have pleasant experiences? No, I think most of them suffer. Is suffering noble and good? Yes, in some cases. How do I reconcile all of these divergent and in some cases diametrically opposed opinions? I reconcile them by saying that these lines I have written here are *written*, and when what is written closes in on a true record of human behavior, it frequently finds that the behavior of humans, however well-meaning, is ambivalent, paradoxical, contradictory, morally ambiguous. Human consciousness evades tidy depictions. Human consciousness lists where it will; one day it's at the movies, next day it's taken up with chess, or baseball, or the best way to win money at the casinos, or how to beat the IRS. One day human consciousness wants to love all the children with HIV, the next day it wants to blow up thousand-year-old religious idols in the desert. To be human is to be, by turns, sacred and profane, magnificent and contemptible, light and dark, mirthful and humorless, and human consciousness can't be contained in most of the vessels that would house it. Heroes and villains are one and

the same, they have the same shape, they are indistinguish-
able, they ride the same color horses, and men in black are
no more likely to kill than are men in lavender; great orators
smack their kids; our leaders are failed family men and
women. That doesn't make them bad. All is ambivalence, all
is complicated and strange, and try getting that into a
movie. Go ahead and try.

MARY YUKARI **waters**

EGG-FACE

Keiko Nakajima was thirty years old, and she had never been on a date. In addition, she had never held a job. The latter might have been acceptable; even in these modern times, many middle-class women in the Kin-nanji district did not work outside the home. But such women were usually married.

"Anything new with that Nakajima girl, the middle one?" some housewife might say while shelling peas with her children on the veranda, or gossiping with neighbors in one of the narrow alleyways leading to the open-air market. There never was. Keiko was spotted strolling in the dusk or running the occasional errand at the market; in the mornings, children on their way to school saw her feeding the caged canary on the upstairs balcony. Like some retired person, neighbors said. Like Buddha in a lotus garden.

Wasn't she depressed? Wasn't she desperate? They waylaid her in the alleys: the young housewives applying subtle pressure; the old women probing bluntly, secure in the respect due their age. Keiko met their questions (Do you want children someday? What do you do in your free time?) with an indecisive "saaa...," a cocked head, and an expression suggesting that such a puzzle had never even crossed her mind before. Comments and advice alike were absorbed with a "haaa..." of humble illumination.

"There's no give and take," declared old Mrs. Wakame. She was a formidable busybody who ambushed passersby from the comfort of her front stoop, where she lingered on the pretext of watering her dozens of tiny potted flowers. "Talking to that girl is like—" old Mrs. Wakame said, then shook her head and quoted an old saying about a sumo wrestler charging through squares of cotton hung from doorways.

But Keiko was not stupid. She was too retiring, even for a girl, but her schoolwork had always been good. Her business degree from Ninjo College would have guaranteed her a job if only this recession, now in its ninth year, had not hit the country just as her class was graduating. Managers had begun to be laid off despite decades of service; quotas for college recruits were slashed below half. Keiko, like many in her class, was rejected repeatedly at interviews the summer before March graduation.

Like her classmates, she had waited for the next interviewing season. Up to that point, she did not attract undue attention. But the following summer, when neighbors made polite enquiries of Mrs. Nakajima as to why her daughter was not interviewing—or at least making do with part-time work—they were told that Keiko would marry directly from home, bypassing the typical three or four years of premarriage employment. Nine years went by, however, and nothing happened.

Perhaps there was an inheritance? There *was* the house, which was all paid off according to the Tatsumi woman, whose husband worked at Mitsui Bank. But split among three daughters, it wasn't much. Moreover, Mr. Nakajima drew but a modest salary at some little export company in Shibu-ken. How much savings could they possibly have after private college tuition for three daughters, not to mention wedding expenses for the eldest? Old Mrs. Wakame had noticed Mrs. Nakajima buying bargain mackerel caught off American shores, as well as low-grade rice from Indonesia and Thailand.

There was little to be gleaned from the other two daughters. The Nakajima sisters, apparently, were not close; Sachiko and Tomoko showed little insight into Keiko's mind and even less interest. They at any rate were leading normal lives. Sachiko, the eldest, had recently married a confectioner's son and was now living in Gion. Twenty-five-year-old Tomoko, unmarried and therefore still living at home, had been dating her current boyfriend for five months. She had landed a bank-teller job after two years of interviewing; each day she rode the #72 bus to and from work, looking like a stewardess in Shinwa Bank's official navy jumper.

"They should have *forced* her to work, for her own good." "Life's just passing her by." "That father should bring home company underlings for dinner. Isn't that how the Fujiwaras met?" Ecstatic approval followed each comment, fanning a glow of well-being that lingered as the housewives went their separate ways. Their ruminations moved in endless circles, like a merry-go-round from which they could disembark at any moment if a better topic came along.

It was out of genuine kindness—as well as curiosity, the kind that drives children to poke sleeping animals—that old Mrs. Wakame phoned Keiko's mother. She felt justified in using the telephone because this time, unlike other outdoor occasions when Mrs. Nakajima had managed to slip away, she had a legitimate favor to bestow. This sense of the upper hand made old Mrs. Wakame's voice expansive. A young man, she told Mrs. Nakajima, a former student of her retired husband, was interested in marriage. Should she act as matchmaker and set up a meeting?

There was a brief silence.

"That is very kind," Mrs. Nakajima said with dignity. "We accept."

Mrs. Nakajima herself had married through a matchmaker, but that was decades ago; nowadays, love marriages were prevalent. As a result, Keiko had received only one other matchmaking offer five years ago, involving an elementary-school principal with forty-three years to Keiko's twenty-five. Trusting in future offers, Mrs. Nakajima had declined without even setting up a meeting. "A middle-aged man! How could I do that to a young girl?" she had said. "It would just crush her spirit."

"What spirit?" said her youngest daughter Tomoko. That scornful remark had hurt Mrs. Nakajima deeply, for of her three daughters Keiko resembled her mother the most.

Today, Mrs. Nakajima and Keiko sat at the kitchen table in the awkward aftermath of old Mrs. Wakame's phone call. It was about four o'clock, and Mr. Nakajima and Tomoko were still at work. Granny was home—she sat upstairs all day, coming down only for meals—but by unspoken assent, they made no move to go to her with the news.

A breeze wafted in through the open window, bringing with it the aggressive smell of fresh grass. Since the last rain, weeds had invaded the neighborhood, appearing overnight, in startling hues of neon, through cracks in the asphalt, from under ceramic roof tiles, even within the stone lanterns in the garden. The garden itself, cut off from the western sun by a high bamboo fence, now lay in deepening shadow.

Also drifting in on the breeze, from the direction of Asahi Middle School, came the synchronized shouts— "Fight! Fight! Fight!"—of the baseball team running laps. It was April again, the start of another new school year.

Instinctively Mrs. Nakajima considered closing the window, turning on the little radio that was permanently set, at cozy low volume, to the easy-listening station. For the shouts were a disturbing reminder that for the past nine years, while Keiko's life ground to a halt, mindless toddlers had been transforming into young adults whose voices now rose with strength and promise. Aaa, each new spring came so quickly!... as if the rest of the world followed a different clock.

But the phone call changed things. Suddenly the air in the kitchen, which still smelled faintly of this morning's prayer incense, altered—attuning itself to that elusive forward momentum of the outside world. For the first time, Mrs. Nakajima dared to hope her daughter's destiny could be saved, like a pan snatched from a stove in the nick of time.

With a sharp, anxious sigh, Mrs. Nakajima pushed herself up from the low table. Keiko, idly prying off the label from a jar of salted plums, glanced up in mild puzzlement.

"That jar's so low already," Mrs. Nakajima said by way of explanation.

"I can buy another jar," Keiko offered. "I'll take my bicycle." She ran errands for everyone in the family, which was only fair since she wasn't working. That had been Mrs. Nakajima's job for many years. She had not minded it for herself, but it smote her to see the same affable subservience in her daughter.

———

According to the résumé, Toshi Funaba was twenty-eight years old—Keiko's junior by two years. He had a business degree from Noraku University, where old Mr. Wakame had taught (hardly an elite school, but a good one), and he held a position as assistant manager at a merchandising company called Sabin Kogyo. Two photographs were enclosed with the résumé, casual outdoor shots: Toshi in a wet suit, sitting on the beach and gazing pensively out over the waters of Kobe Bay; Toshi in a Nike T-shirt, triumphantly holding aloft a small mackerel on a line.

"His hobbies," Mr. Nakajima read over the gentle clacking of chopsticks at the dinner table, "are scuba diving, sailing, dirt biking, and deep-sea fishing."

"Hehhhh...!" Around the table, there was an exhaling of exaggerated awe.

"Expensive hobbies," remarked Granny. She held out the photographs at arm's length, gripping the rim of her eyeglasses with a free hand as if it were a telescope. She noted with a quickening of interest—nothing much, after all, ever happened upstairs—that this boy was better-looking than Keiko.

The entire discussion had an air of unreality. Over the years, it had been an unspoken rule to spare Keiko any reminder of her situation; tonight, however, the practical necessities of Mrs. Wakame's offer unleashed in the family a heady tingle.

Tomoko, born in the year of the tiger, had just had an exhausting day at the bank. This was not the life she had envisioned for herself. Her feet ached. One of these days her ankles would swell up like some old matron's. And tomorrow would be no better, nor the day after that. Oh, what was the point of struggling and coming home spent, only to see Big Sister smiling and doing nothing, *not a single thing,* and getting everyone's sympathy besides? Granny actually gave her spending money out of her pension because "the poor girl has no income of her own." And now a prospective husband was dropped into her lap, a better catch than Tomoko's own boyfriend at the office. It was not to be borne.

"Let's hope you can keep up with him," she said to her big sister.

Keiko cocked her head in her usual evasive way, but said nothing.

Mrs. Nakajima waved away Tomoko's remark with an airy gesture which was at odds with the fierce, helpless glance she shot in her youngest daughter's direction. "Men don't care about that kind of thing, do they, Papa?" she said. Mr. Nakajima grunted, still staring at the résumé. Tomoko chewed stonily. Her red fingernail polish gleamed under the electric light.

"Well, well," Granny said heartily, "that Wakame woman has once again outdone herself."

There had been a time, several years ago, when Tomoko had insisted on knowing all the details of her mother's courtship. "Saa," Mrs. Nakajima had told her, "we dated for three months. He used to visit me once a week on his way home from work. I remember we took lovely walks in the dusk."

"Did you flirt with each other?" Tomoko asked. It had caught her mother off guard. Neither of her other daughters had asked such a bald question.

"Of course not!" Mrs. Nakajima said. "It was nothing like that." The impact of her words, now beyond retrieval, spread out in slow motion to fill the moment.

"He never even took you downtown?" Tomoko was referring to those chic tea rooms where, since before the war, young men in love were known to take their dates.

"I don't recall," Mrs. Nakajima had said shortly. She met

Tomoko's level gaze and felt, for a brief instant, a stab of dislike. "We preferred eating pork buns or fried noodles at one of the local places."

Tonight at the dinner table, Mr. Nakajima expounded on Toshi Funaba's workplace. He had heard good things about Sabin Kogyo. Despite this long recession plaguing the country, Sabin Kogyo had remained stable: its asset-liability ratio was excellent, and the yearly decline of its annual gross revenue was milder than most of its counterparts in the industry. The family fell silent before these indisputable statistics.

"It might really happen, ne!" Mrs. Nakajima whispered to her husband later that night, as they lay down to sleep on their separate futons.

"Nnn, it might!" he replied.

"Kobe's not far," Mrs. Nakajima said. "She can come visit us on the train." They stared up into the dark, thinking.

Mrs. Nakajima had never had a boyfriend before her marriage. Mr. Nakajima had dated sporadically, his crowning achievement being a one-night sexual encounter with a barmaid at the establishment he and his coworkers frequented after work. They had no advice to pass on to Keiko. They did not fully comprehend how they themselves had become linked together, they merely hoped Keiko would grow into marriage as they had—in the same mysterious way she had learned to crawl, then later to walk.

Old Mrs. Wakame was feeling the first stirrings of doubt. Just this afternoon she had met Toshi Funaba and his parents for the first time—something she should have done before approaching the Nakajimas, but at the time she had not been able to wait. A silent young man, she reported to the housewives standing about her front stoop. But not shy. Just silent...

What old Mrs. Wakame did not mention was how much this young man reminded her of her own teenage grandson who had declared, when he was six, "Granny, I love you better than anybody else." That moment still burned in her chest but with pain now. For lately, whenever his parents brought him to visit, he sat before the television, distant and bored. Every so often, he would condescend to utter a strained little "hohhh..." at her best offerings of gossip. Only when he talked to his own friends—Mrs. Wakame had overheard him using her hallway phone—did his voice take on the animated and confidential tones he had once used with her. This young man Toshi Funaba exuded the same air as her grandson.

"Sohh—" said one woman, nodding deeply. "Parents are pressuring him."

He'll liven up, Mrs. Wakame assured them, once he meets Keiko.

The problem, according to one of the housewives, was that matchmaking was not what it had once been. Men who used it these days no longer understood the subtle difference between evaluating an arranged-marriage prospect versus a love-match prospect. This boy Toshi, with his fancy hobbies (neighbors had seen photos; old Mrs. Wakame had made copies), seemed typical of a new breed that confused matchmakers with dating services.

"Soh soh," someone else said, "they grow up watching *actresses* on television."

A Mrs. Konishi, whose own daughter had just gotten engaged (a love match), made a pretty moue of concern. Poor Keiko, she said. In the old days she would have been just fine. Keiko had the qualities of an ideal wife: gentleness, deference, domesticity. Plus a college degree.

Eighty-two-year-old Mrs. Tori, bowed over a trembling cane, lifted her head. Even in our day, she said querulously, men liked women who could at least hold up their own end of a conversation.

Sachiko, Mrs. Nakajima's eldest daughter, came over from Gion on the local bus. It was Thursday. Keiko's date was set for Saturday afternoon.

"I don't understand," Sachiko said to her mother, who had been waiting for her outside in the alley. "Tomoko knows makeup as well as I do. Plus she *lives* here."

"It isn't fitting," Mrs. Nakajima whispered, glancing toward the house, "for younger sisters to be teaching older sisters. Besides..." She lifted her head, its home-permed waves webbed with white hairs, and looked up at her tall daughter. "Besides, Tomoko has the wrong attitude." Her haggard expression gave Sachiko, who had seen little of her family since her own recent wedding, an eerie glimpse of her mother in old age.

In the dining room, which boasted the best natural light, Sachiko now spread out the contents of her plastic makeup pouch onto the large low table. "We'll just do one side of your face," she told her little sister, "so you can see the difference."

"Haaa..." Keiko agreed, nodding but not venturing to touch anything. Mrs. Nakajima retired to the kitchen in high spirits, humming a Strauss waltz.

As children Sachiko and Keiko had played together at this table when Sachiko's more lively neighborhood friends were unavailable, for the sisters were close in age whereas Tomoko was five years behind. Today Sachiko recalled an early memory: a silent house, rain making pinpricks of sound on the broad hydrangea leaves in the garden. In the bracken-filtered light, she and Keiko had drawn pictures or gazed out the window. *Jikkuri-gata,* their mother had teased: characters of contemplation. Time passed. They were—in her memory—silent: mindless, timeless, knowing they were provided for, vaguely registering the faint clatter of the outside world. Dinner noises in the kitchen...an ambulance siren in the distance...

Keiko had managed to remain in that world. Sachiko thought of what awaited her back at home: laundry, cooking, wrapping tea sweets for tomorrow's customers, the already faded romance with her husband, the perpetual polite tension of living among in-laws. She sat on an unfamiliar red floor cushion that must have been purchased after she moved away, and she thought how quickly she had become a visitor in her own home.

Keiko, with self-conscious care, was dabbing her face with a damp foundation sponge. "Egg-face," some boy had once called her in fourth grade, and the name had stuck for the remainder of her elementary-school years. Her mother would pacify her ("An oval face is a sign of beauty! White skin is better than dark!"), while Granny, skilled at self-promotion, remarked, "At least she takes after me in the skin area." In truth there was a certain quality to Keiko's cheekbones, packed high like an Eskimo's, which lent to her face the suggestion of a blank shell. Her other features, overshadowed by this denseness of bone, appeared shrunken in contrast. The children in their unwitting astuteness had caught her essence: that bland surface of her personality which allowed, with minimal effort, deflection of any attack.

"Now some blush." Sachiko handed Keiko the oversized brush. "Put on as much as you're comfortable with. No, right here. The round part of your cheek." Keiko touched the tip of the brush to her skin: once, then twice.

"More than *that!*" Sachiko's voice rose in exasperation. She flicked her own wrist rapidly, suggesting many, many more strokes.

"Ara!" Keiko breathed as a soft stain of pink, barely visible, bloomed on her cheek. "It's pretty." Then, apparently embarrassed by this outburst, she lowered her gaze to the blush compact in her lap. She shut it with a tiny click.

Their mother came in to view the result: a job worthy of the Shiseido ads, in subtle tones of grey and peach. Mrs. Nakajima examined it with a look of wonder; she herself had never gone beyond liquid foundation, adding red lipstick only when she went out. "Lovely," she said, "just lovely. Aren't you glad, Keiko-chan?" Keiko, with an obliging laugh, nodded. "Look at yourself in the mirror!" her mother said, steering her around to face the mirror and looking over her shoulder.

Mrs. Nakajima, peering at Keiko's flushed face in the mirror, understood that a change had taken place. In her daughter's eyes was a look she had seen in alley cats, when they warily approached a proffered treat. It was a look terrible and bottomless in its hope. Mrs. Nakajima's belly shifted in unease, as if her body knew something she did not.

Unsure what to make of this, Mrs. Nakajima put it from her mind. The three of them went upstairs to show Granny. She was hunched over on a floor cushion, watching sumo on television. "There—which side of her face looks better?" Sachiko demanded, pushing Keiko forward.

"Maaa, what an improvement!" cried the old lady, looking up and clapping her hands. "That side, definitely. Look how dewy and white the skin is!"

No one spoke.

"*Granny!*" said Sachiko. Her voice became loud and slow even though there was nothing wrong with Granny's hearing. "We didn't even *do* that side. We did the *other* side." She exchanged a wry glance with her mother. Even Keiko gave a little smile, tucking her hair behind one ear.

After they had gone, Granny turned back to her television set. She could no longer concentrate on the sumo match; she still seemed to hear Sachiko's muffled laughter drifting up the stairs. Maa, so what if her eyesight was no longer perfect? In her own day, at least, she had been a great beauty. Upslanted eyes ("exquisite, like bamboo leaves," someone had said), a face compared with the one in that famous Tondai lithograph, a long shapely neck that was the envy of her village. She had held sway over a dozen eligible suitors, eventually marrying into a professor's family despite her own lack of education. How dare they forget it! Her daughter-in-law, her granddaughters—for all their pitiful fuss over face paint—had nothing to work with. Ridiculous bumpkins! Oh, youth and insolence would leave them soon enough. A nervous tic began throbbing under her left eye.

"How did it go, do you think?" Mrs. Nakajima whispered for the second time to old Mrs. Wakame, who was sitting beside her on the homebound train. "Did he like her, do you think? Will he ask to meet her again?" Keiko was sitting three seats ahead, out of earshot.

The lunch date had taken place at a restaurant called Miyagi whose sushi turned out to be, befitting its seaside location, of uncommonly good quality. Old Mrs. Wakame loved sushi, especially the *kampachi,* which she and her husband could now rarely afford on his pension. But her matchmaking duties came first, so for the first half of the date she delayed eating, chatting instead about everything from weather to chrysanthemums. The auspicious cuisine, as well as the pleasant conversation (mostly among the four parents, although this was to be expected), erased the uneasiness of her earlier meeting with Toshi.

It was further into the lunch, after they had covered jobs and hobbies (Keiko's hobbies were walking and reading) and the table's energy was flagging from the generous portions of yellowtail and hamachi and eel and squid, that Toshi began amusing himself with questions of his own. "Keiko-san, what is your favorite color?" he asked, tapping his cigarette over an ashtray. "Keiko-san, what is your favorite animal?"

Old Mrs. Wakame threw him an uncertain glance but his handsome face looked reassuring, full of the grave manly concern that was so attractive in samurai dramas. And Keiko was holding her own so well, answering each question correctly after a long thoughtful pause, although at times she did present her answers with unnecessary bows that were quick and clumsy, like a child's. So Mrs. Wakame paid them little heed. Hunching over her lacquered box, she applied herself singlemindedly to the sushi she had been waiting for, narrowing her eyes in pleasure as the freshly ground wasabi warmed her sinuses.

She suddenly came to. Toshi's question was ringing in her ears: "Keiko-san, what do you want most in life?" The table was silent, save for the steady clinks of ice in the men's whiskey glasses. Toshi's mother, a fashionably dressed woman, glanced at her watch.

"Saaa—" With all eyes upon her, Keiko cocked her head.

"We all want the same thing, don't we," Mrs. Nakajima broke in, nodding at her daughter as if in agreement. "A long healthy life, happiness..."

With a small predatory smile, Toshi Funaba exhaled cigarette smoke toward the ceiling.

Recalling this now, old Mrs. Wakame sighed and shifted position on her train seat. "Saaa, it went well enough, don't you think?" she said to Keiko's mother. "Who can predict," she added.

They both fell silent, sipping Morinaga Orange Drink from slender cans around which they had wrapped their handkerchiefs.

The train rattled along the tracks, and the city spread out below them: modern high-rises crowding out old buildings of wood and tile, balconies and verandas bedecked with futons hung out to air. The spring air was translucent with smog. All the soot expelled during the day—all the soot expelled during this long depression—was falling back down to earth, the sediment floating in the busy streets. Late afternoon sunlight slanted through it, creating an amber viscosity in which the traffic below would eventually still.

Old Mrs. Wakame stood up to roll down the shade, and her eye fell upon a travel poster displayed above the window: a promotion for some resort showing, in brilliant colors, a lone crane flying over snowfields. It brought to mind the television program she had seen last night, an NHK dramatization of the Crane Maiden legend: a crane, rescued from a trap by an old weaver, returns to him disguised as a beautiful maiden. This role was played by the lovely Junji Mariko in a rare appearance. The credits said so, at any rate, but who could really tell? Her face was averted from the camera, shielded by a fall of glossy hair. She would weave him wondrous silks free of charge, she murmured, as long as he promised never to watch her in the process. "You mustn't peek," she implored. "I couldn't bear for you to learn the secret of my weaving."

Something about that graceful turning away of the head—so old-fashioned, and now extinct—had touched old Mrs. Wakame deeply. And when the weaver, overcome by curiosity, finally peeked through a crack in the shoji screen ("Is that actor Mori Daiji?" asked her husband, exhaling a cloud of cigarette smoke. "Maaa, he's certainly aged."), Mrs. Wakame had uttered a shrill cry of awful nameless regret. She had felt silly afterward. For everyone knew what he would see: a crane, half-plucked and grotesque, feeding its own feathers into the loom . . .

What this had to do with anything, Mrs. Wakame did not know. Again, she shifted position on the plush seat. Images flashed into her mind of Keiko at the lunch table: lipstick smeared on her front tooth, trembling hands with red-painted fingernails bitten to the quick. "I would like children," she had said, as smoke from Toshi's ashtray rose up between them. "I have always wanted children." Remorse hit old Mrs. Wakame like a wave, and she lowered her Morinaga Orange Drink onto the windowsill.

RICK BASS

OGALLALA

They say that everything is always and forever falling apart, disintegrating—*entropy,* the scientists call it—but that even in that falling-apart, there is a regular order and pattern, a logic, which is, I suppose, in the end, mildly reassuring. They say also that because the urge or impulse to create arises from the act of assembling (or reassembling) so many separate pieces, there is always latent, in any creation, the seed for betrayal, dissolution, disassembly. That nothing is ever fixed, and that everything must fall apart, again and again. That this falling is the very thing, the force, that drives the world. That the best we can ever do is to hold on, as all else falls apart, and to try sometimes, in our clumsy fashion, to mash a few of the pieces back together.

Even the most eloquent success, however, is going to have burning within it that seed for falling apart. And what a hell of a thing it would be for that falling-apart seed, rather than the creative, putting-back-together seed, to be the force of the world: the thing that keeps the world moving, that

makes the days move forward. The thing, ultimately, perhaps, that we do best, even if there is always a part in us
somewhere (another kind of seed) that resists that force of
falling-apart.

I left when I was seventeen and a half; I couldn't get out of
Texas fast enough. It wasn't so much that the old man, Pop,
thought I was a fuckup—he was right, I *was*. It seemed as if
there was in me this uncontrollable seed—this *blossoming*,
as I reached adolescence—to disrupt the dreams and labors
of his and Mom's life. For a while, their beef was the best in
the world. They were trying something new at their ranch.
At our ranch. Our neighbors continued on with their old
ways, aiming only for the highest possible volume of meat
produced from the smallest possible amount of land—and
though they sometimes ridiculed the extra attention Pop
and Mom gave their stock, as well as the land itself—resting
huge portions of their ranch for years at a time, and filling
the surrounding skies with the haze of their controlled
burns, and harrowing and composting it some years without even planting—giving back, some years, after the earlier
years of taking—they had eaten some of his and Mom's
Robledo beef, named for the creek that ran through their
ranch, and they had to agree that it tasted different.
     And they had to agree, too, looking at his and Mom's
well-rested and well-fed, well-watered herd, that theirs was a
fine bloodline: that their animals were almost more like
works of art than cattle. Their fields were green and tall
with waves of sweet grass, even as their neighbors' pastures
shriveled and withered. Part of it was the care they gave their
herd, but part of it too came from the bounty of the sweet
and giant underground river, the Ogallala reservoir, which

flowed secret, unseen, down out of Nebraska and the rest of the Midwest, all the way to their ranch. They had spent their lives assembling property that overlay the hidden Ogallala, and then protecting and preserving that water. The great river was drying up, far beneath them—other ranchers' wells were going dry, and entire towns, in farming and ranching communities, were withering and then collapsing, becoming husks, ghosts—but unlike the other ranchers, Mom and Pop knew how much they had, and made sure they didn't use too much. Over the years, they had gathered enough land, and of appropriate topography, so that more water drained into their pastures than that which they took back and used.

What is the nature of excellence, and, once discovered—if it can be discovered—what sustains it, against the falling-apart? Is there a nurturing river that travels beneath us, or one that seeks our defeat—any of us, all of us?

I live now in Portland, Oregon, and work as the company representative for a union of timber millworkers, trying to keep their wages up, and their health insurance, even as the mills all around us are closing, with the timber companies having highgraded the surrounding countryside. We keep having to negotiate and renegotiate, to stay alive, for even just a few more months at a time. The pressure is intense—the foreign pressboard and chipboard manufacturers are *killing* us—and even our own union demands are sometimes a strain on the very thing that birthed our jobs and which, in theory, is supposed to sustain us, the mill itself.

I do my best. I'm proud of my work. In the last ten years, a hundred and twelve mills have closed, but not ours. We're hanging in there. Scrambling, picking up a little wood where we can—importing burned aspen from Alberta, old cedar from Canada, big Doug fir from cutover Montana and

Idaho, even getting wood shipped over from New Zealand, for Chrissakes—and we make a good product, high-quality finish-grade plywood veneer: maybe the best.

Mom and Pop were fierce, even obsessive, with their cattle operations, and while it would be easy for me to say they devoted too much time to the fierce pursuit and development of their craft—the often-brutal, even heartless linebreeding of a gentle cow that produced high meat yields, yet which was drought tolerant, with high calf survival, and above all, delicious. And sometimes it seemed that way to me, briefly: that such excellence lay far below, as if in its own reservoir, while the sweet mundanities of the upper world—family life, lazy picnics, and so forth—existed in another reservoir, up at the surface, and that it was difficult, almost impossible, for a person to be able to access both of those reservoirs at the same time.

But for the most part, I felt included in those pursuits—both above and below the surface—and cannot in all fairness blame any estrangement, my setting-out-on-my-own and choosing another lifestyle, on any lack of attention I might have received as a child, growing up. What I saw instead were two people fully engaged in the world, and in their craft, and if anything, I consider that a gift.

They were the last among their neighbors to take their herd off the expensive winter diet of New Mexico alfalfa hay, and turn them back out onto the spring pasture of new growth; and they were the first, in autumn, to take them off the grass as it began to go dormant, to keep them from injuring the roots.

They were obsessed, I suppose, with their venture, and, as if controlled by some other alien force from above, or perhaps below, it seemed to both me and them that I was intent upon *not* participating in that excellence, and indeed, often, intent upon unraveling.

Driving to class in high school each day, I would as often as not leave the various gates open, totally obliterating whatever specific and crafted combination of breeding and grazing regimes they'd prescribed for the herd. I'd sneak out at night and get liquored up with my friends, and hot-wire the tractor and drive in great big wild loops through the pastures, terrifying the calves and mother cows, and carving up the neat pastures with big deep ruts, and burning out the clutches and motors of the tractor.

After every such spectacle, my parents would have a stern talk with me, and I'd nod my agreement, truly contrite, truly aghast and disbelieving at what I'd done—but then it would be as if there were an electrical current running through me, and once again, like a zombie or a sleepwalker, I'd leave the gate open, or find myself once more out on the tractor, chasing down one of the prize bulls while one of my friends swung a lariat, trying to lasso the terrified beast beneath a full moon.

And it wasn't just what I did which plagued them: it was what I didn't do, as well, and perhaps even more so.

I didn't feed or water the stock, wouldn't participate in the slaughtering, didn't take part in the dinnertime discussions of marketing and price structures and the cost of feed and supplies. I didn't show any interest in the news of the day, the news of the week, or the news of their lives. I could not, would not, be pastured, and could not, would not, support either excellence or order—particularly not their fierce brand of it. They created me, they made me, but they could not control me.

———

Although they had never been rich, back in those days, they had hired illegal Mexican aliens, wetbacks only a few days into their journey from across the Rio Grande, to pick and pile and burn those weeds, for at fifty or seventy-five cents or even a dollar an hour, no one in the country could afford *not* to use them, as perhaps the planters of the South less than a hundred years ago had felt unable to exist, to prosper, without the economic engine, the forced labor, of slavery.

Early in the summers, then, before the immigration laws were tightened, some days there might be dozens of men, women, and children crawling through Mom and Pop's fields, out among the tame cows and calves and bulls, the cattle's tails swishing as they grazed, and the laborers creeping, for the most part silent in the great heat, inching their way north toward what they perceived would be the economic freedom of the cities.

And in the fall, on days when the crackling-hot air grew heavy and sluggish in advance of a storm, and the leaves on trees hung limp with the unaccustomed moisture, the countryside would be filled with the haze and sweet odor of their fields burning, as if from the fires of some active battlefield of cannons and muskets; and though their neighbors disagreed with their practices, claiming that the cattle would for the most part try to avoid the weeds in their grazing anyway, preferring and seeking out the last of the sweet native grasses, they tolerated this eccentricity, this stubborn, perhaps even prideful embrace of near-meaningless excellence.

I tolerated it, too. It was the one thing they did that I liked. I enjoyed watching the fields burn. I was known to set a few—in our fields, as well as our neighbors'—and enjoyed, on a windy night, running just ahead of the flames: vaulting a fence, and running through the scrub brush, panting, back to my jeep, and then driving to a pay phone and calling the VFD.

Arriving back home sooty, breathless.

What could they do but send me away? It was what I wanted; it was what I believed I needed.

Mom and Pop carried with them, at all times, a tattered spiral journal, which they called the Book of Life. In it, they kept notations and measurements of every bull and cow they'd ever owned, notations which were fiercely critical, and which usually condemned a calf to death. They called it "culling," and despite the excellence of the bloodline they were developing, fully 90 percent of each year's calf crop never made the grade.

Nor would they allow their culls—their rejects—to be placed on the open market, or be auctioned. They would have ceded too much control, and would have allowed someone else to come in and seek to combine or recombine some of the same genes and characteristics that Mom and Pop had spent all the many years previous developing, nurturing, summoning.

Instead, they killed the offending offspring, and buried them in the same pastures in which they had been born. As if they were literally nothing more than a crop, in constant need of thinning, rather than sentient, needful creatures.

The cattle-slaughtering, like so much of life, was both beautiful and awful. When it was nearing time for a shipment, and their freezer-aged stock was depleting, Pop would wander out into the fields at night; and as the herd sought him out and followed him in their gentleness, as they always did, he would evaluate them, for the purpose of selecting one of them to begin butchering that night.

Usually, he would have had one in mind for a long while, watching and evaluating, having paired in his mind one certain animal for one certain restaurant—developing that animal further toward that restaurant, in that manner, caring for it with extra attention and calmness, and feeding and fattening and watering it, hosing it down in the heat and brushing and stroking it, and making sure that it fed only in the freshest, most rested pastures, those last several weeks.

But as he walked among his herd at night, he was not above changing his mind at the last moment, or the next-to-last moment; and occasionally he would single out a cow that he had not previously considered, or had considered earlier but rejected, only to choose it again now.

And leading that cow away from the herd then with a bucket of sweet oats, he would walk it into the slaughtering barn, the refrigerated smokehouse with its elaborately designed high-pressure nozzles and floor drains, its block-and-tackle apparatus for spreading and hoisting. Leading the cow into the slaughter pen, he would close the bars and pipes behind it, penning it into the chute.

While the cow still had its head down in the bucket of sweet feed, and after the rest of the herd had drifted on farther, out of the range of knowing, Pop would lift the sledgehammer as he had so many thousands of times before, and would strike the cow so squarely and surely, so precisely, that it never knew what happened, but instead collapsed, sometimes with legs quivering though other times with no other movement at all, other than the falling itself: as if some vital essence that had kept it upright had suddenly disappeared, or had been revealed, just as suddenly, to have never existed in the first place.

The rest of that night, and the next, would be spent skinning and disemboweling and quartering and then butchering the animal, a huge task for any one man. I helped him once, when I was thirteen, then told him afterward that I would not be doing that again. I may be mistaken, but I believe that I also might have called him an old bald-headed sonofabitch. I don't remember a lot from those days, but I do recall the deeply sorrowful look on his face—a thing very much like despair, from a man who had never before failed at anything in his life—but then, if I am remembering correctly, it was as if a mask came over his face, and he simply nodded, as if to say that he would keep on doing it alone, as he had always done it alone.

"It upsets him," my mother said to me once, "that you're not nice to him. That you do these things. Try to be nice to him, at least. Can you do that?"

I shrugged. "Sure," I said, or something like that. "If that's what you want." As if, *No problem,* or, *Why not?*

But I misunderstood, or underestimated, the force of the black river within me: where it came from, and what, if anything, it was about. It was not pure or clean or graceful, and I could only be unruly, I could only seek to tear apart.

When he slaughtered the cattle, no part would be wasted. The entrails would go to an organic farmer who raised hogs (sometimes supplying his pork to a few of the same restaurants with whom Pop did business), and the bones and hoofs went to a woman who did organic gardening, and who used the bones to fertilize her soil. Even the hide and skull were spoken for, making their way to a local artist.

All the rest was eaten: dismembered and separated lovingly, each cut isolating the paired muscles of symmetry, two of everything twining to make one great beast: two loins, two flanks, two sets of ribs. Two shoulders, two shanks and rear; two neck roasts, two backstraps.

It usually took another full twelve hours to do the butchering, so that he would have to do that part of the task the next night, working a second straight night without sleep—and then he would either hang the meat himself, aging it for certain customers according to their various specifications, for a month or longer, or, for the customers whom he trusted to take proper care of the meat, he would ship the butchered meat out immediately, without even freezing it, packing it instead in sealed bags and chilling it on ice.

With this task, too, there could be no postponing, so that on those mornings, he or Mom would have to leave early, driving out to the little airports in Victoria, to send the meat to one of the two Houston airports (there were not yet plans to build a third), where it would then be sent on to New York, Seattle, San Francisco, Paris, Spain, or Germany—wherever it was traveling.

With the Capital Grille, in D.C., he'd done over fifteen million dollars of business across the decades. With another, The Metropolitan in Seattle, more than ten million. Sometimes it was slightly disconcerting to him to see pictures in the news of politicians he did not admire, and whom he had probably helped fatten and strengthen, so that now, by indirect extension, they were all that was left of those earlier herds, and had become, in that strange fashion, his earlier herds—though there were others that he admired, too, who he knew also must have eaten at those restaurants, and been likewise strengthened for their good deeds, rather than for evil: and so it all must have seemed to balance out.

Entering adolescence, I was dimly aware of the increased stresses they were both starting to face: rangeland colonization by fire ants, invasion of noxious weeds, market-flooding by cheap and inferior imported Mexican beef, economic recessions, screwworm, brucellosis, anthrax, hoof-and-mouth, and the vanishing, sinking Ogallala. There probably wouldn't have been more time for me anyway, even if I'd wanted it.

I was already off at college, in New York studying political science and history, when Mom got sick. I know the world doesn't work this way, but for a long time I wondered if things didn't fall apart because I left. I wondered if I had stayed, perhaps things would have turned out differently— would not have unraveled as they did. As if there is always some infinite variety of choices, combinations, and possibilities, and that Pop was right, even the smallest choices matter immensely, and that this is why he watched their herd with increasing zeal, making ever-fiercer and more critical annotations in the Book of Life, while the rest of us slipped away. That it wasn't the sweet blessings of the Ogallala that made his herd so magical, but indeed, his grip on history, his iron hand on the future and on the present.

I don't believe that now—about the infinite variety of combinations, always available to any and all of us. I think that the world and its various repetitions and cycles, its patterns of history, are prone to play themselves out again and again, and that change, even faint change outside the old patterns, is often all but impossible to achieve.

And maybe that's what the old man was trying to do— reaching so deep for change, like some frustrated, lesser god—that he let go of all of the patterns and relative balance and security and repetitions of this world above, and went down into some deeper place.

But he went there alone.

As she was dying, Mom wrote me letters. She told me that when she started getting really tired, too tired to even walk all the way from their cottage to the pond without having to stop and rest for a moment, Pop adjusted by carrying two lightweight aluminum folding chairs with them; and halfway to the pond, when she stopped and could go no farther, he would set the chairs up, and they would sit in the darkness, midway, watching the fireflies and listening to the night. And after some time, she would find the strength to rise, and continue on.

And when her rest periods became longer with each passing week, and her steps shakier, Pop bought her all sorts of vitamins, and took to driving her in the little jeep down to the pond—the jeep's sputtering engine disturbing the crickets and other night sounds, and sometimes frightening into flight the cattle egrets that roosted in the creek that ran alongside the sand road, so that as they drove, snow-white birds would be swirling around them in the night, birds flying in all directions like a windswept funnel of origami; and they would pass slowly through the birds' rising midst, as if through a storm, and on to the pond, Pop desperate to return to the earlier times, digging deeper for them now as if mining them, and Mom wanting only to sleep. They had made a doctor's appointment for her, but the first unscheduled opening had been weeks away.

What did either of them know? There was the suspicion, the first fear, that it was something larger; but they had never been old before, much less ancient, and fiercely, they pushed that fear back, and simply denied it, much as Pop would excise any other unwanted characteristic.

She never wrote, *He misses you.* Instead, she wrote, *Take care of him.* But I didn't even do that.

She said she rarely fished anymore, when they went down to the pond, but instead was most comfortable curled up on the swing under the big oak with a blanket drawn over her, watching him fish, peering out beyond the yellow umbrella of light thrown by the lantern, around which swarmed a wild assemblage of moths.

Some of the moths were plain, though others were quite beautiful, green and red and indigo, as if they had escaped from some collection, some museum keeper's ancient exhibit from centuries before, and had become inspirited, reanimated, and released back into the world.

The cattle, summoned by the sound of the jeep and by the lantern's glow, and the sound of my parents' voices across the water, would gather, too, moving slowly toward them in the darkness, huge and shuffle-footed, cracking twigs and farting and grumbling, sloshing water in the shallows and lowing and mooing; and again, as always, they would gather around Pop, and around Mom on the porch swing, and whether like a phalanx of guardians or supplicants, it would have been hard to say. And they would stand there with their tails swishing, for most of the evening; again, only watching, and waiting.

Sometimes, increasingly, Mom would be too tired to even get back into the jeep to drive home. Occasionally Pop would help her back into the jeep, though other times, he would let her stretch out on the porch swing and sleep there, as if it were a couch, using a rolled-up sweater for a pillow, while he slept on the bare ground next to her, with the cattle still surrounding them.

The lantern would eventually fizzle out, and the moths that had been swarming it would move on to other sources of light; and Mom and Pop would not awaken until dawn—sometimes surely recognizing where they were, though other times, for long moments, the world must have looked completely unfamiliar to them.

———

And when the diagnosis was made, they sought to control that, too, as forcefully as they had the appearance of any other renegade trait—an ill-curved horn, a fetlock in slight disproportion to a forelock, a dewclaw prone to snag and split on rock or gravel, an aging hip ligament that might not bear a bull's ponderous weight—and Pop set aside all aspects of his business and took her to and from Houston five days a week, six hours a day round-trip for the two-hour chemo and radiation session; and he put the breeding operations on hold, that first year, so that in the Book of Life there was a pause, like the annual growth rings of a tree that fail to show up during a drought year.

Back and forth he drove her, driving with the windows down and the wind rushing over their bare arms and through their hair: and sometimes Mom rode in the front seat, nestled in against Pop, though other times he folded down the backseat of their big Suburban and let her sleep back there, on a pallet he had fashioned for her.

Still unwilling to make himself vulnerable to the overhead that would be required in hiring a staff—and unwilling to trust them to do the job, any job, as well as he and Mom could—he nonetheless was forced to hire various local youths to help with the most basic of chores, which he no longer had time to tend to, with his new killer commute—and he would stop often along the way and relay the day's instructions to them from one lonely wind-blasted pay phone after another, often only reaching their answering machines, for the young people usually slept in late in the summer and on weekends: and sometimes, when he returned, he found that the tasks had been done, though other times, they had not.

I know that he was angry that I was not there, assuming those tasks, those duties. Even two thousand miles away, I could feel the anger, radiant and driven, as if on a blast of south wind: Pop furious at my own need or desire for change.

How it had to have infuriated him: the unsurety of arriving back at the ranch in each day's last light, and wondering whether one certain windmill had been turned on, or one group of cows and calves had been turned out to one pasture or another, or whether the oil in the bush hog had been changed, or the alfalfa from New Mexico delivered and safely stacked, neat and dry, became for Pop part and parcel of the larger uncertainty, about whether the doctoring was going to work or not.

Both his and Mom's minds were filled with each day's micromanaged profiles of various blood chemistry signatures, each day's reading wildly different from the day before; and whether each day's reading was different because of the effectivity of treatment, or the disease's natural ebb and flow, neither the doctors nor Mom and Pop really knew.

Arriving home and putting Mom to bed, and then hurrying out into the dusk to do his chores, and backtracking to see whether the other chores had been done—sometimes replicating that work, then, and other times addressing it anew, with the task never begun—was almost therapeutic, for if he could match himself against, and perhaps contain, this smaller disorder, then might not the other larger, looser puzzle pieces of Mom's illness, Mom's cancer, reassemble back into health and strength and wholeness and recovery?

Often, before she got sick, they had sat up in the evenings working on the accounting end of their business, paying bills and ledgering statements—but now by the time he finished his rounds, working by lanternlight, it was always at least midnight, and he would be too exhausted to work with any of it. He'd come in and collapse in bed next to her, too tired to even shower, and would sleep so deeply that sometimes when the alarm went off at 4:00, he would feel rested, for a while. He would rise and shower, do a few more chores, and then they would be on the road before 6:00, Pop sipping coffee, driving through the fog and soft sunrise toward the maw of Houston traffic and Mom's 9:00 A.M. appointment.

Only once did he ever oversleep: he had set the alarm for P.M. rather than A.M., and it was Mom who sat bolt upright at seven, to the terrifying sight of outside light and the melodies of morning birdsong. They threw their clothes on and hurried out the door, ignored the hungry herd's bawls of complaint as they drove away without feeding them, and drove hard, arriving for the treatment only fifteen minutes late—and all the way there, Mom had seemed in many ways more frightened by the thought of missing a day's treatment than she had by the illness itself: terrified, even now, by imperfection, and a job done poorly or incompletely...

I made it home as often as I could, and I saw what I had always known, that she was as brave as he was fierce: the two herdmasters.

As her body failed further, and she became but a vessel for fatigue, rot, and disintegration, they did not give up hope, but did find that their capacity and yearning for sweetness and pleasure was becoming honed to an edge of almost unbearable sharpness. They made time where they no longer had it. Pop would stop by a roadside ditch as Mom napped, and would pull off his boots and socks and wade out into the shallows, amidst skittering crayfish and minnows, as if he were a child again, and would cut a bouquet of roadside flowers, spider lilies and Indian paintbrush and bluebonnets and coral bean, and would place them on the front seat for her in an improvised vase made by cutting the top off a plastic water jug, so that when she awakened, she would be startled by their appearance, and pleased, honored, feeling cherished—and as the flowers' fragrance filled the truck, it would still seem possible, amidst such beauty, that victory would be theirs, and that this challenge, this rebellion, would be quelled and then defeated.

Likewise, nearing the end, some evenings they would go back out into the night, as they once had not so long ago, and they would fish, or just walk, Pop pushing Mom along the sandy trails in her wheelchair, listening to the night sounds.

As ever, the herd would follow them, twigs and limbs and branches cracking underfoot, and Mom and Pop would pass on by the ponds where they had once fished, the porch swing hanging empty now, as if awaiting another, perhaps younger couple, like some self-propelled carnival ride on which the metered time has expired, or, more ominously, like some strangely animate process, akin to that of a Venus flytrap, which needs to lure the living into its maw in order to keep its own self fed—and farther they'd go then, into the woods, down toward the creek where the wild turkeys roosted.

They would stop and pull down a few of the wild pears from trees they'd planted so long ago—though Mom had no appetite, and was usually able to eat but a bite or two.

They would leave the cores and uneaten portion of the fruit on the ground, among the other fallen pears, for the raccoons and ants and caterpillars and skunks and coyotes and foxes and opossums, for the crows and beetles, and for the herd itself—the cows' huge teeth crunching the pears with the sound of small-arms-fire, amidst the cricket-night—and on they'd pass, further into the night, with a bit of space opening up now between them and their herd, as the cattle lingered beneath the wild pears to search out the fallen and discarded fruit.

"You don't think it's been a waste, do you?" Mom would

ask, as Pop pushed her in the wheelchair: his hand on her shoulders, and one of her hands reaching up to hold his. "I don't think it has, at all—I think it's been wonderful, the most exciting and useful life anyone could ever have. But I want to know what you think. Are you satisfied with it, even now?"

"You're going to get better," is all Pop would say when she asked him such questions. And she would pat his hand and say, "I know, I know—but I just wanted to know what you were thinking. Neither of us are going to live forever."

"That's still a long way off," he'd say.

The doctors were still trying. There were half a dozen things still left to try. There could be no denying that she was sicker than she had been a year ago, when she had first begun the treatments—but they still had ideas, some of them experimental and others proven to have occasionally worked. And she was still standing, for the most part, wasn't she? She was sixty-one, he was sixty-two, and it was still a good twenty years before gene therapy would be understood enough to sometimes patch such chromosomal injuries or aberrations.

But there were still some different ideas to try. Truth be told, they both knew there were more ideas left to try than there was time left in which to try them, so that it would be, as it had been their whole life, a matter of choice and selection: but right now, this evening, each sweet-honed evening that they went out into the wild pear orchards, there was still a chance for at least one more try—still the hope that her ravaged body could take at least one more round.

The treatments pulling something deeper and deeper, each time, from within her flaming, desiccated marrow.

I got to be with her the day before she died, for which I'll always be grateful; and Pop was with her the next day. I had already gone on back to Oregon—I had just gotten a job as an intern with the union—and he said that she died strong and brave, calm and steady—that her heartbeats on the monitor had been erratic, as he held her hand, but that then they had stilled to such perfection, such elliptical grace and precision—such peacefulness, is the way I like to imagine it—that he had thought she was getting better, that she was rallying; but a short time later, there was nothing.

And in Oregon, that same morning, in my sleep, I felt that erratic leaping and thrashing, that thumping and wild-bird flightiness, followed briefly by the incredibly sweet peace and calm—the steadiness, the unchangingness—as if, because we would always be connected by blood, there was no amount of distance or time, and no amount of culling, that could change that fact, or separate that which had already been cast and made.

What do any of us do with our time, or any other resource? How best to spend it? I want to believe that the best use of a life is to help craft the world into a finer, more excellent place—but what if the highest good is simply to embrace beauty, and love, and be loved?

I want to believe that near the end of Mom's life, they had the opportunity to discuss these things. I like to believe, too, that he had the opportunity to ask her, one more time, whether she thought they had made the right choices in devoting so much time to the dream of their herd, and its perfection.

Should we have spent more time on each other, I hope he asked her, *should we have spent entire afternoons, random afternoons rather than planned, lying in a blanket in the tall grass, motionless, staring up at clouds? Should we have in-*

*vested more time—thousands of hours, even tens of thou-
sands—in such motionless, such nothingness?*

She would hesitate only the slightest bit before answering *no. No,* she would say again, firmly. *If I could do it again,
I'd do it the exact same way.*

Perhaps they were sitting on the swing, in the late afternoon, in early November, and the herd as always would
have drifted over to be near them. There would be no position Mom could sit in that did not bring her pain, even
breathing brought her pain, and yet she might have laid her
head against his shoulder as she had done in all the years
of health, and said *no* a third time, to be sure that he
understood.

She could not answer for him, but it was her answer,
and she is buried now on his and her ranch in what he
thinks of as the family cemetery, despite the fact that it was
only a family of three and a graveyard of but one.

He fenced the cemetery with oil-field tubing, to keep the
cattle from knocking over the granite headstone—strangely,
it looks like another corral—and he keeps it well-painted,
well-watered, and even now, twenty years later, there are
still fresh flowers at the gravesite, always. I'm no longer in
the will, but I can still go visit. Sometimes when I am in that
part of the country, I cross the fence at night and go visit it
without announcing myself to anyone: not to the ranch's
caretakers or Alejandro. Instead I stride through the tall
grass and among the gentle, precious, valuable cattle like an
immigrant, or an illegal alien. I lay some flowers there on
the grave, and sit for a while, listening to the night sounds,
and then leave.

The grass is taller there, inside the fence, ungrazed for
so long, and on warm days the herd will gather around and

try to graze at the edges of that boundary. The weaning calves can sometimes stick their heads through and nibble at the tops of the long waving grasses, and the cattle like to rub against the unyielding welds of the pipe, itching and scratching.

Sometimes they sleep there, encircling the cemetery, which I'm sure was a bit eerie at first, though surely Pop came soon enough to accept it as commonplace—and it probably became a source of dull sadness to him, many years later, that all of the herd that she had once known was finally gone, and ultimately became comprised instead completely of calves and bulls and mother cows that never saw her, never knew her gentle touch, or her pleasure upon their shared land. It would be a small thing, that knowledge, but a lonely one, and so perhaps he was comforted a little, as I am, by the fact that the herd still, as if through tradition, likes to congregate around her gravesite.

This other life of mine, now, in Oregon: despite being fully grown, a responsible adult (too much responsibility!) of forty-plus years, I still find myself examining this new life, this Oregon life, as if it is not really mine, organically crafted or created, but instead something I have simply found, something I have just wandered into. As if there is still a part of me left back in Texas, in the life I never lived, and the things I never did. As if that life, and those nonevents, are still somehow in me, again like a secret river.

That other, unlived life: how would things be different, now, if Mom had lived? How would they be different, for instance, if I had stayed—if I had never left—or if I had even returned?

In this other life—sometimes I can almost imagine it, and can examine it as one might examine a real and physical, tangible item—a rock or stone, perhaps—I would have been the good son. I would not have burned the fields before they were ready, would not have terrified the herd, would not have left gates open. I would have studied genetics, would never even have become interested in labor law and trade policy.

This other, imagined life, this gone-away or never-was life running always beneath me now like a shadow or hidden stream, beneath the flow of our awkward lives, up here at the surface.

The boy who would replace me showed up looking for work a couple of years later, any work, a wetback only traveling through, literally one in a million, or a million-point-two, who crossed the U.S.–Mexican border each year, looking for better pay, desperate enough to risk their lives for the mere sake of good work, and the astonishing wages of up to fifty dollars a day. It did not matter to any of them how grueling the labor might be.

All our lives, we had been seeing them filtering through the brush country, sometimes in small groups, other times solitary. They ran low and bent-over, carrying no possessions other than a jug of water with which to combat the heat. In the winter they might or might not be wearing a single coat, though in the summer, they often wore brightly colored button-down short-sleeve shirts gotten at a discount store or Goodwill, so that they looked as if they were on their way to some informal, lighthearted summer party—festive reds and lime-greens and yellows and blues—as if believing that, properly dressed, their alienability might be masked.

It wasn't enough, of course. Anyone who saw them hurrying through the ragged country knew immediately that they were fugitives. Sometimes they traveled along the oil and gas pipelines cut through the brushland, though other times they wove through the deeper brush, between catclaw and prickly pear.

Their brightly colored shirts were a liability when the helicopters or Border Patrol passed over, searching for them, and sometimes they would pull the shirts off and wad them up and hide beneath the largest tree they could find, hearts hammering as if pursued by hounds: and yet after the helicopters passed, they would push on deeper, back into the territory that had once belonged to their ancestors. Not necessarily wanting that territory to be returned to them— not in the beginning, and maybe not for another forty or fifty years—but wanting only, in the beginning, to simply survive.

Centuries earlier, some of their ancestors might have marched with Coronado's army, under the flag of Spain, through this same country and then westward, searching for the fabled Seven Golden Cities of Cíbola—a culture, a civilization, went the rumors, constructed entirely of gold (they had heard of this village, and had misinterpreted the Indians' word *cíbola* as meaning *gold*, rather than *buffalo*)— though in the end Coronado's army had become lost and fevered, circling the desert in the near-fruitless search for mere water, the true gold, while vast migratory herds of buffalo numbering in the hundreds of thousands moved slowly away from them, always tracking the water themselves, and knowing where it was: along the Nueces River, and the Guadalupe; the Rio Hondo, and Cat Springs, and Buffalo Springs, and Agua Dulce.

This boy, this alien, was traveling alone, and rather than heading due north as so many did, he was following the creeks, for both their water and their shade, as well as the fact that they provided better hiding cover, and also were pleasing to him to look at, as he had grown up in a land of little water.

There were so many of them, so hungry for opportunity. They were like moths at night, like the vast schools of mullet out in the gulf, like ants or wasps or gnats or midges, or like the snow geese and sandhill cranes that migrated south in the autumn and north again at the end of winter—a constant, natural phenomenon.

They were reclaiming their old territory, their old borders, like a returning tide that can never be denied. In a few more years they would already be—once again—the majority ethnic group in the state, after a hundred-and-seventy-five-year near-absence.

When this boy, Alejandro, saw the Robledo pastures, he became emboldened to stop. Pop's cattle were sleek and healthy, gentle and well cared for—Alejandro had never seen such cattle, as muscled as quarter horses or even thoroughbreds—and the range was sylvan and lush, seeming like a dream, in that otherwise barren country. The silver paint on some of the welded pipe fences was beginning to dull and chip, however, and there were a few clusters of weesatche and mesquite creeping out into some of the pastures, seedlings and saplings that were only a year or two old—and Alejandro reasoned that there might have been some change in ownership, due perhaps to a death, and that in that period of change or upheaval there might be opportunity.

He told me later (once he owned the ranch) that he didn't wade right into the job, but instead wandered the perimeters for a few days, evaluating things, making mental lists of tasks he perceived needed doing. Something about the place seemed unavoidably desirable to him, so that he was prepared to work for free, if only he could stay there, or nearby; if only he could be in that place's presence, daily.

He was starving, as almost all of the migrants usually were, and dared to venture into the little town one day right

at dusk, like a wild animal, where with some of the few dollars he still owned, he bought two loaves of white bread; but
then he went back out into the country, carrying one loaf in
each hand, the plastic bags dangling and twirling as he
walked.

He had never seen fireflies before, there not being
enough moisture in his homeland to sustain them, and with
toxic waves of pesticides applied to sunburnt cotton fields
foreclosing eventually the possibility of almost any interesting or unique specimen of life, save for the unvanquished
boat-tailed grackles and their less-interesting associates,
brown-headed cowbirds—and as he walked down the gravel
road that led out of town, walking freely in the silence of
summer dusk (if he heard a car or truck coming, he would
vault over a barbed wire fence and hide hunkered in a
brambly hedge of dewberries), he marveled at the almost
hallucinogenic off-and-on semaphore of the floating, drifting fireflies. It's entirely possible that he walked through
fields and charred little oak groves that I had set fire to only
a few years earlier.

He followed the individual blinkings of the fireflies for
hundreds of yards at a time, as if his movements were being
directed precisely by some conductor other than himself.
For a long time he was hesitant to touch one, certain that
a creature of such amazing design would be poisonous, or
possess a painful sting—perhaps even an electrical shock,
such as the one from the fence he had crossed earlier in his
journey, his first such experience—but finally he got up
enough nerve to set down his loaves of bread and capture
one gently, in cupped hands, and he was further astonished
to see that the fireflies contained no heat.

If anything, he imagined he could feel a coolness coming from them, and, as with every child before him, he looked

for, and found, a bottle, into which he placed several fire-flies, enough to make a lantern: and he walked with that for a while, the lantern in one hand and the two loaves of bread twisting from the other hand, until he heard a truck approaching, at which point he quickly set the bottle down carefully and then leapt into the hedge.

He listened as the truck slowed before the upright bottle in the middle of the road—he heard people's voices—and he peered through the hedge and watched as one by one the fireflies lifted up out of the openmouthed bottle, ascending back into flight like sparks rising from a campfire—and when the bottle had finally emptied itself in this fashion, growing dark and hollow again, the voices in the truck spoke in tones of quiet and puzzled amazement now, and then the truck drove on, leaving the empty bottle in the center of the road, and Alejandro, a little scratched and torn but with his sacks of bread protected, climbed out of the hedge and continued on his way.

This boy could have been me, if I had stayed. This boy *was* me, the other me—not of blood, but of place. I had caught those same fireflies, as a child: had moved through those same fields.

Raccoons followed him as if he were some nocturnal piper. Things felt hooked together to him here, he said, still loosely connected rather than torn apart. He liked the security of that feeling, as well as the richness of choice and potential, and felt—knew—that already, less than three weeks into his journey, he had waded into the midst of previously unimaginable blessings.

He camped under one of the big live oaks just across the border of Pop's property and listened to the thin trickle of the creek, astounded that there could be water at the surface in this country, even in the summer: not water mined from far below, pumped by windmill, but flowing free of its own accord, part of the living world.

Perhaps he felt governed—summoned—by some other force in the world. Perhaps he felt compelled to make order, to help reassemble things.

He listened to an owl hooting, far away, and to the distant throb and hiss of pumpjacks, a lulling sound, and was startled when another owl answered the first, from almost directly overhead. In his culture an owl could be viewed as a portent of bad fortune, but he chose not to believe that, in this instance. An owl had to live somewhere, and this was a nice dark shady creek.

He listened to it hoot just above him, sometimes answering the other one, and other times calling out to it, when there had been too long a silence—and he heard little fish splashing in the creek, and listened to the creek itself, a rolling sheet of music.

He finally slept, after the owl had flown off to hunt. And in the morning he rose, not stiff but loose as youth itself, and washed off in the creek and then put on a bright red shirt and slicked his hair back, combing it with a sprig of spiny weesatche, and then went up to the house, a couple of miles distant, to ask for a job.

He turned out to be a fierce and hard worker, a good speaker of the English language—a book reader—and a boy, a young man, who did not ask questions. I did not really get to know him until later in life, once the transformation was complete, and he had already been willed the ranch, but on the few times I would be down there visiting, in the years after Mom's death, that was the impression I got even then: that he was exceedingly patient, just waiting.

I was reminded of the way the cattle themselves were drawn to the ashes of the little brush and grass fires that Mom and Pop burned, in the autumn, to rejuvenate their pastures. Even before the flames had fully died out, and then later, while the coals and ashes were still hot, the cattle would wander out into those ashes and then just stand there. Perhaps the heat felt good on their hoofs. No one had ever come up with a good explanation. It was always a strange sight to see, particularly at night, with a herd of cattle surrounded by a burning ring of fire, just standing there patiently: as if yielding, succumbing, surrendering already to the pull of the flames not at all unlike those which would one day cook them on some suburban backyard grill.

Or at least they appeared to be mild and patient in their waiting. Perhaps just beneath that patience, however, writhed a reckless, clamant desire, an insatiability and voraciousness for the green grass that would be coming in the spring, and the herd had no discipline, no ability to wait the six months for its arrival. As if somehow there was ultimately little difference between flickering red flame and cool green meadow.

Pop put him straight to work on the hardest, gnarliest jobs imaginable, and Alejandro labored beyond Pop's wildest hopes and dreams. He put him to work clearing brush on a three-hundred-acre parcel he'd bought from yet another neighbor who'd gone bust, dragged under by the drought— it was Pop's belief that if he cut and picked and burned all the brush, some of the springs might begin to flow again— and that first day, he handed Alejandro the chain saw, a can of gas, a gallon of bar oil, and drove him out into the heated center of the spiny, prickly, thorny, daggered brushland, and turned him loose, never believing Alejandro would last: certain that the demands of the labor would chase him away, as perhaps he believed they had chased me away.

That first day, Alejandro worked too hard, too fast, and burned up the saw's engine, so that for the last two hours he had to cut the brush with the little hand ax he'd thought to take out of the back of the jeep. Pop picked him up at dusk and was surprised nonetheless by the amount of work he'd gotten done—surprised, too, to even see him at all—and he drove him back to the house, where he already had a fire going in the outdoor grill, and a rack of ribs roasting.

Alejandro was ass-whipped, nearly delirious with the pleasure of fatigue, and rode sprawled back in the jeep, looking up at the twilight, the day's progress already a blur in his memory; and Pop remembered that, too, and handed Alejandro a cold beer, which he accepted and drank deeply, with even greater pleasure; and Alejandro marveled at how cool the night air was in the open jeep, passing over his heat-wracked and salt-rimed and brush-scratched body, and he shut his eyes and smiled, grinned, actually, and Pop looked over at him and smiled, felt his heart leap, and knew, or dared to believe, that he had finally found his son.

And although Pop enjoyed the morning ride out to the new pasture with Alejandro each day, he began giving him the use of the jeep, so that he might drive himself, while Pop used his old truck or, occasionally, his horses, to ride the other pastures, checking on his herd, and feeding and watering them, checking their salt and mineral licks and vitamin supplements, worming them, tending to them. Watching them.

The Book of Life always in his glove box, or in his jeans' back pocket. The myriad list of numbers, and the wandering, seemingly random paths of legacy as coiled and complex, across fifty-plus years and thousands of acres, as any one individual's coiled strand of DNA.

The saw still wouldn't work. Alejandro drove it into town at noon on the fifth day and left it with a mechanic there, with instructions to do whatever it took to rebuild it. The mechanic recognized Pop's jeep, as had other people in town, but said nothing, only took the saw and studied it, sniffed it, and told Alejandro that the valves were burned out, it was toasted, he must've run it with too lean an oil mixture or let it get too hot, and that he'd be better off buying a new one.

"The oil mixture was good," Alejandro said. "Is there a better saw that can run hotter, a bigger saw?"

The mechanic studied the ancient, valve-mangled saw Alejandro had brought in: a junker. "Sure, yeah," he said. "For about six hundred bucks."

He had almost no money left. He pawned the junker for five dollars, bought a cheap pair of gloves—the ax had turned his old ones to tatters—and another loaf of bread, an apple, and a banana. He had a dime left, now, with which he bought gas for the jeep, hopefully enough to get back to work—and told the mechanic he'd be in to pick up the new saw after he got paid.

He didn't quite make it all the way back before the jeep sputtered out of gas, so that he had to push it the last couple of miles. It was easy work, however, compared to the clearing of the brush, though he didn't have any water with him, and hated the waste of time. He put a slice of bread on the hood of the jeep and let the sun toast it as he pushed, and left the radio on, listening to the music from a Mexican station, and it was almost like a break, even a brief vacation, as the trumpets blared and the singers crooned.

Not a single car or truck passed, in his half hour of

pushing, and when he got back to the field he drank almost
half a gallon of water, and then, feeling dizzy, sat down in
the sand for a moment, surveying his progress, too tired for
a minute to start in chopping—he needed a full minute's
rest, maybe even two minutes—and for the briefest of in-
stants caught a glimpse of, and imagined, what it might be
like some day to be too old and infirm to work.

He stared out at his clearing—the tangible proof, his protection, against such an awful condition—and the thought
or fear passed, as if absorbed or consumed by the mirage-
shimmers of heat that were rising from the bare and newly exposed ground like the vapors from a crackling fire already lit.

He finished the new property on schedule, two weeks later,
using the ax exclusively, and was paid six hundred dollars on
the nose. He went into town and bought the big new saw—
he had told Pop nothing of the old saw's demise—and when
he handed it to Pop, with the explanation that he had broken the old one, had burned it up, Pop was so touched by
this commitment to integrity, and by the gift of the shiny
new saw, as well as overjoyed by the fact that Alejandro
would not be moving on, that he made the decision to let
Alejandro work with the cattle. He would still employ him
for the grunt work, the grit-and-stone work of muscle jobs—
but he would begin easing him into the cattle business, to
see if he might have an aptitude for it. He would begin letting Alejandro help make notations and observations in the
Book of Life. He would show him how to butcher, slaughter,
and wrap. He would take him to Paris and New Zealand, to
South America and South Africa. The herd would grow even
more refined, so that it would be almost as if they had created a new species...

Would he leave the ranch to Alejandro, then, when he

died? I believe that the idea had ignited within him the moment Alejandro handed him the shiny new saw. And I think that likewise it had been in Alejandro's from that same time. That in his patience, or beneath it, there was a hunger. And I know that I cannot judge that, for I have my own hungers, yet I do judge. I like to think that all the bitterness has leached through me, that there is none remaining—I have my new life, the fight against the big timber corporations' injustice in the Pacific Northwest, as alien a landscape to south Texas as is possible, in this country—and yet some days, still, when I think of all this, there is something left in me, a biliousness, that just will not leave.

I'm sure I know how Pop must have looked at it. He would make Alejandro be a perfect cattleman, if he didn't take to it naturally. He could, and would, shape him, just as he'd been able to shape almost everything, all his life. Everything except the son who left.

Or he believed that he had shaped it: still not understanding that more often than not he, too, was being shaped. Still not seeing that at all. That always, we shape and sculpt each other.

It was not until the fourth week of Alejandro's employment that Pop found out Alejandro was homeless. Alejandro was working in one of the upper pastures, trapping gophers (Pop wouldn't allow poisons in his watershed), and Pop was riding along the creek when he came upon Alejandro's small encampment: a crude ramada made of yucca stalks, and a lean-to of spiny weesatche branches for a closet.

At first Pop thought it was the residue of some passing-through migrants, and was starting to dismantle it, when he recognized one of Alejandro's bright shirts, folded neatly in the yucca-stalk bower, and a pair of his jeans, as well as a pair of cowboy boots he had bought used in town.

Beyond that, nothing—no notepad and pen, no letters to or from home, no books or magazines, no mirror or pictures, nothing to show that he had ever even existed, just an extra change of clothes—no clue, even, in his crude dwelling, about what he did for a living—and Pop had gotten back on his horse and backed away slowly, as if he had come too close to some sacred shrine—though what might be honored in such a novena, he would not have been able to say, only that it was both vaguely familiar and yet completely foreign to him. As if he stood in witness before a path he had taken, but had never realized he had taken—some journey beneath his more visible journey at the surface—or as if the view before him was, more disturbingly, that of a path he had not taken, though it had been available to him, offered to him, though he had rejected it, even though there might have been as many wonders—more wonders, even—along that path, than the one he had chosen.

An uncontrollable divergence: an unbraiding, it seemed somehow, of his own life, and the dreams that he had somehow, through the dint of his own ceaseless and furious labor, managed to convert to brief reality, in the form of his herd—a ghost herd, really, he knew, against the force of time—and his island of sylvan pastures and meadows.

By midautumn of that first year he had deeded to Alejandro the three hundred acres that Alejandro had cleared upon first coming to work for him. He had pulled his old basement and sidewall forms out of the garage, still left over from the days of the construction of his stone cottage, and had given them to Alejandro, who was now building his own cottage on that three hundred acres, working on it every evening after work—working by moonlight, in the cooler temperatures that made such work so pleasurable, even after a full day's labor in the sun.

Some evenings Pop would travel over there to help him—would ferry stones up the ladder to hand to Alejandro on the scaffolding, so that Alejandro did not have to waste his time marching up and down the ladder himself—and it pleased him to see Alejandro's expertise, partly natural and yet partly learned, from previous masonry jobs in Mexico— the young man already far more talented at the task, the craft, than Pop had ever been—so that it was a joy just to watch him work, and to watch the steady rise of the four walls, not so much like grand architecture (though it was that) as natural history revealed, like a geological upwelling of mystery and order and form, grace and beauty and meaning; and though there was always the herd to tend to, the old man found that he liked increasingly to lie in the grass in the autumn twilight and then the moonlight, surrounded by the cool blinkings of fireflies, and to simply watch the laborer labor: watching the wall rise, stone by stone and course by course, with one awkward shape being placed with another to suddenly create supple beauty.

Only twice did Pop even intimate to me that he regretted the way things had turned out: that he believed I had chosen a shadow life, rather than a true or real one.

The first time was when I was back down there not long after Alejandro had started working for him. The three of us outside by the big fire pit, drinking beer and barbecuing a fatted calf, one that, despite being superlative, had just not quite made the grade.

"How long do you reckon you'll be out there, working for that mill?" Pop asked—almost breezily, but not quite.

I was honestly surprised. I truly thought he understood. "Forever," I said, after a moment's pause, and he clammed up, didn't ask anymore about it, not then, nor ever again.

The second intimation was even briefer. It came about five years later, which was only the next time I went back down there. Pop had spent most of the evening bragging how good Alejandro was with the business. This was back before I knew about the change of the will and, I suppose, perhaps even back before Pop knew about it. Perhaps he did not make that decision until that very evening.

We were cooking out again, just him and me, out on the front porch—how many hundreds of meals, or even thousands, had the three of us taken on that same porch, back when Mom had still been living?—and I guess I was getting a little cross with how long he was carrying on about good old Alejandro, because I missed, I believe, some important communication or noncommunication, which probably would have been sufficient between some fathers and some sons. I didn't notice, at the time, that for a moment, he might have been thinking about me, instead of Alejandro.

He was saying something about how there were some things Alejandro couldn't do. I don't recall it exactly—I'm afraid my blood was up a little, and I wasn't doing a real good job of listening—but it's possible that he might even have said that there were some things that Alejandro could never be.

And I think that I might have responded with sarcasm—might have said something like, *That's hard to imagine.*

I do remember that the rest of the night was pretty quiet after that.

It was about a year later when I received a letter from him saying he felt he needed to leave the ranch to Alejandro, in order to—how did he phrase it?—most fully motivate

Alejandro to maintain the high standards of production that had always been Pop's (and Mom's) dream.

He would leave me money, in the will, he said. But he would leave the land to Alejandro. I would be able to visit, he said. He's put language in the will to assure it.

I was taken aback, sure. And I'd have to agree, a worker should be rewarded, as should loyalty. Employees should share in the success of the companies for whom they labor. But still, it took my breath away—*the land*. True, I only got back to it once every five years or so. But still, I was shocked.

I tried not to show it. Sure, there was probably some simmering part inside me, maybe even a thing like rage, or fury. But I think that's mostly gone away. I think now it's just disbelief. It was his own damn ranch, after all. It's a free country. He could do with it whatever he wanted.

In the meantime, more and more of the surrounding ranchers were failing, as was the water supply for the homes in town. More and more often, a homeowner would turn on the faucet to take a shower, or to draw water with which to cook, only to hear the clanking, shuddering dry-heave of empty pipes rattling within the walls, straining to find water where there was none: a hiss and a rasp from the faucet, a rush of hot air, a few grains of sand—glittering like tiny diamonds—and then nothing.

Pop's lands, however, kept their water. His springs continued to prosper, like some biblical paradise. Seeps continued to spring up on their land, particularly after the thunderstorms of hurricane season, even as their neighbors' ranches shone barren like dry bone sockets. On Pop and Alejandro's ranch wildflowers bloomed, and hummingbirds and butterflies whirled, even in midsummer: and the sweet tongue of the Ogallala continued to nurture and nourish them, if no one else; and still, in their reckless surge toward excellence, they dug deeper, became ever-more critical.

Eventually, though, even some of their wells began to diminish. They had to cut back on the size of the herds, and had to rest-rotate the pumping schedules from some of the weaker wells. I'm sure the old man didn't like it a bit—coming up against limitations of any kind, for the first time in his life. The land finally starting to show its age, just like him.

Mom and Pop—and later, Pop and Alejandro—always had a bull named Moses. There was Moses the First, then Moses Two, Moses Three, and so on. He was always the herd bull—the most productive one. Moses One and Moses Two had been gentle, Moses Three had been skittish but efficient, and so on. I lost track of them, though I suppose anything anyone might ever care to know about any of them is all there, recorded meticulously in all the different volumes of the Book of Life—tattered spiral notebooks and sun-faded cloth journals, and oil- and bloodstained diaries, stacked between bookends, one after another, on the mantel above the stone fireplace.

It was Moses Number Eight who gored Pop. It was a smoldering summer, the hottest yet on record. Alejandro called me about it, after he had gotten Pop to the hospital, and after it was established that he was going to survive.

More and more of the wells were going dry, so that they were having to go out and shut them down at all hours of the day and night. Alejandro said that he'd noticed Moses getting testier in the heat. But it never occurred to them that behind Moses's monstrously huge head, and reddened, pinheaded eyes, he might ever conceive of charging across the gap, the gulf, that separated animal from man, servant from owner, captor from captive.

One of the windmills in Moses's pasture had stopped working, Alejandro said, the gaskets burned out either from the incredible heat or from the casing running low on water, and Alejandro and Pop had driven up into his pasture to work on it. It was early evening, with the sun's temper finally beginning to cant downward a bit, like a weapon that is no longer being used to strike directly, but at a reduced angle, causing slightly less damage—though still, the blows fell across the men's backs.

The herd, hoping for treats, or perhaps out of idle curiosity, had followed the little jeep up the hill, irritating Moses from the beginning; he had been lounging belly-deep in the dwindling stock tank, its shoreline cratered and rutted with thousands of deep pockmarks from where he and the herd had been wading in and out of the little pond, with the shoreline still dropping, revealing new mud each day.

(Pop was worried that as the water level dropped, the alkaloids and other minerals in the pond would become more concentrated, and that ten thousand miles away, his customers—particularly the French—would be able to taste the difference. He kept pumping harder, trying to keep the tanks from dropping; but they were all falling now, and it seemed that the losses were not so much through the heartbreak of unprecedented evaporation as instead simply drawing away, back down some fissure in the earth.)

Moses, then, was the last to join them, walking slowly up the slight hill to where his herd already stood around watching the repairs. Both men turned to look at him when he arrived, and would later remark to each other that, if anything, it seemed to them that he was more peaceful, even satisfied, than they had seen him since the escape. As if he had made it back to his own self, or had even made up his mind about some troubling issue, Alejandro remembered thinking. He was getting old, for a bull, and soon they'd have to be bringing in a newer, younger one from another pasture. Maybe the heat was about to break, Alejandro thought. Maybe even the drought itself.

To both men, afterward, it seemed that it had been one specific sound that had set him off: the *clink!* of a wrench, a five-eighths box wrench, being set down on one of the steel stays of the windmill's frame: Pop setting the wrench down perhaps a little too loudly, in the evening stillness, enthused with the simple pleasure and relief of having broken open a rusty nut.

It was precisely as if that sound had thrown a switch: as if, in the metallic clink of metal against metal, some electrolytic transfer had been opened in the bull, some force and power far beyond his own control or even knowing—a rage and destructiveness that had always been in him, brooding, perhaps, over the way the men had bounded and manipulated him, using him only to attain order, always order— and had he not kicked over the open toolbox during his charge, he might have been upon them even before they had time to react.

The speed of the mind in a time of fear—so much broader than it is deep. Alejandro whirled and thought, strangely, he said, of Pop first—as if the old man were his aging father, or even his son, or some other close blood relation—but then he had time to think of himself, too, and to ascertain as well that the old man was fuddling around, rising crookedly and doing something clumsy and wrong, something that might jeopardize Alejandro, if he stopped to try and save him—and still, in the mind's lightning-wide race, there was time to consciously choose, to amend, and to attempt to save himself first—and Alejandro ducked and rolled under the frame of the windmill, and then reached out a hand to Pop, who was still doddering on the other side, just as Moses reached him and hooked one of his horns in under Pop's wizened flank and lifted him into the air as if he were but a sheet of paper, or even lighter than paper.

Alejandro saw how Moses seemed to be suddenly free, in that initial spark-gap of violence, and pleased—there was no other word for it—though when Pop went airborne, arms flailing, limp as a scarecrow's, the pleasure left Moses and he seemed confused again, during that not-so-brief time that Pop was in the air—as if, like some metamorphic Antaeus, he had to have not just his four hoofs in contact with the ground, but also the feet of whomever or whatever he was attacking, to be most fully his own force.

Moses whipped his head around wildly, as if wondering where Pop had gone—enraged at his disappearance—before spying him floating just above; and when Pop descended, Moses caught him in the cradle of his horns, and with the huge boilerplate of his head (as if it were created for only this purpose, and long ago), he drove Pop toward the windmill, even as the noodleweight of Pop was sliding from that nest of horns, like some failed fledgling.

He slammed Pop against the windmill with a force that rocked the frame itself, caused a galvanic shudder and clang to reverberate all the way into the vanes far above—an oddly musical sound, as if musicians were warming up, preparing to play—and strangely, this impact seemed to resuscitate Pop rather than finishing him off: as if the bull had somehow imparted, in the speed of the transaction, some of its own considerable force into Pop's ailing, vanishing body—a crude and temporary grafting of power.

One of Pop's legs was useless, Alejandro said, shattered like bottle glass within him, but the other one still functioned, and he was able to pivot crookedly, like a man or woman tucking his or her shoulder against an oncoming cold wind, just before Moses's third charge; and with a slight hop, he moved to the side just as Moses drove his huge head against the windmill's frame again, missing Pop by inches.

The rest of the herd had been spooked by Moses's initial charge and had bolted a short distance, but now stood scattered, watching; and as Moses wheeled and tried to hook Pop with his horns, trying to mince and perforate him—Pop had crumpled, was bent over double, his body no longer obeying his own commands—Alejandro ran past Moses and slapped him hard, open handed, in the face, and shouted at him, turning his attention from Pop long enough for Pop to crawl under the jeep.

Moses chased Alejandro around the windmill, circling it three times, as if in some child's game, before tiring or becoming confused. He halted, slobbers of drool slinging from his muzzle, bloodied from where he had rammed the windmill. Hiding on the other side of the windmill, Alejandro watched him, and then feinted toward the herd—Moses lunged to that side of the windmill—and then Alejandro darted back to the other side, scooped Pop up and lifted him into the jeep, and then jumped in himself, started it, and roared off, even as Moses was back upon them and running alongside, shoving against the jeep with his head and hooking and rattling his horns against the side.

"Get back, you sorry motherfucker," Alejandro was yelling, shouting at him as if he were nothing more than a bad dog. "Get back, you sonofabitch," he shouted, swatting at him again with his free hand—and soon the jeep was going fast enough that Moses fell behind, and then stopped, knock-kneed and panting, and watched as the jeep sped away.

They drove straight to the hospital in the old jeep, with Pop conscious the whole way. He was spitting up blood, and Alejandro said that he found himself furious, filled with a rage almost equal to that of the bull's, and resolved that after he got Pop to the hospital, he would go back and kill the bull that very afternoon. What a stupid, stupid thing, he thought, to trade a man for a bull. How, in any world of logic or order, could one bull be allowed to erase one man?

"Hold on," he told Pop, who seemed now to be drowning in his pain. He reached over and gripped Pop's near arm hard, not knowing if it was injured or not, but needing to hold him. "Hold on," he said.

The leg was shattered, broken in more places than the doctors could count. Some of the doctors who looked at it were of the opinion that the whole thing should be removed, while others proposed that they wait awhile and see, reasoning that if their efforts at repair failed, they could always come back and do that later.

Once he regained consciousness—the leg set and pinned and screwed and plated in as many places as they'd been able to, seven pounds' worth of hardware, and the plaster cast afterward, around it all—Pop informed them that removing his leg would not be an option, but they shook their heads as if listening to a child, one with whom they had neither time nor inclination to argue, and said that time would decide that, not him or them.

He was in the hospital for three weeks. There was some interior bleeding that was slow to heal, and then some of the smaller fragments of bone began to move, attempting to reassemble themselves, like the miniature action of plate tectonics, or the indomitable urges of anything living to regain its old foredestination, and no matter whether the old way was a cherished one or not.

The pain was worse, now, beneath the cast, and the little fragments of bone had nowhere to go, bumped slowly into one another, collided with those already set in place, as well as the main stem of the remaining bone. Sometimes they succeeded in regaining their approximate earlier positions, nosing back into place like fish tumbling through a current, endeavoring to find a certain eddy in which they could rest— though other times such fragments would end up being swept farther and farther from where they needed to be.

A small piece of bone that belonged in the upper thigh might, at the end of a week's passage, have somehow been shoved and pushed all the way down into the ankle, where, as if despairing, or simply having run out of choices, it sought to emerge through the skin: and the doctors would have to cut off the old cast, remove those trinkets of bone, and then form a new cast, again and again.

Pop kept these little shards of bone in a dish on the windowsill of his hospital room. Alejandro came by to see him every day, just before dark. He said that Moses seemed tame once more, and was acting as if nothing had happened, but they both knew they could never trust him again, and unspoken between them was the concern, even fear, that such a trait might be buried not just deep within him, but within all his progeny, spread across the herd like a secret virus, waiting to blossom, or detonate. Perfection poised to crumble, always, at any instant.

Some days, Pop seemed amazingly strong—as if the trauma had challenged him, and in so doing, strengthened him—though the very next day, he would seem more haggard than ever: as if there was no chance he would survive the injury, and that in fact the injury was not yet over, but was still occurring anew each day—as if Moses kept returning, each day, to charge him yet again, and with the last of Pop's life leaving quickly now, draining away, and with Moses intent upon finishing him off, taking the last of it. Taking back the last of it.

Pneumonia settled into his lungs, picked up from the secret germs hidden throughout the hospital, decades of germs mixing and breeding in every pore, every corner and crevice, and as his fevers spiked yet again, and he trembled and shivered and baked, more projectiles exited his leg, and then the plaster. The dish on his windowsill grew full, and he started a second one. Some of the bones looked like the ancient pieces turned up in farmers' fields by the plow, Indians' bones from centuries ago, as well as those of their quarry, taken by bow and arrow. The clinking of the plow's iron teeth against an arrowhead, as the plow strained the earth, stirring the soil for the return of yet another season.

Pop was home in time for Thanksgiving, having finally stabilized, though in some lower, lonelier place. Everyone could see it. It was as if he was already gone. And strangely, in this leave-taking, the townspeople drew closer to him, gathering around his illness, and the scent of his coming death, like animals coming in closer to the one among them who will tell them what to do, who informs their movements, and even sometimes their existence.

The land down there is still in drought—even his own ranch—Alejandro's ranch—is beginning to grow wild, and fade, and even more farms and ranches are shutting down, or foreclosing. The community is pretty much down to its last handful of survivors, but from what I hear, those who are left are all the stronger for it, and closer—almost like family. And Pop's done what he can, to help keep the basic services provided—schools, libraries, health care, fire department, etc. He won't give them his water, but he continues to tithe some of his wealth. He continues to try to help out the ones who have been strong enough, or lucky enough, to survive, and who have stayed.

Alejandro has taken over the full ranch operations. There is a part of me that understands this—in a way, Alejandro carries more of Pop's vision, and the future, in him than I ever will, despite my having Pop's own blood—though there is another part of me that rages, sometimes, when I examine it too closely: not so much the way things went bad, as instead, the certain paths or avenues that were never taken, or never panned out—though what those paths, those series of combinations, might have been, I cannot say, for it seems to me that I never even saw them, never really had the chance to make a conscious decision one way or the other—choose *this one,* or *that one*—but that instead, those choices remained somehow always beneath me, moving silent and unseen, and somehow, always dwindling, always diminishing.

I suppose I must admit that there is a bitterness in me. I know that it is like some eternal flaw or imperfection, one that should not be tolerated. I know it is like the vanishing Ogallala itself—that I do not know enough peace; and that I have another hunger, too.

The town is waiting for Pop to emerge from his latest illness, so that he can return to being the community's paragon of strength once more. They are planning a feast, a festival, on his curmudgeonly behalf. He, who has saved them with his excellence, his feisty uncompromising ways.

I know, or suspect, that my own myriad, daily compromises and choices might indicate to some a lesser strength of character. Whether that's true or not, I'm not sure I can say, even now. I do know that in my work, I try to save what I can, and let go of what I must let go of—culling, or not culling, in my own fashion. I know I am both bitter and hungry. Everything falls apart, but things can reassemble, too. When he is recovered, I may go down to that feast. I might yet become perfect.

Francine **prose**

THE WITCH

Struggling beneath the thickening snow, the windshield wipers croak *why why why why*, which is what Zip wants to know. Why the hell precisely *is* he out here in a blizzard, on a winding road, at midnight, taking the curves at fifty? It's got to be a bad sign when your wiper blades start talking. Getting killed would be a worse sign, a billboard lit up by that final flash, giant letters spelling it out: Zip's pushed his luck too far. He should have taken early retirement, he's been eligible since July, but he refused—a huge mistake about to be corrected when his patrol car wraps itself around the nearest tree. Right now, he could be home in bed watching TV with Irene, or playing computer games with Charlie, if the kid's still awake, instead of driving through a storm just because Jerry Greco's wife, Marianne, called in crying that Jerry was trying to kill her again.

Wind crashes into the car door, snow weighs down the wipers now barely clearing one frosted saucer of glass. The road is slick as a tablecloth, and naturally Zip has to wonder what's to keep God from yanking it just to see everything slide.

Lately, Zip's been getting superstitious. It's genetics kicking in, like one of those time-bomb chromosomes you pray your kid won't inherit. Zip's grandmother couldn't leave the house without first touching every icon, every raccoon-eyed Virgin, every bearded saint famous for slaying a dragon or bringing the Cyrillic alphabet to the Slavic people. These days Baba would have a diagnosis: obsessive-compulsive disorder. The family's diagnosis came closer: a lunatic and a witch. Zip's mom believed Baba could *do* things; once, when Zip's mom was driving her to a doctor's appointment, Baba started mumbling gibberish and Zip's mom drove off the road. Obviously, Zip comes from generations of thinking that magic spells count for more than, say, driving experience or skill. Twenty years as a state trooper, eighteen of marriage, a kid who's almost fourteen, a lifetime as a normal guy, and Zip's turning into Baba.

Zip sucks on his doughnut-shop coffee. The caffeine doesn't help.

Who says snowstorms are quiet? This one's making a racket, the plop of sodden flakes, the shrieking wind competing with the groans from the trees. As a kid, Zip was scared of driving in weather like this. Then for years he got used to it, and now he's scared again. Some chemical change has turned him into one of those paranoids who think Fate's got nothing better to do than smack you around for staying too long at the party. Is it Fate? Or statistics? You always hear about cops getting killed with two weeks until retirement.

More like water than solid ground, the blacktop slips beneath him. It would help if Zip knew the road, but though he's lived in the county all his life, he hardly ever gets out here. Certainly, he's never been to Jerry and Marianne's. He sees Jimmy at the barracks and at meetings. Maybe once a year, at Christmas parties and such, he talks to Marianne—boozy, sociable conversations that, strangely, he finds himself thinking about later. But they're not the type who give the jolly hot-dog-and-beer summer cookouts. The far edge of the county is the perfect place for the Grecos. They could kill each other every night, and no one but their kids would hear them.

The last time he drove this road, it was a gorgeous spring morning. A little girl had come into school claiming she'd seen a human head in a plastic bag in the woods by her bus stop. A pathological liar. But you have to check this stuff out. The grade-school principal, Sally Mayhew, rode beside him in front, and they both half pretended Sally wasn't gay, unseriously flirting, while the kid in the back babbled on about her mom's movie-star friends, all her dad's new cars, the lady's head with blond pigtails—the little girl had blond pigtails—in the pumpkin leaf bag.

She'd led them to a spot by side of the road. "Oops," the kid said. "She's not here anymore."

Zip is just as certain that there won't be a corpse when, and if, he gets to Jerry Greco's house. Every couple of months, for years, somebody's had to go out there. It's always a little . . . delicate, since Jerry's on the force. Headquarters tries to send Lois Ryan, when she's on duty, because this isn't your high-risk domestic violence, the crackpot waving the broken bottle, it's some chick thing, Marianne Greco loaded on vodka and pills, crying that her life is shit, while Jerry, also hammered, paces around the edges, yelling that Marianne needs to check herself into a dry-out clinic. The whole force knows about it, and they all pretend they don't. It's a small division. They've got to work together.

How can people live like that? Zip can't understand it. When he and Irene have an argument—for example, the one that grew out of her asking why Zip all of a sudden wanted to lose so much weight, the fight that escalated into Zip saying Irene knew goddamn well *she* didn't want him taking early retirement, and Irene saying well, actually, what did Zip plan to *do* with his time?—Zip feels gloomy and tired for days. Some people must like drama. The fighting. The making up.

Marianne and Jerry probably have every reason to want to kill each other. Jerry's got girlfriends all over the county, amazingly, since Marianne's got him on such a short leash that when Jerry's an hour late for dinner she calls in to the station and asks if there's been an accident on the road. Zip's pretty sure that Jerry is harmless. But there's always that guy everyone swears wouldn't hurt a fly until the night he chops up his wife into little tiny pieces. Plus Jerry's a fellow trooper, and if something did happen and Zip got there, let's say, twenty minutes late, the story would be all over the state, he might as *well* retire.

And finally, there's this: Marianne called in, as she always does, and then Jerry called in, as he always does, and said to ignore Marianne, as he always does, and then he called back a few minutes later and said maybe they should send someone out. Which he never does. *Ever.*

Zip turns right, the wheels go left. Zip thinks, I'm dead, until adrenaline jump-starts his instinct and he lets the car do what it wants. The wheel spinning in his hands makes him feel like a circus bear driving one of those tiny cars. But he's not a bear anymore, he's dropped twenty pounds in six months on the "Zip" Ziprilic diet: all the coffee he can drink. His doctor's thrilled, his cholesterol's dropped, Zip likes the way he looks. For the first time in his life, his nickname doesn't seem like a joke. Only Zip's heart doesn't like it. It's been doing this trippy salsa beat, down low, so maybe it's only his stomach. Irene thinks the weight loss means he's having an affair, which he isn't. Though lately he's had the feeling that there *is* less...interference between him and other people, especially women, which is why he could flirt like that with Sally Mayhew as he drove around thinking that he was a lucky guy, a grown man getting paid to cruise a lovely country road with a nice-looking friendly lesbian grade-school principal on a beautiful spring morning.

Tonight Zip feels less lucky as he tries to convince himself that the storm is letting up and that by some miracle he'll find the house. The mailboxes are miles apart and already buried in snow. He'll drive around forever and then get stuck at the bottom of a hill, radio in, freeze his ass off in the car all night until the roads are plowed and somebody comes to get him.

The house should be somewhere around here. He slows down, but not enough to lose the power he needs to get up the inclines.

Suddenly, just as Zip is driving by, a gust of wind lifts the snow off the top of a mailbox, and he sees the name: GRECO. Come on, how freaky is that? Maybe it's God trying to help him save Marianne Greco's life, or Fate sadistically ushering him from one death trap into another.

Through the veiled windshield, clumped with white, Zip makes out your basic prefab split-level—a cheaper and less cared-for version of his own. The Grecos' downstairs lights are blazing, the upstairs windows are dark.

Zip parks at the bottom of the driveway. Later, Jerry can help him dig out. He honks the horn—a big friendly shave-and-a-haircut how-are-ya—just as he was taught during that wasted weekend of Domestic Violence Training.

Don't surprise somebody high on all the ordinary sub-
stances plus the domestic-violence chemicals. Zip can't
imagine hitting Irene, their fights don't go like that, either
she sulks for three days or becomes so logical that, all right,
he's had fantasies of wringing her neck, just to make her
shut up. The fantasy passes in a heartbeat—as it does for
Jerry, Zip hopes. Zip couldn't imagine hurting Irene. Lately
she's seemed so fragile, first the lactose intolerance, then
the wheat allergy. That's why she doesn't want Zip around
the house, it must take her all day to figure out what she
can and can't eat. That's not fair. Zip loves Irene. He wishes
he were with her and Charlie right now. Maybe that's why
he kept working—so he could feel this desperate, lonely
longing to be home.

He puts on his jacket, pulls up the hood, and heads up
the drive. The snow is halfway up his calves and keeps melting into his boots. Thank God he lost the extra weight, it's
tough enough trudging through the drifts, and it's so humiliating to show up huffing and puffing. There's a place by the
front steps from which Zip can see into the living-room window, and that's where he pauses to catch his breath. His
heart is jumping again.

Didn't they hear his car horn? Why aren't they looking
out? Jerry's on the sofa, Marianne on the love seat, both just
sitting there. Stunned. Not talking. Nothing looks torn
apart, Marianne's face is okay, everything fine and dandy.

Except for the two handguns, one on the end table beside Marianne, the other on the couch next to Jerry. Two
guns. Enough bullets for everyone and the kids, as well. If
Zip had any brains, he'd turn around and get back in the car
and take early retirement tonight.

Zip knocks, gently but firmly. Jerry lets him in. How

warm and bright the house is! Shelter from the storm! Jerry flashes Zip a big goofy smile that might be more welcoming if not for Jerry's pointy little cat teeth, which go right along with his caged-bobcat nervous energy, the scary ratio of tension and instinct to brains that has always put Jerry Greco near the bottom of the list of guys Zip would want to work with.

Jerry's T-shirt and jeans look slept in, or grabbed off the bedroom floor. He squeezes Zip's shoulder and says, "Man, am I glad to see *you*. What a night, huh? They're predicting a foot and a half, but what the hell do *they* know?"

Zip follows Jerry into the living room and gets as far as the doorway. That's when he sees the icons jammed into every corner, all the old familiar faces, Our Blessed Virgin of Whatnot, St. Michael and St. George, the two tall guys with the long white beards. What are *they* doing here? He hasn't seen them since Baba died. Obviously, a coincidence. Zip feels oddly dingy. Too much caffeine, for a change. He doesn't want his hands shaking, especially if he has to separate the Grecos from their guns.

Fortunately Marianne and Jerry are too out of it to notice where Zip's looking. So there's no need for a little group excursion down memory lane, back to somebody's Orthodox childhood, that sinkhole of superstition that Zip's been running from ever since. Whereas someone in *this* house—it's got to be Marianne—has never left that place where you tear out big fistfuls of hair, crying to a Madonna who, any moron could tell, has more problems than you do.

Jerry's sunk back into his couch. The spazzy way he keeps reaching out and touching his gun is exactly how Zip's grandmother used to poke you at inappropriate random moments. Might as well add Tourette's syndrome to Baba's diagnosis. His grandmother's got his attention now, from beyond the grave, and while he's spaced out and distracted by this voodoo paranoia, Jerry Greco will pick up his gun and blow them all away. Baba's last little joke.

Baba *was* a witch, which is, come to think of it, what Marianne Greco looks like with her long crazy black hair, her dark eyes ringed with smudged makeup.

Marianne says, "Hey, Zip, good to see you. Would you mind taking off your boots?"

Would Marianne mind go fucking herself? He's not dropping by for a beer! Then he looks down and, sure enough, his boots are seeping grainy black puddles into the grayish wall-to-wall. Zip crouches and unlaces his boots, clumsily shakes them off. He feels like Jack in "Jack and the Beanstalk." He'll never leave here alive. He looks around at this giant's lair— functional, modern, somehow institutional despite the children's sneakers and toys piled up in the corners.

"Jesus, Zip," Marianne says. "You lost a ton of weight."

"No cake," says Jerry. "That's all it took. Am I right?"

"That's all it took," says Zip.

"Please," says Marianne. "Sit down. You want something? Coffee? A beer?"

Zip would love some coffee. "No thanks. You guys called in?"

"Sit." Jerry gestures at a recliner placed conveniently between Marianne's love seat and Jerry's couch. Not so conveniently, as it turns out, because when Zip sits and the couple begins to talk, Zip has to swivel between them while still trying to keep one eye on the guns.

"Well," says Jerry, "we were sleeping."

"*You* were sleeping," says Marianne. "You know I haven't slept in, like, six months."

"You were snoring," says Jerry.

"Fuck you," says Marianne.

"Marianne," says Jerry. "Give Zip a fucking break."

"All right," says Zip. "You guys called into the station. That's what this is about."

"Okay," says Jerry. "I was sleeping. I heard noises downstairs. Someone walking around. Maybe I was still dreaming, but I was sure I could hear the fucker moving from room to room. I asked myself a million times, was I awake, and then I got my gun out of the nightstand, got dressed, and went downstairs to look around."

"Did Jerry say anything to you?" Zip asks Marianne.

Marianne props her elbows on her knees and leans forward. The cuff of her pink terry bathrobe falls back, revealing her thin forearm, on which she's wearing a thin gold bracelet.

"Marianne," says Jerry, "you're falling out of your clothes." Zip looks up just in time to see the tops of Marianne's breasts before Marianne makes a face at Jerry and tightens the sash on her robe. She doesn't look like a pill freak. She and Jerry seem all too sober.

"I don't know," she says. "Maybe I dozed off. Anyway, I finally heard it, too. Footsteps downstairs. And Jerry wasn't in bed. I figured it was Jerry going to get a snack, but I don't know, something felt weird, something *told* me to check for Jerry's gun. It wasn't in his nightstand. So right away I got nervous. What if something happened to Jerry, and it wasn't him down there, but some other guy, some stranger—"

"Wishful thinking, ha ha," says Jerry.

Marianne rolls her eyes. "So I'm not, like, about to yell, *Oh, Jerry, dear. Is that you?* Let the guy know where I am. So I get *my* gun from *my* night table."

Marianne's looking hard at Zip, but strangely, he doesn't notice until she cuts her eyes to the gun and he realizes that he and Marianne are in intense visual communication. He sees Jerry noticing, too. How ironic if Zip, who never cheated on Irene, got blown away on duty by a jealous hothead like Jerry Greco.

Jerry says, "I got her the gun after Lorraine Prentiss got held up down in Reedsville—"

"It wasn't then," says Marianne. "It was when that kid down the road was doing all that half-assed breaking and entering—"

"Craig DeBellis," says Jerry.

"You know something strange?" says Zip. "Last spring, I got this call, this kid from the grade school said she'd seen a human head at her bus stop. Heather DeBellis. Isn't it weird I'd remember the kid's name?"

"Everyone on this road is named DeBellis," says Marianne. "Except us. Gross. Was there a head?"

"No," says Zip. "People imagine things all the time."

"Tell me about it," says Marianne. "Anyhow, I got my gun and kind of snuck downstairs, and I hear this noise and turn toward it, and so help me Jesus Christ I'm just about to aim and shoot when the sensor light, you know, the security light, goes on outside. A deer must have passed or something. And I see it's Jerry, backlit, pointing his gun at *me*."

"We could have killed each other," says Jerry. "We could have fucking killed each other. Man, we came as close as *that* . . ." He pinches the air with his thumb and forefinger.

Something is wrong with this story. Zip's got it. A deer in a snowstorm.

"But you didn't," Zip says. "Kill each other. And the intruder?"

"Must have been the wind," says Jerry. "Listen to it out there."

Zip says, "So Marianne calls in because . . . ?"

"Flipped out. Hormones. As usual. She's like one of those sports cars goes from zero to seventy in six seconds. Totally bananas, crying, blubbering, saying I'm trying to kill her. I don't love her. I hate her. The usual shit. Women. Shit."

Zip can't look at Marianne. "But you weren't trying to kill her, Jerry. And then *you* called in."

"Okay," says Jerry. "This is the hard part. But you're right, I called in, so fuck it, I might as well deal with it. Right? I was scared. I mean it. I thought: You know, if Marianne and I *did* kill each other, there wouldn't be a single person in the whole world, probably not even our own kids, who wouldn't think we'd done it on purpose. Everyone would say: All right. They finally did it. What the hell took them so long? And I'll be honest. That scared the shit out of me. It fucking terrified me, man."

"Terrified," says Marianne. "*Now* he gets fucking terrified."

Zip's a little nervous himself, because *he'd* also been thinking that Jerry and Marianne probably had a million reasons to murder each other, and if they'd wound up dead, accidentally or not, everyone would have assumed that they'd done it on purpose...

"Are you okay?" Marianne asks. "Oh, God, are we freaking *you* out?"

"Yes," Zip says. "I mean no. I'm fine."

"Christ, Marianne," Jerry says. "Zip's a cop. Not a fucking marriage counselor."

As if on cue, a series of shrieks float downstairs. "Daddy! Daddy! Daddy!"

"It's Chris," says Marianne. "For you."

"Duh. I know it's Chris," says Jerry. "Can't *you* go? See what he wants. I'll owe you one."

"One," says Marianne. "You'll owe me *one*. I can tell you what he wants. He wants you."

"Who would *you* want?" she asks Zip. "The dishrag mom who washes your socks and wipes your ass and gets dinner on the table? Or the dad who comes home in a uniform with the snappy hat and gun and handcuffs and shiny badges? What would a seven-year-old boy want? Who would *anyone* want?"

"Okay, buddy," Jerry yells upstairs. "Dad's coming. I'm on my way." He shrugs at Zip, then takes off, leaving his gun on the table. If these were strangers, Zip would pocket the gun, telling the wife he was just holding it for safekeeping. But with Jerry and Marianne, that would be...socially awkward.

Marianne listens with the back of her head till the noise upstairs dies down. She rakes her hand through her hair, then jackknifes forward and wraps her robe tighter. Okay, there's that witch thing, but there's something else, too, some restless dissatisfied energy animating her long skinny body that—if this were any other situation and anyone but Marianne Greco—Zip thinks he might find sexy. Interesting, at least.

Silence. Silence. More silence. Marianne looks at her gun.

Zip says, "How old are the kids now?"

"Besides Chris?" says Marianne. "Zack's fifteen. Patty's eleven. What's Charlie now?"

"Twelve?" says Zip, then thinks: Thirteen.

After another silence, Marianne says, "Seen Lois lately?" But she's not really asking. It's shorthand to find out if Zip knows how often Lois Ryan has driven out here in the line of duty.

"Lois is fine. Off tonight, I guess."

"Lucky her," says Marianne. "You know the real reason he got me that gun? Because he's never home."

Is Zip supposed to admit he knows? "Marianne..." he says.

"Let me talk," she says. "I assume you figured out that Jerry's not being on his side of the bed was not exactly a once-in-a-lifetime event."

"I got that much," Zip says.

Marianne shivers, grabbing her arms, though the house is overheated—as Zip notices, only now. It must cost them a fortune to keep the place like this, with the wind raging out-side, flinging snow against the windows. Zip wriggles out of his jacket, trying not to interrupt the conversation. Mari-anne's shoulders ripple, reflexively mirroring his, and her bathrobe gaps again to reveal a curve of breast arcing under her nightgown.

"Mostly it's fine with me," she says. "I'd rather be alone. You know..." Her pause is a warning. Zip doesn't want to hear what's coming. "I'll bet you think Jerry's a normal guy, a sane, normal guy. That's what everybody thinks, especially his girlfriends. Even the guy's own kids don't know how nuts he is. But trust me. The guy's insane."

"Marianne..." Zip tries again.

"Please, Zip. Don't Marianne me. You wouldn't believe the crazy shit he says. All this stuff"—she waves at the icons—"they're his. Jerry's a believer. I feel like I married my grandmother. And that's the *sensible* part of him. He's way more fucked up than that. He goes into these jealous rages, saying I'm some kind of witch, that I'm making guys think about me, look at me, which wouldn't even make sense even *if* we ever went anywhere where guys *could* look at me. At some point tonight, probably the minute you leave, he's going to come out with some paranoid bullshit about how I brought you here with my magic powers."

Zip misses the next few sentences. Once more he's distracted by Marianne's saying that Jerry thinks she's a witch when he, Zip, has been thinking that's what she looks like. Well, Marianne looks like a witch. Anyone would think it.

"...and it's not exactly like I need a black cat to go out and spy around. My girlfriend calls one day, and it takes me half an hour to figure out she's trying to tell me that Jerry's fucking that teenage nympho slut from the beauty parlor in Loudonberg."

Even Zip knew about that one. Word got around the force that Jerry was giving this big-haired high-school jail-bait free rides in his patrol car.

"You knew, right?" says Marianne.

"You mean Amy Fisher?" Zip likes making Marianne smile.

"So it wasn't exactly top secret. But this time I couldn't stand it. So one day I drive into Loudonberg and walk right into Quickie Cuts, No Appointment Necessary, and tell her I want my hair cut. Of course she knows who I am, I know who she is. It's one of those moments, everybody knows everything, no one says a word. You tell me how ballsy that is, letting some slut your husband's fucking get her hands on your hair."

Zip looks at Marianne's tangled hair. No one's had their hands on it in a while.

"This was last year," says Marianne. "I ask for a trim. We go through the whole charade, she washes my hair, takes off a quarter inch, exactly like I tell her. Finally I check the mirror and say, Perfect, great, could I borrow the scissors? There's this one teensy stray hair I need to get...I liked how she got nervous, but only for a second, because we were both so good at pretending that I just happened to be some woman who wanted a haircut, and she just happened to be some little whore who cut hair.

"I took the scissors and threw them across the room. They landed right between the eyes of this blond model in a poster for some bullshit pixie haircut. And they stuck there, the scissors stuck there, kind of ... twanging in the wall."

Would scissors do that? Zip wonders. You'd have to throw them hard.

Marianne says, "I can't throw. I can hardly play catch with the kids. So maybe Jerry's right, maybe I am a witch. Everyone thinks I am, so I might as well be. But listen, let me ask you: If I *was* a witch, if I had magic powers, why would I let my marriage get to the point where I was flinging scissors around some low-rent beauty parlor in Loudon- ville? The point where I believe that the fucker is trying to kill me. Listen, when I call into the station, I *mean* it, when Lois comes out here, I *mean* it, and then a couple days pass, and I forget until it happens again. You think a witch would live like that? An abused wife lives like that."

Zip can't help it. "Marianne, has Jerry ever ... ?"

"Jesus. Please," says Marianne. "That's not what I'm say- ing at all. If I was using my powers to get you out here, wouldn't I have fixed myself up first? You think I'd look like *this?*"

"You look fine," says Zip. "Anyhow, you and Jerry *called.*"

"I rest my case," says Marianne. "But okay. As I was say- ing. It was like something guided my hand and *put* that scis- sors between the model's eyes on that poster. And it was pretty soon afterwards that bitch dumped Jerry. For which, needless to say, he blamed me."

Marianne leans forward, and now Zip does, too. She

says, "I'll be honest. There's been a million times I wanted to shoot him. But it just so happens that tonight wasn't one of them. But I thought the same thing he did. That if he and I killed each other everybody would think we meant it. I figured *that* out before he did. And Jerry's right. It was scary."

Zip feels something like . . . jealousy. But what could he possibly envy?

"And that's when I thought: he's killing me, and I called in, and Jerry called. And then he called back. How many times has *he* called in when we were having trouble?"

Zip shrugs. What's he supposed to say?

"Never," says Marianne.

There's something Zip's not getting, the step that leads from their *not* killing each other to Marianne thinking Jerry *is*—thinking it seriously enough to call in to the station. But that's how they play it out here. Some people count to ten when they're mad. Others throw dishes. Some pick up the phone and call the troopers their husbands work with.

Marianne makes a cup with her hand and presses it over her eyes. "Jesus Christ," she says. "Do you know how embarrassing this is?"

"Don't be embarrassed," Zip says. "Marriage isn't easy." What the hell is Zip talking about? And what's made Marianne take her hands from her face and stare at him across the room. What is she seeing in his face? Zip doesn't have a clue. Still, there's something exciting about a woman looking that long until Marianne ends their little moment by bursting into tears.

"What am I supposed to do now?" she says, between gulping sobs. "I'm forty-one. I've got three kids. Am I supposed to start over? Look for another guy? Go back to shaving my legs?"

Zip sneaks a look at the fine dark hair climbing up Marianne's calves. Ordinarily, he doesn't like hairy legs. Irene gets hers waxed at the mall, he thinks guiltily—guilty because an unprofessional, inappropriate, tiny...hiccup of lust is making him want to push up Marianne's robe and see. Ordinarily, for that matter, he doesn't like women crying. Irene did lots of crying before her crackpot nutritionist figured out about the wheat allergy. Suddenly, it occurs to Zip: Irene has a crush on that nut.

Zip has heard guys say that when their wives or kids cry, it makes you want to give them something to cry about. Whereas Zip just wants to be somewhere, with anyone else but Irene. That's what women's tears do to him. Yet right now, for some reason, he thinks it would be criminal, pitiless—inhuman—not to get up and cross the room and sit down next to Marianne and put his arm around her.

Under Zip's hand, Marianne's thin shoulder trembles like a hamster, trapped in fuzzy chenille. Marianne leans against him, at which point Zip's soul vacates his body and watches it hugging his co-worker's wife. The only way he can come down is to convince himself he's just seeing a trooper comforting a domestic 911.

"Feel this." Marianne takes his other hand and puts in inside her robe. Zip's hand is twice the size of hers, but it lets itself be led, burrowing into the warm dark place between soft robe and softer skin.

"Feel my heart," says Marianne.

Zip can't feel a thing. And then he thinks he can: a bubble swelling and popping lightly against her rib cage. Or maybe it's his own heart, doing that dance the coffee's taught it.

It started before the coffee. That's why Zip lost the weight.

"Feel how unevenly it's beating," says Marianne. "That's what I mean: he's killing me. I'm not saying that just to *say* it! What else can I do but call in?"

Of course, it's then that Jerry appears, bouncing down the stairs.

"Great," says Jerry, meaning *them*, meaning Zip's arms flying from around Jerry's wife's shoulders and out from under her robe. "Would you look at this? Is this beautiful, or what?"

"Marianne was upset," Zip says, jumping up and springing back to his chair, trying at the same time to keep semifocused on Jerry's gun.

But it's one of those times that Marianne was just describing. Everyone knows everything, and no one says a word. It's clear that Jerry doesn't want to kill Zip. He doesn't want to kill Marianne. If he did, this would be the moment. No one wants to kill anyone, except maybe Zip, who could still get creamed driving home in the storm. Neither of those guns will be fired tonight. Zip can cash it in, and take off.

"I'm really sorry, man," Jerry says. "Dragging you out in weather like this. Shit, I don't know what got into me. Into Marianne. You don't need to drive home in this. Want to spend the night?"

Looking over at Marianne isn't anything Zip can control. And Marianne's staring right back at him. So it's not all in his mind. Something's going on here. No one says it has to make sense. He would give anything to know what Marianne's expression means. But what *doesn't* he know, exactly? It means she wants him to stay. Really, it would be smarter to stay. He could call Irene. Irene would rather he stay over than try to get back in this blizzard.

"That's okay," says Zip. "I'll make it. Don't worry about it."

All this time, he's looking at Marianne, whose disappointment is so visible, it's as if they've had a long affair and he's just told her he's leaving. What's worse is, Zip is horribly sure that the same look is on his face.

"Are you positive?" says Marianne. "You could stay on the couch. Or Chris could sleep with us, he'd love it, and you could have his room."

"Positive," says Zip. "I've got to get back."

"Fine, then," says Marianne.

"I'll walk you to the car," Jerry says. "I'll bring a shovel, just in case."

Doesn't Jerry see what's going on? So what if he does? Zip's leaving. Jerry goes to get his coat. Zip follows him into the hall. Marianne rises, then stops in the living-room doorway, the gold icons winking behind her.

"Well...thanks..." Marianne's voice trails off.

"Don't mention it." Zip's manly response is undermined by the awkwardness of putting on his boots.

"Ready?" says Jerry.

"Drive carefully," says Marianne.

"See you," Zip says, without turning.

But when at last they get outside, and the wet snow whips their faces, it takes all of Zip's self-control not to turn and look back to see if Marianne's watching. The warmth they've brought with them from inside lasts about a second before the cold sneaks under their jackets and their teeth start chattering lightly, a reflex that neither Zip nor Jerry wants the other to see. They take the first few steps boldly, stomping in and out of the drifts, but soon slow up and stagger down the drive, bending almost double against the stinging wind.

"Motherfucker!" Jerry shouts at the wind.

Zip doesn't have to answer. His only job is to get to the

car. Finally he succeeds. He brushes the snow from the windshield and climbs inside.

"Get in," he tells Jerry. "At least while I try to start this."

Jerry props the shovel against the car and slides into the passenger seat. Miraculously, the car starts up and eases forward out of its space.

"Okay, then," says Zip. "Take it easy, man." But Jerry isn't moving.

"I need to tell you something," he says. "About what happened tonight. This is going to sound crazy. But trust me on this. Marianne's a witch. I *told* you, I know it sounds crazy, but I've seen her do shit you wouldn't believe...Listen, the first time I met her mother, this was back in Brooklyn, her mother tells me that when Marianne was a kid, they'd go to church on Sunday, this is in the Orthodox church, where everyone stands up—"

"I know about it," says Zip.

"Her mother tells me that every Sunday, in the summer, a bunch of people would faint, and it was always the people standing directly around Marianne. And she always thought it *was* Marianne. Clearing herself some room. Her own *mom* tells me this, and I don't listen!"

Mother of God, it's Zip's dead grandmother speaking to him in the voice of a not-very-smart and probably crazy cop! Baba always talked like that, blamed the neighbors for souring the milk by looking at her funny. And there was always that same wild look, that same wacky glint in her eyes. Isn't that what Marianne said? *It's like living with my grandmother.* Zip remembers his mother—dead for how long now? Could it really be five years?—telling him how Baba's mumbling made her drive off the road. Zip's attention drifts briefly, but snaps right back when Jerry says:

"How do you think *you* got here tonight? Man, you cannot *believe* how many guys get lost around here, the FedEx man, the UPS man, the electric-meter reader, they're always knocking on the door, Marianne's *bringing* them up here, and I know it's just a matter of time before one of them decides to stay. Or comes back. Or calls her. And if she leaves me, it'll kill me. I swear. Look, I know what you're thinking. I'm not exactly a saint. But let me tell you: there's a difference between nookie and a woman who can make weird shit happen. The mother of your children."

It's not just that Jerry could say this stuff, but that Jerry *believes* it, and the naked longing that creeps into his voice when he talks about Marianne, the love and terror, respect and desire, all knotted and gnarled up together. Jerry doesn't care if Zip hears. He doesn't care who's watching. How slow Zip's been to understand: Jerry loves his wife. He's terrified of losing her, and who's to say he isn't right? Jesus, what went *on* at that house? What happened between Zip and Marianne? Zip feels a bolt of sheer longing sizzling through his chest. Was Marianne at the Christmas party this year? Why didn't he pay attention? It's another year—eleven months—till Christmas comes again. Maybe Jerry's right about her. Some people have strange powers.

Zip says, "I don't know, Jerry. I don't think Marianne's planning to leave you. Like we were saying, people imagine things. And Jerry...there aren't witches, really. No one believes that shit. Your grandmother believed it. Think about it, Jerry—"

"Oh, really?" says Jerry. *"Really?* How *did* you get here tonight?"

"You and Marianne called, remember? Picked up the phone and called. That's a little different from her dragging me out here by magic."

"I mean, how did you find the house, wise guy? This weather sucks. You can't see two feet. The mailbox is covered with snow."

Zip sees an image, clear as a film. Snow gusting off the mailbox just as he drives by. He shakes his head to get rid of it.

"Homing instinct," he says. "Speaking of which..."

"All right," says Jerry. "I'll let you go. Hey, man, listen. This is, like, our little secret, right?"

"Sure," says Zip. "No problem. Who am I going to tell?"

"Okay, then. Drive safely, man. Thanks again. See you at work." Jerry gets out of the car.

"Take it easy," says Zip.

Zip waits with the engine running until he's sure that Jerry's back home. A shiver crawls down the back of his spine. Is it cold—or fear? What if Jerry kills Marianne—and Zip never sees her again? Then he gets out and takes a piss, looking up at the house.

If Marianne Greco were a witch, why would she live in that dump? It's not the gingerbread cottage, not the hut on chicken legs. Because she isn't one, Zip thinks. There are no bolts of magic sparking around that split-level. There was no head in the trash bag. Just people making up stories and telling them until they believe them. No evil vibrations crackling, except between the Grecos, no deer in the security light, no intruder downstairs, no scissors twanging between the eyes of a model in a poster, no grandmother playing with Zip's head from beyond the grave.

How he wishes there *were* all those things. But he knows there aren't. There is only a plain, thrown-together house, not so different from his own, disappearing, inch by inch, under the deepening snow.

margo **rabb**

HOW TO TELL A STORY

There are three things I've learned, so far, in my graduate creative-writing program:

1. Deny, at all costs, that your fiction bears any resemblance to your real life (First Commandment of the MFA program: Autobiography Is Sin);
2. Sleeping with an attractive male classmate who is widely admired by fellow students will yield positive feedback on your stories (attractive male will comment enthusiastically, and admirers will echo his opinions);
3. Tequila shots in the women's bathroom before class enhance your ability to stomach painful criticism of your stories.

   It's my third semester in the Master of Fine Arts program at Southwestern University, which is also known as the Master of Fucking Around, a term affectionately coined by one of our prominent male graduates, whose first book advance was larger than all of the faculty's salaries here, combined.

Today, my story's up in workshop. It's called "The Gift," and is about a nineteen-year-old girl whose mother and father die in a plane crash twenty miles off the coast of Maine. Co-incidentally, my parents died in a British Airways crash off the coast of Maine five years ago, when I was nineteen. Half the workshop knows this about me; half doesn't, including Charles Chester, the professor. In our private, pre-workshop conference fifteen minutes earlier, he'd stared down his nose at me and asked, "Is this *autobiographical*?" His thin arms twitched under his camel-colored, elbow-patched cardigan, which he wears every day (do they give you a crate of those the moment you receive tenure?). Chester is rumored to be around fifty, though he looks ninety. He carries a doughnut-shaped hemorrhoid pillow around with him everywhere, to sit on during our three-hour class. Rumor has it he was once nominated for a National Book Award; I've searched for his books in five bookstores, and all are out of print.

"No," I told him in the private conference. "It's not autobiographical."

If the pre-workshop conference is like being massacred slowly and having your inner organs scrupulously probed and dissected and analyzed, then the twelve-person work-shop is like being a piece of raw steak fed to starving bears, all of them clawing you, chewing you up, and then spitting you out. And afterward, you're supposed to say "Thank you."

As the workshop of my story begins, everyone searches Chester's face for a verdict of what he thinks of the story. He's frowning; this, to my peers, is sufficient proof that my story sucks.

"It's just not believable. I mean—a plane crash?" Howard begins. Howard is the program prodigy. The faculty cream over him. They give him prizes. Awards. Nominations. Scholarships. His last story was about a pedophile who set fire to his own arm hairs. An allegory, the professor had called it.

"I think the plane's okay, the problem is there are too many characters. Why do you have *both* the parents die? How 'bout one?" Stacy asks. "One would be more real. Less dilution of tension. Also, you could probably begin the story on page ten." Stacy has four standard comments: Too many characters, Start on page [5, 10, 15 or 20], That's a red herring, and Show, don't tell. She offers these comments in different random combinations, like lottery numbers. She's learned them in classes at Southwestern and the University of Iowa, where she received her previous MFA (several students in the program are working toward their second degrees, putting off the collective nightmare of having to get a regular job). "Also, you mention this gift thing and then you hardly discuss it directly again: total red herring," she goes on. "And I think you need to *show* the plane crash. Show the *suffering*, the *terror*. Make us cry."

"It did make me cry," Lily says, nearly whimpering, which is her usual tone of voice. "I think it's so sad. I mean, God . . . it's a gem. A real gem. Don't change a thing." I would hug Lily, except she's said the same thing about everyone's stories; we've all written gems.

"Anna, could you please read that page we talked about in our conference, aloud?" Chester asks.

"Okay," I say, trying not to let my voice waver. I'd rather uncap my pen and impale myself in the eye than read this story out loud. Reading a story I've written is like confessing, like being on *The Jerry Springer Show,* except the other guests punch you verbally instead of physically, and instead of breaking up the fight the professor nods encouragingly and takes notes.

"This is from, umm...page three?" I say, my voice sounding like a ten-year-old's.

My fifth day in Deer Bay, I received a letter, a plain white business envelope with no return address. For five days I'd been numb, walking around the streets of this town like a zombie, pacing aimlessly alongside all the other surviving relatives who'd been flown in, along with a bevy of grief counselors, by the airline. There were over a hundred of us "next of kin"; we gathered each morning by the shore to watch the divers try to find the remains of the plane. Every day I stared at the ocean, entranced, as if I expected my parents to miraculously emerge out of it, saying "Oh hi, Amy, we're so glad you waited for us..." as if they'd survived the crash, the days in the ocean, safe in an underwater Atlantis, and were just waiting for the divers to rescue them and bring them ashore.

The days in Deer Bay had been so bizarre and surreal that I didn't even think it odd, at first, to get this unmarked envelope delivered to me there, in the middle of nowhere. The envelope was postmarked from Boston; I'd never even been to Boston. Standing outside the post office, I tore it open: it was a money order for $500, made out in my name.

It took several long minutes for it to sink in: that article in the paper. Someone must have read it, that piece in the *Globe*—I'd done an interview, they were profiling us, the surviving relatives; every day there was a new write-up on one of us. They'd run my picture two days before with the caption *Amy Appel, Orphan Girl*, like I was some kind of musical being advertised, or photo study, or curiosity, or freak. My fingers trembled on the envelope—to think of myself as the kind of person someone read about in the paper and felt so sorry for, they'd send money—it made me angry, to be the object of pity, and frightened, too. Against my will, I'd become a different person. I had no other family, no siblings or aunts or uncles; all my grandparents were dead. The world I'd always known had ended, now, and this week in Deer Bay was the knife that slowly carved my life in two.

"It's like a cheesy TV movie," Brian says to the class, avoiding eye contact with me. "If I saw it on channel nine, I'd turn it off."

"I agree—and the setting has to go. Why Maine? I could see this set in Germany, and maybe during another time period, like during the war," Calvin says.

"That first line—'My fifth day in Deer Bay'—it *rhymes*. My first thought was, What the hell is it, a sonnet?" Howard adds.

The comments go on. I half listen to Sam, the oldest student and a Vietnam vet, who agrees with everything that's been said and wants more *action, action, action*; Helen, Sam's twenty-two-year-old wife, who compares every story to Raymond Carver's; Leslie, bra-size DDD (she informed everyone at the first party of the year), who wants a sex scene. Then there are the silent students, such as Josh, who sit there, as always, in speechless disapproval, as if the story isn't even worth a disparaging comment. Josh drove me home from a party once, earlier this year, then invited himself in for a glass of water, read the spines of all the books on my shelves, gazed thoughtfully at the posters on my walls, kissed me on the cheek, and then practically flew out of my apartment, leaving me thinking, What the *hell* was that?

Despite the "autobiography is sin" clause, I know so much about these twelve people it's horrifying. It's too much, more than peers should know: that Lily was molested by her uncle (four stories); that Sam attempted suicide twice (three stream-of-consciousness pieces); that Leslie's father was an alcoholic (a novel). I know these things are true, because I'm the one who's asked, at parties and bars after class: Did that happen for *real*? And the answer is nearly always an embarrassed *yes*.

Chester interrupts my thoughts and says, "I think this selection Anna has read illustrates the difference between *sentiment* and *sentimentality*. Brian likened this story to a television movie. Why? Let's discuss this concept—*sentimentality*."

Everyone stares at the ceiling.

Surprisingly, Josh speaks. "I disagree," he says, and shrugs. "I disagree with everything that's been said. I don't think it's sentimental, I think it's emotional, and the emotion works, considering the subject. The whole story works—I feel for this girl, this narrator, Amy. That her parents died is totally believable, and heartbreaking, too. The tension of receiving the money...it's a complex, moving story, and I don't think anyone's given it enough credit here."

Miraculous: I can't believe he just said that. Josh comments so rarely that whenever he speaks, everyone listens, and his approval of my work causes a ripple effect.

Stacy pauses, then says, "I do like the description of the town—there are some nice details there."

A few moments later, Calvin adds, "And yeah, the letter... the idea of the letter, that someone sends her this gift that she doesn't want... it's not a bad premise."

A few other people offer some semi-compliments about the story's meager merits; they stare at me, surely thinking I've slept with Josh, viewing me with a new admiration.

Meanwhile, I can't believe that anyone, besides Lily, has actually said something positive about my story. The only time someone's ever said "I think this story works" was when Leslie wrote "Triple Irony," last spring—soon after she'd announced, to a group of us at a local bar, "I want to write a story about a ménage à trois but I've never had one, can anyone help?" During the workshop of that story, Brian and Calvin drew comparisons to Chekhov.

Chester ignores the positive commentary, and as the workshop winds down he embarks on a monologue about the horror of comma splices, then reminds us that there's a reading tonight by Bruce Ryan, who recently won the Pulitzer Prize. Everyone's going to this reading—we've been talking about it all semester. Ryan's book *The Lancet and the Plum*, a collection of short stories about being a military doctor in Vietnam, is taught in all the craft seminars; it's one of my favorite books. Rumor has it that his next novel, which isn't even completed yet, has already been sold for over $1 million. Everyone's so excited, nervous, and frenzied about meeting him, it's as if the messiah's coming to town.

"Don't forget the party after the reading, at my place," Stacy announces to the class, and passes out a map with directions. Stacy's convinced that she and Bruce Ryan are going to have an affair; she's been e-mailing him all year, since she met him at a reading he gave in Iowa City last summer. "He's really an amazing guy, he wants to spend time with me and may even mention me to his agent," she's told us.

Today's class ends just in time, as my pre-workshop shot of tequila is wearing off—Leslie and I had brought the flask, lime, and salt shaker to the girls' bathroom earlier, as we always do. Everyone adjourns to the Slaughtered Lamb, which serves free happy-hour food on Wednesdays. It's our Wednesday tradition: murder each other in class, then celebrate. As I pack my things up, Josh says, "I really did like it, Anna, I think it's an amazing story," and says he'll wait for me in the hall, to walk to the bar.

I'm emboldened by Josh's response, and surprised that I've survived yet another workshop in one piece. I'm also angry at Chester for making me feel horrible about the story for no reason, and I tell him, when it's just he and I left in the room, "Well, some people liked it. You know, I think I may submit this story for the Harden Prize."

The awarding of the Alice Harden Prize is the most significant event of the program: it's $2,000, and based on the story we submit for it, all forty-seven of us fiction writers are ranked from best to worst. From that ranking, it's decided who gets teaching fellowships and nominations for national awards and publications—and, more important, it represents wholehearted approval, and recognition that the winners have talent, and an actual chance of becoming *writers*.

Chester stares at me. "I don't know if it's such a good idea to submit this story for the prize." He sits on the corner of his desk. I wonder how his hemorrhoids are doing. "At least not without a lot more work," he says.

"I've worked on it so long, though. Really—this is like my hundredth draft. And some people, well, one person in workshop definitely liked it..."

"Anna, I have to tell you this. Whatever's happened in your own life"—he stares off at the blackboard, as if this is painful for him, talking to me—"does not necessarily make a satisfying story. Because a thing, an emotion, an event, is true in life, doesn't mean it will be true on the page. If you're going to be a *writer*, you should know what it takes—an ability to create an imaginary world, to separate your fiction from the facts of your own life."

He says the word *writer* almost mockingly, the way one might say *movie star.*

I gaze down at the floor. I sometimes wish that, instead of writing fiction, we were doing something hopelessly esoteric, like writing linguistic analyses of sixteenth-century pig Latin, because then there wouldn't be this tiny chance of making it. Because that's the hope we all have, buried in each of us, somewhere: we all want to make it. Past winners of the Harden Prize have gone on to publish stories in *The New Yorker* and *The Atlantic Monthly* and *Harper's*; they've won Guggenheim, Lannan, and NEA grants and PEN/ Faulkner Awards; they've been to MacDowell and Yaddo and Bread Loaf; they've had their pictures in *Poets & Writers* and their books reviewed in the *New York Times*, and have even, now and then, appeared on the bestseller list. They've achieved my dream—not to be famous, or rich, or eternally remembered, but just to make a living as a writer, to keep telling stories for the rest of my life.

"I thought..." I say, "I'm just trying to tell a good story. I just want to...you know, keep doing this, writing stories, till I can make a living at it—that's all I really want."

He raises his eyebrows, as if I've just told him all I want is to fly to the moon.

"Anna, I'm going to tell you this, because no one else will. Before you make a mistake in planning your future. I don't know if you have what it takes to be a writer. I haven't seen one story of yours which has shown the potential to be published. Frankly, I haven't seen a sign of that ability in your work."

I flinch; it's almost as if he's slapped me, as if he's kicked me in the stomach. This is different from the disparaging comments on my stories: this is my whole goddamned life.

"I'm simply telling you this so that you can make appropriate decisions when planning how you will—as you said—'make a living,'" he says.

I don't know what to say. What can I say? "Well, huh." My face is hot; I look at my shoes and my watch and say, "Oh! Gotta go!" and bound out of the room and down the hall, past Josh and the lingering crowd, down the stairs and into the relentless southwestern sun, and I'm crying, weeping, because it's my heart that's just been trashed and trampled and critiqued, and because everything I've written is true, everything I've ever written is true.

It's not the Alice Harden Prize I've got any chance of getting, but the Weeping Prize, The Girl Who's Cried Most in the English Department. I walk the six long, sun-cooked blocks to my apartment, trying to gather myself back together.

I've attempted to write stories that aren't about losing my parents, about death. That aren't about orphans, or plane crashes, or lost love and feeling alone in the world—and I can't. The events, characters, and dialogue in my stories are only impressions of real life, but the emotions are completely, unmistakably mine.

And the thing is, it's not like I can just make myself stop. It's like a need, a compulsion, *to write*—a constant feeling, whenever I go into a bookstore, of wanting, more than anything, to read a story that will comfort me, a story about a girl who has no parents, who finds herself weeping, for no immediate reason, while standing on line at Safeway or Epic Café or while walking down the street. I want to read about a girl who feels she'll never get better, she'll never survive, and she's not quite an "orphan" like in *Hard Times* and *Oliver Twist,* and she's too old for *The Secret Garden* and too jaded for *Anne of Green Gables,* and it seems there's no one else in the world like her, no one else who's felt *this.* And of course I can't find that story, that book I so want to read, because it doesn't exist, because it's in my head. And what else can you do, then, but write it down?

Ironically, it's not such a comfort once you do write it down—it's usually the opposite. One night in Maine, one of the grief counselors gave us notepads and said, "Write out your sorrow—it'll soothe you." Nancy, who was twenty-three and had just lost her husband and two-year-old daughter in the crash, shouted at the counselor, "Are you *fucked*?" And I think Nancy was right; it is kind of fucked, dredging up all the pain over and over, remembering how I identified my mother only by her watch, and my father, by his college ring. Sometimes, at night, I lie awake worrying that the Greek myths are true, that like the dead warriors in Hades, fated to live for eternity with their bloody war wounds and torn clothes, my parents are now left somewhere with their bodies destroyed beyond recognition, forever. Sometimes I even lie to people, and tell them my mother died of cancer

and my father of a heart attack, because I'm too embarrassed that my life's a newspaper article, because I can't deal
with the fact that I found out my parents had died not from
a phone call from the airline (I had to call them, and it took
hours to officially confirm) but because I saw the crash reported on a news break, interrupting a Sting video I was
watching on MTV.

Why can't I stop writing? Because life can be so absurdly
sickening that I have to rearrange it, alter it, turn it into
fiction.

When I reach my apartment, my mail is waiting for me.
There are the usual bills, a postcard from a friend in New
York, and three envelopes addressed to me, in my own
handwriting: SASEs. Rejections.

I send short stories out like a banshee. At the moment,
I've got stories at eleven places, like little children at foster
homes, trying to get themselves adopted. Right now "The
Gift" is at three magazines, "The Flight" is at four, and "Deer
Bay" and "Longing" are at two places each.

The first two rejections are printed notes, the usual
"Thank you for your submission but we have no use for it,
blah blah blah," one with a *Sorry!* scrawled next to it, to
which I want to scrawl back *Fuck off!* on the little note and
return it to them. I have a file of all the rejections I've received so far, a big fat stack of notes and slips, some of
which I've gotten back after a magazine has kept a story
for two years. Once I received a note stapled to a soiled,
crumpled copy of my manuscript, from the *Partisan Review,*
explaining that their basement had flooded and my manuscript had been submerged under a foot of water; another
favorite, from *The Paris Review,* apologized for the delay in

my story's return, but it had been "misplaced" for six months under an intern's bed.

The last of today's notes, which I open now, is from *The Lion*. It's handwritten:

Dear Anna,

Thanks for your story, "The Flight." While a bunch of us here loved it, the final decision of the editors went against publication. We see too many stories about death, and are looking for something fresher. But please send more work. I enjoy reading your stories, and I hope to publish something of yours soon.

Best Regards,
Tom Westlake

I hope to publish something of yours soon. Tom Westlake. Oh, Tom, what do you look like? Are you single? I'm in love with you, and I will marry you and have your children if you will please, please publish my story.

I take out "The Flight" and reread it, striking out entire pages and writing one more, and before I know it two hours have passed and there's a knock on the door. Leslie, Lily, and Josh are standing there.

"We were worried about you, when you left so quickly and didn't come to the bar," Lily says, and Leslie adds, "We thought maybe Chester tried to rape you, but then we realized he wouldn't have the equipment for that."

I smile and say I'm okay. I can't bring myself to tell them what Chester said to me, but I show them Tom Westlake's rejection slip, and everyone agrees it's certainly encouraging, there's no doubt, and Lily gives me the latest creative-writing-program news: "The word at the Lamb was that

they're going to have Bruce Ryan judge the Harden Prize—
it won't be decided by the faculty at all."

We walk to the reading together. "You should submit
that story from class today," Josh says.

"Or just give Bruce Ryan a little extra attention tonight,"
Leslie says. "Wonderbra time."

I'll tell you something: there's a fashion problem plaguing
writers. Bruce Ryan is wearing a Hawaiian shirt with four
buttons undone, and his chest is covered in so much gray fluff
it looks like a limp squirrel is napping between his pecs. He
wears the kind of tinted eyeglasses serial killers wear, and
a glittery bracelet that I think I saw on Puff Daddy at the
Grammys. Someday, as a public service, I'm going to start my
own company, Makeovers for Writers. Perhaps I could get
NEA funding. Or at least a guest-speaking spot at Bread Loaf.

Ryan is reading a new story, which unfortunately bears
no resemblance to his previous work; it's about a lecherous
History professor with a predilection for groping female students. I wonder if *this* is autobiographical. The fact that our
future in the program lies in his hands is not a comfort. I
glance around the auditorium. In the back two rows sit the
fiction faculty: there's the director of the program, Frank
Ogden, who, according to program legend, punched out
the former director in a fistfight; his wife, Karen Warren,
who looks like she's perpetually sucking a lemon; Charles
Chester, who towers over everyone because he's perched on
his hemorrhoid pillow; Christopher Mann and Joseph Wil-
son, whose stomachs protrude so far past their shoes it appears they've eaten all their remaindered books.

I know I'm harsh. You must, dear reader, be thinking:
She's judgmental, our storyteller. She's an unreliable narrator.

There are too many characters.

Too many red herrings.

She should've started on page ten.

The reading finally ends, Ryan climbs down from the stage, and Stacy kisses him on the cheek. She scrambles off to prepare for the party, and a tanned, hefty man with a face like a baked ham slaps Ryan on the back, fraternity-brother style. Eventually, the two men make their way to the back of the auditorium, where Leslie, Lily, and I are standing. Baked-ham man sticks his arm out at me. "Carlos," he says, and shakes my hand too tightly. "And I guess y'all know Bruce Ryan."

We introduce ourselves. "You probably know Carlos already too, though you don't realize it," Ryan says. "The character Costas in *Lancet and Plum*? You're talking to him."

I remember Costas from the book—daring, emotional, sympathetic. I hadn't pictured him looking like something from the meat case.

"Hey—you girls like a ride to the party with me and Ryan?" Carlos says, and before we know it, we're all piling into Carlos's red sports car.

Ryan opens the door to the front seat for me. "You," he says, poking my arm. "*You're* a good writer."

"But you haven't read any of my work," I say.

He clutches my arm firmly. "I can *tell*."

Up close, Ryan's face looks like it's made of leather. He's lizardy. Worn. Thin. He spits when he talks. As we drive to the party, he lets loose a litany of nonsequiturs: he used to be macrobiotic, but now he eats only green vegetables and steak; he will work only with female editors who are under thirty-five; his ex-girlfriend tried to kill him by poisoning his gin and tonic; girls in one-piece bathing suits should be arrested for prudishness. The man needs a verbal editor, and then he needs to be knocked in the head. How's it possible that he wrote such a beautiful book?

Carlos drives at about eighty miles an hour. "So you girls are writers, huh?" he says. He seems to get a kick out of this idea, as if we're a circus act.

"We are," Leslie says, giggling. When any powerful man is present, Leslie's entire frontal lobe has a meltdown. "What do *you* do?" she whispers to Carlos.

"An editor at Harvard Press," Ryan answers for him. "I got him the damn job." Ryan flicks Carlos's hair three times from the backseat, like a Boy Scout secret signal. "He's looking for new writers, girls, you know."

I'm in the front seat, next to Carlos, and as if on cue, Carlos pinches my knee. I gape at him, and in the backseat I see Ryan, who's sandwiched between Leslie and Lily, squeeze them both simultaneously. I can't believe this is happening. It's *The Benny Hill Show,* set in academia. All three of us women sit in their car, motionless, stunned, disgusted.

As we cruise through a stop sign, Carlos squeezes my knee again, and leaves his hand there. "What the hell are you doing?" I say.

"What do you mean?" Carlos asks, offended.

"Get your hand off my knee."

He looks at Ryan in the rearview mirror and rolls his eyes. "Jeez-us," he mutters, and ignores me until we reach Stacy's house.

When we get there, I think of leaving immediately, but I'm strangely drawn to this scene. I'm perplexed by how this man whom I once idolized for writing this amazing book— a book I read three times, which I slept with under my pillow—could be . . . a creep.

Everyone's here at the party—all the students, and the faculty. The faculty seem impressed but intimidated by Ryan;

they gaze at him, surrounded by his harem of aspiring-writer girls, like the wallflowers staring at the popular kids at a school dance. I find Josh and tell him about the knee-pinching. He's too shy to go beat Carlos up, which would be the proper male thing to do, so we amble around the yard, observing. An MFA party is like a chemical experiment; you never know what new material might form. It's only been going on five minutes, but already almost everyone seems drunk. Leslie strips down to her bikini and swims through the pool. Calvin and Helen wrestle by the palm trees.

Around midnight, the faculty leaves; the students get in and out of the hot tub to talk to Ryan and his sidekick Carlos. The hot tub has become Ryan's office, his own version of Fonzie's bathroom. Ryan's wearing skin-tight Speedo bathing trunks, which reveal far more than any of us want to see; his chest is puffed out, his legs spread as if this is a *Playgirl* shoot. I haven't exchanged a word with Carlos or Ryan since we were in the car. Josh takes his shirt off awkwardly; he's built like a Calvin Klein model but seems nervous about baring his body. He voices what I'm thinking: "This man is judging us. Let's go in."

"I love that one story, of your wife, when she first becomes ill..." Lily is saying to Ryan as the water gurgles around her skirted bathing suit.

"I don't have a wife," he smirks. "I've never been married. It's bullshit! All of it. You *kids*. It's a fucking story. Have you ever heard of *make-believe*?"

Howard, perpetually sober, is perched on the edge of the tub, fully clothed, with just his feet dipped in. His hands shift clumsily, as if he wishes he could be taking notes. "What is it that made you become a writer?" he asks Ryan in earnest.

"To get laid!"

Even Howard seems depressed by what Ryan's turned out to be; he soon leaves, looking mournful and dejected, and Lily goes with him. Not long after, there's a commotion in the house; Stacy investigates, and reports that Calvin, Leslie, and Brian have wound up in her bed; she has to get them out. Josh gets up to make himself another drink. This leaves me alone with Ryan and Carlos. I'm quiet, not wanting to say anything to them, sitting far away from them at the opposite end of the tub. I repeat to myself that my status in the program is in this man's gnarly hands.

The two men are quiet, too. Carlos stares at me for an uncomfortably long time.

"Hey, I know who she is," Carlos says, suddenly. "I know who you are. Stacy mentioned what you write about—I *knew* I recognized you. That girl from the *Globe*. The plane-crash girl. God! I can't believe I remember that. Your parents were blown up," he says matter-of-factly.

Blood rushes to my head. Ryan's gazing at me, sickly amused. I'm nauseous and dizzy; I want to throw up. I'm sure that tomorrow I'll wake up and know exactly what to say at this moment, but right now I can't think of anything.

I stand up and silently leave. I walk slowly toward the house, dazed, not knowing where to go.

Josh sees me. "Are you okay?" he asks. He sets down his drink. "Do you want me to take you home?"

I nod. We're quiet for most of the drive, until Josh says, "You know, I think Ryan lied to us—I read in a magazine once that he was married, and his wife did die, just as she does in his book, but he doesn't like to talk about it. It can't be easy to have thousands of strangers knowing the most intimate details of your life and thoughts. It almost justifies him being an asshole."

"Almost."

We reach my house; he turns off the ignition. "It's all true in your story, isn't it?" he asks.

"Some things." I don't feel like talking about it now. Josh is one of the few people in the program whose stories aren't exactly tragic—he's written about losing a bike race, and his parents missing his soccer games, and having ex-girlfriends from families less wealthy than his. And now that he's driven me home on two occasions, the entire program will be convinced we're having a full-fledged affair. I'm not even sure I want to kiss him. He's almost too good looking, too pretty— teeth so white they're distracting.

"Do you know what Leslie said about you once?" he says. "'I envy her,' she said. 'I envy her being free.'"

"What does that mean?"

"Not having parents. No one yelling at you to get a normal job, no one sending those not-so-subtle hints that you're not good enough, 'Why can't you get an MBA or go to law school or med school or at *least* go for a Ph.D.?' 'How will you ever make money? What are you going to do with your life? When are you going to grow up?' My parents say it all the time."

I want to say: do you know what it's like, whenever someone mentions *parents, family*? How often it comes up in casual conversation, at parties, on trains, whenever someone asks why I don't fly; even on my computer, when I begin a letter with "Dear," Microsoft Word automatically suggests "Dear Mom and Dad" to save extra typing. How every time I go out with a new guy I ask him, What do your mom and dad do?, secretly hoping he'll say at least one of his parents is dead (or both—maybe both—then I'd really fall in love).

There's a huge gulf between the words I think and the words I want to say. So I sit there, unsure of what to say or do, until he clasps my hands and kisses me, pulling me toward him in the front seat of his Ford pickup.

I know I've become a writer when I think, while we're kissing, *Well, whatever comes of this, I can always put it in a story.*

The Harden Prize is announced, and Howard's won it again, so all of us, except Howard, are commiserating at the Slaughtered Lamb on a Sunday night, staring into our beers.

"Sometimes I wonder why I'm doing this," Calvin says. "Sometimes I don't know why I'm in the program."

"I hate how we call it 'the program,'" Helen says. "It sounds like AA or something. I was at the food co-op the other day and this guy said, 'You're in the program, right?' People around me looked at me like I was nuts, like he'd just asked if I was in a cult or something, like the Scientologists or the Moonies."

Josh offers to drive me home again, but I live nearby, and I tell him I'll walk. I feel like being alone. I keep thinking about what he said, that night in his truck, about people envying me; I can't stop thinking about it. An answer to it has been welling up in my head, and I have to get it out, I have to write it down. It's almost two A.M. when I get back to my house, but I can't sleep. I take out "The Gift," cross out the ending of the latest draft, and write:

The summer after the crash, I spent two weeks with my boyfriend Colin, my first boyfriend after my parents died—he invited me to join his family on their vacation to the South Carolina shore—and his mother looked at me so queerly when she met me, cocking her head to one side and squinting, almost suspiciously, and asking for "facts" about my family history, as if I was a foundling her son had adopted, a charity case. During that week there was a hurricane warning, and she was disturbed that no one called to assure that I was fine. She couldn't fathom that I had no relatives; she came from a Southern clan with four generations still living. "Nobody's phoned you the whole time you've been with us!" she said one night, tactlessly, distrustfully, warily. At nineteen, legally an adult but still a teenager, I had no grownups checking on me, no one for her to okay things with, to get approval from. At the end of the week, I overheard her talking about "my son's girlfriend" to her cousin on the phone. "Colin has such a big heart!" she said, as if it required a particularly large heart for me to be loved.

After that summer I returned to school, and life went on, and eventually I got used to explaining to new friends and boyfriends and teachers and employers that my parents were dead. And through those years I never cashed that money order; I kept it stashed in the pages of my journal, waiting for the time when I could look at it and not double over in pain. It's stashed in my journal still.

I don't know where these paragraphs have just come from—I've barely thought of this old boyfriend, or his mother, or those weeks in South Carolina, for five years—I never even knew why I'd kept that money order all these years until I saw the reason before me on the page.

I think now that my writing is as dear to me as a family would be, and crazy as that sounds, I think writing requires the same kind of attention, of commitment, of love, that people do. To be faithful to a story even when it fails me, to come back to it again and again when I worry that I may never make it work, that it may always disappoint me, that everything I've put into it could be lost—to know this, yet still keep writing—what could that be, if not love?

And I think, maybe, that none of us really knows—not Ryan or the faculty or any of the students—how to tell a story. Because when I sit down, like this, in the middle of the night, pen in hand, something outside of myself tells me to keep going, for hours, to never, never stop... until it's not me writing the story anymore, but the story writing *me*.

peter **greenaway**

105 YEARS OF ILLUSTRATED TEXT

The Pillow Book was a film made in 1996 to throw another stone in the pond of my anxiety that we have not seen any cinema yet. We have only seen 105 years of illustrated text. And recorded theater. And theater is primarily a matter of text. In practically every film you experience, you can see the director following the text. Illustrating the words first, making the pictures after, and, alas, so often not making pictures at all, but holding up the camera to do its mimetic worst. Though Derrida said the image has the last word, in cinema, we have all conspired to make sure the word has the first word. Godard said that once you have that check in the bank, that check you earned by bamboozling the bank manager into being impressed by your text, then throw that text away and start all over again. An object conceived and perceived in words is going to stay that way. And if that really really is the case, and it works in words, why waste time and patience and money making the conversion?

Now, all of this is a sort of treacherous thing to say in a magazine dedicated to narrative in the movies—dedicated in fact to that very uncomfortable premise that in the movies you have apparently got to have text before you can have pictures. Which is bad. Because cinema is not an excuse for illustrated literature. But then I am primarily a painter, and my prejudice is that painting is the prime visual art and the very best painting is non-narrative.

So it is good to say all this in the enemy camp—is this the enemy camp? Of course it is not, because we know this to be that state of things in the cinema we have arrived at after 105 years of striving for better things. In a strange way, the desire to manufacture this magazine is proof of what I am saying. Because we all know that literature is superior to cinema as a form of storytelling. It empowers the imagination like no other. If you want to be a storyteller, be an author, be a novelist, be a writer, don't be a film director. Cinema is not the greatest medium for telling stories. It is too specific, leaves so little room for the imagination to take wing other than in the strict directions indicated by the director. Read "he entered the room" and imagine a thousand scenarios. See "he entered the room" in cinema-as-we-know-it, and you are going to be limited to one scenario only. The cinema is about other things than storytelling. What you remember from a good film—and let's only talk about good films—is not the story, but a particular and hopefully unique experience that is about atmosphere, ambience, performance, style, an emotional attitude, gestures, singular events, a particular audio-visual experience that does not rely on the story. Besides, nine times out of ten, you will not remember the story. And if you do, and you tell it, and you are talking in words, then you are back to literature, and the cinematic experience is not communicated that way. Because for the moment we have not found anything better, and because we are lazy, the narrative is the glue we use to hold the whole apparatus of cinema together. There is much to say that D.W. Griffith, proud manufacturer of *Intolerance,* took us all in the wrong direction. He enslaved cinema to the nineteenth-century novel. And it is going to take a hell of a lot of convincing to go back, right the wrong, and then go forward again. But I have hopes. I do really believe that we are now developing the new tools to make that happen. Tools, as Picasso said of painting, that will allow you to make images of what you think, not merely of what you see, and certainly not of what you read.

However, you have got to go very slowly. John Cage, composer, painter, and all-round thinker and cultural catalyst, said that if you introduce twenty percent of novelty into any artwork, watch out—you are going to lose eighty percent of your audience at once. He said you would lose them for fifteen years. Cage was interested in fifteen-year cycles. But he was hopelessly optimistic. The general appreciation, for example, of Western painting has got stuck around Impressionism, and that was 130 years ago, not fifteen years ago.

So, bearing all this long-term anxiety in mind, the first provocation with the film *The Pillow Book* is that it is called *The Pillow Book.* Never put the word "book" in a film title. I have done it twice. Deliberately. (*Prospero's Books* was the other.) If only to draw attention to my anxieties. What itches, needs scratching.

Pillow-books were a genre literature in Japan for over a thousand years. In the beginning they were bedside diaries kept in a drawer in your wooden pillow, to which you added important considerations before going to sleep with, so to speak, your head on them; then they became aphrodisiacs for sleepless lovers, and then they became sex manuals for bored lovers, and then they became sex primers to initiate the innocent. The film *The Pillow Book* could be thought of as functioning on all four levels; it offers what you might say are the profound thoughts, it hopes to titillate sexual fantasies, it demonstrates new ways to do it, and it offers you a checklist of the basics.

The particular pillow-book I chose to homage, though not at all to illustrate, was a classic written by a tenth-century royal courtesan, Sei Shōnagon. It is a loose book, impressionistic, hardly coherent as a continuous narrative. It is full of descriptions of court life, and the retelling of court gossip and descriptions of fashionable shrines and how to get there by the most elegant means. It is a piece of writing replete with those typical Japanese wistful and melancholic evocations of ephemerality. It was written a thousand years ago almost exactly to the year the film was made, and it was written by a woman. To be literate a thousand years ago in the West was pretty uncommon; to be literate and a woman, very unlikely; to be literate, female, and quite brilliant, a well-nigh Western impossibility. Sei Shōnagon feels modern, almost a proto-feminist in such a paternalistic age that women at court stayed, for the most part, silent and still and available indoors all their lives. She said much, and she said two electrifying things from the still darkness of her domestic prisons. She said them of course very much in her own way, but she said there were two things in life that were absolutely essential, and life would be unbearable without them: the sensuous body and literature. My crude summation would be sex and text. Both have the X factor. She said them with longing and her longing stayed with me. How can we arrange to have these two desirable items, and how can we arrange to have them always together?

Well, I tried, at least to make them as indivisible as possible for the length of a film. The plot, characters, and dialogue of *The Pillow Book* are mine. Not Sei Shōnagon's. Why illustrate a great piece of writing whose very advocacy and evocation and efficacy lies within its very existence as writing? I am paying homage to a great piece of writing, not illustrating it, not even interpreting it. Not illuminating it. A good filmmaker should be a prime creator—a composer, not a conductor.

The desire to celebrate Sei Shōnagon and her thoughts about sex and text, and the anxiety that we have not seen any cinema yet, but only 105 years of illustrated text, need a vehicle of organization. Conventionally, in the sort of cinema we have had so far, though hopefully will not need to have in the future, we apparently need to make that vehicle a narrative. Our thoughts are essentially of the contemporary, but we are nothing without memory and comparison, so I constructed a two-tiered narrative of the present and of the past. In the beginning was the word, and a very young Japanese girl has a birthday greeting written on her body by her father. So comprehensive was this gesture of love and ownership and blessing that the Japanese girl, maturing in the 1990s, wants her lovers to write on her body in a similar fashion. She, like me, learns that text and sex were also desirable commodities for that paragon of Japanese classic authorship, Sei Shōnagon. Armed with Sei Shōnagon's good sense and wise desires, our heroine searches to find out whether a good calligrapher can indeed be a good lover, and can the opposite also be true? The film engages in her search. It is a catalogue movie, with a list of sexual and calligraphic encounters intertwined. Sex and text in one. All the film purports to do is deliberate on this one idea, and all its cousins and relatives. What, why, how, when? Is the body an alphabet? Can flesh really be paper? Is there immortality in text? Is the spine of a book the same as the vertebrae of a man? What is the word-price of fleshly love? Can text be jealous? Can books fuck with books and make other books? Is blood ink? Is the pen a penis whose purpose is to fertilize the page? Can she who was the paper become the pen? And if the body has made all the signs and symbols of the world, passing from thinking brain to moving arm to gesturing hand to stiff pen on silent paper over thousands of years, what now—when we all write on keyboards? Have we severed a most important link? Is there ever now going to be a necessary evolutionary future for letters and words? And if words were made by the body, where is there a better place to put those words than back on the body?

The film has written and spoken dialogue in twenty-five languages—English, French, Japanese, Mandarin, Cantonese, Vietnamese, Latin, Hebrew, necrotic Egyptian...and it has written calligraphic text on paper, wood and flesh, on flat and curved surfaces, vertically and horizontally, on both living and dead flesh, in neon, on screens, in projection, as sub-title, inter-title, and sur-title, as High Art and low art, as advertisement and banker's check and registration plate, on photograph, on blackboard, as letter correspondence, as photocopy facsimile, and spoken, chanted, and sung, with and without music...a mocking challenge. You want text? Cinema wants text? Cinema pretends to eschew text? Then we can give you text to mock that smug suggestion that cinema thinks it is pictures.

Enough. Where are there models for a more perfect image-text marriage?

Japanese hieroglyphs may be a good model for reinventing the desperately in-need-of-being-reinvented cinema. The history of Japanese painting, the history of Japanese calligraphy, and the history of Japanese literature are the same—all grow and have grown together; what you see as an image you read as a text. What you read as a text, you perceive as an image. This was certainly my major aim and model in the film *The Pillow Book*. Get the *Titanic* sailing correctly before you worry about the deck chairs. Indivisibility between text and image. Eisenstein saw the possibilities back in the 1920s. His theories of montage assimilated the dual image-text role of the Oriental ideogram. No middlemen. Image and text come together hand-in-hand. Cinema does not seem to have wanted to learn from such an encouragement. We have encouraged ourselves to need perhaps too many middlemen, too many translators. Most of them lazy. My fictitious Japanese lover's less-than-great calligrapher is Ewan McGregor's Jerome, a translator. St. Jerome was the first major translator of text for the modern world—though his business was to convince us about Christianity. What is it that cinema is trying to convince us of? Christianity and the cinema both desire happy endings. Heaven and a golden sunset. Perhaps, sadly, in the end, cinema is only a translator's art, and you know what they say about translators: traitors all.

THE AFFAIRS OF EACH BEAST

The dogs had gone feral. They roamed the countryside in packs, their claws grown long, their fur thick and unbrushed and tangled with thistles. When the soldiers began marching at dawn, Leksi counted each dog he spotted, a game to help the time pass. He quit after forty. They were everywhere: crouched and watchful in the snow; racing through the shadows of the towering pines; following the soldiers, sniffing their boot prints, hoping for scraps.

The dogs unnerved Leksi. From time to time he would turn, point at the closest ones, and whisper, "Stay." They would stare up at him, unblinking. There was something strangely undomestic about their eyes. These dogs lacked the wheedling complicity of their tamed brothers; they were free of the household commandments: *Do not shit in the kitchen. Do not bite people.* A silver-haired bitch still wore a purple collar, and Leksi imagined that the other dogs mocked her for this badge of servility.

Of the three soldiers, Leksi, at eighteen, was the youngest. They marched in single file with ten-meter intervals between men, Leksi in the rear, Nikolai in the middle, Surkhov in front. They wore their gray-and-white winter fatigues, parkas draped over their bulky packs to keep everything dry in case of snowfall. *We look like old hunchbacks,* thought Leksi. His rifle strap kept slipping off his shoulder, so he ended up holding the gun in his gloved hands. He still wasn't used to the rifle. It never seemed heavy when he picked it up in the morning, but by noon, when he was sweating through his undershirt despite the cold, his arms ached from the burden.

Leksi, along with all of his school friends, had eagerly anticipated enlistment. From the age of fourteen on, every girl in his class had been mad for the soldiers. Soldiers carried guns, wore uniforms, drove military vehicles. Their high black boots gleamed when they crossed their legs in the outdoor cafés. If you were eighteen and you weren't a soldier, you were a woman; if you were neither soldier nor woman, you were a cripple. Leksi had not been back to his hometown since enlisting. He wondered when he'd get to cross his legs at an outdoor café and raise his glass to the giggling girls.

Instead he had this: snow, snow, more snow, snow. It all looked the same to Leksi, and it was endless. He never paid attention to where they were going; he just followed the older soldiers. If he were ever to look up and find them gone, Leksi would be lost in the wilderness, without any hope of finding his way out. He could not understand why anyone would want to live here, let alone fight for the place.

He had first seen the Chechen highlands a month before, when the convoy carrying his infantry division across the central Caucasus stopped at the peak of the Darial Pass so that the men could relieve themselves. The soldiers stood in a long line by the side of the road, jumping up and down like madmen, pissing into the wind, hollering threats and curses at their hidden enemies in the vast snowy distance.

He had been cold that afternoon, he had been cold every morning and night since then, he was cold now. He was so cold his teeth were cold. If he breathed through his mouth, his throat hurt; if he breathed through his nose, his head hurt. But he was the youngest, and he was a soldier, so he never complained.

Surkhov and Nikolai, on the other hand, never stopped complaining. They shouted to each other throughout the morning, back and forth. Leksi knew that armed guerrillas lurked in these hills; he heard they were paid a bounty for each enemy they brought to their chief, the *vor v zakone*, the "thief-in-power." The bodies of Russian soldiers were sometimes found crucified on telephone poles, their genitalia stuffed into their mouths. Their severed heads were left on the doorsteps of ethnic Russians in Grozny and Vladikavkaz. Leksi couldn't understand why Surkhov and Nikolai were so recklessly loud, but they had been soldiers for years. Both had seen extensive combat. Leksi didn't question them.

"Put Khlebnikov in charge," Surkhov was saying now, "and he'd clean this place up in two weeks. There's twelve pigfuckers here that tell all the other pigfuckers what to do. You put Khlebnikov in charge, he'd get the twelve, *ping ping ping*." Surkhov made a gun with his thumb and forefinger and fired at the invisible twelve. He wasn't wearing gloves. Neither was Nikolai. Leksi got colder just looking at their bare red hands.

Surkhov was skinny but tireless. He could tramp through deep snow for hours without break, bitching and singing the whole way. His face seemed asymmetrical, one eye slightly higher than the other. It made him look perpetually skeptical. His shaggy brown hair spilled out from below his white watch cap. The caps were reversible—black on the inside for nighttime maneuvers. Leksi, whose head was still shaved

to regulation specifications, felt vulnerable without his hel-
met, which he had left behind after Surkhov and Nikolai
kept throwing pebbles at it. None of the older soldiers wore
helmets. Helmets were considered unmanly, like seatbelts,
fit only for UN observers and French journalists.

Nikolai's hair was even longer than Surkhov's. Nikolai
looked like an American movie star, strong-boned and blue-
eyed, until he opened his mouth, which was jumbled with
crooked teeth. If the teeth bothered him, it didn't show—he
was constantly flashing his snaggle-toothed smile, as if daring people to point out the gaps. Nobody ever did.

"They'll never bring Khlebnikov here," said Nikolai.
"You're always talking Khlebnikov this, Khlebnikov that, so
what? Never. Khlebnikov is a tank. They don't want tanks
here. This..." and here Nikolai gestured at himself and
Surkhov, their march, ignoring Leksi, "...this is not *relevant*.
This is a *game*. You want to know the truth? Moscow is happier if we die. If we die, all the newspapers rant about it, the
politicians get on TV and rant about it, and then, maybe,
they begin to fight for real."

Whenever Nikolai or Surkhov said the word *Moscow* it
sounded profane. Actual curses rolled from their tongues,
free and easy, but to *Moscow* they added the venom of a true
malediction. Most of the older soldiers spoke the same way,
and the intensity of their emotion surprised Leksi. Nikolai
and Surkhov took almost nothing seriously. Surkhov would
read aloud the letters he got from his girlfriend, affecting
a high-pitched, quavering voice: "I long for you, darling, I
wake in the morning and already long for you," and then he
and Nikolai would burst into laughter. One night Nikolai described his father's long, excruciating death from bone cancer, and then shrugged, sipping from a mug of coffee spiked
with vodka. "Well, he outlived his welcome."

A week ago they had been marching down an unpaved road. They walked in the tracks of an armored personnel carrier because the grooved and flattened snow gave better traction. They came across a skinny, dead dog, and Surkhov dragged it by its front paws into the center of the road. Blackbirds had pecked out the eyes and testes. Surkhov, one hand on the back of its neck, lifted the dog's frozen corpse onto its hind legs and used it as a ventriloquist's dummy to sing the Rolling Stones.

"I can't get no sa-tis-fac-tion, I can't get no sa-tis-fac-tion, I have tried, I have tried, I have tried, I have tried, I can't get me no..."

Nikolai had laughed, bent over at the waist, hands on his knees, laughing until the blackbirds circling overhead winged away. Leksi had smiled, because it would be rude not to smile, but he could not look away from the dog's eyeless face. Someone had shot it in the forehead; the bullet hole was round as a coin. One of the soldiers from the APC, taking target practice.

Leksi was deeply superstitious. His grandmother had taught him that the world was full of animals and that the animals all knew each other. There were secret conferences in the wild where the affairs of each beast were discussed and argued. A boy in his school had pegged a pigeon with a slingshot, killing it instantly. A year later the boy's older sister died in a car accident. Leksi did not believe it was an accident; he was sure the other birds had conspired and gained their revenge.

"Aleksandr!"

Leksi looked up from the snow and realized that he had fallen far behind Nikolai. He rushed forward, nearly tripping. Carrying the rifle disrupted his balance. When he was again ten meters behind the older soldier, he stopped and nodded, but Nikolai summoned him forward with curling fingers. Surkhov squatted down and observed them from his position, grinning.

"Who's watching my back?" asked Nikolai, when Leksi approached him.

"Me. I'm sorry."

"No, again, who's watching my back?"

"Me."

Nikolai shook his head and looked at Surkhov for a moment, who shrugged. "Nobody's watching my back," said Nikolai. "You're watching the snow, you're watching the dogs, you're watching the sky. So, okay, you are an artist, I think. You are composing a painting, maybe, in your head. I appreciate this. But then tell me, if you are making this painting, who is watching my back?"

"Nobody."

"Ah. This is a problem. You see, I am watching Surkhov's back. Nobody can attack Surkhov from behind, because I would protect him. But who protects me? While you paint this masterpiece, who protects me?"

"Sorry."

"I will not die in this shit land, Aleksandr. You understand? I refuse to die here. You guard me, I guard Surkhov, we all live another day. You see?"

"Yes."

"Watch my back."

Only after they began marching again, after Surkhov and Nikolai began singing Beatles songs, replacing the original lyrics with obscene variations, did Leksi wonder who was watching his own back.

The three soldiers stopped less than a kilometer downhill of the mansion, at the edge of a dense copse of pines. A high wall of mortared stones surrounded the property; only the shingled roof and chimneys were visible from the soldiers' vantage point. A long field of snow lay between them and the house. The shadows of the tall trees stretched up the field in the last minutes of sunlight.

Surkhov took the binoculars back from Leksi and stared through them. "They can watch the entire valley from there. No smoke from the chimneys. But they know we'd be looking for smoke."

Nikolai had pulled a plastic bag of tobacco and papers from Surkhov's pack; he leaned against a tree trunk now and rolled a cigarette. Leksi could roll a decent number if he were warm and indoors, sitting down, the paper flat on a table-top. He was always amazed that Nikolai could roll them anywhere, in less than a minute, never dropping a flake of tobacco, no matter the wind or the darkness. Nikolai could roll a cigarette while driving a car over a dirt road and singing along with the radio.

He gripped the finished product between his lips while returning the plastic bag to Surkhov's pack. Leksi lit it for him and Nikolai inhaled hungrily, his stubbled cheeks caving in. He released the smoke and passed the cigarette to Leksi.

"Intelligence said no lights in the house the last three nights," said Nikolai.

Surkhov spat. "Intelligence couldn't find my cock if it was halfway up their ass. Fuck them and their patron saints. Aleshkovsky told me some of them flew a copter to Pitsunda last weekend, for the whores. We're down here freezing our balls off and they go whoring."

"So," said Nikolai, "they send three men. The way they see it, (a) the place is empty, we take it, fine, we have a good observation post for the valley; (b) half the terrorist army is in there, we're dead, fine. All at once, we are relevant. We are martyrs. The real fighting begins."

"I don't want to be relevant," said Leksi, handing the cigarette to Surkhov. The older soldiers looked at him quizzically for a moment and then laughed. It took Leksi a second to realize they were laughing with him, not at him.

"No," said Nikolai, clapping him on the back. "Neither do I."

After nightfall they unrolled their sleeping bags and slept in turns, one man always keeping watch. Leksi pulled the first shift but could not sleep after Nikolai relieved him. Every few minutes a dog would howl and then his brothers would answer, until the hills echoed with lonely dogs calling for each other. An owl screeched from a perch nearby. Leksi lay in his bag and stared up through the pine branches. A half-moon lit the sky and he watched the silhouetted clouds drift in and out of sight. He lay with his knees pressed against his chest for warmth and flinched every time the wind blew a stray pine needle against his cheek. He listened to Nikolai puffing on another handrolled cigarette and to Surkhov grinding his teeth in his sleep.

In a few hours he might be fighting for a house he had never seen before tonight, against men he had never met. He hadn't insulted anyone or fucked anyone's girlfriend, he hadn't stolen any money or crashed into anyone's car, and yet these men, if they were here, would try to kill him. It seemed very bizarre to Leksi. Strangers wanted to kill him. They didn't even know him, but they wanted to kill him. As if everything he had done was completely immaterial, everything he held in his mind: the girls he had kissed; the hunting trips with his father; the cow he had drawn for his mother when he was seven, still hanging in a frame on her bedroom wall; or the time he got caught sneaking glances over Katya Zubritskaya's shoulder during a geometry test and old Lukonin had made him stand up right there and repeat, louder and louder, while the students laughed and pounded their desks: *I am Aleksandr Strelchenko and I am a cheat, and not even a good cheat.* These memories were Aleksandr Strelchenko, and so what? None of it mattered. None of it was real except here, now, the snow, the soldiers beside him, the house on the hilltop. Why did they need the house? To observe the valley. What was there to observe? Trees and snow and wild dogs, the Caucasus mountains looming in the distance. Leksi curled up inside his sleeping bag and pictured his severed head resting on a Grozny doorstep, his eyes the eyes of a dead fish on its bed of ice.

At 3 A.M. they climbed the hill. They left their packs behind, wrapped tightly in waterproof tarps and buried below the snow, marked with broken twigs and pinecones. The moon was bright enough to make flashlights unnecessary. Surkhov and Nikolai seemed like different people now; since waking they had barely spoken. They had blackened each other's faces and then Leksi's, pocketed their watches, reversed their caps.

They reached the stone wall and circled around to the back gate. If there were any guard dogs, they would have already begun barking. That was a good sign. They found the back gate unlocked, swinging back and forth in the wind, creaking. That was another good sign. They crept onto the property. The grounds were sprawling and unkempt. A white gazebo stood by an old well; the gazebo's roof sagged from the weight of the snow.

The house's large windows were trimmed in copper. No lights were on. The soldiers took positions by hand signal: Surkhov approached the back door while Nikolai and Leksi lay on their stomachs and aimed their rifles past him. Surkhov looked at them for a moment, shrugged, and turned the knob. The door opened.

Nobody was home. They attached their flashlights to their rifle barrels and split up to check both floors and the cellar, slowly, slowly, looking for the silver gleam of a trip wire, the matte gray of a pancake mine. They searched under the beds, in the closets, the shower stalls, the wine racks in the cellar, the modern toilet's water tank. When Leksi opened the refrigerator he gasped. The light came on.

"Electricity," he whispered. He couldn't believe it. He walked over to the light switch and flicked it up. The kitchen shined, the yellow tiled floor, the wood counters, the big black stove. Surkhov hurried in, his boots thundering on the tiles. He turned off the light and slapped Leksi in the face.

"Idiot," he said.

When the search was completed, Nikolai radioed their base. He listened to instructions for a moment, nodded impatiently, signed off, and looked up at the other two, who were gathered around him in the library. "So now we sit here and wait."

The walls were bookshelves, crowded with more books than they were meant to hold, vertical stacks of books on top of horizontal rows of books. Books were piled in corners, books lay scattered on the leather sofa, books leaned precariously on the marble fireplace mantle.

Leksi's face was still flushed from embarrassment. He knew that he had deserved the slap, that he had acted stupidly, but he was furious anyway. He imagined that Surkhov slapped his girlfriends that way if he caught them stealing money, and it burned Leksi to be treated with such disrespect, as if he were unworthy of a punch.

Nikolai watched him. "Look," he said, "you understand why Surkhov was angry?"

"Yes."

"Did you check the refrigerator before you opened it?" asked Nikolai. "Did you check to see if it was wired? And then you turn on the lights! Now everyone in the valley knows we are here. You need to pay attention. You never pay attention and it's going to get you killed, which is fine, but it's going to get us killed also, which is not fine."

Surkhov smiled. "Tell me you're sorry, Leksi, and I'll apologize too. Come on. Give me your hand."

Leksi was unable to hold grudges. He extended his hand and said, "I'm sorry."

"Fool," said Surkhov, ignoring Leksi's hand. He and Nikolai laughed and walked out of the library.

They washed off the face paint in a blue-tiled bathroom, using soap shaped like seashells, drying themselves with green hand towels. Afterwards they searched the rooms for loot. Leksi took the second floor, happy to be alone for a while, pointing his flashlight at everything that interested him. In one grand room, where he assumed the master of the house once slept, he stared in wonder at the bed. It was the biggest bed he had ever seen. He and his older brother had slept in a bed one-third this size until his brother got married.

Blue porcelain lamps stood on the night tables. A tea cup sat on a saucer beneath one of these lamps. The cup's rim was smudged with red lipstick, and some tea had spilled into the saucer.

A heavy black dresser with brass handles stood against one wall. On top of the dresser were pill bottles, a brush tangled with long gray hairs, a china bowl filled with coins, a cut-glass vial of perfume, a jar of pungent face cream, and several silver-framed photographs. One of the photographs caught Leksi's eye, an old black-and-white, and he picked it up. A raven-haired woman stared at the camera. She looked faintly bored yet willing to play along, the same expression Leksi saw on all the beautiful young wives in his hometown. Her dark eyebrows plunged toward each other but didn't meet.

Leksi had the eerie sense, examining the photograph, that the woman knew she would be seen this way. As if she expected that a day would come, years and years after the shutter clicked, when a stranger with a rifle strapped to his shoulder would point his flashlight at her face and wonder what her name was.

He checked the other rooms on the floor and then went downstairs, not realizing that he was still holding the framed photograph until he entered the dark library. He saw a match flare and he pointed his flashlight in that direction. Surkhov and Nikolai were sprawled on the leather sofa, their boots and socks kicked off, their stinking bare feet on the glass-topped coffee table. They had removed their parkas and sweaters; their undershirts were mottled with sweat stains. They were smoking cigars. On the floor beside them was a heap of silver that glowed cool and lunar when Leksi aimed his flashlight at it: serving trays and candlesticks, tureens and ladles, napkin rings and decanters. Leksi wondered how they expected to carry all that loot home with them. Maybe they didn't, maybe they just liked the sight of it, the piled treasure. A two-foot-tall blond china doll wearing a white nightdress sat on Nikolai's lap. His hand was massaging the doll's thighs. He winked at Leksi.

"Aren't you hot?"

It was true; Leksi was hot. He had been cold for so long that the heat had been welcome, but now he leaned his rifle against a bookcase, carefully set the photograph on the mantle, and shrugged out of his parka.

"They must have run off in a hurry," said Surkhov. "Left the electricity on, left the heat on." He inspected the glowing ash on the tip of his cigar. "Left the cigars."

Nikolai leaned forward and lifted a wood cigar box off the coffee table. "Here," he said to Leksi. "Take your pick."

Leksi selected a cigar, bit off the end, lit it, and lay down on the rug in front of the dead fireplace. He turned off his flashlight. They puffed away in the darkness and did not speak for a time. It was very good to lie there, in the warm house, smoking a good cigar. They listened to the wind gusting outside. Leksi felt safer than he had in weeks. The other two were tough on him, it was true, but they knew what they were doing. They were making him a better soldier.

"Leksi," said Surkhov, sleepily. "Leksi."

"Yes?"

"When you opened the refrigerator, what did you see?"

Leksi thought this was probably another trick. "Look," he said, "I'm sorry about the—"

"No, what was inside the refrigerator? Did you get a look?"

"Lots of stuff. A chicken."

"A chicken," said Surkhov. "Cooked or uncooked?"

"Cooked."

"Did it look good?"

For some reason Leksi thought this was a very funny question and he began to laugh. Nikolai laughed too, and soon all three of them were shaking with laughter.

"Ay me," said Nikolai, sucking his cigar back to life.

"No really," said Surkhov. "Did it look like it'd been sitting there for months?"

"No. It looked very good, actually."

Leksi lay on his back with his hands behind his head and thought about the chicken. Then he thought about his feet. He unlaced his boots and pulled them off, and the wet socks as well. He shone his flashlight on his toes and wiggled them. They were all there. He hadn't seen them in a long time.

"Well," said Surkhov, sitting up. "Let's get that chicken."

They ate off bone-china plates, with silver forks and wood-handled knives, at the long dining room table. The sun was beginning to rise. The crystal chandelier above the table refracted the light and created multicolored patterns on the pale blue wallpaper. Nikolai's blond doll sat in the seat next to him.

The roasted chicken was dry from sitting in the refrigerator, but not spoiled. They chewed the bones, sucking out the marrow. The soldiers had found a nearly full bottle of vodka in the freezer and they drank from heavy tumblers, staring out the windows at the valley that opened before them.

The snow and trees, the frozen lake in the distance, everything looked beautiful, harmonious and pure. Nikolai spotted an eagle and pointed it out; they all watched the bird soar high above the valley floor. When they were finished eating they pushed the plates to the center of the table and leaned back in their chairs, rubbing their bellies. They exchanged a volley of burps and grinned at one another.

"So Aleksandr," said Nikolai, picking at his teeth with his thumbnail. "You have a girlfriend?"

Leksi took another drink and let the alcohol burn in his mouth for a moment before answering. "Not really."

"What does this mean, not really?"

"It means no."

"But you've been with women?"

Leksi burped and nodded. "Here and there."

"Virgin," said Surkhov, carving his name into the mahogany tabletop with his knife.

"No," said Leksi, undefiantly. He was not a liar and people eventually figured this out. Right now he was too warm and well fed to be goaded into irritation. "I've been with three girls."

Nikolai raised his eyebrows as if the number impressed him. "You must be a legend in your hometown."

"And I've kissed eleven."

Surkhov plunged his knife into the table and shouted, "That's a lie!" Then he giggled and drank more vodka.

"Eleven," repeated Leksi.

"Are you counting your mother?" Surkhov asked.

"I'm a very good kisser," said Leksi. "They all said so."

Nikolai and Surkhov looked at each other and laughed. "Excellent," said Nikolai. "We're lucky to have such an expert with us. Could you demonstrate?" He reached over and grabbed the doll by its hair and tossed it to Leksi, who caught it and looked into its blue glass eyes.

"I don't like blondes," said Leksi. The other men laughed and Leksi was very pleased with the joke. He laughed himself and took another drink.

"Please," said Nikolai. "Teach us."

Leksi supported the doll by the back of its head and leaned forward to kiss its painted porcelain lips. He kept his eyes closed. He thought about the last real girl he had kissed, the eleventh, the night before entering the army.

When Leksi opened his eyes Nikolai was standing, hands on his hips, frowning. "No," he said. "Where is the passion?" He grabbed the doll by the shoulders and pulled it from Leksi's hands. He stared angrily at the doll's face. "Who

do you love, doll? Is it Aleksandr? No? Is it me? I don't believe you. How can I trust you?" He cupped the doll's face in
his palms and kissed it mightily.

Leksi was impressed. It was a much better kiss, there
was no question. He wanted another chance but Nikolai
tossed the doll aside. It landed on its back on the oaken sideboard. Surkhov clapped and whistled, as if Nikolai had just
scored the winning goal for their club team.

"That is a kiss," said Nikolai, wiping his lips with the
back of his hand. "You must always kiss as if kissing will be
outlawed at dawn." He seized the vodka bottle from the
table and saw that it was empty. "Surkhov! You drunk bas-
tard, you finished it!"

Surkhov nodded. "Good vodka."

Nikolai stared sadly through the bottle. "There was
more in the freezer?"

"No."

"There's all that wine in the cellar," said Leksi, looking at
the doll's little black shoes dangling over the sideboard's edge.

"Yes!" said Nikolai. "The cellar."

Leksi followed Nikolai down the narrow staircase, both of
them still barefoot. The cellar was windowless, so Nikolai
turned on the lights. The corners of the room were cob-
webbed. A billiards table covered with a plastic sheet stood
against one wall. A chalkboard above it still tallied the score
from an old game. In the middle of the floor a yellow toy
dumptruck sat on its side. Leksi picked it up and rolled its
wheels; it would make a good gift for his little nephew.

One entire wall was a wine rack, a giant honeycomb of
clay-colored octagonal cubbies. Foil-wrapped bottle tops
peeked out of each. Nikolai pulled one bottle out and inspected the label.

"French." He handed it to Leksi. "The French are the whores of Europe, but they make nice wine." He pulled out two more bottles and they turned to go. They were halfway up the stairs when Nikolai placed his two wine bottles on the step above him, drew his pistol from his waist holster, and chambered a bullet. Leksi did not have a pistol. His rifle was still in the library. He held a bottle in one hand and a toy truck in the other. He looked at Nikolai, not sure what was happening.

"Leksi," whispered Nikolai. "How do they play pool with the table jammed against the wall?"

Leksi shook his head. He had no idea what the older man was talking about.

"Get Surkhov. Get your rifles and come down here."

By the time Leksi had retrieved Surkhov from the dining room, their rifles from the library, and returned to the cellar staircase, Nikolai was gone. Then they heard him calling for them. "Come on, come on, it's over."

They found him standing above an opened trapdoor, his pistol reholstered. He had shoved the billiards table aside to get to the trapdoor, a feat of strength that Leksi did not even register until a few minutes later. The three soldiers stared down into the tiny subcellar. An old woman sat on a bare mattress. She did not look up at them. Her thinning gray hair was tied back in a bun and her spotted hands trembled on her knees. She wore a long black dress. A black cameo on a slender silver chain hung from her neck. Aside from the mattress, a small table holding a hot plate was the only furniture. A pyramid of canned food sat against one wall, next to several plastic jugs of water. A short aluminum stepladder leaned against another wall.

"Is this your house, grandmother?" asked Surkhov. The woman did not respond.

"She's not talking," said Nikolai. He crouched down, grabbed the edge of the door frame, and lowered himself into the bunker. The woman did not look at him. Nikolai patted her for weapons, gently but thoroughly. He kicked over the pyramid of cans, checked under the hot plate, knocked on the walls to make sure they were not hollow.

"All right," he said. "Let's get her out of here. Come on, grandmother, up." The woman did not move. He grabbed her by the elbows and hoisted her into the air. Surkhov and Leksi reached down; each grabbed an arm and pulled her up. Nikolai climbed out of the bunker; all three men stood around the old woman and stared at her.

She looked back at them now, her amber eyes wide and furious. Leksi recognized her. She had been the young woman in the photograph.

"This is *my* house," she said in Russian, looking at each man in turn. She had a thick Chechen accent but she articulated each word clearly. "*My* house," she repeated.

"Yes, grandmother," said Nikolai. "We are your guests. Please, come upstairs with us."

She seemed bewildered by his polite tone, and let them lead her to the staircase. When Nikolai retrieved his wine bottles she pointed at them. "That is not your wine," she said. "Put it back."

He nodded and handed the bottles to Leksi. "Put them back where we got them."

When Leksi came upstairs he heard them talking in the library. He went there and found the old woman sitting on the sofa, rubbing her black cameo between her fingers. It was hard to believe that she had once been beautiful. The loose skin of her face and throat was furrowed and mottled. At her feet was the piled silver, glittering in the sunlight that poured through the windows.

Surkhov had pulled a leather-bound book from a shelf and was skimming through it, licking his fingertips each time he turned a page. Nikolai sat on the floor across from the woman, his back against the marble side of the fireplace. He held an iron poker in his hands. The silver-framed photograph still rested on the mantle. Leksi waited in the doorway, wondering if the old woman saw her picture. He wished he had never moved it. There was something terribly shameful about forcing the beautiful young woman to witness her future. The vodka, which Leksi had drunk with such pleasure a few minutes ago, now burned in his stomach.

"Don't do that," said the old woman. The soldiers looked at her. "This," she said angrily, licking her fingertips in imitation of Surkhov. "You will ruin the paper."

Surkhov nodded, smiled at her, and returned the book to its shelf. Nikolai stood, still holding the poker, and gestured to Leksi. He ushered him out to the hallway and closed the library doors behind them. They went into the dining room. The dirty plates, littered with broken chicken bones, still sat in the middle of the table. Nikolai and Leksi looked out the high window at the snow-covered valley.

Nikolai sighed. "It is not a pleasant thing, but she is old. Her life from now on would be very bad. Give her back to her Allah."

Leksi turned and stared at the older soldier. "Me?"

"Yes," said Nikolai, spinning the poker in his hands. "It is very important that you do it. Have you shot anyone before?"

"No."

"Good. She will be the first. I know, Aleksandr, you don't want to kill an old woman. None of us do. But think. Being a soldier is not about killing the people you want to kill. It would be nice, wouldn't it? If we only shot the people we hated. This woman, she is the enemy. She has bred enemies, and they will breed more. She buys them guns and food, and they slaughter our men. These people," he said, pointing at the ceiling above them, "they are the richest people in the region. They have funded the terrorists for years. They sleep in their silk sheets while the mines they paid for blow our friends' legs off. They drink their French wine while their bombs explode in our taverns, our restaurants. She is not innocent."

Leksi started to say something but Nikolai shook his head and lightly tapped Leksi's arm with the poker. "No, this is not something to discuss. This is not a conversation we are having. Take her outside and shoot her. Not on the property, I don't want the blackbirds coming here. Bad luck. Take her into the woods and shoot her and bury her."

They were quiet for a minute, watching the distant lake, watching the wind-blown snow swirl above the pine trees. Finally Leksi asked, "How old were you? The first time?"

"The first time I shot someone? Nineteen."

Leksi nodded and opened his mouth, but forgot what he had meant to say. Finally he asked, "Who were we fighting back then?"

Nikolai laughed. "How old do you think I am, Aleksandr?"

"Thirty-five?"

Nikolai smiled broadly, flashing his crooked teeth. "Twenty-four." He pressed the poker's tip against the base of Leksi's skull. "Here's where the bullet goes."

When they brought her into the house's mudroom and told her to put on her boots, she stared up at the soldiers, her hands trembling by her side. For a long while she stared at them, and Leksi wondered what they would have done to her if she had still been young and beautiful. And then he wondered what they would do if she simply refused to put her boots on. How could they threaten her? Would they shoot her there and carry her into the woods? He hoped that would happen, that she would fall down on the floor and refuse to rise, and Nikolai or Surkhov would be forced to shoot her. But she didn't, she simply stared at them and finally nodded, as though she were agreeing with something. She sat on the bench by the door and pulled on a pair of fur-lined boots. They seemed too big for her, as if she were a child trying on her mother's boots. She tucked the black cameo on its silver chain inside her dress and pulled on a fur coat made from the dark pelts of some animal Leksi could not name.

A heavy snow shovel hung on the wall, blade up, between two pegs. Surkhov took it down and handed it to the old woman. She grabbed it from him and headed out the door without a word. Leksi looked at his two comrades, hoping they would tell him it was all a prank, that nobody would be killed today. Nikolai would punch him on the arm and tell him he was a fool, and everyone would laugh; the old woman would pop back into the mudroom, laughing— she was in on it, it was a great practical joke. But Surkhov and Nikolai stood there, still barefoot, their faces expressionless, waiting for him to leave. Leksi walked out the door and closed it behind him.

The old woman dragged the shovel behind her as if it were a sled. The snow came up to her knees; she had to stop every minute for a rest. She would take several deep breaths and then continue walking, the shovel's blade bouncing over her footprints. She never looked back. Leksi followed three paces behind, rifle in hand. He followed her out the back gate and told her to turn right, and she did, and they circled to the front of the property and then down the hill.

Every time she stopped, Leksi would stare at the back of her head, at the gray bun held in place with hairpins, with growing fury. Why had she stayed behind in the house when everyone else had left? She hadn't been abandoned. Somebody had helped her down into the subcellar; somebody had dragged the billiards table over the trapdoor. It must have been pure greed, a refusal to give up the trinkets she had accumulated over the years, her crystal and her silver and her French wine and the rest. The others must have urged her to come with them. She was stubborn; she would not listen to reason; she was a fanatic.

"Why did you stay here?" he finally asked. He had not meant to speak with her; the question came out unbidden.

She turned slowly and stared up at him. "It is *my* house," she said. "Why did *you* come?"

"All right," he said, pointing the rifle at her. "Keep moving." He did not expect her to obey him, but she did. They were walking down to where the three soldiers had hidden their packs, about a kilometer away; Leksi would carry them back up and save Surkhov and Nikolai a trip. It would be hard going, carrying three packs uphill, but he thought it would be much better than this walk downhill. Because Leksi did not doubt for a second that what he was doing now was a sin. This was evil. He was going to shoot an old woman in the back of the head, watch her pitch forward into the snow, and then bury her. There was nothing to call it but evil.

He had long suspected that he was a coward. His older brother would tell him ghost stories in the night and Leksi would lie awake for hours after. Sometimes he would shake his brother awake and make him promise that the stories were lies. And his brother would say, "Of course, Leksi, of course, just stories," and hold his hand until he fell asleep.

"They chose you because you are the baby," said the old woman, and Leksi squinted to look at her through the glare of sunlight reflecting off the snow.

"Just walk."

She hadn't stopped walking, though, and she continued talking. "It's a test for you. They want to see how strong you are."

Leksi said nothing, just watched the shovel skip down the slope.

"They don't care if I live or die, you must know this. Why should they? Look at me, what can I do? They are testing you. Can't you see this? You are smart, you must see."

"No," said Leksi. "I'm not smart."

"Neither am I. But I've lived with men for seventy years. I understand men. Right now, they are watching us."

Leksi looked up the hill, to the mansion at its crown. He suspected she was right, that Nikolai was watching them through his binoculars. When he turned back the old woman was still trudging forward, her breath rising in vapors above her head. She seemed to be moving more easily now, and Leksi decided that she was in better shape than she had pretended, that her constant pauses were not caused by exhaustion but rather by an attempt to delay what was going to happen. He understood that. He, too, dreaded the ending.

"But at the bottom of the hill," the old woman said, "they won't be able to see us. That is where you can let me go. They expect you to. If they wanted you to kill me, would they have let you go by yourself? Why would they want you to take me so far away, out of sight?"

"They don't want the blackbirds to come near the house," said Leksi, and when he said it he realized it made no sense. He was going to bury her. Why would the black-birds come? Besides, Nikolai was not a superstitious man.

The old woman laughed, the gray bun at the back of her head bobbing up and down. "The blackbirds? That is what they said, the blackbirds? This is only a joke, boy. Wake up! They are playing with you."

"Grandmother," said Leksi, but he couldn't think of anything else to say. She stopped and turned again to stare at him, smiling. She still had all her teeth but they were yellowed and long. The sight of the teeth infuriated Leksi; he rushed down the hill and jabbed the muzzle of his rifle into her stomach.

"Keep walking!" he yelled at her.

When they were halfway from the bottom she asked, "How will my grandchildren know where to come?"

"What?"

"When they come to visit my grave, how will they know where it is?"

"I'll put a marker up," said Leksi. He had no intention of putting a marker up, but how else could he answer such a question? His fury had already disappeared and he was disgusted with himself for letting it go so quickly.

"Now?" she asked. "What's the good of that? When the snow melts the marker will fall."

"I'll put one up in the spring." He knew this must sound as ridiculous to the woman as it did to him, but if she thought his assurance was preposterous she gave no sign.

"With my name on it," said the old woman. "Tamara Shashani." She spelled both names and then made Leksi repeat it.

Leksi had known a girl named Tamara in school. She was fat and freckled and laughed like a braying donkey. It seemed impossible that this woman and that girl could share a name.

"And my hometown," added the old woman. "Put that on the marker, too. Djovkhar Ghaala."

"You mean Grozny."

"No, I mean Djovkhar Ghaala. I was born there, I know the name."

Leksi shrugged. He had been in the city four days ago. The Chechens called it Djovkhar Ghaala; the Russians called it Grozny. The Chechens had been driven out; the city was Grozny.

"Tell me," said the old woman. "Do you remember everything?"

"Tamara Shashani. From Djovkhar Ghaala."

Leksi followed behind her, eyes half closed. The sunlight's glare was making his head hurt. The shovel's blade carved a little trail in the snow and he tried to step only in that trail, not sure why it mattered but anxious not to stray outside the parallel lines.

"Do you know the story of when the Devil came to Orekhovo?"

"No," said Leksi.

"It's an old story. My grandfather told me when I was a girl. The Devil was lonely. He wanted a bride. He wanted company for his palace in Hell."

From the manner in which the old woman spoke, Leksi knew that she had told the tale many times before. She never paused for thought; she never needed to search for the right phrase. He pictured her sitting on the edge of her children's beds, and then her grandchildren, reciting their favorite adventure, the story of when the Devil came to Orekhovo.

"So he gathered his minions, all the demons that wandered through the world spreading discord. He brought them into the meeting hall and asked them to name the most beautiful woman alive. Naturally, the demons argued for hours. They never agreed on anything. Brawls broke out as each championed his favorite. The Devil watched, bored, tapping his long nails on the armrest of his throne. But finally, after tails had been chopped off and horns broken, one of the senior demons stepped forward and announced that they had chosen. Her name was Aminah, and she lived in the town of Orekhovo."

Leksi smiled. He had heard this story before, except that in the version he knew the beautiful woman lived in Petrikov and was called Tatyana. He tried to remember who had told him the story.

"So the Devil mounted his great black horse and rode to Orekhovo. It was a winter's day. When he got there he asked a child he met on the road where the beautiful Aminah lived. After the boy gave directions, the Devil grabbed him by the collar, slashed his throat, plucked out his blue eyes, and pocketed them. He threw the boy's body into a ditch and continued on his way."

Leksi remembered that part. Don't talk to strangers, that was the lesson. He looked uphill and saw that the mansion was no longer in view. If he did let the woman go, who would know? But she would seek out her people and tell them that three Russians had occupied her house. Perhaps there would be a counterattack, and Leksi would die knowing that he had orchestrated his own doom.

"When the Devil found Aminah's house, he hitched his horse to a post and knocked on the door. A fat woman opened it and invited him inside, for the Devil was dressed like a gentleman. She stirred a pot of stew that bubbled above the fire. 'What are you seeking, traveler?' she asked. 'I seek Aminah,' said the Devil. 'I have heard of her great beauty.'

"'She is my daughter,' said the fat woman. 'Have you come to ask her hand? Many suitors wait upon her, yet she has refused all. What do you have to offer?' The Devil pulled out a purse and undid the strings. He dumped a pile of gold coins onto the floor. 'Ay,' said Aminah's mother. 'At last I am wealthy! Go to her, she is at the lake. Tell her I approve of your suit.' When the woman sat on the floor and began counting her gold, the Devil crept up behind her and slashed her throat. He plucked out her blue eyes and pocketed them. He ladled himself a bowl of soup and ate until he was full, and then he left the house and mounted his black horse."

Never invite a stranger into the house, thought Leksi. *And never count your gold while someone stands behind you.* The more he considered it, the more he doubted that the Chechens would attack the house. Why should they? Any direct assault would result in a quick reprisal, so they couldn't keep the house if they did take it. There was too much risk involved for such a cheap reward: three Russian soldiers without vehicles or artillery.

"The Devil came to the lake and saw his prize. His demons had done well: Aminah was more beautiful than all the angels the Devil had once consorted with. The lake was frozen over and Aminah sat on the ice pulling on her skates. 'Good afternoon,' said the Devil. 'May I join you?' Aminah nodded, for the Devil was handsome and dressed like a gentleman. He walked back to his horse, opened his saddlebag, and pulled out a pair of skates, shined black leather, the blades gleaming and sharp."

When Leksi listened to the story as a child he asked how the Devil had known to bring his skates. Whom had he asked? His mother! He could picture it now; she was sitting at the edge of the bed while Leksi and his brother fought for the blanket. He asked how the Devil knew to bring the skates, and his brother groaned and called him an idiot. But his mother nodded as if it were a very wise question. He could have pulled anything from that saddlebag, she told Leksi. It was the Devil's saddlebag. If he had needed a trombone he would have found it there.

"Aminah watched the Devil carefully," continued the old woman. "She watched him sit down on the ice and pull off his boots, and she saw his cloven hooves. She looked away quickly, so he would not catch her spying. They skated out to the center of the lake. The Devil was fantastic. He carved perfect figure eights, he pirouetted gracefully, he sped across the ice and jumped and spun through the air. When he returned to Aminah's side he pulled a necklace of great blue diamonds from his pocket. 'This is yours,' he told her, placing it around her neck and fastening the clasp. 'Now come with me to my country, where I am king. I will make you my queen, and you will never work again. All of my people will bow before you, they will scatter rose petals before your feet wherever you walk. Anything that you desire will be yours, except this—when you take my hand and come to my land, you can never go home.'"

Leksi and the old woman were walking in a narrow gully now, over slippery stones. Snow melted in the sun and streamed weakly over the rocks. It was treacherous footing but the old woman seemed to handle it with ease; she was agile as a goat.

"Aminah smiled and nodded and pretended that she was thinking about it. She skated away at a leisurely pace, and the Devil followed behind her. She skated and skated and the Devil pursued her, licking his sharp teeth with his forked tongue. But he did not know this lake, and Aminah did. She knew it in summer, when the fish leapt up to catch flies and moths, and she knew it in winter, when the ice was thick in some places and thin in others. She was a slender girl and the Devil was a big man; she hoped he was as heavy as he looked."

Listening to the story now and remembering how it ended, Leksi felt sorry for the Devil. Was the Devil really so terrible? True, he had murdered the innocent boy on the road. But Aminah's mother had deserved it for selling her daughter so cheaply. And what the Devil desired—who could blame him? He wanted to marry the world's most beautiful woman. What was wrong with that?

Just let the old woman go, thought Leksi. *Just let her walk away. The odds are good she'll never make it to shelter before nightfall. I'd be giving her a chance, though, and what more could she ask of me? That would be mercy, to let her walk.* But then Leksi thought of Nikolai. Nikolai would ask how it had gone and Leksi would be forced to lie. Except he could not imagine lying to Nikolai. Leksi never lied; he wasn't good at it. He pictured Nikolai's face and Leksi knew he could never trick the older soldier. And he could not go back to the mansion and admit that he had disobeyed a direct order.

"Finally, Aminah could hear the ice beginning to crack beneath her skates. The Devil was right behind her, reaching out for her, his fingernails inches from her hair. Just as he was about to grab her the ice beneath him gave way and he fell with a cry into the freezing water. 'Aminah!' he yelled. 'Help me!' But Aminah skated away as fast as she could. She reached the edge of the lake, took off her skates, put her boots on, and left the town, never to return."

She kept the diamonds, thought Leksi. Maybe they turned back into eyeballs. He remembered being disappointed, as a child, that the Devil could be so easily trapped. Why couldn't he just breathe fire and melt all the ice?

The runoff from the melting snow had created a shallow

stream in the gully that rose halfway up Leksi's boots. He worried about falling and twisting an ankle—how could he climb back uphill with a sprained ankle? Still, it was less exhausting than trudging through the wet snow. He remembered waking early on summer mornings with his brother, searching under rocks in the woods for slugs and beetles, pinning them on fish hooks, wading into the polluted river, and casting their lines. They never caught anything, the waste from the nearby paper plant had poisoned the fish, but Leksi's brother would tell jokes all morning, and then they would lie on the riverbank and talk about hockey stars who played in America and actresses on television.

"What happened next?" Leksi asked the old woman. He couldn't remember if there had been an epilogue.

The old woman stopped walking and looked skyward. A blackbird squawked on a pine branch above them. "Nobody knows. Some say the Devil swam under the ice and back to Hell. They say that every winter he returns, looking for Aminah, calling out her name."

The Devil really loved her, decided Leksi. He always rooted for the bad men in fairy tales and movies, not because he admired them but because they had no chance. The bad men were the true underdogs. They never won.

Leksi and the old woman stood motionless, their breath curling about their heads like genies. Leksi heard growls and turned to see where they came from. In the shadow of a great boulder twenty meters away three dogs feasted on a deer's still-steaming intestines. Each dog seemed to sense Leksi's gaze at the same time; they lifted their heads and stared at him until he averted his eyes.

Leksi looked uphill and realized they were no longer standing on a hill. Panicked, he searched for footprints, but there were none on the gully's wet stones. How long had they walked in the stream? Where had they entered it? All the tall pine trees looked identical to him; they stretched on for as far as the eye could see. Nothing but trees and melting snow littered with broken twigs and pine cones. The dogs watched him and the blackbird squawked and Leksi knew he was lost. He strapped the rifle over his shoulder, pulled off a glove, and began fumbling in his parka's pockets for his compass. The old woman turned to look at him and Leksi tried to remain as calm as possible. He pulled out the compass and peered at it. He determined true north and then closed his eyes. It didn't matter. He had no idea in which direction the house lay. Knowing true north meant nothing.

The old woman smiled at him when he opened his eyes. "It's an old story. Of course," she said, letting the shovel's long handle fall onto the wet rocks, "some people say there is no Devil."

Leksi sat on the bank of the now bustling stream. If he could organize his thoughts, he believed, everything would be all right. Unless he organized his thoughts he would die here in the nighttime, the snow would drift over his body and only the dogs would know where to find him. He stared at his lap to rest his eyes from the glare. Feeling hot, he laid his rifle on the ground and shrugged out of his parka. The sun was heavy on his face and he could feel his pale cheeks beginning to burn. He listened to the countryside around him: the dogs snarling at the blackbirds; the blackbirds flapping their wings; the running water; the pine branches creaking. He sat in the snow and listened to the countryside around him.

When he finally raised his head the old woman was gone, as he knew she would be. Her shovel was half-submerged in the stream, its handle wedged between two rocks, its metal blade glinting below water like the scale of a giant fish. The sun rose higher in the sky and the snow began to fall from the trees. Leksi stood, pulled on his parka, picked up his rifle and started wading upstream, searching for the spot where his footprints ended.

He hadn't gone far when he heard a whistle. He crouched down, fumbling with the rifle, trying to get his gloved finger inside the trigger guard.

"Relax, Leksi." It was Nikolai, squatting by the trunk of a dead pine. The tree's bare branches reached out for the blue sky. Nikolai tapped off the ash of the cigar he was smoking. He was in shirtsleeves, his rifle strapped over one shoulder.

"You followed me," said Leksi.

The older soldier did not reply. He squinted into the distance beyond Leksi and Leksi followed his gaze, but there was nothing to be seen. A moment later a single gunshot echoed across the valley floor. Nikolai nodded, stood up and stretched his arms above his head. He picked a bit of loose tobacco off his tongue and then tramped through the snow to the stream. Leksi, still in his crouch, watched him come closer.

Nikolai pulled the shovel out of the water and held it up. "Come over here, my friend."

Leksi heard singing behind him. He wheeled about to find Surkhov marching toward them, singing "Here Comes the Sun," twirling a silver chain with a black cameo on its end.

Nikolai smiled and held out the shovel. "Come here, Aleksandr. You have work to do."

karen e. bender

ANYTHING FOR MONEY

Each Monday at eleven o'clock, Lenny Weiss performed his favorite duty as executive producer of his hit game show, *Anything for Money*; he selected the contestants for that week's show. He walked briskly across the stage set, the studio lights so white and glaring as to make the stage resemble the surface of the moon. In his silk navy suit, the man appeared to be a lone figure on the set, for his staff knew not to speak to him, or even look at him. He had become the king of syndicated game shows for his skill in finding the people that would do anything for money, people that viewers would both envy and despise.

The assistants were in the holding room with the prospective contestants, telling them the rules: No one was allowed to touch Mr. Weiss. Mr. Weiss required a five-foot perimeter around his person. No one was allowed to call him by his first name. No one was to be drinking Pepsi, as the taste offended Mr. Weiss. Gold jewelry reminded him of his former wife, so anyone wearing such jewelry was advised to take it off.

He stood by the door for a moment before he walked in, imagining how the losers would walk, dazed, to their cars, looking up at the arid sky. They would try to figure out what they had done wrong, they would look at their hands and wonder.

Then he walked in, and they screamed.

He loved to hear them scream. They had tried to dress up, garishly; polyester suits in pale colors, iridescent plastic shoes. The air reeked of greed and strong perfume. Some of the women had had their hair done especially for the occasion, and their hair shimmered oddly, hardened with spray.

"Pick me!"

"We love you, man!"

"We've been watching since the beginning!"

A woman in a T-shirt that said *Dallas Cowboys Forever* lunged forward, grabbed his arm, and yelled, "Lenny!"

"Hands OFF Mr. Weiss!" shouted the security guard.

There was always one who was a lesson for the others. The door slammed and the woman was marched back to her life. They all listened to her heels clicking against the floor, first sharp and declarative, then fading. The others stood, solemnly, in the silence, as though listening to the future sound of their own deaths.

They were all on this earth briefly; for Lenny, that meant he had the burning desire to be the king of syndicated game shows, one of the ten most powerful men in Hollywood. He did not know what the others' lives meant to them, but just that they wanted what he had.

Now he needed to choose his contestants. They would be the ones with particularly acute expressions of desire and sadness; they would also have to photograph well under the brilliant lights.

"All right!" He clapped his hands. "You want to be rich?

You want other people to kiss your ass? Well, listen. You're going to have to work for it. Everyone!" He knew to change his requests for each new group; he did not want any of them to come prepared from rumors off the street.

"Unbutton your shirts!"

He knew this one was more difficult for the women, but that was not a concern to him. Some of the people stiffened, pawed gingerly at their buttons. Others tore through their buttons and stood before him, shirts loose.

"Take off your shirts!"

He lost a few more with this request. Others removed their shirts as though they had been moving through their lives just waiting for such an order. They stood before him, men and women, in bras and bare chests, some pale, some dark, some thin-shouldered, some fat.

"Repeat after me. Say: I am an idiot."

He heard the chorus of voices start, softly.

"Louder! Again!"

Their seats had numbers on the bottoms; he knew immediately whom he would call back. He would call Number 25, the woman with the lustrous blonde hair, and number 6, the man with the compulsive smile. Lenny clapped his hands.

"Thank you. My assistant will contact those who we have chosen." Lenny turned, almost running down the hallway. He walked around for fifteen minutes before he could get back to work.

He had grown up in Chicago in the 1930s, the only child of parents who had married impulsively and then learned that neither understood the other; Lenny dangled, suspended, in the harsh, disappointed sounds of the house. His father died suddenly when Lenny was eight. Lenny's mother moved them to Los Angeles and got a job as a secretary at one of the movie studios. The boy was shocked by the clarity of the desert light, the way it made everything—the lawns, flowers, cars—appear stark and inevitable. His mother was the only person he knew in the world, and at first, when he walked to school he was crazy with fear that she had also disappeared. He pretended he was collecting clouds to make a wall around her, and when the sky was cloudless he pretended he was sick. Then his mother brought him to the place where she worked. He sat on the floor watching her, and then everything else going on around her, too.

When he graduated high school, he became an errand boy on a soap opera, then a writer. He enjoyed making bad things happen to other people: troubled marriages, sudden illnesses, kidnappings. He married a woman who was impressed by his job and descriptions of various actresses on the set. They had a child, a girl. Then one day the producers gathered all the employees into a windowless conference room. "There's no more show," they said.

It was a bad time for hiring in any field, and he and his wife had little savings. He looked for work for six months without luck, setting his sights lower and lower, but already there was an odor of desperation on him. One night, his daughter was screaming with pain from an ear infection, but he was afraid to go to a doctor for what it could cost. The child's pain so horrified him that he bolted out of the house.

He did not stop running for several blocks. Strangers walked down the street, their wallets bulging with money he wanted. The money was so close to him, he could almost smell its green dusky smell. His teeth were clenched very tightly, and his jaw hurt. Suddenly, he had an idea: he could rob a liquor store. He had thought about how to do this when he wrote his soap operas. The simplicity of this idea made him stop in astonishment. He could wear a stocking over his face and stuff a bottle in his jacket pocket as a gun.

There was a liquor store a few blocks away, and he stumbled toward it. Lenny stood outside the liquor store for a long time, the clear red letters announcing *LIQUOR* into the night air. He sobbed softly. His tongue tasted like a dry, bitter leaf. The other customers entered the store, noble in their morality and their innocence. He had become this: a man who would do anything for money.

Later, he would tell people that this was the moment he became God—for he had saved himself. *Anything for Money* could be a show in which contestants could do terrible, absurd things to receive vast amounts of money.

The next day, he waited for six hours in the waiting room of his former employer. When Lenny saw the head of programming, Mr. Seymour Lawrence, come out, he hurtled toward him, thrusting out a proposal. "Read this," he told Mr. Lawrence. Lenny did not know why the man decided to listen to him, though he understood, in an honest part of himself, that it was simply a grand moment of luck. Later, he chose to describe this as a sign of his own inherent glory. Mr. Lawrence took the thin sheet of paper, folded it in half, and stuck it in the pocket of his blazer. Lenny watched him walk off. A month later, Mr. Lawrence bought the idea for the show.

Now he was 65, the show's executive producer, and his limousine took him from the studios to his home in the hills above Los Angeles. As a young man, he had never quite believed the success of *Anything for Money,* the way his longing formed itself into homes, boats, cars. He used to wake up, his heart pounding as though he was running an immense race. His daughter and wife were mere shadows to him, for he needed to get to the studio with an almost physical craving. He was there from eight in the morning to ten at night.

Thirty years ago, his wife, Lola, left. He blamed his wife's leaving on her excessive demands; many of his colleagues' wives had left them, too. The few times he had seen her since she left him, she looked entirely unfamiliar to him. It seemed that he had not been married to her but a lookalike who resembled her. She had come up to him at a party and said, softly, "You never knew anything true about me." When she said this, he felt a deep wound, as though his honest attempts at goodness had been misunderstood. All his attempts at romance had been deeply clichéd—he bought her diamonds, midnight cruises, silk gowns. "All I wanted," she said, "was a poem written about my eyes." He stood before her like a little boy. Did this mean they had not loved each other?

His memories of his daughter were glazed with exhaustion. Charlene stood, naked, in the bathtub, water streaming down her tiny body, a pale angel absolutely convinced of her own glory; he could not believe she had come from him. Sometimes Charlene ran to him and clung to him with such fierceness, he felt a crumbling inside him. He was afraid she would see in his eyes the weakness of a lame dog and would laugh at him. She was a toddler running, stiff-legged across the lawn, running as though the lawn were clouds and would tear apart if she stepped too hard; then she was six and running, legs outstretched, like a small antelope, in gaudy, colorful clothes; then his wife left and he could not see her running. She was gone.

Charlene believed that he had kicked them out of the house. That was what Lola had told her. He tried to explain to her that that was not the truth, but she said, bluntly, "Mom said she asked you thirty times to stay at home for my five-year-old birthday. And you did not." He did not remember any of these requests. He had thought he belonged to a family, but his wife and daughter had become strangers who could not be trusted.

Charlene had decided that he did not want her; but he had decided that she did not want him. She called him only to request money, which he always gave her. He once heard her on a talk show denigrating him with a fictional story: "My father was so self-centered he had a special mirror only he could look into. If anyone else did, he'd tell us it would crack." Much audience laughter. Lenny would not hear from her for months, and then get a long letter, dissecting injuries done during her childhood; she had been arguing with him in her mind the whole time. Then, when he called her to discuss the letter, she would hang up on him.

The calls came more frequently immediately after Lola's death. His ex-wife had died in a car accident fifteen years ago; she was gone and his remnant feelings for her were interrupted—he still had not divined whether they had loved each other or not. For a short time after the accident, Charlene called him, frequently; she seemed to hope that, as her only living parent, he would have the capacity to read her thoughts. He sensed then how remote she felt from other people. When he could not read her thoughts, she reacted with anger so forceful it was as though he had told her he hated her.

Over the last fifteen years, he heard about her mostly through gossip items in the paper: *Charlene Weiss sub eatery sinks. Charlene Weiss briefly hospitalized for alcohol abuse. Charlene Weiss has fling with Vance Harley, hunky new sitcom star. Charlene Weiss has daughter, Aurora Persephone Diamantina Weiss.* A quote from the happy new mom: "I have reached a pinnacle of joy."

She did tell him about Aurora. She had become pregnant from one of her many suitors and decided to have a child on her own. He received an elaborate birth announcement, a silver card with a photo of the baby girl swathed in white robes like a tiny emperor. The inscription below the picture said *Aurora: A Child Who Will Be Loved.*

For thirty years, he lived alone in his mansion on top of the Santa Monica Mountains; he had told his architect that he wanted to feel as though he could touch the entire city. He could see all the way to the Pacific Ocean, the expanse of ocean like black glass, all the way to the luminous blocks of downtown, to the cars pouring, twin rivers of red and white lights moving east and west, north and south. His loneliness had buried itself deep within him, and he experienced it as the desire to be in the seat of every car. The architect had set his living room at the edge of a hill, so that when Lenny looked out his twenty-foot-high glass windows, he almost believed he could fall into the trembling party of lights. He stood there many nights, his mouth hot with longing so primitive he could not name it; he was aware only of his quiet desire to thrust himself into the dark air.

The call came when he was having a limo meeting with the producer of the talk show *Confess!* His maid's voice floated over the speakers.

"Mister Weiss," Rosita said. "Come home."

"Why?" he said to the air.

"A child is here."

"What child?"

"Aurora."

Everything inside him went still.

When they reached his house, Lenny stepped out of his

limo. His home was made of pale marble, and clear white wavelets from the swimming pool shimmered on its empty walls. Black palms, bathed in blue light, swayed in the warm wind. The bushes in his gardens had been trimmed to the shapes of elephants, giraffes, bears, and they made a silent, regal procession through the darkness. He stood for a moment, in the quiet that he had made, before he went inside.

The girl stood at the top of the stairs. He would not have been aware of her but for the ferocity with which she stood there, as though she had dreamed herself in this position for years. She was gripping the railing, staring at him. Her face was dim, but he could see her fingernails holding the rail— they were an absurdly bright gold. She ran down the stairs so fast he thought she might fall. She was standing in front of him, breathing hard.

"Grandfather, you're real," she said.

His legs felt insubstantial as water; he stepped back. He looked at Aurora. He believed she would now be about twelve years old. Her face had the hard, polite quality of someone who had been scheming quietly and fervently for a long time. Her auburn hair reached halfway down her back. She had Lola's eyebrows, two arched *U*s that gave her an alert, surprised expression. She had Charlene's dark blue eyes. They were the color of steel, and moved around restlessly, but had a hard gaze when they settled on something. He knew because they were also his eyes.

"Hello," he said. He offered his hand. She shook it vigorously. He still had on the phone headset he usually wore so as not to miss any calls.

"What are you doing here?" he asked.

"I was sent."

"By who?"

"My mother."

She handed him a letter. The letterhead said:

> BUENA VISTA REHABILITATION CLINIC
> *Your Secrets Are Ours*

Dad—
I am here for the next three months.
Take care of Aurora.
She likes chocolate.
I'm so tired.

Charlene's signature resembled a tiny knot.

The letter's tone was so polite he knew that someone had been watching her as she wrote it.

"Is this where your mother is?"

She nodded and moved toward the living room window. "I read about this!" she exclaimed. "Your view. In a magazine about houses. It's even bigger in real life."

He wanted to stop her. She was standing against the window, pressing her fingers against the glass. He saw her make a breath on the glass, a pale oval, and the intimacy of the action made him want to walk away.

Two large suitcases sat in the foyer. He gestured toward the suitcases. "Carlos can take these up for you."

Aurora darted up to one and grabbed the handle. "No!" she said. "I want to do this one myself."

The bag was not actually a suitcase, but a large, green canvas sack. It bulged with odd, unidentifiable objects.

"You can't carry that yourself," he said.

She looked pleased, as if she'd predicted he would say this. "Then you help me."

He did not remember the last time he'd carried anyone's bag. "Rosita, call Carlos," said Lenny.

"No," Aurora said. She stood up straighter. "I want you."

Rosita brought him a dolly and he pushed the bag into the elevator. The girl walked beside him, fiercely gripping the bag handle. The elevator rose to the second floor and the three of them walked and pushed down the hallway, Aurora gripping the handle of the bag the whole time with a nonplussed expression, as though she were walking a dog. When they got to a guest room, he stopped.

"You can stay here," he said.

She walked in, dragged the bag into a corner. "Thank you," she said.

"Good night," he said.

Her eyelids twitched. "I'm not sleepy yet."

He began to back away. "Hey, look," he said. "I'm sorry. You'll have to entertain yourself. You know." He lifted his hands helplessly. "Sweeps. Nielsens. I don't have time for baby-sitting. Rosita," he said. "Aurora will be visiting us. Please bring her a hot chocolate."

Aurora stepped back and looked down. She wrapped her arms around herself, tightly. She looked as if she had fallen from the sky.

He did not know what to say to her.

"Rosita, add some whipped cream to her chocolate," he said.

Lenny woke with a shudder in the middle of the night. He sat, his heart pounding, in his bed. Then he got up and went to the kitchen. He sat in the blue midnight and drank a glass of milk.

He heard footsteps—peering out of the doorway, he saw

Aurora in the foyer. The girl was walking barefoot, in her long johns, through the enormous room. She made almost no sound and moved through the darkness in a careful, fevered way. She did not merely look at the grand hallways, but went up to the statues, lamps, and touched them tenderly, getting to know them. She moved urgently, disappearing into room after room.

He fled back to his room. He felt shaken, furious, wondering if he should wake Rosita, call the police. The girl had simply been walking through his house. Now it seemed that the clock was melting, the curtain could burst into flames. He lay awake for a long time, unable to get to sleep.

He woke up at six, far earlier than he believed the girl would wake up. After he made his way down the stairs, he realized that his headset was gone. He had left it on the kitchen table after his midnight glass of milk, and its absence made him feel broken off from the news of the day. He rang Rosita and asked her to look for it. He would give himself twenty-five minutes for breakfast. About ten minutes into his breakfast, Aurora walked in. She stood in the doorway; she looked as if she was trying to decide whether she should bow or curtsy or just barrel ahead.

"Hello, grandfather," she said.

"Hello."

Her face was heavy with exhaustion, but hopeful. She sat at the other end of the table. Before she did this, she moved a large crystal urn of flowers to the floor.

"What are you doing?" he asked.

"I want to be able to see you when we talk."

He eyed her and ate a forkful of eggs. Rosita placed a croissant before her. Aurora was staring at him, drumming her fingers on the tablecloth.

"I have a question."

"Yes?"

"How does it feel to be syndicated in forty-three countries?"

"Forty-four. Somalia just signed on."

"Forty-four."

"Very good."

"Your first episode of *Anything For Money* had the biggest television audience ever."

"That is true."

"How did you get Ringo Starr to do a guest spot?"

"He asked to come on." He looked up. "Is this an interview?"

"I've read one hundred twenty-seven articles about you. In all the major magazines. More on the Internet. On the authorized sites." She went through four slices of bacon. "Is it true that you only stock water in the back of the set so that contestants will get hungry and meaner?"

"No." He lifted the paper in front of his face. "Anything you need, ask Rosita."

"I would like an office."

He lowered the paper. "For what purpose?"

"The production of my feature film."

He folded the paper.

"I am currently in pre-production."

"You are twelve years old," he said.

"I know," she said, as though that was a compliment. "I have read many books on the subject. I am writing a script. If you want to know the title, I can—"

He marched out of the dining room; she followed. He walked too fast. He was not used to waiting for another person, and he could sense her trailing behind him, trying to catch up.

He pushed open two doors embossed with a gold pattern identical to the doors of Il Duomo in Florence and walked into a room that overlooked the rose gardens.

"Your office," he said.

She seemed surprised that her request had been obeyed so easily; then she walked in, hands clasped behind her back like Napoleon inspecting the troops. She walked to the window and looked outside. The morning sun fell in wide bright strips across the lawn, so that the pink and cream-colored roses gleamed like satin.

"Do you require use of a phone?"

"No," she said.

"A fax machine?"

"No, thank you."

She rose up on half-toe and then abruptly down again; later, he realized this was the gesture she used when she had more on her mind that she wanted to talk about, as though she were trying to make herself physically taller, give herself stature to ask for what she wanted.

"Your office," he said. "Now. My headset."

"Your what?"

"My headset. I need it." He smiled, trying to appear more relaxed than he felt. "Hey, I could be missing my biggest deal."

"I don't have it," she said, curtly. She sat stiffly in the office chair, like an executive calling a boardroom to order. "Now. Tell me your opinion. I want to describe the sky over a new planet that has been created by the explosion of a supernova. Should it be pink or yellow or blue?"

"Blue," he said, helplessly.

She spun the chair. "Thank you. I have to get to work."

————

Lenny drifted through his day at work with a dazed feeling. When he left, the sky was dark and furred with purple clouds. He told the chauffeur not to drive him home immediately, but around the city, and sat quietly in his seat, like a child who had been instructed to be still.

When he got home, he found the staff assembled in the living room. They were holding pieces of paper. Rosita was wearing a large pot holder on her head. Carlos was wearing a cape. He saw other staffers, whose names he did not remember: a gardener wearing a chiffon scarf around his neck, the pool man. Aurora was standing on a chair in front of them. They were listening to her.

"Rosita!" Aurora announced. "Your turn!"

"You, Count! You have cursed me!" She indicated her pot-holder hat.

"It is what the forces requested," said Carlos, in a science-fiction-y voice.

"Hello," said Lenny.

There was a stunned silence. Rosita swiped the pot holder off her head. Carlos removed his cape and bowed deeply.

"What is going on?" asked Lenny.

"We're rehearsing," said Aurora.

"For what?"

"My movie." She smiled. "They are all so good at their parts. I didn't know they all wanted to be actors!"

He had not known they had any other aspirations at all. He studied them. They looked away, trying to erase the animation in their faces.

"Thank you, all," she said. "Rehearsal's over."

He heard murmurings of thanks. Carlos took Lenny's briefcase and walked, morosely, up the stairs.

"Rosita! I want my dinner," he said.

"Can I have mine, too?"

"You haven't had dinner?"

"I wanted to wait."

"Children shouldn't eat at nine o'clock," he said. It occurred to him that he had no idea when a child should eat dinner.

"I always wait for my mom to come home."

"When is that?"

"Six. Nine. Ten. Sometimes never."

"What do you eat when it's never?"

"Whatever's around. Ritz crackers. Mints."

"Rosita, give her some dinner," he said. He went to his room.

He entered his bedroom and changed into his silk sweat suit. Then he looked for his favorite comb. It was not in his bathroom or his bedroom; nor could he locate his cologne. Standing in the middle of his bedroom, he wondered what the hell was going on. He went to the balcony and listened; she was still eating dinner. He walked down the hall to Aurora's room and opened it. The sack was on the floor; he unzipped it. It was full of little paper bags. Opening one marked *MY GRANDFATHER LENNY,* he found his headset and his comb and cologne. Lenny looked into the other bags. One was marked *MADAME FOURROUT* and inside was a postcard of Paris, a snapshot of what appeared to be a friendly baker, and a wooden spoon. Another bag said *SAM FROM OXFORD* and there was a snapshot of a college student and a silver pen engraved with the initials SNE. There were men and women of all ages and nationalities, and their toothbrushes, lipstick, office supplies. The people represented in the bags were from Paris, Milan, Athens,

Buenos Aires, everywhere that Charlene and Aurora had lived.

He zipped up the green sack and walked out of the room, embarrassed by what he had just done. Embarrassment was an unusual feeling for him, and he did not know what to do with it. Then his stomach clenched up in a way that was so acute it was like a physical pain; he had to sit down for a moment and wait for it to go away. In that bag, he saw the history of his own loneliness. He did not know why she had taken these objects from these people, but he believed he understood in some way, as well.

Lenny did not come to the table for another half hour. He was shaken and did not want her to see him. But when he came into the room, she was still there; she was waiting for him.

She was eating with painstaking slowness, carefully scraping the sauce from the poached salmon off the plate, pouring the sauce in an intricate design onto the grilled tomato. He was not used to anyone waiting for him at the dinner table. He was used to the mobs surging, gray-faced, in the holding room, staffers pacing, tense, outside his office. She was spelling her name in the sauce: AURORA.

He strode in quickly and took his seat. She had removed the urn again.

"I was a little hungry," she said.

He could see, suddenly, that she was enormously tired, that she had been kept awake, or kept herself awake, far longer than she should have.

"So," he said. "Time to get to know each other." His laughter fell into the room. Rosita brought out a tray filled with glistening pieces of sushi. "Where were you and Charlene most recently?"

"Paris. Vienna. Argentina. We had a fine time—"

"What do you do there?"

"I hang around. I'm very sociable."

"What does your mother do?"

"She is a busy woman." She shook much more salt on her dinner than was necessary.

"Doing what?"

"Many people want to know her." Her hand waved grandly in the air. "You know she started her own line of baby clothes. Le Petit Angel. She was going to work with Christian Dior—"

"Before she got thrown into rehab?"

"No!" she cried out, and her voice curved, suddenly, into a wail. They stared at each other, fearful, as though an intruder had entered the room. She looked into her lap and pressed her hands against her face. Then she glanced past him and said, quickly, "I . . . I want to talk about success. I want to be a success. I have my own theory—"

"What is that?" he asked.

She sat up straighter. "Success is about keeping your eyes open. Being organized. Having a plan. Getting to know people—"

"Success is luck," he said. "Some people are winners. Some are not."

She gazed at him with an expression that straddled opportunism and love.

"I have created the most successful show on television. One quarter of the world watches my show." His voice was husky, honeyed; he wanted to convince her of something. "The ones who win, they're lucky. They get the question they know how to answer, or they called the office the moment we needed to fill a show."

"What about the unlucky ones?" she asked.

"The losers. Some people are winners, some are not. But we need them, too. So people are grateful not to be them."

She was listening.

"We're choosing contestants tomorrow in Las Vegas for a special episode there. To be broadcast opposite the Super Bowl." He punched the air enthusiastically. "Why don't you come see how I do it."

He could not look directly at the joy in her face; it blazed, with a terrible brightness.

He took her in his private jet, the jet that he had Lockheed build for him on a special and secret assignment, a jet that was bigger and faster than anything that John Travolta or Harrison Ford owned. The plane flew with an exquisite smoothness, as though it were cutting through cream. The earth fell away, the ocean a swath of silver, Southern California suddenly tiny and silent and unreal; he looked out the window and he felt a sweet relief blow through him, as though the daughter who had shunned him had never existed, as though no one lived there at all.

He took a break from the planning session and grandly walked her around the plane, making sure the staff was watching. "This is my granddaughter Aurora—I'm telling her how to become a success. Aurora, here is the plane sauna. My staff tells me that any person of any stature must have one of these on a plane. Over here, here's the plane game room, this is the biggest pool table in the sky—"

They landed in Las Vegas and set up their camp on a full floor in the MGM Grand. On the show, the contestants were going to run naked through a large, slippery pit filled with bills, trying to grab as many as they could. However, they would be allowed to use only their teeth. Some of the bills would be ones, but some would be thousand-dollar bills. Most of the plane trip had been consumed with discussion of whether to use olive oil or Crisco for the pit. The contestants would have to look good naked, be good at sliding on curved surfaces, and have large mouths. Hundreds of people showed up and were funneled to a conference room, where they were instructed to wait until Lenny arrived. He told Aurora to sit in the room with the contestants so that she could hear his staff prepare them.

The group looked like they'd been up late for too many nights—their eyes were rimmed violet, their hair desert-burned. They had been around the prospect of instant luck for too long, and they looked worn but grimly entitled.

Lenny walked in. "All right!" he shouted. "You want to do Anything for Money? Show me!" Their hungry eyes were set on him. "You, what's your name?"

"Lily Valentine."

"What are you worth, Lily Valentine?" He pulled a wad of bills from his pocket. "Five dollars? Ten? A hundred?" He flicked the bill against her nose. "A thousand?" He let the bill fall to the floor. Everyone eyed it.

"You'll be worth two of those if you can sing for me."

Lily's face flushed. "Sing?" she asked. She was in her forties, with pink-blonde hair.

"'The Star-Spangled Banner.' Praise your great country."

She took a breath and released it. "O—ooh, say can you see—"

"I can't hear you, Lily."

"By the dawn's early light." She had closed her eyes.

"Stop!" he said. An aide scooped the thousand-dollar bill off the floor.

"You call that singing?"

Lily began to cry.

"Are you winners or losers?" Lenny shouted at the group. "What are you worth? Just a few bucks?" He listened to his voice boom. "Bye, Lily, go home—"

There was a shuffling behind him. Aurora was standing up, hands balled into fists.

"STOP it!" Aurora yelled at him, and ran out of the room.

Everyone was still; Lenny burst through the door. She was walking with stiff steps down the hotel hallway.

"Stop!" he yelled. "Why did you do that?"

She spun around. "Why were you such a jerk to her?"

"Hey," he said. "This is how I choose."

She backed away, her face new and hard with fury. Fear flashed, brightly, inside him.

"What can I say?" he said, walking toward her. He held up his hands. "This is what I do."

She turned and began to run from him.

"Wait," he said.

He did not know where that word came from. He did not know why he wanted her to stop. He simply wanted to know something.

"Aurora. Please stop," he said.

He remembered how, as a toddler, Charlene would run around the garden, kissing the flowers, the grass, the air. He remembered how she would run up to him and kiss him, her mouth wide open, as though trying to swallow his entire cheek.

"Aurora. Why did your mother send you to me?"

Aurora stopped. Her voice was hoarse. "I didn't have anywhere else to go."

He stood, dizzy, watching her run from him; then he told his staff to take over for the afternoon. He walked through the hotel, past the slot machines, where the sounds of people hoping to change their lives were as loud as a thousand bees; he continued through the cocktail lounge, the cigarette smoke a silver fog, then through the numerous gift shops, filled with cheap and ugly artifacts priced so extravagantly the gamblers had to believe they had ascended to a superior place. Then he pushed through a hotel exit and stared, trembling, empty, at the aqua sky. He was so lonely each breath hurt. He had nowhere else to go.

It was dusk when he found her. She was sitting on a bench, staring at a fountain surrounded by arcs of blue light. He walked toward her slowly. He did not know what he wanted, but he felt just as he had many years before, when he was about to rob the liquor store—as though he wanted to change the universe. Then what he had wanted was practical. The universe he wanted to change between himself and his granddaughter was entirely different. It was a universe of feelings, and he did not know how to live in it.

"Aurora," he said.

"What do you want?" she asked.

He stood in front of the girl: an expensively dressed man, sweaty, against a dark sky. "I'd like to talk to you," he said.

She shrugged.

He sat down and leaned forward, clasping his hands. He did not know how to begin. "What's the title of your movie?"

"Why?"

It was the only question he could think of to ask.

"*Danger,*" she said, a thrilled edge to her voice. "This is the poster. It'll have a picture of an exploding world. There will be huge clouds of smoke. People from other planets will pick up stranded earthlings in their rockets. The saucers will fly through violet rain—" Aurora's face seemed naked as a baby's. She awaited his response.

"*Danger*," Lenny said, slowly, for it seemed like a beautiful word. "*Danger*. It is a great idea."

The next day, the jet took them back to the mansion. They walked the grounds together and Lenny showed Aurora the whole estate, but mostly he listened to her tell him about her film. The girl spoke quickly, desperately. The plot of *Danger* was unclear but enthusiastic. It involved runaway missiles, a child army, aunts possessed by aliens, and other complex subplots. Lenny's contribution to the conversation was not to interrupt. If he did, the girl became furious. Aurora had thought through many of the marketing elements: the poster, the commercial. She became so passionate during her description of the trailer for *Danger* that she got tears in her eyes.

He was not sure what to do together. His jet took them to Hawaii one weekend to swim with sea turtles, and to London the next for a lavish tea. He imagined intimacy would be like the sensation he had when the jet swung up into the sky, a feeling of vastness; but she was not interested in the green sea around Hawaii, the heavy, sweet cream spooned on a scone. Instead, she wanted to know the most peculiar details about him. What was his favorite color? What was his favorite vegetable? What kind of haircuts did he have as a child?

One day, she asked him what he was most afraid of in the world.

"You first," he said.

"Spiders," she said.

"Snakes," he said.

She looked dissatisfied. "Something better," she said. "Earthquakes."

These were lies; he did not know what he feared.

"Ticking clocks," she said.

"Why?"

"When my mother doesn't come home," she said. "I listen for ticking clocks. I can hear them through walls."

"When does she not come home?"

"I get scared I'll be awake forever. I think I hear them down the street."

She covered her face with her hands in a small, violent motion. She held them there for a moment; when she lifted her hands, her face was blank, composed. "Tell me what you're afraid of," she said, and it was an order.

"I don't know," he said.

"You have to say something."

"I have to think," he said, but he could not describe his gratitude at the question, for no one had ever asked him this before.

That night, Lenny could not sleep. He went to the kitchen at 2 A.M. for a glass of milk; again, he heard the girl's footsteps. He watched her walk lightly through the foyer again. He waited until she had left and then followed her through the silent house. Aurora crept like an animal across the gleaming cold tile until she reached one of his coat closets. She knelt and picked up some of the favorite pieces of his wardrobe—his Armani loafers, his Yves St. Laurent gloves. She did this quickly, with a kind of efficiency, picking up items and dropping them. Suddenly, she grabbed two shoes and a glove; lightly, like a ghost, she ran back to her room.

For a while, he stood where he had watched her; he wanted her to take everything. He wanted to follow her, uttering words of impossible tenderness, words he could never say to his own child: I want to give everything to you.

He still had not figured out what he was most afraid of when, about a month later, she did not come to breakfast. He was surprised by her absence, but thought she was just sleeping late. He called from work to check in.

"She has the flu," said Rosita. "She's sleeping. Children get sick."

He found it difficult to concentrate on his work, and came home early to see her. She was groggy with fever, but she mostly slept. The pediatrician said to give her fluids and not to worry.

A week later, she woke up, coughing; she could barely breathe. The pediatrician told him to take the girl to the emergency room.

They were borne together on a stale, glaring current of fear. The children's wing of the hospital was like a haunted house: babies screamed as nurses held them down to take blood from their arms, children wheeled out from operations lay, eyes glazed, tubes rising out of their mouths. The parents walked slowly, like ghouls, beside the gurneys rolling their children out of surgery. They were not who he had planned to meet that day.

Aurora was with him and then she was in the pediatric intensive care unit. The flu had developed into pericardiomyopathy—an illness of the heart. The doctor brought the residents around Aurora's bed to instruct them on Aurora's condition, for it was so rare it had never happened in the hospital before. Lenny could not watch this. He tried to call Charlene at the clinic, but an administrator got on the line and said, primly, "She left. She ran away two days ago with another patient."

"Ran away?" he asked. "Why didn't you call me?"

"We were waiting to see if she called us." She paused. "We assume no responsibility once they leave the premises. There were mutterings about South America."

"Find her," he said, "or I'm suing you for so much money your head will spin."

"What do you propose we do, Mr. Weiss? Send our counselors to South America? She wasn't ready. We can't force her. We'll let you know if she contacts us."

In his life, he had commanded budgets of millions of dollars; negotiated with businessmen on every continent of the globe. Now he had to act as Aurora's guardian and he stumbled wildly across the hospital linoleum, as though the floor were made of air. He tried to ensure that Aurora would get good care from the nurses by offering them spots on his show. "We're having a special episode. Pot of five hundred thousand dollars. You'd have a one-in-three chance." Standing at the large smoky windows in the waiting area, he stared out at the cars moving down the freeways. Closing his eyes, he tried to change the course of the day, to will the cars to go backward, but they pressed ahead, silver backs flashing, leaving him standing there, alone.

When Aurora had stabilized a week later, the doctor called him into his office. The office was filled with diplomas and drab orange chairs. Lenny perched on the edge of the chair like a child. The doctor read the chart that Aurora's pediatrician had sent him: "She was in Thailand two years ago," he said.

"Her mother took her there," Lenny said.

The doctor read the name of a disease Lenny did not know. "She wasn't properly treated. Her heart was damaged. This flu did more harm."

Lenny remembered a postcard Charlene had sent from Bangkok: *Having a super time. Aurora loves curry. River rafting next week.* He felt faint and a little sick.

"The news is bad," said the doctor. "She needs a new heart."

Lenny could not breathe. A sharp pain went through him, immense and shocking because its source was wholly emotional; it came entirely from his love.

"We'll put her on the transplant list," said the doctor.

"List?"

"She has to wait her turn."

He had not waited on any list for over thirty years. Lenny stood up. His hair was uncombed and his face gray with exhaustion, but he felt the large, powerful weight of his body in his expensive suit. "What's your job here, doctor?"

"I am the head of pediatric cardiology." He was a slim man, slightly balding. His eyelashes were long and curling. His desk glimmered with crystal paperweights.

Lenny turned away from the man's desk. He was talking fast. "Let me ask you. What do you need in your wing?" Lenny asked.

"Excuse me?"

"Let me tell you how I see the new wing of the hospital," said Lenny, glancing at the doctor's nametag. "The Alfred J. Johnson wing. Twenty million dollars. A children's playroom. Top equipment. A research lab. Endowed chairs." He listened to the hoarse, meaty sound of his voice. "I am the producer of *Anything for Money.* Look at me."

The hospital sent Aurora home with vague instructions: take it easy; no strenuous exercise. She felt weak, but she did not know how ill she was, and Lenny did not tell her. He did not allow himself to think about her weakened state. Instead, he indulged in feelings of pride at his wealth and ability to bend the rules. When he received the official letter, a few days later, he wanted to frame it, for it seemed to reflect some magnificence in his soul. The letter said: *Aurora Weiss is number one on the list for available heart transplants. Please remain at this address.*

Lenny called the doctor every day. He gave Lenny ghoulish harvest reports: a young boy killed in a car accident, a murdered teen. But none of these hearts had the right antigens that would match Aurora's; they had to wait for the correct heart.

Waiting was what fools did; he decided to take things into his own hands. He stayed up all night, making calls. He spoke into a phone that did automatic translating to doctors in Germany, Sweden, France. His price soared. Thirty million dollars to be number one on the list. New wings. Top equipment. Huge salaries. High-tech playrooms. He shouted these offers into the phone at 2 A.M., imagining Aurora and Charlene's gratitude that he had saved Aurora, how they would tell everyone that Lenny had saved his granddaughter by calling every doctor in the world. When sweetness did not work, he tried threats: sending investigators in to check on their records, lawsuits. But no one had the correct heart.

Aurora came into the room one night when Lenny was making his calls. She stood in her pajamas, staring, as he shouted into a phone.

"What's wrong?" she asked.

He put down the phone.

When he told her that her heart was not well and how he was going to help her, she went still; she seemed to have been waiting for years for someone to tell her that she was damaged. "I'm going to find one," he said. "You know me. People know me and they want to help—"

She went pale, for she saw through this immediately. "I'm sorry!" she cried out. "Sorry, sorry—"

He saw, at once, how his daughter had behaved as a mother.

"Aurora. I'll save you," he said. "I swear it."

But she did not let him touch her—she backed away from him with a dim expression, as though she were already disappearing, and believed this was what people had truly wanted from her all along.

He skipped work. He was sleepless. The right heart was not appearing for her. He tried to think about who would give up their heart for millions of dollars. Drug addicts, the terminally ill—but their hearts would not be in good enough shape. He sat behind the dark glass of his limo, grimly watching girls play soccer, wishing one of them would trip. He imagined taking his Mercedes sports car out and plowing it into a group of teenage boys running on the sidewalk, killing enough of them to give Aurora more of a chance.

He proposed to his staff a special episode: "Who Will Die for Money." They would audition people willing to give up their hearts for a staggering pot of $5 million. His staff thought it was a PR stunt and called an audition. The holding room filled with an assortment of the homeless, individuals not in the best of health, and well-dressed, shifty types who seemed to think there was some way to obtain the money without dying.

They were all busily filling out their names and addresses when he got a call from Rosita.

"A heart has arrived on the doorstep," she said.

He rushed home.

A man identified himself as a cardiac surgeon and a purveyor of black-market hearts. He was from Ukraine. Dr. Stoly Michavcezek sat in Lenny's living room, an ice chest on his lap.

"Whose heart was this?" asked Lenny.

"A man. Olympic-quality gymnast. Fell on mat and dead."

"And you could operate? How long has he been dead?"

"Few hours. Payment up front."

They transferred the heart to Lenny's enormous Sub-Zero freezer; then Lenny brought in a specialist from Cedars Sinai to look at the heart.

"This isn't a human heart," the doctor said. "This is the heart of a chimp."

When he returned to the studio, the prospective contestants had all been dismissed and black-suited men from the Legal Department were waiting in his office.

"Lenny," said one. "This has got to stop."

Aurora worked on her movie obsessively; she spent much of her time in her room. When they had a meal together, he did most of the talking; he lied about how close he was coming to saving her. "There's a doctor in Mexico," he'd say, "a small hospital. International laws, they're all we have to get around—" She ate very little and watched him like a child who had disbelieved adults her whole life.

One night, she burst out of her room and ran to her seat at the table. "My plot has changed," she said. "Listen. There are seventeen aliens from the planet of Eyahoo. They have legs in the shape of wheels and heads like potatoes. Their planet is very slippery and they move very fast on their wheels. Often they bump into each other. Their heads are getting sore."

He listened.

"They need a new cousin who can make their planet less slippery. Their cousin is named Yabonda and she lives on a neighboring planet. She has long legs with huge feet that are very absorbent, like paper towels. They want to learn how to have feet like her. Now. Do you think they should maybe invite her to Eyahoo for dinner or just come and kidnap her?"

She leaned back in her chair, clasped her hands tightly, and watched him.

"What would happen with each?" he asked.

"If they asked her to dinner, she would be transported in a glamorous carriage made of starlight."

"Uh-huh."

"If they kidnapped her, it would hurt." She stretched her fingers wide, as though trying to hold everything. "Tell me," she said, sharply.

When Aurora had learned about her condition, she stopped stealing. Lenny began leaving things out for her—his cell phone and toothbrush and car keys—in the hope that she would take them, but in the morning, they remained where he had put them. He missed her midnight rambling through the mansion, waking up to see which objects of his she would find precious.

One night, he heard her footsteps padding down the hall.

Lenny jumped out of bed and followed her. This time, Aurora seemed to have no particular direction, but went around the foyer like a floating, circling bird. Then she saw Lenny. They stared at each other in the dusk of the hallway, and the shocked quiet around them made Lenny feel that they were meeting for the first time.

"Something's going to happen to me," said Aurora, and she began to cry. "I don't know what to take."

It sounded as though the house were made of her cries. They echoed through the empty hallways. The girl knelt to the floor and threw up. The child's distress made Lenny feel as though he himself were dissolving. Lenny lowered himself beside her and put his hand on the girl's back.

"Take me," said Lenny.

The girl stared at him.

"I'll go with you," said Lenny.

"Where?"

"Wherever. I'll go, too."

"How can you go?"

"I can find a way to do it."

He did not know how to stop these words; they were simply pouring out of him. "Please. I'm telling you. Take me."

"I don't want to be by myself," said Aurora.

"You won't be," said Lenny. "I'll be there, too."

When the dawn came, he was sleeping on the floor beside Aurora's bed. He woke up, his promise only a vague cold sensation—then he remembered what he had said.

He got up quietly, and left the room.

It was just six in the morning. Lenny walked to his garage and got into his red Ferrari convertible. He shot up the Pacific Coast Highway, feeling the engine's force vibrate through his body. The highway stretched, a ribbon reaching through the blue haze to the rest of the world. He felt poisoned by the girl's presence in himself and wanted to get her out. He kept going north, the early sun melting the haze.

By 8:00, he had hit Santa Barbara. The main street was filled with a lustrous golden light, and the people strolling the sidewalks looked so contented and purposeful he wished they were all dead. He thought of the way Aurora stood on half-toe when she wanted something, the sweet, terrible optimism in the girl's walk when she headed down the hallway, ready to go about her day. He wanted to get out of his car and rush out among the strangers and find a woman and have sex with her in an alley. He wanted to strip naked and run, singing, into the ocean. He wanted to slam his car into a restaurant and be put in jail. He drove back and forth down the main street for a while, hands trembling on the steering wheel.

He turned the car and roared toward where people knew him best: the studio. At 10 A.M., he walked through the doors and stood in the shadows, watching. Eight contestants were white-lit, hitting buzzers, shouting out answers to questions, and the producers and crew were scrambling noisily in the dark around the stage.

Lenny stared at the brilliant stage set. On this stage, he had seen a man auction off his wife's bra for thousands of dollars; he had seen children thrust their parents' faces into vats of whipped cream for five hundred bucks. He had stood in this brightness, watching others dimly fall around him.

"Lenny," he heard. "Hey, Lenny—"

Now he stood in this corridor, a strange, familiar fear sour in his mouth. He understood, suddenly, what would be unbearable. He did not want to be here alone.

Lenny had to turn around several times before he saw where the exit was. Pushing through the metal doors, he ran into the parking lot, jumped into his car, and drove home.

When the Ferrari floated up to the mansion, Aurora was sitting on the stairs. The girl was still, as though she had been sitting there for a hundred years. Her blue eyes were fixed on Lenny as he began to walk up the stairs.

"I thought you weren't coming back," said Aurora.

"I had to do an errand," Lenny said.

He sat beside Aurora on the stair.

"We could have a house together," the girl said. Her fingers dug into Lenny's hand. "It could be just like your house. We could sleep beside each other, so you always know that the other's there."

Lenny looked out at the yard. Stars seemed to have fallen into the lawn. It was dark and wet from the morning rain and the brightness of the sky seemed to be caught in the grass. He looked over his yard to the hazy brown air over the city, to the people eating sandwiches or telling jokes or cursing or waiting at stoplights or saying goodbye. They seemed so far away. He did not know what any of them were made of, what his daughter was doing, how much money he had.

"I have a new plot idea," she said. "To help Yabonda."

"What do you mean?"

"Her paper towel feet have dried out," she said. "Whenever she lifts her feet they make a weird crackling sound. Everyone on her planet wants her to go away. They can't stand the noise her feet make. It keeps them all awake. There is mayhem and murder." She jumped up and put her hands on her hips; she was trembling. "She meets Glungluck, a kindly alien who was kicked off her planet because her ears, which resemble long straws, suck up everything around them, and people were losing their purses and keys."

"Go on," he said.

"They make a neighborhood," she said. "They add other sad aliens, Kogo and Zarooom. They build big walls around their neighborhood, made of glass roses. The only aliens who can move in are other losers. They all have had bad luck. In their neighborhood, they can talk to each other. They make up songs and have contests. Nobody wins. When the good-luck aliens try to see through the wall of roses, they are jealous and lonely."

He looked at her face. Her forehead was gray and creased, like an old person's.

"I'll produce," he said.

He did not stop looking. He had kept the audition slips of the people who had been willing to give up their hearts for $5 million and he was meeting one, Wayne Olden, secretly, for lunch at a Fatburger in Hollywood to check him out. He was planning to take him in for a full medical exam; after that he would hand over organ-donation forms. Lenny had not figured out how he would kill the man, particularly to maintain the integrity of his organs. They were finishing up a hot dog when he received a call.

"I'm not feeling so well," said Aurora.

"What's wrong?"

"I don't know."

Lenny jumped up.

"I have to go," he said to the man.

"You're kidding," said the man.

"Here," said Lenny, throwing him a thousand-dollar bill. "That's for lunch."

The man looked disappointed. "I thought I was going to get five million bucks!"

Lenny's Mercedes raced home. It was late afternoon, the shadows long and dark against the grass. She was sitting in a T-shirt and shorts by the pool. The late sun made her face look gold.

"What's wrong?" he asked.

"I don't know. I just wanted to see you," Aurora said.

He sat beside her.

"I don't know what to have for dinner," she said.

An expression of surprise crossed her face. It was as though she were witnessing a private, obscene act. Her arm jerked once and she fell out of her chair. She lay still on the grass, her eyes staring, empty, quiet, at the sky.

He said the child's name. Again. Again. Aurora. Pink geraniums heaved in the warm wind. Aurora. He had not been able to answer Aurora's question. The answer pressed out of him like a knife inside his gut. He wanted to tell her that they could have hamburgers for dinner.

He picked Aurora's body up and carried her through the green exuberance of the garden.

Now Lenny was saying another word: Wait. He was in a great hurry. Wait. His voice felt like a shout but it was almost a whisper. The world around him had become silent. It seemed the sky had lowered. He could not stand too tall.

He carried Aurora to his car and put her in the front seat. He seat-belted the girl in and covered her with a jacket. He did not want the child to get cold. He got into the driver's seat and started the car. Wait. He had to belt the girl in more tightly so that she would not slide. His hands were trembling so hard he could not hold the wheel.

The police found them later, a man in his sixties and a girl. They were slumped in the car that had driven suddenly off the cliff in Malibu and crashed on the Pacific Coast Highway. The car had landed in the center of the highway, straddling the center divider, and traffic was slowed in both directions. The white and red lights from the cars made two rivers of brightness as the drivers glided north and south along the coast. Now the cars appeared to be following each other, stopping and starting, stopping and starting, as the drivers passed the wreckage and peered into the darkening night.

T. E. holt

'Ο Λογος

VIDETUR QUOD AUTHOR HIC OBIIT.

The first case of which any record survives was reported in a small-town daily in upstate New York. Tabitha Van Order, the brief item reads, age five, was brought into the county hospital's emergency room with "strange markings" on her face and hands. "She was playing with the newspaper," her mother reported. "I thought it was just the ink rubbed off on her." But the marks did not respond to soap or turpentine. At the hospital, initial examination determined that the marks were subcutaneous, and the child was admitted for observation. They looked, according to the triage nurse, as though someone had been striking the child with a large rubber stamp. "They look like bruises," the emergency-room physician told the *Journal* reporter. The department of social services was looking into the case.

This alone might not have warranted even three inches on page 8 of a sixteen-page paper. What attracted the attention of the editor at the county desk (whose sister, a nurse in the ER, had phoned in the story), and earned Tabitha's case even that scanty initial notice, was one peculiar feature of those bruises, one fact about the case that stood out from the face of an otherwise unremarkable, seemingly healthy little girl. It was not that, over the next several days, the marks did not fade, nor exhibit any of the changes of hue or outline usual in a bruise—although this was puzzling. Nor was it the child's silence, which she maintained three days with a patient gravity that impressed the most casual of observers. What claimed the attention of everyone who saw the child over the three days of her illness was the unmistakable pattern in those marks. They formed a word.

A word, certainly: no one who saw doubted for an instant what they saw. And it was something more, as well. Everyone struck with the sight of that pale, silent face and that black sign reported the same response: each said that the shock of seeing it for the first time was almost physical. It was as if, the nurse on the day shift recalled, seeing it, you felt it on your own face—"like a blush." And indeed, after the initial shock, something like embarrassment did set in: the nurses could never bring themselves to utter the word, either to the child or among themselves; the physicians during their morning rounds half averted their eyes even as they palpated the affected areas. And although *bruises* were discussed day and night across the desk at the nursing station; although *palpable purpura* were the subject of long discussions in the cafeteria; although everyone down to the orderlies hazarded a guess as to the nature of the *marks,* the *word* itself went euphemized, persistently elided.

After embarrassment followed another response, something of which communicates itself even now in the tone of that first newspaper article, a kind of delicacy, a reticence over the details of the case: a hush. That respectful silence grows ambivalently louder in the two pieces that in as many days followed, lengthened, and moved forward toward page

1. As for the child herself, she made no complaint, nor in fact did she utter any word at all until just before the end, when she was heard to pronounce, in tones audible as far as the nursing station, the word spelled out by the bruise across her hands, cheeks, jaw, and (most plainly) forehead. She spoke the word in a piercing falsetto three times, and then, before the nurse could reach the room, the child coded, the physician's assistant said, and died.

I learned much of this, of course, later, by which time several of the principals—the nurses, the orderlies, the mother, and the physicians—were beyond the reach of my own inquiries. But I believe the editor told me as much of the truth as he knew before he died.

Which was more than he told his readers. Even in the third article, which appeared on the fourth day following Tabitha's admission to the hospital, and where the headline type has grown to fifty-four points, the text is most significant for what it does not say. It does not tell the precise form of those bruises that darkened across the child's features in her last twelve hours and then faded completely within minutes of her death—although the darkening and the fading both are faithfully set down. Nor does it transcribe the syllables the child voiced three times before she died—although the fact of her crying out is also given. It does not even mention that the bruises formed a word.

There was this aspect of the affair notable from the start: that embarrassment that overcame all who saw the word, as if the thing were shameful. Not, I believe, for what it said, but for being so patently, inscrutably significant: for being *a sign*. Few people could bring themselves, at first, even to acknowledge what they saw. It was as if an angel had planted one bare foot in Central Park, another on the Battery, and cast the shadow of a brazen horn over Newark. If such had happened, how many minutes might we suppose to have elapsed before anyone could have brought himself to turn to his neighbor and ask: Do you see? How could any of us discuss it without feeling implicated? So it was in the case of Tabitha's word: it was too plainly part of a world we no longer knew how to address.

But there was more to this evasion, of course, than meets the eye, and it is this that I find truly remarkable about the case. It is the function of that evasion, and the unmistakable conclusion it urges, that most impresses me: that everyone who saw the word, immediately, *without* understanding, without conscious thought or any evidence at all, knew that to see the word in print was sentence of death.

No one, at the time, had any empirical reason for suspecting such, but in every account, even the first, I trace an instinctive recognition that the word carried the contagion. It was several months, of course, before the means of transmission was identified, through the work of the Centers for Disease Control and Prevention in Atlanta and Lucerne, and ultimately the heroic sacrifice of the interdisciplinary team at the École des Hautes Études en Sciènces Sociales in Paris. So how do we find, in this first written record, the prudence that spared until a later date so many lives? And how do we balance that seeming prudence with the other inescapable fact about the word: that as the end approached, all seemed seized—as was Tabitha herself—with an impulse to speak it. It was as if the word struggled to speak *itself*, as if in answer to some drive to propagate that would not be denied.

The elucidation of the mechanism was complicated by the discovery that mere speech was harmless, as was hearing: it was the eye through which the plague entered, and

the eye only. The hand that wrote, so long as the person behind it did not look, was spared (with the notorious exception of the blind, who took the illness in Braille, and broke
out before they died in portentous boils). But to see the
word in print (ink or video, it did not matter) was to sicken,
and invariably to die.

Experimental studies were hampered, of course, by a
number of complicating factors, not least of which was the
obvious difficulty in conducting tests on other than human
subjects. A late attempt was made, by some accounts, to in-
corporate the word into the ideogrammatic code taught to
chimpanzees at the Yerkes Center for Primatology; results
were fragmentary, the experiment ending prematurely with
the incapacitation of the staff. One significant datum did
emerge from all studies, however: illiteracy was no defense.
Even those incapable of deciphering the dialogue from
comic strips were found to be susceptible. The only excep-
tions were those functioning, for whatever reason, below the
mental age of thirty months.

But all of this knowledge came later. Although this most
important aspect of the disease did ultimately receive full
measure of publicity, in the case of Tabitha Van Order the
initial reports were mute. Indeed, were it not owing to the
early curiosity of one researcher in virology at a nearby university, the epidemiological particulars of this first case
might have passed almost entirely unrecorded. This virolo-
gist, one Taylor Salomon, happened to have been a patient
on the same floor as the child, incapacitated with pneumonia, which she had contracted while at work in her laboratory. On the day that Tabitha gave up the ghost in a room
four doors down from hers, Professor Salomon was sitting
up in bed for the first time in two weeks, taking some clear
broth and attempting to organize notes from her research.

The attempt was futile, owing to the extreme weakness that had kept her semi-conscious for the previous two weeks, and was disrupted forever by the unearthly cry that heralded Tabitha's demise. Professor Salomon was fortunate in this, however: her own illness had kept her from visiting the child's room, or even glimpsing her mottled face through the open door, before the marks had faded entirely away. And the research project that had hospitalized Professor Salomon soon faded from her thoughts as well, supplanted by a new question as soon as the nurse appeared, visibly shaken, in answer to the professor's call.

The nurse could relate the sequel of the child's cry, but not its meaning; she could only echo, with the distracted air that had come to typify the medical staff in the last hours of Tabitha's life, the helpless distress of her colleagues at finding their patient so unaccountably dead. To Salomon's more pertinent questions about the disease's course and etiology, the nurse could only wring her hands and look back over her shoulder, as if she harbored a guilty secret. Her curiosity piqued, Dr. Salomon managed to rise from her bed and stumble down the hall before the orderlies arrived to wheel the body away. The marks had apparently disappeared no more than five minutes before her arrival.

Luck was with her again, in that her appearance in the room was followed almost immediately by that of the medical examiner. The examiner, already irritated at the interruption of lunch, was inclined to order Salomon from the room, and her recitation of her credentials did nothing, at first, to soothe him. But being in no mood to take up the investigation himself, his irritation was no match for Salomon's persistence, and in the end he agreed to provide the samples she required. In an additional example of the good fortune that marked so much of Salomon's involvement with the

case, the ME's cooperative attitude was not shared by the
hospital staff, which refused to release the child's chart to
anyone but the ME, citing doctor-patient confidentiality. But
the samples, Salomon felt, would prove more valuable than
any M.D.'s scribble, and she was content with the oral recitation of the child's history she eventually wrung from the
nurses. The samples, iced and isolated according to proto-
cols, waited another two weeks before Salomon was able to
return to her lab, where she found, of course, nothing. The
blood, nerve tissue, and other fragments of Tabitha's clay
were apparently those of a healthy five-year-old girl, and
nothing an extremely well-funded laboratory could bring to
bear on them was able to add anything to the story.

Stymied in the laboratory, Salomon turned to a col-
league in epidemiology, and, swearing him to secrecy, initi-
ated field studies of the child's home, school, and other
haunts. The season was late spring; the child's backyard
abutted on a swamp: insect traps were set and their prey examined (at this point the impromptu task force expanded to
include an entomologist). Once again, nothing significant
appeared.

Time was running out for Salomon and her hopes of
scoring a coup. Five weeks after Tabitha's admission to
the hospital, the child's mother, the triage nurse, four orderlies, the emergency-room physician's assistant, three floor
nurses, and two doctors were admitted with livid bruises on
the palms of their hands, cheeks, jaws, and (most plainly)
foreheads.

In this first wave of cases, the disease exhibited additional symptoms, not observed (or not reported) in the case
of Tabitha Van Order. In the triage nurse, onset was marked
by a vague dreaminess that overtook her at work one morning. By lunchtime, she was incapable of entering insurance

information correctly on her forms, and by midafternoon she had wandered from her desk. She was found on one of the high floors of the hospital, staring out a window at the lake, where a sailboat regatta was in progress. It was only at this point that the marks on her face were noticed. At about this time (the precise time is unavailable, owing to the nurse's absence from her desk), Julia Van Order arrived at the emergency room, brought in by a neighbor who had found her laughing uncontrollably in the street outside her home. The third symptom, glossolalia, was observed in two of the orderlies and one physician, who were admitted over the course of the evening. By midnight, there were twelve patients on the floor.

Recognizing an incipient epidemic, the chief of infectious disease imposed strict quarantine that evening. Staff on the floor were issued the customary isolation gear, and strict contact precautions were imposed. Who could blame the man for not issuing blindfolds? Such measures were in fact tried, much later, but by then, of course, it was much too late. He failed as well to confiscate pens.

Professor Salomon, on hearing of these new admissions, realized that her time was running out, and did the only thing left to her. After one visit to the hospital, during which she conducted interviews with those of the victims able to respond, she wrote up as full a description of the disease as she could, took her best guess (which turned out, in the end, to be wrong) as to its cause, sealed the four typewritten pages in a dated envelope, and sent the sealed article, with a cover letter, to *The New England Journal of Medicine*. It was not at that time the policy of the *New England Journal* to accept so-called *plis cachetés*, the practice having fallen into disrepute over a generation earlier, and Salomon's contribution might have been returned unopened had it not been for yet another fortuitous circumstance.

A reporter specializing in science and medicine was visiting Salomon's university that week, lecturing graduate students in journalism. On the day he was scheduled to return to New York, he happened to hear of the dozen deaths that had occurred the previous night at the county hospital. Sensing a career opportunity, he filed a story, complete with an interview with Salomon, and the item ran prominently in the Health section of the following week's issue.

The reporter, who had conducted his interviews with the hospital staff over the phone, and filed in the same way, was fortunate. Professor Salomon was not; time had in fact run out for her in more ways than one. Before she died, however, she had the satisfaction of seeing her report in print, its publication in the *New England Journal* spurred on by the article in *Time*.

In the four weeks that followed the first wave, mortality in the county was misleadingly low. The local daily never having printed the word, the contagion was spread almost exclusively among the hospital staff, in whom the disease lay latent for the month of July. At the end of the first week of August, the marks broke out over the hands, cheeks, jaws, and (most prominently) foreheads of approximately eighty-five doctors, nurses, orderlies, speech therapists, and social workers, most of whom were brought in by their families in various stages of confusion, euphoria, and glossolalia.

In this second wave, observers reported yet another symptom, which followed those exhibited in the first wave in a distinct progression. Whether the onset was marked by dreamy confusion, giddiness, or fluently unintelligible speech, within twelve hours all such symptoms had lapsed into one:

an uncontrollable paranoia, in which the sufferer was convinced that every object in the world, animate or inanimate, was involved in a vast conspiracy to do the patient harm.

Without exception, in this stage of the disease its victims spoke continuously for periods of up to twenty-four hours, offering elaborately detailed descriptions of the delusional system in which they were enmeshed. And without exception, the attending physicians reported that they had at times to fight off the conviction that their patients' dreams were real. Who can blame them? Confronted with an undeniable health emergency, swift to spread, invariably fatal, and marked at its heart by the inscrutable symbol of the word, little wonder that those who struggled to understand the disease struggled as well with fear. Unlike their patients, who had evolved an explanation for the menace within them, their doctors had no such comfort, and could only watch their patients die, and wonder helplessly if they had contracted the plague as well.

For plague, by the end of the first week of September, it had become. There is little point in going over the statistics of that hellish week: the figures beggar comprehension, and mere repetition will not suffice to make them meaningful. Certainly their import was dulled by the more immediate, personal tragedies that struck almost every household in the country at that time. And as the numbers grew to embrace other nations, other languages, their meaning became in no way more intelligible. No more than did the word, which, as it appeared in different nations, took on different forms, but everywhere with the same effect.

At this time, little remains to report, but I would like to offer before I close two or three items that strike me as signifi-

cant. The first, as I have hinted, was almost lost in the events
that followed so quickly on the disease's emergence into the
public eye. But Professor Salomon's team, in the weeks between her death and theirs, continued its research into the
origins of the contagion. And though the trail had by then
grown cold, the scent was not so faint that they could find in
this an excuse for the failure of their investigations: the disease was untraceable, they claimed, because *it had no physical cause.*

And here I find one of the most pathetic effects of this
disease—the kind of case in which its action was so griev-
ous because so clearly marked. One of Salomon's survivors,
a geneticist, whom I had known slightly during our years together at the university, and who was one of the few men I
have ever met who might have deserved to be called a ge-
nius, telephoned me on the day the disease took hold of him.
While I kept him on the phone, in the thirty minutes before
help arrived I listened as he spun out the delusion that had
come on him with the word. The spectacle, if I may call it
that, of a mind of this caliber reduced to raving brought me
close to tears.

But I feel obligated to report what he said to me that day,
in part because it was my only immediate contact with a vic-
tim of the plague. And also because one aspect of the encounter still strikes me, somehow, as significant. *I believed.*
All the time I was speaking to him, I found myself fighting off
conviction. Naturally, the feeling passed, but I still find myself, several weeks later, struggling with a sense of opportunity missed: I felt at the time, and still in my weaker moments
do, as though I had come close to penetrating the mystery of
the word. This is, of course, one of the effects most frequently
reported by those attending on the dying.

The disease, my caller insisted, was not, properly speaking, a plague. That is to say, it was not spread by any of the infectious mechanisms. The word was not a pathogen: it was a *catalyst,* and the disease itself immanent in humanity at large. He had deciphered a sequence, he claimed, in the human genome, which matched, in the repetitive arrangement of its amino acids, the structure of the word. It seemed the word, processed in the temporal lobe in the presence of sufficient quantities of norepinephrine—the quantities released at levels of anxiety commonly associated with fear of bodily harm—acted as a trigger for this hitherto unnoticed gene. The gene, once stimulated, distorted the chemical function of the cerebral cortex, and the result was the familiar progression of stigmata, hallucination, convulsion, death.

It was, of course, palpable nonsense. I did not tell him so. Pity restrained me. He needed me, he went on, to spread the word. I chided him, gently, on his phraseology. His response was impatient to the point of fury. I had to help, he insisted: my own expertise in linguistics dovetailed so neatly with his findings. The two of us, he said, could broadcast the key needed to unlock a cure. I allowed him to speak as long as he needed to, until the ambulance arrived and the receiver was quietly set down. Triage, in those days, was performed upon the spot.

The man's ravings were, of course, merely one more instance of the paranoia that marks the final hours of the victims of the plague. But, like all paranoid fantasies, these had some germ of truth in them, and it tantalizes me. If we accept that the disease came into this world without phenomenal cause, another possibility remains. The disease is, I grant, born in the brain. But it is not the product of any mechanism so vulgar as genetic coding. It is purely a product of the human mind.

I offer this as a message of hope. For if the plague had its origins in the human mind, might it not be fought by the same powers of mind that called it forth? Tabitha had been "playing with the newspapers," her mother reported. So, this night, have I. I have before me the pages, already growing yellow, of the *I——Journal* in the first weeks of June. I visited the newspaper's offices last night, forced to break in with a wrecking bar. The streets of the town were still, but for someone singing in the upper floor above a nearby shop. The words of the song were unintelligible: only the tune came through, a wandering melody, almost familiar.

I have spread them out here before me, these pages from the morgue, my fingers trembling, the paper brittle, my breath unsteady in my chest. I read the stories there: they are the old familiar ones, always the same. Family burned in a fire. Two held in convenience-store murder. Ultimatum issued over Balkan genocide. Plague in the Middle East. Old news. These portents and omens reduced to columns of fading ink.

I know, of course, the risk I am taking. I know only too well how fragile has been the chain of circumstances that has protected me from the infection. I listen even now to the stillness outside my window and am awed by the hush there, and what it says to me of my own great fortune. It is a mournful silence, broken only by the eternal singing of the katydids. They call, as they always have, of the coming of winter: mournful, and yet somehow pleasant, as all melancholy is.

But before I digress again, I would report the last significant item I have in my possession, and then I must go back to my own work, which has been too long interrupted. The information is this. In the later stages of the plague, the word disappeared. Almost as if it were no longer necessary, the last victims sickened, raved, and died without any visible sign of illness. I have a theory, of course. And although there is no means at my disposal to prove it even to my own satisfaction, I am convinced it is true.

The word, whatever it meant, whatever form it took in whatever language, was not the carrier of plague: not in any of the ways we sought to *understand.* Understanding was beside the point: for how could Tabitha, herself unlettered, have understood? The answer, plainly, is that she did not. I can imagine the scene vividly, even now, as the child turned the pages of the newspaper, rehearsing in her thoughts such anxieties as she had heard adults around her voice over pages such as these. Anxieties she did not understand, yet could not help but share: anxieties that, for all she knew, were made of words. Words she could not understand, but still she searched among them for some clue, some *answer* to the riddle of her life.

Children are suggestible, reader. To go from fear of unintelligible danger to a physical expression of that fear required only one word, any word, any arbitrary sequence of letters that happened to come to her as she "read." That word, written in blood on her features, took her to the hospital, confirming all her fears—fears that conspired, after three days and nights of what must have been pure, unremitting terror, to stop her heart.

Do you doubt me, reader? What more would you have? Letters of fire across the sky? A voice speaking prophecy in your sleep? A look in the mirror at your own forehead? A list, perhaps, of the ways death can come to you, even as you read here, safe in your home?

What is it you want? The word?

———

I give you this, and then I must be gone. All you need is here before you—and the knowledge that what kills us now is any word at all, read in the belief that words can kill.

I know this now. I have been convinced for several days.

'Ο Λογος

'Ο Λογος

'Ο Λογος

Jennifer Egan

GOODBYE, MY LOVE

When Ted Hollander first agreed to travel to Naples in search of his missing niece (longing to get away, to look at art), he drew up for his brother-in-law, who was footing the bill, a plan for finding her that involved cruising the places where aimless, strung-out youths tended to aggregate—the train station, for example—and asking their denizens if they knew her. "Madeline. American. *Capelli rossi,*" red hair, he'd planned to say, had even practiced his pronunciation until he could roll the *r* in front of "rossi" to perfection. But since arriving in Naples, he hadn't said it once.

Today, after more than a week of not looking for Madeline, he visited the ruins of Pompeii, scrutinizing early Roman wall paintings and small, prone bodies scattered like Easter eggs among the columned courtyards. He ate a can of tuna under an olive tree and listened to the crazy, empty silence. In the early evening he returned to his hotel room, heaved his aching body onto the king-sized bed, and phoned his sister, Beth, Madeline's mother, to report that another day's efforts had gone unrewarded.

"Okay," Beth sighed from Los Angeles, as she did each afternoon. The intensity of her disappointment endowed it with something like consciousness; Ted experienced it as a third presence on the phone.

"I'm sorry," he said. A drop of poison filled his heart. He would look for Madeline tomorrow. Yet even as he made this vow, he was reaffirming a contradictory plan to visit the Museo Nazionale—the Orpheus and Eurydice in particular, a Roman marble relief copied from a Greek original. He had always wanted to see it.

Mercifully, Hammer, Beth's third husband, who normally had an array of questions for Ted that boiled down to one very simple question: am I getting my money's worth? (thus filling Ted with truant anxiety), either wasn't around or chose not to weigh in. After hanging up, Ted went to the minibar and dumped a vodka over ice. He brought drink and phone to the balcony and sat in a white plastic chair, looking down at the Via Partenope and the Bay of Naples. The shore was craggy, the water of questionable purity (though arrestingly blue), and those game Neapolitans, most of whom seemed to be fat, were disrobing on the rocks and leaping into the bay in full view of pedestrians, tourist hotels, and traffic. He dialed his wife.

"Oh, hi hon!" Susan was startled to hear from him so early in the day—usually he called at dinnertime. "Is everything okay?"

"Everything's fine."

Already, her brisk, merry tone had disheartened him. Susan was often on Ted's mind in Naples, but a slightly different version of Susan—a thoughtful, knowing woman with whom he could speak without speaking. It was this slightly different version of Susan who had listened with him to the quiet of Pompeii, alert to faint reverberations of screams, of sliding ash. How could so much devastation have been silenced? Where had it gone? These were the sorts of questions that had come to preoccupy Ted in his week of solitude, a week that felt like both a month and a minute.

"I've got a nibble on the Suskind house," Susan said, apparently hoping to cheer him with this dispatch from the realm of real estate.

Yet each disappointment Ted felt in his wife, each tiny internal collapse, brought a corollary seizure of guilt; many years ago, he had taken the passion he felt for Susan and folded it in half, so he no longer had a drowning, helpless feeling when he glimpsed her beside him in bed, her ropy arms and soft, generous ass. Then he'd folded it in half again, so when he felt desire for Susan, it no longer brought with it an edgy terror of never being satisfied. Then in half again, so that feeling desire entailed no urgent need to act. Then in half again, so he hardly felt it. His desire was so small in the end that Ted could slip it in his desk or a pocket and forget about it, and this gave him a feeling of safety and accomplishment, of having dismantled a perilous apparatus that might have crushed them both. Susan was baffled at first, then frantic; she'd hit him twice across the face, she'd run from the house in a thunderstorm and slept at a motel; she'd wrestled Ted to the bedroom floor, laughing and crying both, wearing a pair of black crotchless underpants. But eventually a sort of amnesia had overtaken Susan; her rebellion and hurt had melted away, deliquesced into a sweet, eternal sunniness that was terrible in the way that life would be terrible, Ted supposed, without death to give it urgency and shape. He'd presumed at first that her relentless cheer was partly mocking, another phase in her rebellion, until it

came to him that Susan had forgotten how things were between them before Ted began to fold up his desire; she'd forgotten and was happy—had never not been happy, as far as
she knew—and while all this gave him new respect for the
gymnastic adaptability of the human mind, it also made him
feel that his wife had been brainwashed. By him.

"Hon," Susan said. "Alfred wants to talk to you."

Ted braced himself for his moody, unpredictable son.
"Hiya, Alf!"

"Dad, don't use that voice."

"What voice?"

"That fake 'Dad' voice."

"What do you want from me, Alfred? Can we have a
conversation?"

"We lost."

"So you're what, five and eight?"

"Four and nine."

"Well. There's time."

"There's no time," said Alfred. "Time is running out."

"Is your mother still there?" Ted asked, a bit desperately.
"Can you put her back on?"

"Miles wants to talk to you."

Ted spoke with his other two sons, who had additional
sports scores to report. He felt like a bookie. They played
every sport imaginable and some that (to Ted) were not: soccer, hockey, baseball, lacrosse, basketball, football, fencing,
wrestling, tennis, skateboarding (not a sport), golf, Ping-
Pong, Video Voodoo (absolutely not a sport, and Ted refused
to sanction it), rock climbing, roller blading, bungie jumping (Miles, his oldest, in whom Ted sensed a joyous will
to self-annihilate), backgammon (not a sport), volleyball,
Wiffle ball, rugby, cricket (what country was this?), squash,

water polo, ballet (Alfred, of course, and not a sport), and most recently, tae kwon do. At times it seemed to Ted that his sons took up sports merely to ensure his presence beside the greatest possible array of playing surfaces, and he duly appeared, yelling away his voice among piles of dead leaves and the smell of woodsmoke in fall, among iridescent clover in spring, and through the soggy, mosquito-flecked summers of upstate New York.

After speaking to his wife and boys, Ted felt drunk, anxious to get out of the hotel. He seldom drank; booze flung a curtain of exhaustion over his head, robbing him of the two precious hours he had each night—two, maybe three, after dinner with Susan and the boys—in which to think and write about art. Ideally, he should have been thinking and writing about art at all times of the day, but a confluence of factors made such thinking and writing both unnecessary (he was tenured at a third-rate college with little pressure to publish) and impossible (he taught three art history courses a semester and had taken on vast administrative duties—he needed money). The site of his thinking and writing was a small office wedged in one corner of his shaggy house, in whose door he had screwed a lock to keep his sons out. They gathered wistfully outside it, his boys, with their chipped, heartbreaking faces. They were not permitted to so much as knock upon the door to the room in which he thought and wrote about art, but Ted hadn't found a way to keep them from prowling outside it, ghostly feral creatures drinking from a pond in moonlight, their feet in the carpet, their fingers sweating on the walls, leaving spoors of grease that Ted would point out each week to Elsa, the cleaning woman. He would sit in his office, listening to the movements of his boys, imagining that he felt their hot, curious breath. I will not let them in, he would tell himself. I will sit and think about art. But he found, to his despair, that often he could not think about art. He thought about nothing at all.

At dusk, Ted strolled up the Via Partenope to the Piazza Vittoria. It was teeming with families, kids punting the ubiquitous soccer balls, exchanging salvos of earsplitting Italian. But there was another presence, too, in the fading light: the aimless, unclean, vaguely threatening youths who trolled this city where unemployment was at 33 percent, members of a disenfranchised generation who skulked around the decrepit palazzi where their fifteenth-century forebears had lived in splendor, who smoked hashish on the steps of churches in whose crypts those same forebears now lay, their diminutive coffins stacked like firewood. Ted shrank from these youths, though he was 6′4″ and weighed in at 220, with a face that looked innocuous enough in the bathroom mirror, but often prompted colleagues to ask him what was the matter. He was afraid Madeline would be among them, that it was her, eyeing him through the jaundiced streetlight that permeated Naples after dark. He left the piazza quickly, in search of a restaurant.

Madeline was seventeen when she'd disappeared, five years ago. Disappeared like her father—like Howie, the berserk financier with the violet eyes, who'd walked away from a bad business deal a couple of years after he and Beth divorced and was not heard from again. Unlike Howie, Madeline had resurfaced a handful of times, demanding money in far-flung locales, and twice Beth and Hammer had flown wherever it was and tried in vain to intercept her. Madeline had shimmied out of an adolescence whose catalog of afflictions had included anorexia, bulimia, LSD, heroin, a fondness for keeping company with derelicts (Beth reported, helplessly), four shrinks, family therapy, group therapy, and two suicide attempts, all of which Ted had witnessed from afar with a horror that had gradually affixed to Madeline herself. As a little girl, she'd been lovely, bewitching, even— he remembered this from a summer he spent with Beth and Howie on Lake Michigan. Later, at the occasional Christmas or Thanksgiving, she was a glowering presence. Ted steered his boys away from her, afraid that her self-immolation would touch them, somehow. He wanted nothing to do with Madeline. She was lost.

Ted rose early the next morning and took a taxi to the Museo Nazionale, cool, echoey, empty of tourists despite the fact that it was summer. He drifted among dusty busts of Hadrian and the various Caesars, experiencing a physical quickening that verged on the erotic in the presence of so much marble. He felt the proximity of the Orpheus and Eurydice before he saw it, sensed its cool weight across the room but prolonged the moments before looking at it directly, reminding himself of the events leading up to the moment it described: Orpheus and Eurydice newly married and wildly in love; Eurydice dying of a snakebite while fleeing the advances of a shepherd; Orpheus descending to the underworld, filling its dank corridors with music from his lyre, as he sang of his longing for his wife; Pluto granting Eurydice's release from death on the sole condition that Orpheus not look back at her during their ascent. And then the thoughtless moment when, out of fear for his bride as she stumbled in the slippery passage, Orpheus mistakenly turned and looked.

Ted stepped toward the relief. He felt as if he'd walked inside it, so utterly did it enclose and affect him. It was the moment before Eurydice must descend to the underworld a second time, when she and Orpheus are saying goodbye.

What moved Ted, what crushed some delicate glassware in his chest, was the quiet of their interaction, the absence of drama, even tears, as they gazed at each other, touching gently. He sensed between these two an understanding too deep to articulate: the hushed, unspeakable knowledge that everything is lost.

Ted stared at the relief, transfixed, for thirty minutes. He walked away and returned to it. He left the room and came back. Each time, the feeling was the same.

He spent the rest of the day upstairs among the Pompeian mosaics, but his mind never left the Orpheus and Eurydice. He visited it again before leaving the museum.

By now it was late afternoon. Ted began to walk, still dazed, until he found himself among a netting of backstreets so narrow they felt dark. He passed churches blistered with grime, decrepit palazzi whose squalid interiors leaked sounds of wailing cats and children. Coats of arms still hung above their massive doorways, soiled, forgotten, and these staggered Ted: symbols once so urgent, so defining, made meaningless by nothing more than time. He imagined the slightly different version of Susan walking near him, sharing in his astonishment. As the Orpheus and Eurydice relaxed its hold on him, he became gradually aware of a subterranean patter around him, an interplay of glances, whistles, and signals that seemed to include nearly everyone, from the old widow crouched on the church steps to the kid in the green shirt who kept buzzing past Ted on his Vespa, grazingly close. Everyone but himself. He scanned his surroundings for an exit.

From a window, an old woman was using a rope to lower a basketful of Marlboros to the street. Black market, Ted thought, watching uneasily as a girl with tangled red hair and sunburned arms removed a packet of cigarettes and placed some coins in the basket. As it swung upward again, back toward the window, Ted recognized the girl as Madeline.

So acutely had he been dreading this encounter that he felt no real surprise at the staggering coincidence of its actually taking place. Madeline lit one of the Marlboros, brow creased, and Ted slowed his pace, pretending to admire the greasy wall of a palazzo, so as not to reach her. When she began walking again, he followed. She wore black jeans and a sleeveless white T-shirt, and she was thin but no longer emaciated, as before. She walked erratically and with a slight limp, slowly, then briskly, so that Ted had to concentrate in order not to overtake her or fall behind.

He was sliding into the city's knotty entrails, a poorer, untouristed area where the sound of flapping laundry mingled with the dry, bristly chatter of pigeons' wings. Without warning, Madeline pivoted around to face him. She stared, bewildered, into his face. "Is that?" she stammered, "Uncle—"

"My God! Madeline!" Ted cried, wildly mugging surprise. He was a lousy fake.

"You scared me," Madeline said, still disbelieving. "I felt someone—"

"You scared me, too," Ted rejoined, and they laughed, nervous. He should have hugged her right away; now felt too late.

To fend off the obvious question (what was he doing in Naples?), Ted kept talking: where she was going?

"Visit a friend," Madeline said. "What about you?"

"Just...walking!" he said, too loudly. They had fallen into step. "Is that a limp?"

"I broke my leg in Tangiers," she said. "I fell down a long flight of steps."

"I hope you saw a doctor."

Madeline gave him a pitying look. "I wore a cast for three and a half months," she said, "an old-fashioned plaster kind. Two hundred and four people signed it—there was literally not one iota of space left."

The swarm of detail stymied Ted. "Then why the limp?" he finally asked.

"I'm not sure."

She had grown up. And so uncompromising was this adulthood, so unstinting its inventory of breasts and hips and gently indented waist, the expert flicking away of her cigarette and whispery creases alongside her eyes, that Ted experienced the change as instantaneous. A miracle. Her face was triangular and mischievous, pale enough to absorb hues from the world around her—purple, green, pink—like a face painted by Lucien Freud. She looked like a girl who a century ago would not have lived long, would perhaps have died in childbirth. A girl whose feathery bones did not quite heal.

"You live here?" he asked. "Naples?"

"A nicer part," Madeline said, a bit snobbishly. "It's a palace compared to this. What about you, Uncle Teddy?"

He named the town.

"Is your house very big? Are there lots of trees? Do you have a tire swing?"

"Trees galore. A hammock no one uses."

Madeline paused, closing her eyes as if to imagine it. "You have three sons," she said. "Miles, Ames, and Alfred."

She was right; even the order was right. "I'm amazed you remember that," Ted said.

"I remember everything," Madeline said.

She had stopped before one of the seedy palazzi, its coat of arms painted over with a yellow smiley face. "This is where my friend lives," she said. "Goodbye, Uncle Teddy. It was so nice running into you." She shook his hand with damp, spidery fingers.

Ted, unprepared for this abrupt parting, stammered a little. "Wait, but—can't I take you to dinner?"

Madeline tilted her head, searching his eyes. "I'm awfully busy," she said, with apology, and then, as if softened by some deep, unfailing will to politeness, "But yes. You may."

It was only as Ted pushed open the door to his hotel room, the medley of 1950s beige tones that greeted him after each day he spent not looking for Madeline, that he was assailed by the sheer outlandishness of what had just happened. It was time to make his daily call to Beth, and he imagined his sister's dumbstruck jubilation at the avalanche of good news since yesterday: not only had he located her daughter, but she'd seemed clean, reasonably healthy, mentally coherent, and in possession of at least one friend (not counting the two hundred and four people who had signed her cast)—in short, better than they'd had any right to expect. And yet Ted himself felt no such elation. Why? he wondered, lying flat on the bed with arms crossed, shutting his eyes. Why this longing for yesterday, even this morning—for the relative peace of knowing he should look for Madeline but failing to do so? He didn't know. He didn't know.

The implosion of Beth and Howie's marriage had proceeded spectacularly the summer Ted lived with them at their Lake Michigan house while he oversaw a construction site two miles away. Apart from the marriage itself, the casualties by summer's end had included the majolica plate Ted brought Beth for her birthday; sundry items of abused furniture; Beth's left shoulder, which Howie dislocated twice, and her collarbone, which he broke. While they raged inside the house, Ted would take Madeline outside, through the razor-edged reeds, to the beach. She had long red hair and blue-white skin that Beth was always trying to keep from burning. Ted took his sister's worries seriously, and always brought the bottle with him when they went out to the sand—sand that was too hot in the late afternoons for Madeline to walk on without screaming. He would carry her in his arms, light as a cat in her red and white two-piece, would set her on a towel and rub cream onto her shoulders and back and face, her tiny nose—she must have been five—and wonder what would become of her, growing up among all this violence. He insisted she wear her white sailor hat in the sun, though she didn't want to. He was in college, working as a contractor to pay the bills.

"A con-trac-tor," Madeline repeated, fastidiously. "What's that?"

"Well, he organizes different workmen to build a house."

"Are there floor sanders?"

"Sure. You know any floor sanders?"

"One," she said. "He sanded our floors in our house. His name is Mark Avery."

Ted was instantly suspicious of this Mark Avery.

"He gave me a fish," Madeline offered.

"A goldfish?"

"No," she said, laughing, swatting his arm. "A bathtub fish."

"Does it squeak?"

"Yes, but I don't like the sound."

These conversations went on for hours. Yet often, Ted had the uneasy sense that the child was spinning them out as a way of filling the time—to distract them both from whatever was going on inside that house. And this made her seem much older than she was, a tiny little woman, knowing, world-weary, too accepting of life's burdens even to mention them. She never once alluded to her parents, or what it was she and Ted were hiding from out on that beach.

"Will you take me swimming?"

"Of course," he always said.

Only then would he allow her to doff her cap. Her hair was long and tangled and silken; it blew in his face when he carried her (as she always wished) into Lake Michigan. She would gird him with her thin legs and arms, warm from the sun, and rest her head on his shoulder. Ted sensed her mounting dread as they approached the water, but she refused to let him turn back. "No. It's okay. Go," she would mutter grimly into his neck, as if her submersion in Lake Michigan were an ordeal she was required to endure for some greater good. Ted tried different ways of making it easier for her—going in little by little, or plunging straight in—but always Madeline would gasp in pain and tighten the grip of her legs and arms around him. When it was over, when she was in, she was herself again, dog paddling despite his efforts to teach her the crawl ("I know how," she would say, impatiently. "I just don't want to."). Splashing him, teeth chattering gamely. But the entire process unsettled Ted, as if he were hurting her, forcing this immersion upon his niece when what he longed to do—fantasized about doing—was rescue her. Wrap her in a blanket and secret her from the house before dawn. Paddle away in an old rowboat he'd found. Carry her down the beach and simply not turn around. He was twenty. He trusted no one else. But he could do nothing, really, to protect his niece, and as the weeks seeped away, he began to anticipate summer's end as a dark, bad thing. Yet when the time came, it was strangely easy. Madeline clung to her mother, barely glancing at Ted as he loaded up his car and said goodbye, and he set off feeling angry at her, wounded in a way he knew was childish but couldn't seem to help, and when that feeling passed it left him exhausted, too tired even to drive. He parked outside a Dairy Queen and slept.

"How do I know you know how to swim, if you won't show me?" he asked Madeline, back on the sand.

"I took lessons with Rachel Costanza."

"You're not answering my question."

She smiled at him a little helplessly, as if she longed to hide behind her childishness but sensed that somehow, it was already too late for that. "She has a Siamese cat named Feather."

"Why won't you swim?"

"Oh, Uncle Teddy," she said, in one of her eerie imitations of her mother. "You wear me out."

Madeline arrived at his hotel at eight o'clock wearing a short red dress, knee-high black patent leather boots, and a regalia of cosmetics that sharpened her face into a small, ferocious mask. Her narrow eyes curved like hooks under the candied-red mass of her hair. Ted glimpsed her across the lobby and felt reluctance verging on paralysis. He had hoped urgently, cruelly, that she wouldn't show up.

Still, he made himself cross the lobby and take her arm. "There's a good restaurant up the street," he said, "unless you have other ideas."

She did. "You leave the planning to me," Madeline averred, blowing skeins of smoke from the window of a taxi and haranguing the driver in halting Italian as he shrieked down alleys and the wrong way up one-way streets to the Vomero, an area Ted had not seen. It was high on a hill. Reeling, he paid the driver and stood with Madeline in a gap between two buildings. The flat, sparkling city arrayed itself before them, lazily toeing the sea. Hockney, Ted thought. Diebenkorn. John Moore. In the distance, Mount Vesuvius reposed benignly. Ted pictured the slightly different version of Susan standing nearby, taking it in.

"This is the best view in Naples," Madeline said challengingly, but Ted sensed her waiting, gauging his approval.

"It's a wonderful view," he assured her, and added, as they ambled among the leafy residential streets, "This is the prettiest neighborhood I've seen in Naples."

"I live here," Madeline rejoined, but Ted felt nearly certain she was lying.

"Looks expensive," was all he said.

Madeline explained that she was getting into retail. "I have these friends that're starting up a business selling all kinds of stuff," she said. "Wigs, cell phones, key chains. We're already making money."

"I'm surprised you can work legally in Naples."

She grinned. Though one of her front teeth was chipped, the rest looked healthy, surprisingly white. "No one works legally in Naples," she said.

They reached an intersection thronged with what had to be college students (strange, Ted thought, how they looked the same everywhere), boys and girls in black leather jackets riding on Vespas, lounging on Vespas, perching, even standing on Vespas—the density of Vespas made the whole square seem to pant, and the fumes of their exhaust worked on Ted like a mild narcotic. It was dusk, and a chorus line of palm trees vamped against a Bellini sky. Madeline threaded her way among the students with brittle self-consciousness, eyes locked ahead.

In a restaurant on the square, she asked to be seated by the window. Then she ordered the meal: fried zucchini flowers followed by pizza. Again and again she peeked outside at the youths on their Vespas. "Do you know them?" Ted finally asked, though clearly she did not; they'd hardly glanced at her as she passed.

"Students," she said dismissively, as if the word were a synonym for nothing. "Kids."

"They look about your age."

"Age is a relative thing, Uncle Teddy," Madeline said, aiming a neat pipette of smoke over his head, "when you've done and seen as much as I have."

"I'm eager to hear about that."

"Oh, it's exhausting, and I've told it all so many times," she said, with mannered weariness. "I want to hear about you. Are you still a professor of art history? Are you a world's expert on something?"

Unnerved by her precise memory, Ted felt the bubble of anxiety that rose in him whenever he spoke about his work. "I'm omnivorous, I guess," he said, sounding stuffy and dull to himself. "Right now I'm writing about the impact of Greek sculpture on the late nineteenth century."

Madeline listened, eyes narrowed. "Your wife, Susan, her hair is blonde, right?"

"Susan is blonde."

"Does she dye it?"

"Excuse me?"

"I bet she highlights it," Madeline said. "There's a place in New York, can you believe? Highlights cost $350. I still read American magazines," she said, as if to persuade Ted that her information was good. "Do you love her? Susan?"

This cool inquiry landed somewhere near Ted's solar plexus. "Aunt Susan," he corrected her.

"Aunt." Chastened.

"Of course I love her," Ted said quietly.

Dinner arrived: pizza draped in buffalo mozzarella, buttery and warm in Ted's throat. After a second glass of red wine, Madeline began to talk. She had started out in London, she said, then flown to Hong Kong and entered mainland China on a boat. "Later I sneaked into Tibet on a bus," she said, "dressed as a monk. I rolled up my hair in a sock. My friends wanted me to cut it off, but I said no way, this hair is all I've got!"

"Are those the same friends you're working with here?" Ted asked. "Did you all come to Naples together?"

"Oh no," Madeline said. "I have no idea what happened to those people. Some of the girls, when I saw them again in Hong Kong, they were turning tricks."

The phrase skipped off her tongue with an ease Ted found troubling. "You're saying they're prostitutes?"

"It happens," she said. "You run out of money, run out of things to sell. Guys, too, but not as often. A guy can always haul wood or something." There was a studied quality to her blasé, as if she believed her knowledge of prostitutes, like her travels to Tibet, were inherently impressive. Ted felt a flicker of distaste, the plucking of a string. She was his niece, he reminded himself. She was Madeline.

"I've met rich people, too," she assured him. "I've been on yachts four times. Well, one was a sailboat. Or can a sailboat also be a yacht?"

"I'm not a connoisseur of yachts," Ted said grimly. "Or sailboats."

"I've met almost every kind of person there is," Madeline went on, "and I write down things about each different one, and then the next time I meet that kind of person, I know exactly what they'll do."

"Really. You can predict their behavior." His sarcasm was palpable.

"Literally," she said. "Like the other day, I met this girl on the beach, and she said her family would take me to the circus with them if I came back the next day at the same time. And I said, now tell me exactly what time, because I knew her type from before, I had it written down. And she told me six o'clock. So I came to the beach at six o'clock, and no one was there!"

She said this triumphantly, but Ted pictured Madeline arriving alone to an empty beach. "That's awful," he said.

"It wasn't awful," she said sharply. "It was exactly what I thought."

"Then why show up at all?"

"To see if I was right!" she said, then lapsed into disheartened silence. Outside it was dark, the teenagers had long ago dispersed. "We might as well go," she said.

The night had brought a chill, but Madeline didn't have a coat. "Please wear my jacket," Ted urged her, removing the worn, heavy tweed, but she wouldn't hear of it. He sensed her wish to remain fully visible in her red dress. The boots exaggerated her limp.

After a walk of many blocks, they reached a generic-looking nightclub whose doorman waved them listlessly inside. By now it was midnight. "This place is owned by friends of mine," Madeline said. "I keep saying I'll come, but I never have any time!"

They might have been anyplace in the world: black walls, neon purple light that leeched into everything white; a beat with all the variety of a jackhammer. Even Ted, no connoisseur of nightclubs, felt the tired familiarity of the scene, yet Madeline seemed electrified. "Buy me a drink

Uncle Teddy, would you?" she said. "Something with an umbrella on top."

Ted shoved his way toward the bar. Being away from his niece felt like opening a window, loosening an airless oppression. Her pretensions and bragging, her insincerity—all of it exhausted and dismayed him. She'd been through so much, yet emerged without knowledge or wisdom—she was less, not more, than she would otherwise have been. He felt angry, as if she'd broken a promise.

Madeline had saved for him a soft stool at a low table, a setup that made Ted feel like an ape, knees jammed under his chin. As she hoisted the barbaric umbrella drink to her lips, he noticed slivers of pale scar tissue on the inside of her wrist, accentuated by the purple light. He took her arm in his hands and turned it over; Madeline allowed this until she saw what he was looking at, then yanked her arm away. "That's from before," she said. "In Los Angeles."

"Let me see."

She wouldn't. And to his own amazement, Ted reached across the table and seized her wrists in his hands, wresting them over by force. Madeline resisted, and as he twisted her shaking arms, Ted knew he was hurting her and took a certain angry pleasure in it. Finally she surrendered, averting her eyes while he splayed her forearms on the table and studied them in the cold, weird light. Amid the red streaks his own hands had made, they were scarred and scuffed like furniture, bumps and knots and cuts that should have had stitches, but obviously had not.

"A lot are by accident," Madeline said. "My balance was really off—that's how I broke my leg."

"You've had a bad time." He wanted her to admit it.

"I hardly remember it."

"Try."

There was a long silence. Finally Madeline said, "I thought I saw my father. Isn't that stupid?"

"Not necessarily."

"I looked across a room—bam—I saw his hair. Or his legs, I still remember the exact shape of his legs. Or his hands. That way he used to tilt back his head when he laughed—do you remember, Uncle Teddy?"

"I remember."

"Everywhere," she said. "Everywhere. And I thought it might really be him, like maybe he was following me to make sure I'd be okay."

Ted let go of her arms, and she folded them in her lap. "Did you see him in Tibet?" he asked.

"Two times. Once, I went by a food stall and he was eating soup. But I kept walking, because I thought if he knew I saw, he might go away. Another time he passed me on a bike—I thought he did," she corrected herself. "It was stupid. I've been childish for most of my life, Uncle Teddy."

"You were a child," he said. "That's different."

Madeline made a face. "An awful child," she said, derisively. "A ridiculous little girl."

Ted flinched as though she'd struck him. "How can you say that?"

"Well, no one exactly stuck around."

"Your mother's around," Ted informed her over the thudding of his temples. "She's been sitting at home five goddamn years, waiting for the phone to ring."

"She can't help me," Madeline said.

"You were a wonderful little girl." Belligerent, insisting—he didn't care. "A beautiful, sweet little girl." He felt as if Madeline had destroyed that child, snuffed her out.

They sat in silence. Ted felt the gimlet gaze of his niece upon him. "Uncle Teddy," she finally said. "What are you doing here?"

It was the question he'd been dreading from the first, yet the answer slid from him like meat falling off a bone. "I'm here to look at art," he said. "To look at art and think about art."

There: a sudden, lifting sensation of peace. Relief. He hadn't come for Madeline, it was true. She made no difference.

"Art?" Madeline said.

"That's what I like to do," he said, and smiled. Smiled at his niece, forgave her all in one magnanimous instant. "That's what I'm always trying to do. That's what I care about."

In Madeline's face there was a shift, a slackening, as if some weight she'd been bracing herself against had abruptly been removed. Then the artifice seemed to drain from her all at once, leaving a wan, dispirited girl of twenty-two, slumped on a stool. "I thought you came to look for me," she said.

Ted watched her from a distance. A peaceful distance.

Madeline lit one of her Marlboros, and Ted noticed for the first time that her nails were red; she'd painted them since this afternoon. After two drags, she squashed it out.

"Let's dance," she said, a heaviness about her as she rose from her stool. "Come on, Uncle Teddy," taking his hand, herding him toward the dance floor, a liquid mass of bodies that provoked in Ted a frightened sensation of shyness. He hesitated, resisting, but Madeline hauled him in among the other dancers and instantly he felt buoyed, suspended. How long had it been since he'd danced in a nightclub? Fifteen years? More! Hesitantly, Ted began to move, feeling hulking, bearish in his professor's tweed, moving his feet in some approximation of dance steps until he noticed that Madeline was not moving at all. She stood quite still, watching him. And then she reached for Ted, encircled him with her long arms and clung to him so that he felt her modest bulk, the height and weight of this new Madeline, his grownup niece who had once been so small, and the irrevocability of that transformation loosed in Ted a jagged sorrow, so his throat seized and a painful tingling fizzed in his nostrils. He cleaved to Madeline. She was gone, that little girl, gone with the passionate boy who had loved her.

Finally she pulled away. "Wait," she said, not meeting his eyes. "I'll be right back." Disoriented, Ted hovered amidst the dancing Italians until a mounting sense of awkwardness drove him from the floor. He lingered near it, waiting for his niece. Eventually, he circled the club. She'd mentioned having friends there—could she be talking to them somewhere? Had she gone outside? Anxious, befuddled from his own umbrella drink, Ted ordered a San Pellegrino at the bar, and only then, as he reached for his wallet and found it gone, did he realize that she'd robbed him.

Sunlight pried open his sticky eyelids, forcing him awake. He'd forgotten to close the blinds. It had been five o'clock by the time he'd slept, after hours of helpless wandering in the Vomero, where he'd solicited an array of lousy directions to the police station; after locating it finally and relaying his sad tale (excluding the identity of the pickpocket) to an officer with oiled hair and an attitude of pristine indifference; after procuring a ride to his hotel (which was all he'd really been after) from an elderly couple he met at the station, whose passports had been stolen on the Amalfi ferryboat.

Now Ted rose from bed with a throbbing head and stampeding heart. A confetti of phone messages strewed the

table: five from Beth, three from Susan, and two from Alfred ("lost," read one, in the broken English of the hotel
clerk). Ted left them where he'd thrown them. He showered,
dressed without shaving, drank a vodka at the minibar, took
more money from the room safe. He had to find Madeline—
now, today, instantly, and this imperative, which had seized
him at no specific moment, assumed an urgency that was
the perfect inverse of his earlier avoidance of it. There were
other things he must do—call Beth, call Susan, eat—but
doing them now was out of the question. He had to find her.
Had to find her.

But where? Ted deliberated this question while downing
two espressos in the hotel lobby, letting the caffeine and
vodka greet in his brain like fighting fish. Where to look for
Madeline in this sprawling, malodorous city? He reviewed
the plans he'd never executed before—approaching kids at
the train station, the youth hostels, but no, no, he'd waited
too long for any of that. There was no more time.

Without a clear plan, he took a taxi to the Museo
Nazionale and set off in what seemed the direction he'd
walked the day before, after viewing the Orpheus and Eurydice. Nothing looked the same, but surely his state of
mind could account for the difference, the tiny metronome
of panic now ticking within him. Nothing looked the same,
yet everything looked familiar—the stained churches and
slanting crusty walls, the bars the size of hangnails. After
following a narrow street to its wriggling conclusion, he
emerged onto a thoroughfare lined with a gauntlet of weary
palazzi, their bottom floors gouged open to accommodate
cheap clothing and shoe stores. A breeze of recognition fluttered over Ted. He traversed the avenue slowly, looking right
and left, and finally spotted the coat of arms painted over
with a yellow smiley face.

He pushed open the diminutive rectangular door cut into the broad, curved entrance built to receive coaches and horses, then followed a passageway into a cobbled court-yard still warm from recent sunlight. It smelled of melons and garbage. A bandy-legged old woman wearing blue kneesocks under her dress bobbled toward him, hair in a scarf. "Madeline," Ted said, into her faded wet eyes. "American. Capelli rossi." He tripped on the *r* and tried again. "*Rossi,*" he said, rolling it this time. "*Capelli rossi.*"

"No, no," the woman muttered, shaking her head and puffing out her cheeks. As she began to lurch away, Ted followed, slipped a twenty-dollar bill into her soft hand and inquired again, rolling the *r* this time without a hitch. The woman made a clicking noise, jerked her chin, and then, looking almost sad, gestured for Ted to follow her back the way he'd come. He did, filled with disdain at how easily she'd been bought, how little her protection was worth. To one side of the front door was a broad flight of stairs, glim-mers of rich, Neapolitan marble still winking up through the grime. The woman began climbing slowly, clutching the rail. Ted followed.

The second floor, as he'd been lecturing his undergradu-ates for years, was the *piano nobile,* where families bran-dished their wealth before guests. Even now, littered with molting pigeons and stuccoed with piles of their refuse, its vaulted arches overlooking the courtyard were still illu-mined by some vestigial splendor. Seeing him notice the architecture, the woman said, "Bellissima, eh? Ecco, guar-date!" And with a pride Ted found oddly moving, she threw open the door to a big dim room whose walls were stained with what looked like patches of mold. The woman pulled a switch, and a lightbulb dangling from a wire transfigured the moldy shapes into painted murals in the style of Titian and Giorgione, robust naked women holding fruit; clumps of dark leaves. A whisper of silvery birds. This must have been the ballroom.

On the third floor Ted noticed the first of the youths like the ones he'd been avoiding in Naples, two boys hunched in a doorway, sharing the butt of a cigarette. A third lay asleep under a straggling assortment of laundry: wet socks and underwear pinned carefully to a wire. Ted smelled dope and olive oil, heard a mutter of subterranean activity, and realized that this palazzo had become a rooming house. So, he thought, amused by the irony of finding himself amidst this demimonde, here we are. At last.

On the fifth and top floor, where servants once had lived, the doors were smaller, set along a narrow hallway. Ted's elderly guide stopped to rest against a wall, eyes closed, breath whistling in her chest. In the course of the ascent, Ted's contempt for her had been supplanted by gratitude— what effort that twenty dollars had cost her! How badly she must need it. "I'm sorry," he said, "I'm sorry you had to walk so far." But the woman shook her head, not understanding. She tottered partway down the hall and rapped sharply on one of the narrow doors, speaking in Italian. When the door opened he saw Madeline, half asleep, dressed in a pair of men's pajamas. At the sight of Ted her eyes widened, but her face, that pale triangular mask, remained impassive. "Hi, Uncle Teddy," she said mildly.

"Madeline," he said, realizing only then that he, too, was breathless from the climb. "I wanted to . . . to talk to you."

"No problem."

The woman's gaze jumped between them; abruptly she turned and began her precarious journey back downstairs. Ted watched her go, but the moment she rounded a corner,

Madeline shut the door in his face. "Go away," she said. "I can't talk to you now, I'm busy."

"I will not," he said. "I will not go away." He moved nearer the door, flattening his palm against the splintery wood. Across it, he felt the angry, frightened presence of his niece. "It's true, what you told me before," he reflected. "You live in a palace."

"I'm moving someplace better any day."

"When you pick enough pockets?"

There was a pause. "That wasn't me," she said. "That was a friend of mine."

"You've got friends all over the place, but I never actually see them."

"Why would you?" she said haughtily. "Why should they want to see you?"

"Retail! Now I know what that means."

"I'm not a thief!" she insisted in a high, thready voice.

"You do a beautiful impersonation."

"Fuck you. I don't care what you think. Why can't you leave me alone?" She sounded close to tears.

"I'd like to," Ted said. "Believe me."

But he couldn't. Even when he heard Madeline burrowing deeper inside her apartment, he could not bring himself to leave, or even really move. Finally he bent his knees and slid to the floor. By now it was afternoon, and an aureole of musty light issued from a window at one end of the hall. Ted rubbed his eyes. He felt as if he might sleep.

"Are you still there?" Madeline demanded through the door.

"Still here."

"Go to hell."

I believe we're there, Ted imagined saying.

For a long time, hours, it seemed (he'd forgotten his watch), there was silence. Occasionally Ted heard other, disembodied tenants moving inside their rooms. He imagined he was an element of the palace itself, a sensate molding or step, whose fate it was to witness the ebb and flow of generations, to feel the palace relax its medieval bulk more deeply into the earth. Another year, another fifty. Twice he stood to let other tenants pass, strung out–looking girls with jumpy hands and cracked leather purses. They hardly looked at him.

"Are you still there?" Madeline asked, from behind the door.

"Still here."

She emerged from the room and locked the door quickly behind her. She wore blue jeans, a T-shirt, and plastic flip-flops, and carried a faded pink towel and a small bag. "Where are you going?" he asked, but she glanced at him and stalked down the hall without comment. Thirty minutes later she was back, hair hanging wet, trailing a floral smell of soap. She opened her door with the key, then hesitated. "I mop the halls to pay for this room, okay? I sweep the fucking courtyard. Does that make you happy?"

"Should it?" he said. "Does it make you happy?"

The door shook on its hinges.

As Ted sat, feeling the evolution of the afternoon, he found himself thinking of Susan. Not the slightly different version of Susan, but Susan herself—his wife, on a day many years ago, before Ted had begun to fold up his desire. Riding the Staten Island Ferry, Susan had turned to him suddenly and said, "Let's make sure it's always like this." And such was the intermingling of their thoughts that Ted knew exactly why she'd said it: not because they'd made love that morning or drunk a bottle of Pouilly-Fuissé at lunch; not because they were stealing a weekend alone in New York, but because she had felt the passage of time. And Ted felt it, too, then, in the leaping brown water, the scudding boats, the wind—motion, chaos everywhere—and he'd held Susan's hand and said, "Always. It will always be like this."

Recently, he'd mentioned that trip in some other context, and Susan had looked him full in the face and replied, in her new, sunny voice, "I don't remember going to New York." Amnesia, he'd thought. Brainwashing. But, of course, (he now saw) she'd been lying. That was all. He'd let her go, and she was gone.

"Are you there?" Madeline called, but Ted didn't answer.

She opened the door and stuck out her head. "You are," she said, sounding more grudging than angry. Ted looked up at her from the floor and said nothing. "You can come inside, I guess."

He hauled himself to his feet and stepped inside her room. It was tiny. A single bed, a desk, a sprig of mint in a plastic cup filling the room with its scent. The red dress, hanging from a hook. The sun was just beginning to set, skidding over the tops of houses and churches and landing in the room through a single window by the bed. Something hung there, in the window: a crude circle made from what looked like a coat hanger, dangling on a string. Madeline sat anxiously on her bed, and Ted recognized, with brutal immediacy, what he'd somehow failed to see until now: how alone she was in this foreign place. How empty-handed.

As if sensing the movement of his thoughts, Madeline said, "I used to know a lot of people. But it never really lasts."

On the desk lay his wallet, a picture of Beth in a small round frame. There was a stack of books, most of them in English. *The History of the World in 24 Lessons. The Sumptuous Treasures of Naples.* At the top, a worn volume entitled, *Learning to Type.*

Ted turned to his niece and seized her slender shoulders, two bird's nests in his hands. The prickling sensation ached in his nostrils. "You can do it alone," he told her. "You can, Madeline. But it's going to be so much harder."

She didn't answer. She was looking at the sun. Ted turned to look, too, staring through the window at the riot of dusty color. Turner, he thought. O'Keeffe. Paul Klee.

On another day more than twenty years after this one, Ted, long divorced, a grandfather, would visit Madeline in Arizona. He would stand with his niece in a living room strewn with the flotsam of her teenage children and watch the western sun blaze through a sliding glass door. He would think of Naples, and feel again the jolt of surprise he remembered—the relief, the delight—when at last the sun dipped into the center of Madeline's window and was captured inside her circle of wire.

Now he turned to her, grinning. She was doused in orange light.

"See?" Madeline said, eyeing the sun. "It's mine."

A HOT TIME AT THE CHURCH OF KENTUCKY FRIED SOULS AND THE SPECTACULAR FINAL SUNDAY SERMON OF THE RIGHT REVREN DADDY LOVE

At the Revren Daddy Love's funeral—a long, loud service where they alternated tween dancin and weepin—a swarm of rumors buzzed through the pews. Women leaned across husbands and whispered to each other about Daddy and Sister Gayl and Lil Henny and Big Angela and Tish and Babs and on and on til what everyone was really saying was *Girrrl, every pair of female lips in this con-gre-gayshun done tasted Daddy's sweet juice.*

The Deacon preached, "The Revren took from our wallets!... Took from our wives!... Even took from some a our daugh-ers!"

"Wellll..." they called back.

"Was he the way he was because he wanted to be or because we wanted him to be? We'll never know."

"Tell it..." they said.

"But that's no nevermore cuz now that he gone we all gone be a lil poorer. Yes, I say, we's all a bit poorer t'day! Cuz Black currency ain't money. No! It's joy! The twenty-dollar bill of our currency... is *theater.* The dramatic theater of daily life. The ten-spot is rhythm. The fiver is hope, the deuce is freedom, and the dollar is good, hearty laughter."

"*Preach!!!*" they yelled.

"And, of course, the C-note is love. So by our math, the Revren Daddy Love was...a *multi*millionaire. And, the Revren Daddy Love was...*a big spendah!*"

At the wake, the rumors flew, and a gaggle of questions chased after them. The married women arranged fresh potato salad and hot corn bread, the unmarried women gulped the good champagne out plastic cups, and everyone wondered aloud, *You think Daddy took all he could get or gave everythin he had?*

The Revren Daddy Love caused much discord, but none on two subjects: first, Daddy was colossal. Freckles on his hi-yalla skin as large as dimes, a belly as great as a jumbo TV, a mouth that made mailboxes jealous, and a frame so titanic he would just swallow a girl up with one of his patented post-service hugs. No matter how rotund she was, Daddy could still hug her in surround-sound stereo because Daddy was super-sized, as though God had intended him to be quite literally larger than life.

Second thing everyone knew about Daddy: in every crevice and crack of his giant body Daddy Love did love women. All women. Daddy's love was as blind as faith and as democratic as the sun. Any woman, regardless of shape or style, could come to Daddy and find herself ecstatically baptized by those eyes, eyes the color of pure honey, eyes that shot an electric current through a girl's body and loved her better than most men could with their hands. It was the affirmation, and *all* the affirmation, a female needed to know she was magnificently woman. Women saw how seriously Daddy Love appreciated them, and, wildly appreciating his appreciation, they rewarded him and rewarded him with no regard for vows or jealousies or the horde of rewards he was getting from a horde of rewarders. But was it really Daddy getting the reward? For a week or two afterwards her husband would feel happier having her around, her family would eat better, and her entire house, no matter how small and drab, would seem a touch brighter, as though someone had installed a window that moved throughout the day to capture as much sunlight as possible.

Was his flock particularly lost or uniquely found? The center of those conversations was the church choir, Love's Angels. Those twenty-one women joined not for the singing, which was third rate on a good day, but for the special confession ritual.

Daddy always said his choir had to be held to a higher standard and when they sinned they had to receive special attention. On Sundays just before service, an Angel who had sinned would go to Daddy's office and confess. They would talk about what she'd done and why she'd done it. Then, the Angel would raise her skirt until her bottom was bare and free. Daddy would remove his belt and apply a slow battery of stiff thwacks to those bare, free cheeks with a sharp, stinging force that was said to make her brown skin wiggle hotly and then, for a fraction of a moment, sing out, in torrid pain, a sound like high, tortured notes from a muted trumpet. Angels confessed almost as often as their singing cheeks allowed. And on those rare occasions there was space for a new member, women waged war to get in.

That's how things were at St. Valentine's Blessed Temple of Godly Love, Sanctified Ascension, and the Holy Glissando, located in Brooklyn, at the corner of Grace Street and Divine Avenue, in an abandoned Kentucky Fried Chicken.

Now it may be easier to believe we could have a Black president, a nigger boycott on Cadillacs, and an all-white

NBA all at once, than to believe in a single abandoned Kentucky Fried Chicken in Brooklyn, USA, but it's true. What happened is someone at headquarters gave some franchisee the green light to build a three-floor KFC palace even though there were, within reasonable walking distance of the corner of Grace and Divine, three KFCs, two Church's Chickens, one Roy Rogers, one Kennedy Fried Chicken, one General Tso's Fried Chicken, and two Miss Mannie Mack's Fried Chickens (one of which shared space with Al's Fried Chicken Shack). Guess someone upstairs just couldn't stand that franchisee's ass.

Only three days after the KFC palace opened, corporate paid a visit to their new pride and joy and quickly realized their geographical error. In a panic, they commanded the ill-fated franchisee to make up the competitive difference by frying his chicken in a heavier, thicker oil and three and a half times as much of it. Years later, the star-crossed franchisee would crumble during cross-examination in his trial on federal civil rights violations and admit that corporate had indeed hollered, *"Deep-fry those niggers!"* He was all but thrown underneath the penitentiary when, through pathetic tears, he conceded that yes, he had noticed the vile smell of his toilets, and yes, he'd heard about the jolt in sales of Pepto-Bismol, and—yes, yes, oh God, yes!—eyewitnessed three men, on the very same day, crashing to the floor from heart failure right inside the store, and yet he still continued to deep-fry even though he said to himself, "Ah thinks the chicken is comin out a lil too greazy."

It ain't take long for Daddy Love and his followers to turn that mountainous grease pit into a church. There was already a tall red steeple, lots of seats, tons of parking, and plenty of private office space. In the beginning most felt it wasn't too bad using bits of leftover chicken in communion to signify the body of Christ. And after a while people came to like using the drive-thru window for confession. But Daddy never did have that greazy kitchen cleaned out properly. He just slapped some thick wooden boards on top of it and built his pulpit over that. Bet he'd like that decision to do over.

You might have never known the building had been a KFC if not for the sixty-foot sign that displayed the KFC logo and a portrait of Colonel Sanders. The pole that held up that sign withstood every sort of abuse they subjected it to until they were convinced that the pole and the portrait had been constructed to outlast that KFC palace, America, and maybe even Earth. So every Sunday they filed into service under the unchanging halfsmile of that good ol neo-massa Colonel Sanders. That's just one of the reasons why only Daddy Love and his most loyal devotees ever called the church by its real name. To everyone else it was the Church of Kentucky Fried Souls.

After ten years at Kentucky Fried Souls Daddy Love had become a ghetto celebrity. He was known for his curious congregation, his unique vision of the Bible, and his way of riding slowly through the neighborhood in his 1969 convertible white Bentley, chauffeured by one of his Angels, passing out fives to the little boys and tens to the little girls. But first and foremost, Daddy was known for his preaching. He preached with a dynamism that hypnotized and bewitched, employing rhythm and volume, intensity and repetition, moans, grunts, hollers, hums, and a raw spiritual force beamed down from up on high to give his sermons wings that you could grab ahold of and go with him as he took flight, transcending English, while you nestled inside his truth—strings of words dipped in a magic that let him say crazy things no other preacher could say and pull you into a new awareness that would make you do crazy things, that, if you really knew how to listen, might make your life a little better.

There was no place you could go in Black New York where they ain't know about Daddy. But he had grown tired of being a local legend. He wanted to float in the rare air. He'd stepped up to the plate and seen the fence separating those who were legends for a certain generation and those who had crossed over into history, and he wanted to smack a grand slam. He wanted to ascend the Black imagination and fly at the altitude of C. L. Franklin and Adam Powell and Martin King, those spiritual pilots who rest atop the Black imagination like nighttime stars: brilliant patches of light with a sort of everlasting life that we can look up to for direction anytime we lose our way. He would get there with one magnificent, never-to-be-forgotten performance, an extraordinarily epic manifesto-sermon punctuated with an impossibly dramatic flourish that would come together to form a story passed down from generation to generation and lift him into that rare air. On the last Sunday of his life Daddy Love arrived at Kentucky Fried Souls two hours early.

As the congregation filed in, the warm clack and click of fine Sunday shoes could be heard over the light sounds of the choir quietly singing "Love Me in a Special Way" and the organist and drummer and electric guitarist and three-man horn section backing them. Once they were seated a hush came over them. There was a long, silent moment that neither a nervous cough nor a baby's cries dared break, then Daddy Love emerged from his office on the third floor, escorted by two busty and freshly absolved Angels. He raised his large chin slightly, pursed his giant lips delicately, and, with a voice smooth and bassy like jazzy tuba riffs, said simply, "Love is here."

He was wearing what amounted to, despite their obvious lavishness, a lounging robe and house slippers. The slippers were thick, plush, and fire-engine red, with a busy logo across the front. The robe, made of rare silk, was a matching fire-engine red with thick black trim and long ends that draped on the floor below him. A black belt knotted tightly about Daddy Love's giant stomach pulled it all together. The combined worth of every single item worn by any family in attendance was not as great as that one robe. No one knew whether Daddy wore it out of vanity, or because he knew we needed to see him look like a prince, or both.

To thunderous applause, Daddy made his way down the stairs, an Angel on each arm, with a walk that combined a bull's brute, a rooster's righteousness, and a pimp's peacock. When he finally came to the lip of the pulpit, Daddy reached down and snatched a bit of his billowing robe off the floor, sucked in his great stomach, and squoze himself through the doorway of the pulpit. He then faced the podium and placed his hands on its far edges, giving him the appearance of total authority over that spiritual cockpit. He looked out at his flock and said with bottomless earnest, "Praise the Love."

They cheered and Daddy eased into his sermon. "Back in the day Love knew a man who'd died and gone to heaven. This man had been married for decades and loved his wife dearly. But in matters of love he was something of . . . a microwaver. He liked that quickfast heat, that fast food, that slambang dunk. He took more time in choosing his words when he spoke than in pleasing his wife when the conversation ended!"

"Oooooh chile!" the women called back.

"When he arrived at the pearly gates and got through the line to see Saint Peter, the good saint told him, 'You've led a good, clean life and been an upstanding member of human society. But you are not yet ready. God has made it clear: there will be no microwavers in His heaven.'"

"No microwavers up there!" the women said.

"The man knew there was no appealing God's will, so he came back to earth and came to see Love. He said, 'Daddy Love, I have been turned away from the gates of heaven! What did I do?' Love sat down beside him and said, 'It's not what you did do—it's what you did *not* do. We'll sit and talk about loving in a Gawdly way and you'll go out and practice loving in a Gawdly way and one day Heaven will again summon you and this time you'll stroll right in.'" Daddy gingerly opened his heart-red Bible. "We started in the Song of Songs, chapter three, verse five. It is written, 'Daughters of Jerusalem, I charge you by the gazelles and by the does of the field: Do not arouse or awaken love until it so desires.'"

Daddy Love gazed out over his flock and those light eyes began narrowing slightly and everyone knew that the Word was about to take him over. "Do not...*arouse*...or *awaken*...love...until *it*...so desires. Brothers and dearly beloved sisters, what's that mean?"

"Tell us what it mean, Daddy!" someone called out.

"It means you can't...hurry...love," he said tenderly. "It means we must let love grow naturally. To surrender— yes, surrender, my brothers—to love's pace. For that is the only way to truly love our sisters in...a Gawdly way."

The women let out a tremendous mmm-hmmm.

"So Love told his friend that the only way God would want us to love is in a *slow, tender*—that's right—tender way that surrenders to love...that doth not arouse love until *it so* desires..."

"*So, SO tender!*"

"...and Love told his brother, 'While you're in the kitchen, stirring up love, adding spices, you got to let that love cook at its own pace. Cuz that's the only way to get some tender food, you got to let the slow heat have at it for a good, long while!' Can Love get just one witness?"

"Bring us through, Daddy!" they cried out.

"So you're laying there in your...*kitchen*," he said, and slowly closed his eyes and smiled, winning laughs. "And you're there, stripped of society's shields—*Love's talkin bout clothes.* And you're admiring some of God's sublime handiwork..."

"Oh YES!" a man cried out from the back.

"...and you're letting things simmer and bubble and it's getting hot but love's still not done cooking and you're trying to keep from arousing love until *it* so desires...So what you gon do?"

"Teach em how to cook, Daddy!"

"Follow me now..."

"We right behind ya!"

"...Love knows the way!"

"Oh Lord, Love does!"

"...Patience...my brothers and beloved sisters, *patience...* is *Gawdly!*" Daddy Love cried out. "So, watch Love now: linger," he said softly, "before you love." The women murmured their assent. "The good book tell us, 'For love is as strong as death, its jealousy unyielding as the grave. It burns like blazing fire, like a mighty flame.' Now that's true, but love won't burn like blazing fire if you don't handle it properly. Linger before you love!" And then, his mammoth form shaking like a riot, Daddy thundered, *"BE NOT MICROWAVERS, MY SONS, BE OPEN-FLAME GRILLERS! Linger before you love! My God wants His heaven filled with love barbequers who let* the coals roast and the flames lick *and waits* until the sweetest and highest and most uncontrollable of feminine moans has been extracted and then say unto themselves, Ah, I have just...gotten...*started!*" Love shot his arms above his head as though he had scored a miraculous touchdown and the women broke into ecstatic screams and hysterical dances because they knew the coming week would be a good one and they began celebrating right away, halting the sermon for ten long, loud minutes.

"I can feel the dungeon shaking!" Daddy said with a broad smile as they finally quieted. A man in the third row smiled sweetly at his wife and relocked his fingers within hers. "I can feel them chains a-falling clean off!" Laughter sprinkled through. "But Love's got more. Stay with me!"

"WE AIN'T GOIN NO PLACE, DADDY!" a sister cried out, and even Love had to laugh.

"Love once knew a woman who'd died and gone to heaven! In her years on earth she'd been chained by the manacles of repression and the shackles of inhibition. She'd been something of a ram, banging her head against those who loved her, and something of a jellyfish, stinging those who got too close, and something of a praying mantis, loving a man and then devouring him."

The church moaned.

"When she got to heaven Saint Peter said, 'You ain't ready.' So she went to Daddy Love and Daddy Love went to the Good Book.

"Good book say... 'The spirit of God dwelleth within you,' and that is true. Oh yes, that spirit dwelleth within *you*," he said, and his eyes landed in the front row on a well-preserved woman under a faded scarlet hat, "and...*you*," gazing at a woman seated next to her with long braided hair flowing from a sun-yellow beret, "and mos definitely...

you," freezing on a girl, her tight ponytail held in place by an unblemished white ribbon. It was Lily Backjack, a favored Angel, who had seemed as pure as a new day, who had then abruptly left the church and, soon after, high school...For a moment Daddy's eyes locked onto the slight bulge in her stomach and he let out the first part of a very deep breath and a single drop of sweat quivered at the edge of his eyebrow, then broke away and soared down toward his Bible.

"The spirit of God dwelleth within all! So if you want to feel the spirit of God, to experience the full grip of God's love, you must grip another of God's creatures firmly! You must lock onto another body in which God dwelleth and experience that love...*wildly!*"

"Lock onto me, LAWD!!!"

"So one day many years later this sister was called back to heaven. Things had not gone so well her first time there, but she was unafraid this time. On earth she been as free as an eagle and she knew she would get into heaven. When she got to Saint Peter he took her to see God because he himself wanted to ask her about her time on earth. And when she got to the Father and found herself at the trial of the millennium, she was asked one question: 'Did you, in your time on Earth, did ya love your fellow human beings...in a Gawdly way?' *Oh Lord*, my brothers and beloved sisters, when that question comes to you, you've got to be able to say to your Lord a resounding 'Yes Lawd! Yes Lawd! *A thousand times I did!* Yes Lawd!' Can Love *get* an Ayy-men?"

"Praise JEEE-SUS!"

"But this time she was ready for the Almighty's question and she told the King of Kings: 'My Lord, I have let freedom ring! I have let freedom ring from the bedroom to the backseat, in the ocean and in dark caves and in midair, inches below your home, in first class—*I have let freedom ring!*' And the Lord smiled on her then and gave her wings and I tell you now, her time in heaven was as long and fruitful *as the very member of our Maker must be! HAAALL-LAY-LOOO-YAAAAAHHHH!!!"*

And with that they unleashed a roar that tested the walls, and the organ and the drums and the guitar and the horns leapt into the thunder with righteous riffs and hardly a body was seated for everyone was dancing, wild and free, clogging the aisles and shaking the tables, rocking their asses and flapping their hands madly in the air. They had not a care in the world, certainly not that it was Sunday morning and it seemed no different from Saturday night.

As Daddy came down from the pulpit, the organist led Love's Angels into song and they followed as one, in high, soulful church voices.

"Ain't no way...
for me to love you...
if you won't let me!
It ain't no way
for me to give you all you need,
If you won't
let me give all of me!"

One sister stepped forward and took the lead: *"I know that a woman's duty... is to haaave and love a man..."*

"Looovve..." the other Angels backed her up.

"...But how can I, how can I, how can I..." she sang with her hands windmilling furiously, *"give ya all the things I can... if you're tying both of my hands?"*

"Tie me..." the Angels sang.

"It ain't no way...!" the leader sang, then opened her eyes and saw Daddy standing by her side, his massive body filled with the spirit, his shoulders trembling.

"... *For me to lovvve you,*" she sang into Daddy's eyes. "*If you won't ... let me.*" Daddy then began rocking from heel to toe, heel to toe, gaining momentum like a child on a swing, then he bent low and leapt a full foot into the air.

With his prodigious size no one expected to see Daddy Love hold even that much sway over gravity, so none was prepared for what came next. Daddy Love, empowered by momentum, bent again, deeper this time, and leapt into the air. First he was a foot off the ground, then two, then four, then six, the titanic Daddy Love, robe still fastened tightly round his ginormous body, floating up and up, ten feet, twenty, his eyes closed, his hands outstretched, his face as peaceful as a just-fed baby. The music had stopped, the Angels were silent, and the church was filled with statues, mouths agape at their gargantuan leader hanging placidly, fifty feet in the air, almost close enough to touch the ceiling.

A woman, her mouth still open, touched her husband gently, as if full consciousness of the moment might end it. "It's a miracle," she whispered.

Then, someone stirred. Lily Backjack. Even hanging fifty feet in the air, with his eyes closed, Daddy Love could feel her stare, so cold ain't nothin in hell could burn you worse.

As Lily walked up the aisle toward the stage, her white ribbon floating and her belly protruding, everyone scrambled out her way. Daddy just hung there, high above them, frozen. All you could hear was the hard, steady *clack, clack* of her tall black vinyl boots. When Lily reached the stage she grabbed hold of one of the thick wooden boards and gave it a malevolent jerk to make a sliver of space. It was all she needed. She reached into her pocket, pulled out a single match, looked up at Daddy Love, and forced a smile his way. "Now, alla thems will know," she said, "whether or not I *loveded* you." She lifted up the sole of her right boot and in one fluid arc lit the match against her heel and dropped it into the small void. Pools of old, nasty chicken grease waited to suck it in. Lily turned with a flip of her curly hair and began walking back down the aisle. For three seconds, that *clack, clack* of her boots was the only sound. Then, an evil boom. As Lily, pushing a tortured smile through a river of tears, continued walking down the aisle and out of the building, the entire stage turned suddenly into a giant pool of tall, magenta flames.

Through the four seconds it took to clear the church, Daddy Love stayed calm. And during the following four seconds, as the stage grew and grew into a vast barbeque pit over which he hung like a giant, meaty, hi-yalla, free-range, Perdue chicken, Daddy refused to panic. But when he saw three men—who had disappeared just before he began to fly—burst from behind the curtain at the back of the stage, sprint through tall waves of fire, and race out the door trailing bright yellow, only then did Daddy Love lose his cool. He began to shake and wriggle, but he could only twist and turn and help himself be cooked more evenly. He could not loosen the wires that held him up. He could not lose altitude, could not free himself from the invisible cross he'd put himself on. An edge of robe drooped down and a flaming tongue leapt up, a hungry shark, and bit into it. He reached down and snuffed out that small blaze, but the fire was growing fast, climbing the walls and scrambling round the floor, dancing, wild and free, broiling the aisles and wrecking the tables, appearing to be flapping its hands madly in the air without a care in the world.

Daddy Love looked out over our burning church and saw that in the corner there was someone left, a boy lying on the floor, clutching his ankle, cringing in pain, the joint spilling blood that was a red much fuller and blacker than that of the yellowish red of the fire racing toward him from all sides.

"Daddy! Fly down! Save me!" the boy screamed out.

Daddy struggled again to free himself and succeeded only in making his robe fall full open so the boy could see he had on a cheap pair of white cotton briefs.

"Daddy!" the boy bawled like a babe. "Save me, Daddy! Aaahh!"

Then Daddy Love stopped squriming, wiped his sweaty face, closed his eyes, and bowed his giant head in prayer. He felt not the fire leaping and licking from all sides at his toes and neck and ass, but only the need to call on the Lord. "Father!" he screamed out above the deafening cackles of the burning building. "Have I strayed? Have I gone wrong in trying to give my flock the sunshine they need to get through, to get through the days, to get through the jungles keeping them from happiness? Hath I erred in trying to use your name and your teachings to show my flock how to be happier and freer and more loving? Have I not employed your name to make lives brighter? Lord, any mortal can see a man's fall, but only you know his internal struggling, the tears shed in the midnight of his soul. Please Lord, don't take the boy. Reach down and touch us now!"

Daddy looked into the corner, but a blindingly yellow patch of flames had taken it over. Inside his giant chest, hot tears began shaking loose. Then he looked up. The boy was floating slowly and calmly in the air, ten feet, twenty, forty, up toward the ceiling, out of the reach of the fire on each wall, snatching out at him and missing. Soon he reached the ceiling. Fire had chomped at almost every inch of wall and crevice of floor and the boy floated through a fire-eaten hole in the ceiling and landed on a part of the roof. He looked back through the hole at Daddy Love, fire from everywhere closing in on him as he dangled helplessly in midair. Daddy looked at the boy and mouthed, *Don't linger now.* The boy leapt from the roof half a moment before it caved in and landed squarely on the KFC sign. As they crowded in the parking lot around Kentucky Fried Souls and watched the walls of the church crash in on one another, leaving the immense palace a huge pile of blackened rubble, a rumor began slithering through the crowd—*Girrrl, Daddy ain't gilded lil Lily…was that no-good Bishop!* Meanwhile, the boy sat safely, waving gleefully, sixty feet up, atop the portrait of that good ol neo-massa Colonel Sanders, as a fractured but breathing memory of Daddy Love began its ascent into rare air.

FIALTA

From where I stand, on the bridge overlooking the Chicago River, the city looks like a strange but natural landscape, as if it arises as surely and inevitably from the hands of life as does a field of harvest wheat or a stand of red firs. After all, the city was designed by country boys—Mies van der Rohe, Rook and Burnham, Frank Lloyd Wright, Louis Sullivan— all wild and dashing country boys, dreaming up the city in the soft thrum of the countryside.

But the buildings that most reflect nature, at least Midwestern nature in all its dark and hidden fertility, are those by Franklin Nostbakken, the so-called architect of the prairies, that great and troubled mess of a man I once knew.

Three years ago, when I was a senior at Northwestern, I sent Nostbakken a packet of drawings and a statement of purpose. Every year Nostbakken chooses five apprentices to come live with him on the famous grounds of Fialta, his sprawling workshop, itself an architectural dream rising and falling over the gentle hills of southwestern Wisconsin. My sketches were of skyscrapers, set down with a pencil on pale blue drafting paper. They'd been drawn late in the night, and I knew hardly anything about how to draw a building, except that it ought not to look beautiful; it ought to be spare and slightly inaccessible, its beauty only suggested, so that a good plan looked like a secret to be passed on and on, its true nature hidden away.

Two months later I received back a letter of acceptance. At the bottom of the form letter there was a note from Nostbakken himself that read, *In spite of your ambition, your hand seems humble and reasonable. I look forward to your arrival.*

I had been reading, off and on, that year, a biography of Nostbakken, and this moment when I read his handwriting was one of the most liberating of my life—in fact, so much so it was almost haunting, as if a hand had leapt out of the world of art—of books and dreams—and pulled me in.

My first evening at Fialta was referred to as Orientation, but was really a recitation by one of the two second-year apprentices, named Reuben, of What Nostbakken Liked, which was, in no particular order, mornings, solitude, black coffee, Yeats, order, self-reliance, privacy, skits, musicals, filtered light, thresholds, lightning. *Piña coladas,* the woman sitting beside me—Elizabeth—said quietly. *Getting caught in the rain.*

"Fialta," Reuben continued, "is dedicated not to the fulfillment of desire but to the transformation of desire into art." We were sitting in the Commons, a beautiful, warm room that doubled as our dining room, our office, and our lounge. There was an enormous fireplace, windows streaming with slanted and dying light, and a big wooden table, whose legs were carved with the paws of beasts where they touched the floor. There was a golden shag carpet, and stone walls. It was high up, and the views were spectacular, but the room was intimate. So this statement regarding desire seemed almost heartbreakingly Freudian, since the room and all of Fialta, with its endless private corners and stunning walkways and fireplaces, seemed to ask you at every turn to fall in love, yet that was the one thing that was not permitted. Reuben went on to say, "Nostbakken does not tolerate well what he calls over-fraternization. He sees it as a corruption of the working community if people, well..." And there was a nervous moment. Reuben seemed to have lost his footing. Nobody knew what to say until a tall woman in the back, whose name would turn out to be Indira Katsabrahmanian, and whose beauty would turn out to be the particular rocks on which Reuben's heart would be dashed, spoke up: *"Sodo-sudu."* Reuben raised his eyebrows at her. "Fool around," she said, with a slightly British accent. "It means to not fool around."

Reuben nodded.

So, no love affairs. As soon as this was declared, it was as if a light had turned on in the room. Until this point, everyone had been so focused on the great absent man himself and his every desire that nobody had really looked around that carefully. But at this mention that we could not fall in love, we all turned to see who else was there. Each person seemed suddenly so interesting, so vital, a beautiful portal through which one might pass, secretly. And this was when I saw Sands, who was, with Reuben, returning for her second year at Fialta. When I try to call forth my first impression of Sands, it is so interpreted by the light of loss that what I see is somebody already vanishing, but beautifully, into a kind of brightness. And as Nostbakken's beloved Yeats said of Helen, how can I blame her, being what she was and Fialta being what it is?

As we left that evening, I talked briefly to Reuben and to Elizabeth, whose nickname became Groovy in those few moments, owing to her look, which had a hundred implications—of Europe and Asia, of girls, of tough guys, of grannies. And I then fell in step beside Sands as she walked outside. It was slightly planned on my part, but not entirely, which allowed me to think that the world was a little bit behind me and my desire. It was mid-September, and in this part of the country there were already ribbons of wintry cold running through the otherwise mild evenings. We had a brief, formal conversation. We discussed Fialta, then Chicago. I had thought I was walking her home, but it seemed that we were actually, suddenly, winding up a pathway toward Nostbakken's living quarters.

"Oh," I said. "Where are we going?"

"I'm going up to check on him." She pointed way up to a sort of lighthouse circling above us.

"Nostbakken?"

"Yes." There was light pouring out the window.

"Oh sure, go ahead," I said.

She smiled at me and then walked off. And I turned to walk back to my room, slightly horrified at myself. *Go ahead*, I repeated to myself. *Oh, hey, go ahead.* This is the whole problem with words. There is so little surface area to reveal who you might be underneath, how expansive and warm, how casual, how easygoing, how cool, and so it all comes out a little pathetic and awkward and choked.

As I walked home, I turned back and saw through the trees again that window, ringing with clarity and light above the dark grounds, the way the imagination shines above the dark world, as inaccessible as love, even as it casts its light all around.

That evening I lay in bed reading Christopher Alexander, the philosopher-king of architects: *The fact is, that this seeming chaos which is in us is a rich, swelling, dying, lilting, singing, laughing, shouting, crying, sleeping, order.* I paused occasionally to stare out the large window beside my bed, which gave way to the rolling hills, toward Madison's strung lights, and, had I the eyes to see, my hometown of Chicago burning away in the distance. Reuben knocked on my door. We were roommates, sharing a large living room and kitchen. Reuben was the cup full to the brim, and maybe even a little above the brim but without spilling over, as Robert Frost put it. If one of the skills of being properly alive is the ability to contain gracefully one's desires, then Reuben was the perfect living being.

"I forgot to give you your work assignment," he said.

The literature on Fialta I received over the summer had mentioned grounds work, which I had assumed meant carpentry or landscaping, but now Reuben informed me that I would be in charge of the cows and the two little pigs.

"There are animals here?"

"Yes. Down in the barn."

"There's a barn?"

"Yes. At the end of the pasture."

"Of course," I said.

He was already bowing out of the door when I asked what I was to do with them.

"Milk the cows, feed the pigs," he said, and ducked out.

I should never have sent in those skyscrapers, I thought to myself as I fell asleep. Those are what got me the cow assignment. You can feel it as you sketch plans, the drag in the hand, the worry, the Tower of Babel anxiety as the building grows too high. There ought not to be too much hubris in a plan. But this is not a simple directive either, since a plan also needs to be soaring and eccentric and confident. But still humble. A perfect architect might be like a perfect person, their soul so correctly aligned that it can ascend with humility. Humble and dashing, those two things, always and forever.

You could say that Fialta was not quite in its prime. Its reputation was fading a little, and all its surfaces tarnishing, but so beautifully that Fialta was a more romantic place than it must have been even at the height of its influence, something that could be said of Nostbakken as well. Early success as an architect and a slide into some obscurity had given his reputation a kind of legendary, old-fashioned quality, even though he was still only in his late fifties. At seven o'clock, at the dimming of the next day, he stepped into the Commons for our first session. He had the looks of a matinee idol in the early twilight of his career, and he seemed more substantially of the past than anybody I've ever met, so that even now, when I remember him, it is in black and white. He is wistful in my memory, staring off, imagining a building that might at last equal nature—generative and wild, but utterly organized at the heart.

That night, when we all met in the Commons at Fialta, Nostbakken entered and said only this: "We have a new project. It's what we were all hoping for. It's a theater, along a city block in Chicago, surrounded on two sides by a small park designed by Olmstead. I'd like the theater to think about the park."

Sands and Reuben nodded, so the rest of us did as well. "Yes, well," he said. "You might as well begin." He put his hands together, in a steeple, as he stared at us—Reuben, Sands, myself, Indira, and Groovy—taking each of us in briefly, and then he left.

Reuben immediately then took his position at the blackboard that was usually pushed against the wall. He and Sands began, and the rest of us very slowly joined in until Reuben had covered the blackboard with phrases, what they called patterns for the building—*sloping roofs, alcoves, extended thresholds, hidden passageways, rays of light, soulful common areas, the weaving of light and dark, clustering rehearsal rooms, simple hearths, thick walls, a dance hall, radiant heat, filtered light, pools of light, arrows of darkness, secret doorways*...

I was already developing a rule to never look at Sands, in order to not give myself away and make her nervous. But there was something in her—some combination of joy and intelligence and seriousness—that seemed unrepeatable to me. Her voice had a vaguely foreign sound to it, a rough inflection left over from someplace in the world that I couldn't quite locate. Her clothes were as plain as possible and her hair pulled back in a ponytail, all as if she were trying to overcome beauty, but this would be like lashing down sails in a high wind. You might get a hand on one stretch, but then the rest would fly away, billowing out.

At one point Reuben and Sands got into an argument. Reuben suggested that the building ought to be cloaked in some sense of the spiritual.

"Reuben," Sands said. "I'm so tired of all our plans having to be so holy. It's such a dull way to think of buildings. And especially a theater."

Reuben looked a little amused. "Maybe we're going to have to divide up again," he said.

"Divide?" said Indira, who up until now had stayed

silent. When she spoke, her earrings made tiny, almost imperceptible bell sounds.

"Last year," Sands said to her, "we had to divide into those who believe in God and those who don't."

"Just like that?" I said. "You know, people spend their whole lives on this question."

"It's just for now," Sands said. "I don't think He'll hold you to it." She already knew I'd be coming with her. And I did, risking hell for her, complaining all the way. The two of us worked in a tiny glass balcony, a little limb off of the Commons. That first night Sands did most of the drawing, and I stood aside and made my suggestions, sometimes saying them more and more emphatically until she would finally draw them in. "Fine, fine," she'd say. We started over many times, a process that previously had seemed to me an indication of failure, but to Sands it was entirely normal, as if each building she called forth introduced her to other buildings it knew, and so working with her could be sort of an unwieldy process and you had to be willing to fight a little to get your way, but ultimately it was like walking into mysterious woods, everything related and fertile but constantly changing, and always there was the exhilarating feeling that one was continually losing and then finding the way.

More than anything, what I wanted was to enter into the rooms she drew, which would be like entering her imagination, that most private, far-flung place. By midnight we brought our draft to the others. It looked crazy, like big Russian circus tents connected by strings of light, like a big bohemian palace, but also very beautiful and somehow humble. I stood there while the others looked at it and felt as though I wanted to disown any participation in it whatsoever, and at the same time I was quite proud.

"It's so beautiful," Groovy said. Indira and Reuben nod-ded. And then they showed us theirs, which was austere and mysterious, rising out of the ground like it had just awoken and found itself the last thing on earth.

And we laid out the two buildings on the table and looked at them. They seemed so beautiful, as things can that are of the imagination and will never really be in the world. One had to love these figments, so exuberant in their pos-tures and desires, trying to assert their way into the world.

"Yours is beautiful," Sands said, softly.

"*Yours* is," Groovy said. "God wouldn't even come to ours. He'd go to yours."

"Definitely He would go to yours," Sands said.

"If He existed," I said.

"Now He's really mad," Groovy said, and Sands laughed a little, putting her hand like a gentle claw on my elbow. I can feel to this day her hand where it gripped my elbow whenever she laughed. Each of her fingers sent a root sys-tem into my arm, that traveled and traveled, winding and stretching and luxuriating throughout my body, settling there permanently.

The next morning on our way to breakfast, Reuben and I saw Indira in the distance, making her way down the path to the river that wound about Fialta. There was already a rumor floating among us that Indira was a former Miss Bombay. I couldn't imagine this; she was so serious. She had a large poetry collection in her room, and an eye for incred-ibly ornate, stylized design. Nostbakken had set her to work immediately on the gates and doorways for the theater. Watching her now, slipping down through the fall leaves, one could see the sadness and solitude that truly beautiful women inherit, which bears them quietly along. "Hey!" Reuben surprised me by calling out, and he veered away from me without even a glance back.

A woman reading is a grave temptation. I stood in the doorway separating the Commons from our tiny kitchen, named Utopia for its sheer light and warmth, and hesitated for a long moment before I cleared my throat. Sands looked up. She was wearing glasses, her hair pulled back in a dark ponytail. She said hello.

"What're you reading?" I asked.

"Oh, this is Vitruvius—*The Ten Books of Architecture.* Nostbakken lent it to me."

"It's good?"

"I suppose. He's asked me to think about the threshold."

"The threshold. That's romantic."

She stared at me. Probably men were always trying to find an angle with her. Her face was beautiful, dark and high-hearted. "What do you mean by romantic?" she said.

This was really the last thing I wanted to define at this moment. It seemed any wrong answer and all my hopes might spiral up and away behind her eyes. "Well, I guess I mean romantic in the large sense, you know. The threshold is the moment one steps inside, out of the cold, and feels oneself treasured on a human scale."

"That's pretty," she said. She was eating Cheerios and toast.

"You know, I never found out the other night where you are from," I said.

"From? I am from Montreal originally."

"You went to McGill?"

"Laval," she said.

I knew Laval from pictures in architecture books. In my books it had looked like a series of dark, wintry ice palaces. "And how did you get from there to here?" I asked.

"Nostbakken came and gave a lecture. I met him there."

My mind was at once full of the image of her and Nostbakken in her tiny cold Canadian room, its small space heater whirring out warmth, the animal skins on the floor and the bed, the two of them eating chipped beef from a can or whatever people eat in the cold, her mirror ringed with pictures of her young boyfriends—servicemen from across the border, maybe—and then of them clasped together, his age so incredible as it fell into her youth.

"Is he in love with you?" I asked.

"Not in love, no," she said. Which of course made me think that his feelings for her were nothing so simple or banal as love. It was far richer and more tangled in their psyches than that—some father/daughter, teacher/student, famous/struggling artist extravaganza that I could never comprehend.

And then Groovy approached, jangling her keys. Her hair had all these little stitched-people barrettes in it. It was bright blonde, and the little primitive people all had panicked looks on their faces, as if they were escaping a great fire. "Nostbakken wants to see you," she said to Sands.

Sands started to collect her books and her tray, and Groovy turned to me. "I heard you're taking care of those cows," she said.

"Yes. And you?"

"Trash," Groovy said. "All the trash, every day, in every room."

"That's a big job. How about you?" I asked Sands.

"She's his favorite," Groovy said.

"So, no work then?" I asked.

"Oh, it's a lot of work, trust me," Groovy said, winking a little lewdly, and then Sands smiled at me a little, and then they both left me to my breakfast.

There was a chair in one corner of the Commons that was highly coveted. It had been designed by one of Nostbakken's former apprentices and it was nearly the perfect chair for reading. That night I was just about to sit in it with my copy of Nostbakken's biography when Groovy came out of nowhere and hip-checked me. She sat down. She was reading Ovid.

"Chivalry's dead," I said, and sat in one of the lesser chairs across from her.

"On the contrary," she said, settling in. "I was helping you to be chivalrous."

"Well then, thank you."

She was sucking on a butterscotch candy that I could smell all the way from where I sat.

"How's that book?" she said.

"It's pretty interesting," I said. "Except the woman writing the book seems to have a real bone to pick with him. It's like the book's written by an ex-wife, or something."

"Does he have ex-wives?"

"Four of them," I said.

"He's hard to love, I bet."

"I expect so. The book says he loves unrequited love, and once love is requited he seeks to make it unrequited."

"I see that a lot," Groovy said.

"Really?"

"Yeah, everybody loves a train in the distance."

Which is when Sands appeared. "Choo-choo," I said. Groovy smiled.

"What's up?" Sands asked. She stood behind Groovy, touching her hair, absently braiding it.

"He's lecturing me on unrequited love," Groovy said.

"What's his position?" Sands smiled at me. "Pro or con?'

"Very con," I said.

"Pro," Groovy said. "Look at him. It's obviously pro. It's practically carved in his forehead."

Fialta did exist prior to Nostbakken. It was originally a large house atop a rolling hill, in which a poet of some significance lived in the late nineteenth century. Apparently Walt Whitman, both Emerson and Thoreau, Jones Very, and even Herman Melville had passed through these walls during the years that America became what it is, when the individual stepped out of the light of its community and every life became, as Philip Larkin later said, a brilliant breaking of the bank. Nostbakken's father had been a member of this circle of friends and had bought the house from the poet in the year 1947; Nostbakken had grown up here as an only child. His parents had cherished him so fastidiously that he had no choice but to grow up to be, as his biographer put it, the ragingly immature man that he was, his inner child grown wild as the thorny vines that clung to the spruce down near the river.

Nostbakken went to school on the East Coast, lived for awhile in New York City in his twenties, and then returned to Fialta and built his workshop here, presiding over it in his brimming room, up about a hundred turning wooden stairs, where I joined him every Tuesday afternoon at five. We would speak privately up here about my sketches, most of which involved Sands, about our plans for the theater, and also just about architecture in general. If you read about Nostbakken these days you will learn that as a teacher he can be offhand, blunt, manipulative, domineering, and arrogant, and though this is all true, his faults stood out in relief against the very lovely light of his generosity, like trees along a dimming horizon. He would turn his moony, moody eye on a sketch and see things I had never imagined—sunlit pools, fragrant winding gardens, gathering parties, cascading staircases. He would see people living out their lives. He would see life on earth. I would emerge from these sessions with him wanting desperately to run and run to catch up with his idea of what I might do, and in this way he created within me an ambition that would long outlast our association.

"What I was thinking," Sands was saying to me, while she leaned over our drafting table to turn on the bent-arm lamp, "was that we might bring the theater's balcony about two hundred and fifty degrees around. Wouldn't that be beautiful, and just a little strange?"

As she reached for the lamp, her body was crumpling up a map we had laid out of Chicago. "You're crumpling the map," I said.

"What?" She turned her face to me. It was riveting—dark and light in equal measure. Her skin had a kind of uneven quality to it that brought to mind childhood and all its imperfections, sun and dirt.

"Oh, nothing," I said. Would that the city be crumpled and destroyed by such a torso breaking over it—the Chicago River bursting its banks and running into the streets, the skyscrapers crashing down, the light extinguished suddenly by that gorgeous, obliterating darkness. We had until morning together to produce a plan that met a number of Nostbakken's and the client's specifications, which included these words—*bold, rich, witty,* and *wise.*

"It doesn't sound like a building," she said.

"I know, it sounds like my grandmother in the Bronx."

By the time we fell out, after finishing three reasonable drafts of interiors to show Nostbakken, it was nearly sunrise and we went to Utopia, made ourselves cinnamon toast and coffee. I picked up the slop bucket that I set out on the kitchen floor every night with a sign above it for donations. This morning there was warm milk in which carrot shavings and potato peels and cereal and a lone Pop-Tart and some strips of cheese singles floated.

Sands accompanied me down through the field to the barn, which sat at the foot of the campus. We stood in the doorway as the shafts of sun fell through the high windows. The four cows were in their various stages—lying and dreaming and chewing and standing.

Sands stood quietly, peering at the cows. The standing cow looked back balefully.

"This one is Anna," I said. And then I introduced the rest—Ellen, Lidian, Marie. "Groovy named them for Nostbakken's former wives. She's been reading Ovid, where women are frequently turned into heifers when the men can no longer live with them, or without them."

"And now they're trapped down here forever."

"Punished for their beauty."

The cows lived so languorously from one day to the next that their being banished women seemed entirely possible. I was moving aside some hay so that I could set down the little milking stool. I looked over to Sands, at her blackened form in the bright doorway. She moved then and the sun unleashed itself fully into the barn. Daylight. For a moment Sands disappeared, but then coalesced again, this time sitting against the door frame.

There was some silence as I struggled to elicit milk from the cow, a project that is part Zen patience, part desperate persuasion, and finally I did it. *"Yay,"* Sands said softly. Some doves fluttered from their eaves and out the door.

"Nostbakken told me that if I wanted to build well, I should study the cows," I told her.

"What did he mean?" she asked.

"No idea."

We both stared for a moment.

"They have those short legs," I said. "Under such huge torsos."

"But good heads," she said. "They've got good, well-balanced heads on their shoulders."

"I suppose."

"Maybe he meant to make a building the way a cow would, if a cow could, not one that looks like a cow."

"So, like a barn then," I said. "Something nice."

"Maybe they're quite glamorous thinkers. Maybe something jeweled and spiritual, like a temple in India, or Turkey."

"Yes," I said. I shifted my chair to the next cow.

"Are cows monogamous?" she asked.

"Don't know, but I expect so."

"Why?"

"Look at them. They're so big and slow."

"Yes, and look at their eyes."

I patted the cow, and the cow responded by not caring. I looked over at Sands. The sun had risen high enough that it was no longer blinding me. She was slumped sleepily against the door frame, with her feet kicked up against the other side. Clasped in the V of her body was Fialta rising in the near distance, steam rising from it, brimming over with its internal contradictions.

———

Nostbakken had in his office an enormous telescope, one of those through which you can actually discern a little of the moon's surface, but instead it was pointed at the earth.

"May I?" I finally asked one October day.

"Please," he said, and I looked down through it at the river, at the waves breaking softly on the banks, which were made of autumn leaves.

"Your work has been getting better and better," he said, behind me.

"Thank you."

"These beams are good. Where did they come from?" He was pointing at one of my drawings.

This was sometimes hard to do, to trace where elements came from in a sketch. It was not unlike pulling apart images from a dream.

"I guess from the barn," I said, which was true, though I hadn't realized it until now.

"Of course," he said. "I saw you walking down there today. How's that going, by the way? How are the cows?"

He must have seen me, trudging in my sleep through the dark field. It made me a little nervous, and anyway the question seemed doubly intimate, since I half believed the cows really were his banished wives. "They're doing well," I said.

"Let me show you something," he said. And from a long drawer he pulled out a series of drawings of Fialta. I had never seen any of his sketches before. It was almost impossible to read them, the lines were so thin and reedy, and they seemed all out of proportion to me, so that Fialta looked like it was blowing in the wind, or maybe going up in flames. He slid out the plan for the barn and laid it out in front of us. "Here she is," he said. "I built it in 1967."

"The summer of love, sir."

"Yes, it was."

One of the things Nostbakken had been struggling to teach us that fall was that a building ought to express two things simultaneously. The first was permanence, that is, security and well-being, a sense that the building will endure through all sorts of weather and calamity. But it also ought to express an understanding of its mortality, that is, a sense that it is an individual and, as such, vulnerable to its own passing away from this earth. Buildings that don't manage this second quality cannot properly be called architecture, he insisted. Even the simplest buildings, he said, ought to be productions of the imagination that attempt to describe and define life on earth, which of course is an overwhelming mix of stability and desire, fulfillment and longing, time and eternity.

The barn, even in this faint sketch, revealed this. It knew. "It's beautiful, sir," I said.

"Thank you," he said.

It seemed only right, I thought, as I spiraled down into the evening air alone, that the cows had such a place to live, since they themselves seemed hybrids of this earth and the next, animals and angels both.

The tradition, Reuben informed us, was that apprentices put on a show for Nostbakken at Thanksgiving. At first we were going to do a talent show, but nobody could drum up a talent. And then we were going to write skits, but they all ended up involving each of us doing bad impressions of him. And then we landed on the idea of putting on a play. He could be in it, too. We'd give him a part to read at the performance, which was to take place at Thanksgiving. We decided first to do *King Lear*, and then *Measure for Measure*, and then Beckett, and then *Arcadia*, and ruled all of these out as we started to cast them. Finally, Reuben suggested *Angels in America*.

"There's no women in it," Sands said, when Reuben suggested it.

"There's gay men," I said to her, "and one woman."

"Gay men are not the equivalent of women."

"Nostbakken likes women better than men," Groovy said.

"Everybody does," Sands said.

I frowned. "So rude," I said to her.

Still, we decided to do *Angels*, with women playing the parts of the gay men, and then, through some hysterical fair play, I ended up with the part of the woman. Indira would be the angel, hovering above gender, and *sodu-sudu* entirely.

If you did want to know what Nostbakken believed about women, all you had to do was step into the women's wing at Fialta, with its great circular common room. There were no walls at all. We were all sitting around the enormous wooden table at the room's center. We were drinking sugar gin, and from here, it was as if the room seemed to believe that women were so in love with other women that they needed no walls at all. Probably when there were no men in the room they passed right through each other as well.

"What was that you read me from Vitruvius?" I asked Sands. "That the walls of his Utopia were made of respect and interest only?"

"So much for a room of her own," Sands said.

"My therapist would be appalled at this room," Groovy said.

"You have a therapist?" I asked. "Where is he, out in the woods?"

"He's a little gnome."

"You sit on his mushroom, talk about your boundary problems," I said.

"You think I have boundary problems?" she said.

I had been joking, but now that the question was put to me, I foolishly answered it, "Well, a little, I guess."

Sands looked at me, horrified.

"In a good way," I said. "It's charming."

"I think you have boundary problems," Groovy said. "There's such a thing as too-strict boundaries, you know. You're all cut off from everybody."

"I am?" I felt just the opposite. I felt like I bled all over everything, in an unseemly fashion, and my feelings for Sands were exacerbating this.

The conversation continued, with allegations and drunken accusations, all led by Groovy and me, the two most insecure parties in the group. Finally the phone rang for Indira, and she stepped into the kitchen to speak. None of us could understand the language, but her voice became louder and more upset as the conversation progressed.

Groovy brought out the cake she'd made for us, an Ovid cake. "It has in it all the foods mentioned in the *Metamorphoses*—cranberries, walnuts, cinnamon, cloves," she said.

"There are marshmallows in Ovid?" I asked, after I took a bite.

"Oh, those," Groovy said. "Those are my signature."

"She puts marshmallows in everything," Sands said. And then Indira returned to the room, apologizing as she sat down. "I'm supposed to be getting married in two months."

"What?" we all said.

"Yes. But I don't want to."

Reuben looked stricken. "It's an arranged marriage?" he said.

."Well, sort of."

"Who arranged it?"

"I did, actually. But it was four years ago, before I went to Princeton and my fiancé to Penn. We planned to return to Bombay and get married, but I fell out of touch with him. Meanwhile, our fathers have joined businesses, and everybody awaits my arrival."

We talked about this for a while, and tried to strategize ways out. By the time midnight rolled around, Sands caught up to me in the kitchen and suggested we peel away, go to the river.

And what is a love affair if not a little boat, pushing off from shore, its tilting, untethered bob, its sensitivity to one's quietest gestures?

"I would love an arranged marriage," Sands said. I was pushing us away from the edge with my oar, breaking apart the thin skein of ice forming there.

"No you wouldn't."

"Yes. I'd like to have a family so involved that they were planning the wedding and I just had to show up, the treasured bride." And then she rose in the boat, and as she stood it was as if the world shifted off course and was just careening back and forth, drunkenly. The trees shook with interest. She stretched and yawned, lifting her arms. Her sweater lifted, so that a narrow strip of her stomach showed. It was like burnished wood, pierced with a ruby. She looked almost psychedelically pretty there, in the tunnel created by the trees over the river.

I would have kissed her then, struggled up through the ranks of myself to do this one true thing, except I made the mistake of glancing up first, through the ragged arms of trees. And there was Nostbakken's room alight. A cold wind reared suddenly, and I could feel minuscule shards of ice embedded in it. By the time the river froze, we would no longer be together, and I could feel in the air already the terrible possibility.

The next afternoon, how could I help but think he had seen us, through his telescope, since when I entered for my tutorial, the first thing he did was lift my sketches to the light and say, "I don't think you and Sands are working well together at all anymore."

"Why?"

"I used to see Sands all over the page, and now I don't see her here at all."

I didn't think this was fair, nor particularly true. "Maybe our work is starting to become similar."

"Oh." He looked at me sarcastically. "The two become one then, is that it?" He actually leaned up against the telescope then. If either of us had looked through it, probably we would have seen the river shrinking, crackling, crystallizing itself into ice.

We had one rehearsal, a run-through in the Commons. Reuben was the director. Nostbakken was going to be given the most expansive part in the play, the part of the dying Prior. And Indira was the angel, of course. Sands had made wings. If I hadn't loved Sands before the wings, I would have now, for they were made of the feathers and down of creatures that had to be imaginary—white and brown and long. Picture her in the dewy morning coming off the hill to wrestle down a figment, tear off its feathers, later affixing them with glue to bent clothes hangers and panty-hose straps, and there you have Sands, and everything about her.

Sands and Groovy played the parts of Louie and Joe, respectively, two gay men. Their interpretations of men were hilarious—strangely deep throated and spliced through with their ideas of gayness, which were like streams of womanliness running through so that the men seemed like crazed combinations of both genders.

I played a luminous, heartbroken, and uptight woman whom Joe had abandoned. I took her husband's rejection of her quite seriously, tried to imagine exactly how it would feel as I swished in my housecoat along the floor of the Commons.

After the rehearsal, I was sitting in the sheepskin chair, minding my own business, when Sands and Groovy came along to deliver their verdict on my performance. "You don't really have being a woman quite right," Sands said.

"What do you mean?"

"Well, you need to feel it inside."

"I can feel it inside," I said.

"You looked kinda stiff."

"No, I didn't. That was my interpretation."

"You gotta loosen up." Sands reached down to shake my shoulders a little.

"You do," I said, and I reached for her, and I brought her to me. Her body was such a mysterious rolling landscape in those moments, it turned and turned and turned, and I could feel her falling into my lap. I don't know what I would have done then, some minor consummation of my feelings for her, but Nostbakken stepped into the room. It was very odd to see him in daylight. Sands stood up, not too quickly, but definitely a little shaken.

"Where is Indira?" he said. "Her father has called me."

"I'll find her," I said. I thought she might be back in the room with Reuben, and I knew he would be mortified if Nostbakken knew this.

And I did find them there, sitting across from each other at Reuben's folding table, two beautiful solitudes greeting each other across a little distance, playing cards.

I think it would have been possible to maintain this little world, always on the edge of fruition, if we hadn't spent Thanksgiving together, hours on hours together, if we hadn't consumed so much sugar gin, if we hadn't put on such a beautiful play. It was a snowy day. Dinner was planned for nightfall, which was 5 P.M. in these parts. Nostbakken would be arriving at four-thirty, at the dimming of the day. So we all met to cook in Utopia at one, after a morning of working alone on our sketches of the theater.

For the first hour we mostly drank. Sands enforced a game of Monopoly, and then we began to cook. Groovy made little pancake hors d'oeuvres, studded with cloves and cinammon. Reuben and I were in charge of the turkey and the ham and the smaller game hens. Indira was in and out, miraculously cooking gorgeous yams and some exotic bean dish at the same time she was dissolving a multimillion-dollar marriage deal in Bombay on her cell without even breaking a sweat. She just kept rearranging things with her long, bronze hands, which I guess is what cooking is.

Sands relaxed in the Commons, reading a book. She had been to town early in the morning to get the drinks and seemed to believe this exempted her from any further partic-ipation in the meal, except for leaning against the doorjamb every now and then to read us a passage from her novel, which today was *Justine*, by Lawrence Durrell: *"Certainly she was bad in many ways, but they were all small ways. Nor can I say she harmed nobody. But those she harmed most she made fruitful. She expelled people from their old selves."*

"That's you, all right," I said.

"It's me, too," Groovy said.

"It's totally you," Sands said, complimenting her.

I was trying to break open the plastic surrounding the turkey, surprised and humbled by all the blood that poured out as it opened. "How does anybody eat after they've cooked a meal?" I said.

"Welcome to being a woman," Sands said.

"Well," I said, "we have to kill them. That's hard work."

"Nobody killed that," she said. "It wasn't ever really alive."

"It was," I said, newly in touch with animals from my months in the barn. I held out the turkey a little. "It had its days in the sun."

Sands smiled at me for a few long moments in which I arranged our whole future. We would live out our long chain of days at Fialta, secretly but not so secretly in love, and then we would move together to Chicago, or New York City, and live in our own private warren of rooms together. And our life would be made up of the gentle separations and communion of marriage. A line from a book Indira had given to Reuben ran through my mind, a sad line, I realize now, but it didn't even occur to me then that it was. *It was good to be alive when you were alive.* My dream, as I stared at Sands, was crosshatched by our friends—Groovy, Indira, Reuben—moving back and forth between us, carrying on.

So, finally, the table was set, and the beloved guest had arrived, exuberant and windswept. He lifted his cup to us, and we drank, our bodies growing warmer as the day grew colder outside, whiter and whiter. The table was laid with the creatures, all burnished a coppery gold. And in the fireplace the log, like another little beast at work on itself, turned and turned as the air filled with the smell of fire. We lifted our cups back to Nostbakken. If you have ever felt that

the table at which you sit contains everything and everybody that matters to you, like a little boat, then you know
how I felt. It doesn't feel secure at all, but rather a little tipsy.
It is unnerving to love a single place so much. There are no
anchors to the world outside, the cities in the distance, the
country around you. There is just this: the six of you afloat
so happily in the temporary day.

After dinner, we cleared away the dishes and then set about
the scene from the play. "Okay," Sands said to Nostbakken,
"you have a part." She handed him a Xeroxed copy of the
play. "This chair you're sitting in? It's your bed. You're
dying." She touched his shoulder when she told him this.
My eyes settled on her hand, on his shoulder. And his eyes
settled on my eyes.

And then the play began. Reuben narrated to Nostbakken what came before: love, disappointment, the crude
beautiful drama of sex, Sands and Groovy vamping at love,
Sands carrying on like a girl making fun of a boy making
fun of a girl, with a painted mustache. She was so ridiculous
and beautiful, I thought I might die. Beyond the play, the
day darkened. The backdrop was the icy arms of trees, the
lift of starlings against the falling sun, the day dying. When
Indira's part came, we had to shout for her. She was in
Utopia, arguing on her cell. She hung up the phone and
came in. She began to cry as she delivered her line, which
gave her part a weird veracity: *"Heaven is a city much like
San Francisco—more beautiful because imperiled."* We carried on for a few seconds, but then realized she actually was
crying, standing there.

"What's the matter?" Sands asked.

"My father, he's sick. They just told me. I have to leave
tomorrow."

"Oh no!" Groovy said. And we all murmured. I looked over at Reuben. *What will you do now, Reuben? What display now? What will spill out of you now?* He stood so still, as the heartbroken always do, and then he went to her. He touched her wing, the safest, least intrusive part.

"Let's continue," Indira said.

And so we did.

"Since you believe the world is perfectable you find it always unsatisfying." This was Sands, as Louis. And then she kissed Groovy, as Joe. They kissed, as men kiss. I staggered inwardly. And the play wound through its tragedies easily until Nostbakken's final, deathbed lines. *You are all fabulous creatures, each and every one. And I bless you: More life.* Behind his head thousands of birds took flight. He raised his arms, though dying. He loved the play, you could tell. The wind howled. And then he stood up to go hug Indira.

Since Sands hadn't cooked, it was her duty to clean up. I helped her clear away the dishes. We made an enormous pile of dirty dishes and plates and heaps of food on the silver table at the center of Utopia. There were also the three empty carriages of bones. "I can't believe that about Indira," Sands said.

"I know. It's hard to believe."

"And now she'll have to get married. That's a real primal fear, you know, for women. I can remember as a girl having dreams about having to get married."

"You're so unromantic, I can't even stand it."

"Me?" she said.

"You."

She was leaning against the silver table, looking down at the turkey drumstick that she was tearing apart in her hands, to eat, when I stepped up, finally, and against all better reason, kissed her. Tomorrow, Indira would be gone, and who could predict what would happen then, when one of us was gone? Time was ticking away, the snow was falling. Sands's mouth tasted like ten thousand things—berries and wine and pumpkin and something too human to define. I placed my hand on her spine as it arched back over the table, and then the door swung open. I turned to see Nostbakken, my arm lifting Sands so that we stood before him, my arm around her. He was smoking a cigar, and some of its smoke was spiraling up around his head. He stood still for a moment and then said, "Oh, is that right? Well, then. Okay. That's fine."

He walked toward us then. "First, let's clear away the bones," he said. "Let's make some room, then, for you two. Let us clear away the bones!" And with that, he swept his entire arm over the silver lake of the table, so that everything flew—all the bodies breaking up in the air, a flurry of bone and gristle, of life sailing apart.

Later that night I went looking for Sands. She had kissed me, told me to wait in Utopia, and ran after Nostbakken. "I'll try to solve it," she said to me. But then she did not come back for over an hour. I went to the women's wing and found Groovy there, helping Indira to pack. And then Reuben came out of Indira's room as well, carrying an empty cardboard box. He wasn't saying anything, so I blurted, "Indira, why are you going? Please don't go. Please stay."

Indira looked at me sweetly, indulgently, as if I were a small child. She hugged me.

And then I went to Nostbakken's. The light was falling down out of the building, onto the snow, that's how bright it was. It was too high for me to see anything, but I stood out in the snow for a long time. I must have stood there for close to an hour. It was ridiculous, I knew, and pathetic, but that light was more warm and significant than any I'd ever known in my life, and I knew that when I turned to go there would be nothing, only the cold and the never-ending drifts of snow.

By the next morning, our dinner was dissolving in the slop bucket—the little pancakes, the heads of fish, the turkey breast, the potato shavings. I poured a cup of coffee, picked up the pail, and walked down through the snow and darkness. The beasts were still asleep, and one startled when I opened the door and the cold sun fell over her. Eventually the snow began to fall—enormous lotus flakes that I watched from inside the barn. I milked the one cow for a while and as the sun rose higher I was finally getting warm. The barn was waking up around me, the building itself shifting and ticking away as the light forced itself through the million tiny chinks. As I milked I tried to think of a way to stay in love with Sands and stay at Fialta. In the moment Nostbakken flung his hand across the table, I had known he would never be reconciled to this. I don't believe there was anything illicit particularly in his feelings; in fact, it was probably their very purity that made them so searing, so intolerant. He was her teacher, and she his student, and they met up there in a perfect illumination high above the regular world. Another cow shuddered awake beside me and looked up at me, half in sympathy, half in resignation to all my shortcomings, which is the very look cows always give, which is their whole take on the world.

And then the door opened. The cold dim day rushed in, and, along with it, Sands. She was wearing a nightgown with a parka over the top, her hair in one long sleepy braid. She looked like she was fulfilling and making fun of my dreams all at once. "You look like a farmer's wife," I said.

"And you the farmer. He wants to see you," she said. Some doves in the rafters fluttered and made a break for the open door, wheeling then around the corner. Fialta was burning away in the distance. From this distance, it looked already to be stirring—composed, as Auden said all living things were, of dust and Eros. It was clear what would happen. I would leave; Nostbakken would fall—the full, staggering weight of him!—in my arms and hug me as he told me I had to leave. But there was still the morning. Her hair and skin were the only moments of darkness in the brightening barn. I kissed her again. One of the cows made a lowing sound I'd not heard before, which sounded like a foghorn in the distance. They'd seen it all before, this whole drama; their large hearts inside them had broken a hundred times before today. The barn smelled exactly like the very passage of time. The cows took their own fertility so practically, as the pigs did joyfully, and the doves beautifully. I already knew then that I'd be forced to leave Fialta; I could practically have predicted my leaving to the hour, but my heart was caught up in the present, whirring away and still insisting that this was the beginning, not the end. And so that's how I felt hardly any grief at all, lying alongside Sands on the crackling, warm hay at the foot of that makeshift paradise, as the cows watched on, remembering human love.

CONTRIBUTORS

steve Almond's fiction has appeared in *The Missouri Review, Playboy, The Southern Review,* and the *Pushcart Prize* anthology. His debut collection of stories, *My Life in Heavy Metal,* was published in 2002.

rick bass is the author of sixteen books, including *Colter: The True Story of the Best Dog I Ever Had.* He lives in the Yaak Valley of Montana with his wife and two daughters.

karen e. bender is the author of *Like Normal People,* published in 2000. Her fiction has appeared in *The New Yorker, Granta, Story, The Kenyon Review,* and *The Iowa Review,* and has been anthologized in *The Best American Short Stories* and the *Pushcart Prize* collection. Her short stories have been read as part of the "Selected Shorts" series on National Public Radio.

pinckney benedict has published two collections of short fiction, *Town Smokes* and *The Wrecking Yard,* and a novel, *Dogs of God.* His stories have appeared in, among other magazines and anthologies, *Esquire, O. Henry Prize Stories,*

New Stories from the South, Ontario Review, and *The Oxford Book of American Short Stories.*

DAVID BENIOFF's first novel, *The 25th Hour,* was published in 2001.

ADRIENNE BRODEUR launched *Zoetrope: All-Story* with Francis Ford Coppola in 1997 and was the editor in chief through 2002. She is now the founding editor and serves on the editorial board.

FRANCIS FORD COPPOLA is a filmmaker who has won five Academy Awards, three of which were for his screenwriting, and lists among his credits noteworthy films such as *The Godfather* and its sequels, *The Conversation, Apocalypse Now, Rumblefish,* and *Bram Stoker's Dracula.* He was the publisher of San Francisco's weekly *City* magazine in the 1970s and launched *Zoetrope: All-Story* with Adrienne Brodeur in 1997.

JENNIFER EGAN is the author of two novels, *Look at Me* (a finalist for the 2001 National Book Award) and *The Invisible Circus,* and a short-story collection, *Emerald City.* Her fiction has appeared in *The New Yorker, Harper's, Ploughshares, GQ,* and elsewhere. As a journalist she is a regular contributor to *The New York Times Magazine.*

ALICIA ERIAN's first collection of short stories, *The Brutal Language of Love,* was published in 2001. Her fiction has appeared most recently in *Playboy, The Iowa Review, Open City, The Sun, index,* and *Nerve.*

PETER GREENAWAY started making his own films in 1966. These include *The Draughtsman's Contract; The Belly of an Architect; The Cook, the Thief, His Wife, and Her Lover; Prospero's Books;* and *The Pillow Book.* His most recent film is *8¹/₂ Women.*

T. E. HOLT's fiction has appeared in *Triquarterly, The Georgia Review,* and *O. Henry Prize Stories,* among other places. He is working on a collection of stories and a group of personal essays about things that happen in hospitals. He occasionally practices medicine.

ʀᴇʙᴇᴄᴄᴀ ʟᴇᴇ has published stories in *The Atlantic Monthly* and is at work on a novel titled *The City Is a Rising Tide*.

ʀɪᴄᴋ ᴍᴏᴏᴅʏ's most recent publication is a nonfiction genealogical narrative, *The Black Veil*. He is the author of the novels *Garden State, The Ice Storm,* and *Purple America,* and two collections of stories, *The Ring of Brightest Angels Around Heaven* and *Demonology*. He is the coeditor of an anthology of essays, *Joyful Noise: The New Testament Revisited*. His short work has appeared in the *New York Times, The New Yorker, Harper's, Esquire, The Atlantic Monthly,* and the *Village Voice*.

ꜰʀᴀɴᴄɪɴᴇ ᴘʀᴏsᴇ is the author of ten novels, including *Hunters and Gatherers, Bigfoot Dreams,* and *Primitive People,* two short-story collections, and a collection of novellas, *Guided Tours of Hell*. Her latest book, *The Lives of the Muses: Nine Women and the Artists They Inspired,* was published in 2002. She is a contributing editor of *Harper's* and writes regularly on art for the *Wall Street Journal*.

ᴍᴀʀɢᴏ ʀᴀʙʙ's stories have been published in *The Atlantic Monthly, New England Review, Shenandoah, Glimmer Train, Seventeen,* and *American Fiction*. They have also appeared in *Best New American Voices 2000* and *New Stories from the South* and have been broadcast on National Public Radio.

sᴛᴀᴄᴇʏ ʀɪᴄʜᴛᴇʀ is the author of *My Date With Satan,* a collection of stories. Her fiction has won many awards, including the National Magazine Award and three Pushcart Prizes.

sᴀᴍᴀɴᴛʜᴀ sᴄʜɴᴇᴇ was the managing editor of *Zoetrope: All-Story* from 1997 through 2001, when she became the magazine's senior editor. She now serves on the editorial board.

TOURÉ is the author of *The Portable Promised Land,* a collection of short stories, and *Soul City,* a novel that will be published in 2003. He has written for *The New Yorker, The New York Times Magazine, Playboy, Callaloo,* and the *Village Voice,* and is a contributing editor of *Rolling Stone.*

MARY YUKARI WATERS's fiction has appeared in *The Best American Short Stories, The O. Henry Prize Stories, The Pushcart Book of Short Stories: The Best Stories from a Quarter Century of the Pushcart Prize,* and various magazines. Her story collection, *The Laws of Evening,* will be published in May 2003.